JUSTICE DENIED

Book 1 of ***The Hudley Saga***

V. M. Gopaul

Trish,
Allah-u-Abha.
May God bless you
[signature] Gopaul

UNITY UW WORKS
NEWMARKET, ON

Praise for *Justice Denied*

An incredible story of true love fighting against all odds, Gopaul has laid bare a harsh reality so few are willing to see.
~ *Infinite Pathways Press*

… a fast moving story that engages the reader instantly. The characters are real and believable and we become immediately immersed in this real moving drama.
~ *Saundra Arnold*

From page one you had my full attention, filled with deep concern for all the characters in peril.
~ *Susan Haines*

As an Iranian individual and particularly because of my religious background, also condemned by the Iranian Government and its religious leaders, I felt very much connected to the story.
~ *Mandana Sabet*

Books by V. M. Gopaul:

JASON McDEERE NOVELS
Tainted Justice

RECREATING A BEAUTIFUL SOUL SERIES
7 Ways to Obtain Divine Gifts & Powers
Family Values

JUSTICE DENIED

2nd Edition

For more information, visit http://www.vmgopaul.com

ISBN 978-0-9682976-7-4
E-ISBN 978-0-9682976-3-6

Cover Design: Christopher Watts

Acknowledgments

My profound appreciation goes to MJ Moores who skillfully edited *Justice Denied* and made many important suggestions to enhance reader experience. Her contributions have definitely made the story clearer, more interesting and tighter.

A huge thanks to Orang Momeni for giving me valuable insight into a teenager's life in Tehran, and one who had an encounter the Iranian Revolutionary Guard.

Many readers took the time to read the manuscript as it was being developed. I appreciated your feedback, which has made this book a better product and would like to personally thank Frances Gopaul, Mandana Sabet, Saundra Arnold, Nanci Pattenden, Sonya Schmoll, and Susan Haines.

Chapter 1

An unexpected light flashed off the passenger side-mirror. Orie looked out the window on his right as a Toyota Land cruiser maneuvered into the next lane.

A speaker blared, "Pull over, now." The flickering white and red beam came from the vehicle's roof. Mouth half open, Orie grabbed the armrest and squeezed. *This can't be happening.*

"*Lanatie*," the curse slipped, thoughtlessly.

Through the Land Cruiser's window, one of the Ayatollah's boys from the Army of the Guardians waved his hand, signaling Ahmad to pull over.

Orie felt an uncontrollable shaking to his left. He hit Ahmad on the shoulder and pointing at his friend's legs, shouted, "Pull yourself together!"

Ahmad's foot smashed onto the brake pedal; the car jolted to a stop. In the back passenger seats Foad and Kamran spoke the same phrase over and over with their heads lowered, as if praying.

Within seconds, four men empowered by their green khaki uniforms and machine guns surrounded the car, now parked on the side of the road in a business complex.

Now, Orie *did* pray—*Please God, don't make this the worst day of my life*. Struggling to regain his senses, he gasped for a breath he didn't realize he held and gripped the armrest tighter.

A stocky man motioned the teens out onto the side walk.

"Empty your pocket," the Guardian, holding a tray, ordered. Hands dug out coins, bills and pieces of paper.

Another Guardian flung open the glove compartment and shifted through the car maintenance manual. The third checked the trunk, then moved to the front and unlatched the hood.

Leaning forward with his head hovering over the hot engine, the Guard's eyes tracked the empty spaces as his right hand moved around the engine block, wires, and carburetor.

The forth Guardian unhooked the back seat and ripped off the lining.

What are they looking for? Orie tried to follow every move of the search without being conspicuous. But the Ayatollah boys came out empty handed. The guards surrounded their prey. Orie risked a sigh of frustration.

The stocky Guard faced the youths who huddled together, their backs against two large wall-pictures of the Ayatollahs—a common sight in Tehran.

The Guardian shook his head and said, "Where are you going?"

"To get a movie," Orie replied.

The man examined the faces in front of him. "Do you go to school?"

"Yes," the boys said.

"Whose car is this?"

"My father's," Ahmad's voice trembled.

Then the questions changed.

"Are you Muslim?"

Silence fell.

"What are you? *Armeniye*." In Parsi *Armeniye* was synonymous to Christianity.

"No," Ahmad said.

The Guardian's facial muscles tightened. Eyes bulging, he yelled, "What the hell are you?"

Silence.

He scrutinized each of the four boys' faces one by one. Then he jabbed Kamran's shoulder with the muzzle of his gun.

"Who are you?"

His paled face showed the hopelessness of a rabbit in a lion's den. Orie's childhood friend said one word, barely audible. But the Guardian, two inches from his face, knew it well.

Orie's heart sank. His mouth became dry. *No, no, no.*

"Dirty bastards," the Guardian's voice ground out the words; his stare hardened. "You are under arrest."

All four boys were cuffed and shoved into the cargo area of the cruiser. Crammed into the back of the vehicle, they dared not complain as the SUV carried on through normal, slow Tehran mid-day traffic. The air-conditioning ran full blast to compensate for the heat and humidity, but the boys never felt it.

Not knowing exactly where they were going, thoughts jumbled for prominence in Orie's mind. *Where are they taking us? Will they torture us? Will I see my family again?* The voice of his father echoed restlessly, *"Where is Orie? Where is Orie?"* Just as it did every evening when the man returned home.

His father fondly called him Orie; his full name was Orang Dareini. Abbas Dareini did not have a job, but went out every afternoon as he could not stand being at home listening to his wife complain. Orie's mind clung to those simple, loving memories in an attempt to keep his sanity as he sat between his friends with the promise of a movie and laughter completely gone.

The vehicle stopped in front of a building that looked like a hospital. The boys were yanked from the vehicle and separated. Orie, accompanied by the stocky guard, was taken to an office in the basement. Trapped in the clutches of a hungry vulture.

***

A stocky agent, calling himself Amin, closed the door and unhooked the cuffs from Orie's hands.

"Sit!"

"Look at me!"

Orie lifted his gaze.

Only the two of them occupied a room barely large enough to house the small veneer-topped table. On one wall pins held up the oversized picture of the living Ayatollah at each corner. A bare lightbulb hung from the ceiling. Other walls held score marks and peeling paint. The air tasted stale.

Amin got on his feet, and with slow steps walked around to the other side of the table and leaned forward.

"You are a dirty people. But don't worry,"—Amin placed his hand on Orie's shoulder—"You have a chance to redeem yourself. Think hard on what I am about to offer you." The words rolled past his lips with unmistakable resolve. He took a deep breath, filling his massive barrel chest, as if to give the young man time to reflect. "Just say that you are a Muslim and you will become clean." He paused. "Do you understand what I'm saying?"

At that moment the haze shrouding Orie's brain dissipated as his chest filled with the energy of his fierce devotion. Nothing could persuade him to dismiss his beliefs. But he was trapped.

Please God, you don't have to challenge me this way. Do not force their hand in this matter.

"I don't have anything against Mohammad. I believe in my religion, too, and live by it. I'm not doing anybody any harm. My parents, God bless them, always taught me and my sisters to be good to others."

Amin stood, removed the gun from his shoulder, and placed it on the table. Orie's gaze shifted to the black, scuffed weapon then back to his captor.

"You are still young. This is your only chance. If I were you, I'd take advantage of this opportunity. Think. Think clearly. Think about your future."

Orie lowered his head, avoiding eye contact with the interrogator. "I am not changing my religion. I won't say I'm Muslim." This wouldn't save his life, but if he was lucky it might just save his soul.

Amin shook his head and raised his eyebrows at Orie's resistance. He sank back onto the wooden chair. Pulling open a drawer from the rickety table, he grabbed a pad and pencil, and dropped them squarely on the rusty-brown stain next to his gun.

He fired questions at Orie about his parents, sisters, friends, and neighbors all the while scribbling the boy's answers. The agent circled the details around family names. On a clean sheet, Amin wrote a few paragraphs, then pushed it in front of his subject.

"Sign it."

Orie scanned it. It started with names of his family members, including those living in Iran and the US. When he read the last sentence he shook his head. "This is a confession that I am a Muslim, which I am not. With all due respect, I can't sign this."

For another half-hour the exchange continued. With every question the knot in Orie's stomach grew. Adrenaline-spiked fear rose like mercury in his veins.

Orie held his ground.

Amin's facial muscles tightened with every refusal until the man left the room without warning.

Five minutes later, he and two others re-entered. One guard ordered Orie to step into the corridor. A nurse passed by.

Must be a hospital used by the Army of Guardians.

Amin shoved a white band around Orie's eyes, knotting it at the back of his head. A zip-tie handcuffed both wrists behind his back. Blindfolded, Orie marched out of the basement pushed by the butt of a gun. His shins hit the edge of a vehicle, maybe even the same Land Cruiser he arrived in. He fell into the cargo area.

As each of his friends jostled in beside him, Orie's relief increased, knowing they were still alive. The vehicle drove off.

***

The Land Cruiser stopped a long while later. Orie had lost all sense of time and place.

"Get out!"

Still blindfolded, one by one, each of the boys were dragged from the vehicle by their shirt collar. A coarse hand led Orie somewhere outside. Far above his head a crow cawed, flapping its wings hard. How he wished the bird could take a message to someone. Orie shuffled his feet, directed only by that hand. He didn't know exactly where his friends were, but from their voices they weren't too far away.

"Squat."

Hands still strapped behind his back, Orie obeyed.

"Move! Move!"

When Orie did not respond to this confusing command, the guard kicked him in the back, kidneys, and chest. Feet and fists pummeled his body for a long time—too long. Orie lost track of time again. Gone was his sense of direction as the cloth over his eyes soaked blood from the slice above his brow.

Now and then, a gust of wind blew, chilling the damp shirt clinging to his spine—his pullover now ragged and torn. Determined not to show weakness, Orie took the abuse. But he was emotionally drained and worried.

Am I going survive this?

His voice broke, "Why are you doing this? I haven't done anything wrong."

No reply except for a kick to his shoulder followed by another shout, "Move!"

Dust collected in the crevices of his mouth. He tried to spit but had no saliva.

Footsteps approached.

"Get up!" A new voice yelled.

Orie staggered but rose, holding his raw wrists away from his back. A presence loomed behind him, not a person but a wall. The wind gusted again. Anger shot like ice through his veins. Silence reigned except for his racing heart and shallow gasps, which increased as spikes of pain flared up from bruises on his ribs and spine.

His fingers grazed concrete, slipping into small crumbling holes. He shuddered. *From bullets? What are they going to do?* He drew in a pain-laced breath. *Am I going to die?*

More footsteps approached. A sudden blare of music made him sick to his stomach. The words, "Khamenei, you are the chosen one. Khamenei, you are our prophet," repeated endlessly over Persian classical instruments. Minutes stretched and disappeared leaving only aching ear drums. His body vibrated with music he did not want, but could not stop.

Before this, if asked about religion, usually Orie felt uncomfortable and preferred to change the subject. Now, he felt trapped—he had no choice but to face the reality of his decisions.

Is this it?

His mind fogged as thoughts upon thoughts churned with no hope of reaching a conclusion. The music was too loud. Every sound ignited a piercing pain just below his skull where a thick trickle of moisture flowed. He dared not wipe it away.

The music stopped.

Orie tensed until the strain left him breathless. He collapsed. His body shuddered from head to toe.

Footsteps scuffed closer. With every motion the new guard shouted, "Kafar," renouncing Orie as an unbeliever. The man shoved the boy into a kneeling position.

"I am *Ali Mohmed*," he said. "Your religion is wrong. No one is better than Mohammad."

Orie sensed heat close to one damaged ear.

In a low voice Ali said, "Here is your chance." With carefully pronounced words he repeated, "Here is your chance—your people are not allowed to attend university. By becoming Muslim, we can give you a proper education. You can become somebody in life, rather than remain a *dog*." The disgrace of the term jarred Orie. "This is your chance. Tell me now."

The unspoken pressure pushed him to answer. In as subdued a manner as he could muster, Orie replied, "I respect what you are saying."

He blinked his eyes under the now filthy, blood-soaked blindfold, to push back tears, and pressed his lips tight to stop from crying out.

His physical energy had drained with every word Ali spoke. Orie prayed silently for the strength to persevere. He had to be true to himself, he couldn't be otherwise.

And then he knew.

Carefully, Orie planned his words so as not to offend his tormentor. Lowering his voice, purging any trace of arrogance, he fortified his spirit though still convinced Ali would harm him if he did not conform.

"My religion does benefit me."

"You bastard! You don't understand. I am here to *save* you. Give you a better future."

"What can I say?" Orie pleaded. "I have to be honest with myself. I believe in my religion; the way you believe in yours."

Ali paused before speaking, "I am capable of killing you and dumping your body. No one will know what happened to you, not even your family."

"I know."

"All you have to say is 'I am a Muslim,' and you are a free man. Is that so difficult?"

The shock felt like Orie's soul crashing into the back of his skull. Ali's words made him reel but the ache awakened a hibernating bear.

"What benefit does that have?" he whispered. "In my heart I am who I am. If I convert to Islam, it will be for you, not Mohammad. Do you want that?"

"It does not matter! I don't care about your heart."

Silence.

"Just say you are a Muslim, and you will be free." The words were slow, but firm.

"I can't."

"Then I'll kill you like the *dog* you are."

Orie staggered at the arrow-like impact of this man's words. A group of feet marched forward.

Ali yelled, "Get ready! Load your weapons." A mechanical clicking echoed before he commanded, "Ready."

In his mind's eye, Orie saw death coming; he tasted blood from the gun wounds on his face. His mind scrambled with worry about his father—his Baba's heart problem. Then to his *Maman*, his sister Laila, in the US, and his older sister, Nagar at home. The thought of being killed by *Sepāh* made his stomach roil.

But as Orie accepted his fate, the metaphysical barriers he had drawn crumbled. Indistinct shouting echoed nearby. Muffled cries of pain reached his damaged ears, followed by uncontrollable weeping. His friends endured the same punishment.

A hail of bullets rang out. A loud thump resounded, like a sack of wheat dropping. Then, Ahmad's voice cried, "Please don't kill me!"

Another volley of shots.

Another muffled drop.

Guns loaded, slides pulled. Ali yelled, "Aim."

Orie felt as though he stood outside of himself, waiting for the bullets to pass through his body. He'd never thought about death before today, not seriously. He struggled to remember the few teachings he'd learned about the end of the physical life and entering the spiritual realm.

I can't remember. Why can't I remember? He licked his cracked lips tasting a metallic tinge. *Should I change my mind?* All he had to do was say he was a Muslim.

He opened his mouth, hesitated. Instead, he drew a last, lung-piercing breath.

But the shot never came.

Different muscles twitched at random. Chaos ruled Orie's body. The adrenaline fled and dampness spread in his pants. Then, the strangest sensation—like a spirit entering inside him to cradle his heart. He felt every beat as though a great drum from the heavens thundered inside. He breathed again, in short bursts.

After a time, someone approached.

"I am with you. I understand. I want to give you another chance," Ali said.

But Orie did not understand. What was it to this man if he were Muslim or not?

Emboldened he said, "You feel bad for me. You're the one putting me in this position. You have a choice just as much as I do—you *don't* have to do it. My answer isn't going to change. Please, just make it quick."

"You don't take my warnings seriously, do you?"

Ali signaled for the execution squad to resume. Once again, came the order to ready the gun and aim.

Orie murmured a prayer, "Is there any remover of difficulties, save God."

He waited. Seconds drifted into what seemed a millennia. It was quiet except for the howling of the wind. His heart went numb inside but the moment evoked thought. His friends were silenced forever, and he was about to lose his life because of a stupid movie. No. Because of someone's desire to change another person's belief. He shivered.

A radio squawked.

"Move!" A deep voice demanded of the executioners, an uprising had erupted somewhere in Tehran and help was urgently needed.

"I'm not done with you," Ali snarled.

A guard dragged Orie across the yard to a cell in Evin prison.

Chapter 2

Jake Hudley pulled the white '94 Oldsmobile Ciera into his driveway and shut the vehicle off. The engine sputtered for ten seconds, gasping for air, and then died. Since his return from Afghanistan two weeks earlier, the misfiring had been on his mind. A tune-up would have to wait until he found a job.

Gaining employment in Lackland, Texas, a military town, was as challenging as it was crowded with recently unemployed veterans like himself. But that was a worry for another day. This evening all Jake wanted was to do was relax.

He slid out of the car to unbuckle his son, Dillon, from the back seat. When Jake set the two-year-old free he ran towards Megan, his older sister of five, who had already jumped out of her seat. When Jake crossed the drive to his doorway behind his children, all three raced to the fridge to quench their thirst.

It was close to 6:00 pm, and the air still burned. The April weather was hotter than usual. *Where's the Arctic air when you need it?* Megan pulled out a jug of orange juice and poured it into two glasses Jake placed on the table. As he pulled out a can of ice tea for himself, he caught sight of Laila sobbing on the phone in Farsi.

Must be having a conversation with her mother in Iran. He paid her no mind. Happy or sad story, she always shed tears when talking with her relatives. *In my family no one cries, except at funerals—but no wailing.*

Jake sank into the sofa and grabbed the remote to watch the battle between the Texas Rangers and the New York Yankees. While away on assignment, he missed watching his favorite sports.

He followed the players on the ten-year-old Panasonic screen, but after a few minutes Laila's sobbing turned into bawling. She mumbled in Farsi so he couldn't make any sense of her concern. His glance kept shifting between the game and his wife. Something didn't feel right.

The bases were loaded with none out. His team, The Rangers, was toughing it out; with just one more run, they could win the game. Eyes still fixed on the play, determined not to miss any action, Jake put his ice tea on the table and walked backwards over to Laila.

The crying turned hysterical. With one hand holding her head, face lowered behind silky waves of brown hair, her other hand gripped the phone making her knuckles white. Laila's delicate frame shook with such force she had trouble keeping the phone to her ear.

"Honey, what's wrong?" Jake asked.

Megan and Dillon jumped down from the table with a wobble of juice glasses, ran to their mother, and wrapped her in their tiny arms.

Laila hung up the phone. "They've arrested Orie." She wailed again, collapsing down onto the floor sobbing into the children's bodies.

"Arrested! Who arrested him?" Jake squatted, placing his hand on her cheek. "Who? Who did this to your brother?"

Gingerly, Jake lifted Laila to her feet and guided her to the chair next to the kitchen table. He sat in the next chair holding her hand, their knees touching.

She lifted her face. Bright red circled her cheeks as the tears swelled from her amber-brown eyes.

"The Army- of- Guardians," Laila uttered between sobs.

"Oh, them." *This is serious*. "How do they know that it was *Sepāh* who picked Orie up?" Jake was familiar with the Army of Guardians, they often crossed the Iran-Afghan border chasing suspects.

"My parents aren't sure. Orie was out with friends to rent a movie and never came home. Where would he go? They checked with everyone. Orie and three others are missing." Laila barked out another sob.

Holding her hand to her forehead, she finally let the tears take her. Jake drew her and the chair forward, wrapping his steady arms around her petite frame, made all the more fragile in her emotional state.

"Did your father call the authorities to find out more information before jumping to conclusions? I know you're concerned, Lalouska, but you need more concrete facts. Orie's a teenager. Maybe he went somewhere without telling your parents."

Even when they met, six years ago back in college, the constant paranoia of her family confused him to no end.

"My parents are afraid to call the ministry office. They've been checking the hard line newspapers."

Jake rubbed his chin across the top of her head. "What? That doesn't make sense. Why the newspapers?" A hint of annoyance touched his voice. This felt similar to dozens of false alarms in the past. He pulled away from yet another overreaction: his eyes glancing back to the game as his hands slid down her arms.

"Nothing makes sense in Iran. The regime uses the media as a tool to let Iranians know about dissidents and targeted groups," Laila explained, trying to curb her emotions long enough to clarify. "I should go home."

Jake's grip tightened around her hands.

"Back to Iran?" He shook his head. "No. I've only been home for fourteen days. Dillion barely knows me and Megan's memories are fuzzy at best. They need two full-time parents right now. My father was away a lot when I was a kid and my mother, sister, and I had a hard time with that. I don't want that to happen with us." Laila nodded. Jake knew she felt the same way but sometimes her emotions got the better of her. His two-year stint in the Middle East had come at the worst possible time—two months before giving birth.

She took a deep breath, trying to compose herself. “My mother and sister sound desperate. They don’t know who to call for help.”

He threw his hands in the air, “How can you help them?”

“I don’t know exactly. At least by being there I could give them moral support.”

Jake arched his eyebrows and ran his fingers over his blond brush-cut. “We can’t afford it. Even if we could, it’s a bad idea. Once you land in Tehran, who knows what’ll happen; they could arrest you too.”

“Okay, okay. You’re right. We’ll have to wait and see.” She wiped her face with the back of her hands, patted the kids on the head and went to finish the dishes, a way to calm down. Jake watched her taunt back muscles shift under her blouse as she loaded more plates into the hot water. He hated seeing her like this and it only ever happened when her family called.

Jake pulled the kids closer, Megan on one side and Dillon on the other. He ruffled their hair and kissed their foreheads. A quiet moment passed as everyone dealt with the family situation differently. Then he nudged both of them, “Go finish your drinks.”

Back watching the game, Jake squinted at the numbers and symbols on the 28-inch screen. The score was even and the other team battled for ground in the tenth inning. The pitchers on both sides were at the top of their game fighting for the win.

The inning ended and the Yankees didn’t score. Relief washed over him as he downed the rest of his iced-tea. Adrián Beltré was up at bat—the best player on the Rangers. The best in the league according to Jake.

The shatter of a glass on ceramic floor filled the air. Silence hung heavy until Dillon burst into tears.

“Mom!” Megan yelled.

“Jake, help the kids. My hands are wet.”

With one eye still on the game, he headed to the disaster zone. Orange juice puddled around pieces of glass on the floor next to Dillon’s chair. He picked Dillon up and rocked him in one arm, the poor guy upset from the crashing noise. His son pulled away at first, but as his little arms reached for Laila he noticed her eyes shut. Jake hugged his son into his shoulder then cleaned up the mess with his free hand. It never got any easier watching Dillon reject him, but he aimed to fix that over the coming weeks as he searched for a job.

By the time he returned to the game, it was over. He lingered to see the final score. The Rangers had won!

"Yes." He pumped his fist in the air. *There must be a God somewhere.* The elation from Rangers' win quickly evaporated.

The kitchen noise drew his attention. Megan and Dillon babbled over who got to take the next sip of juice from Megan's glass at the table by the back patio door as mugs clinked and clattered in the sink at the island just behind the couch. Laila's face drowned in her sadness. He hoped Orie was not in any real danger.

***

Laila Hudley leaned into the counter holding the plug for the kettle, her mind as foggy as a spring morning. She stood still for a moment, lost in thought, barely registering that Jake had poured a cup of coffee and planted himself in a chair with the paper. The flick of its bottom unfolding brought her back to the present. She plugged in the kettle to make a cup of tea then approached her husband.

"Did you sleep well, Hon?" She leaned into his shoulder and rubbed his back with her hand.

"Yeah." He gulped a mouthful of the hot liquid and put the cup down. He always managed a good night's sleep. The same would be true if the house had been engulfed in a fire storm. His vivid blue eyes lifted up towards her face as his hand reached her side.

"And you?"

"Tossed and turned."

"What time should we leave?" He was talking about the *other* event which kept her awake most of the night. It was time to honor the winner of the national Military Spouse of the Year Award. Sandra Hall, wife of Chief Master Sgt. Hall from Joint Base in San Antonio, brought the top honor home. People talked about it everywhere—in coffee shops, around dinner tables, at bingo halls—the town exuberance was comparable to the home team bringing in the big prize.

This morning's issue was a tough one to crack. Avoidance generally worked best at this hour on a Sunday; the excuse Laila gave herself this time was coping with the stress of her missing brother. It was getting down to the wire though. The event started in a few hours and a decision had to be made.

She sighed, unable to procrastinate anymore. While the children were still in bed, the time was ripe to speak her mind. Laila knew she'd never be chosen as the Military Spouse of the Year, which irked her more than a little, so attending the function in any capacity never sat well with her.

The military population in the surrounding the area was all white except for a few African Americans. Being Iranian-born made everyone suspicious of Laila. Even the US passport officers had given her extra scrutiny when she came over for school fifteen years ago—far more than other travelers got.

The whistle from the kettle jolted her into action. A warm cup of Iranian tea would help settle her nerves. She opened the cupboard, pulled Darjeeling and Earl Grey bags from two canisters, and placed them together in a teapot. Sliding over a container, she shook some cardamom into the pot and let it all steep.

Turning to Jake she said, "You go and I'll stay home with the kids."

"No, no." He waved his hand and shook his head as he scanned the news. "We need a night out together. Besides, I don't want to go alone." His chin muscle tensed and a shadow crossed his face as he looked over at her.

Laila knew it would be unfair for Jake to skip the whole event. He'd been looking forward to it since he got home. He'd gone two years with only sporadic contact with her and the kids and any semblance of a normal life. This would be time to see his friends, meet new spouses, and reconnect. With his father being a retired general, Jake had grown up in the military system since he was born, moving from place to place every three years or so. He'd told her how events like these helped make every new community feel like home. And he was home now.

After going back and forth over all the feelings, issues, concerns, and desires, they finally decided not to attend the first part of the celebration but arrive at noon instead, for the second part. That way Jake could meet his friends and exchange news. Then, after a few hours of socializing, they could leave. But all that hinged on Jake's mother babysitting the kids. Laila shook her head. She'd kept her distance from Jake's family once Dillon was born—didn't want his mother interfering again like she had with Megan. She knew they meant well, but inevitably arguments ensued.

Laila pushed back rising nausea the closer they got to the event as Jake maneuvered the Olds down familiar streets. She watched the car's digital clock register quarter-to-twelve. Traveling on W. Military Drive, she took a deep breath when she saw Garcia Motors, a way to relax her mind and body before Jake turned into the Cumberland Golf Club parking lot. Besides the recreation this facility offered, it was used for weddings and special events like the one to honor Sandra Hall.

The excitement of this event had spread to every household. More than the usual number of American flags hung from homes or from poles on the lawns of local businesses. Laila had to give them credit; the population of Lackland could use a bit of good cheer with the morale being low of late—too many wounded troops returning home and looking for work outside the military.

Jake parked the family car and Laila eased out of the front seat. He folded her arm over his as they walked towards the entrance lined with balloons and artificial flowers. She smoothed her black skirt and white top with her free hand. The shawl wrapped around her arms was a precaution in case the air conditioning made the place unbearably cold. She stole a glance at her husband and smiled in spite of herself. He looked smart in his casually pressed pants, blue shirt she bought him for his birthday two and half years ago—his favorite color—and a jacket. The cloth could have used ironing, but neither wanted to bother with it just before heading out the door. Still, he cut a handsome figure all the way from his chiseled jaw, to his wingtip shoes.

They passed through the doorway into a hall holding nearly two hundred guests. The ladies wore elegant silk blouses and high-end brand name skirts or dresses as the lights glittered off jewelry not usually adorned, and the men stood resplendent in their military uniforms. Laila glanced down at the paltry excuse for glad-rags she'd agonized over for nearly an hour before dressing. She hugged Jake's arm closer and let the strength and heat of his body remind her what was truly important—a long overdue night out with her husband.

The first part had just ended and a line dotted with well-wishers lead to the guest of honor, Sandra. *I should go congratulate her as well.*

Elegantly draped in a sapphire blue dress, Sandra's thin body gave the appearance of being ten years younger. Winning this award boiled down to being seen by the side of her well-decorated military husband: attending all the functions with him, being approachable, and most importantly doing notable charity work.

Laila gave Jake's arm a squeeze then slipped from his side. He looked at her. His piercing blue eyes sent happy shivers through her body. She smiled and inclined her head toward Sandra. He flashed her his wicked grin and winked as she turned to walk down the middle aisle, both sides flanked by rows of chairs. The farther she walked into the room, the more the volume of chatter rose. She refrained from placing a finger to block her ear. Groups held happy faces, exchanging greetings and laughter. She should be this carefree, and yet …

Laila waited in the line until her turn came. A necklace with turquoise, one of her favorite stones, rested perfectly on Sandra's collar bones. Her dirty-blond hair with lighter streaks was neatly coiffed. Laila continued admiring the dress as the bodies ahead of her slowly thinned out. With two kids and trying to fit in extra courses from the university, Laila knew she'd never own a dress like that. Still, she had two wonderful children. Sandra had none.

When her turn came, Laila timidly extended her arm for a hand shake.

Sandra surprised her by swinging both her arms around into an embrace. After a quick squeeze, she held Laila's hands.

"Laila, so good to see you!"

She stammered, "Ah, you too. You too."

"All the work you're doing with race relations and interfaith, very exciting."

It seemed Sandra knew more about Laila than she expected.

"Thanks. Congratulations. Great honor for Lackland. Hope we can get together for tea sometime."

With a broad smile, Sandra replied, "Certainly. Look forward to it. Let's do that for sure."

"Sure." Laila stepped off to the side, letting the next person in line step forward, and went to look for Jake. On the way she peeked at the displays of finger food and drinks, all lined up on a table.

She skipped the egg and meat sandwiches and placed a spinach and artichoke in puff pastry on a paper plate. As a vegan, she didn't expect too many choices available for her. Instead, she picked out garnishes such as celery sticks, twirls of carrot peelings, and radish roses.

After taking a bite of the pastry, she scanned the room. Since the last check the noise had increased several decibels. Laughter and loud talk filled the air. But this isn't where she wanted to be. She couldn't enjoy the joyous occasion with her heart tugging between the kids and her family in Iran. She knew she needed this time with Jake but really, this day was for him.

Making her way through the crush of bodies, Laila found Jake with Andy Burke. Both had been very good friends since Jake moved to this area after turning fifteen. Before Jake's Afghani assignment, the guys went out at least a few evenings a week; it irked Laila at the time, as she needed him at home to help with Megan and the chores. And whenever he managed to place a call during his stint overseas, he never failed to ask after Andy. *Men.*

Laila barely finished exchanging greetings with Andy when Stevie Wonder's "I Just Called" chimed in Laila's purse. On impulse, a shiver ran through her body. The next second her stomach clenched and she froze wondering who it could be. In the third second, she decided to ignore the call. Ultimately though, she changed her mind.

"Excuse me; I have to take this." She dug her cell out. The display read Negar, her sister in Iran.

Chapter 3

Laila rushed to the front entrance where the noise lessened compared to the chatter and music inside the banquet hall.

"What is it?" she asked with a finger blocking the sound to her other ear.

Negar sobbed, fighting to catch her breath.

"What's happened?"

Her sister struggled to get even one word out, making choking noises across the line.

"Negar, what is it? Where's Orie?"

"Not Orie. Abba's sick."

A blast of pins and needles took over her body. Laila's mind became numb. She didn't want to hear what her sister had to say, but she couldn't avoid it either.

"How serious?"

Negar burst into a wail.

"Negar, *tell* me. What is it?" Laila took a few steps towards the parking lot and leaned against a lamppost, the phone pressed tight against her ear.

Her sister managed to control her emotion, however slight, and quavered, "He had a heart attack."

"Heart attack. No. Please God." *I can't take this anymore.* "When?"

"Around dinner time. We took him to the hospital. The doctors are doing some tests. Maman is still there. I came home to call you."

Jake's calm, rational voice echoed in her head, *your family panics first and thinks later.* "Negar, go to the hospital and find out how *serious* it is and call me back. I don't care what time."

"Yes. I will." There was a long pause. Laila felt the weight of it.

"What else?"

"Maman asked if you could come home."

Every muscle pulled taunt, including her lungs. Laila forced a long, slow breath before replying. "I have to talk to Jake first. Go and find out about Abbas. Okay? *Insa-allah*, it's not too serious."

After hanging up, she clamped her forehead with her fingers. A deep, draining sadness filled every cell of her body as a burst of wailing clawed the back of her throat; she desperately needed the release. Instead, she swallowed the instinct, went to the porch, looked out to the road and inhaled lungfuls of air. She tried the routine over ten times but her emotions only magnified. As she clung to the post supporting the porch overhang, two couples walked out of the hall and made to light up cigarettes.

She needed some*one* to lean on. Jake. He wasn't far away in a distant land anymore. No, just steps away. She needed him, her best friend, to shore her up emotionally. Needed the weight and warmth of his arms.

When she stepped inside, the noise bombarded her senses. The air had become stuffy and overpowered with food smell. In a corner, a woman played Yankee Doodle on the piano, men in highly decorated uniforms gathered in clusters about the hall carrying on animated conversations, while others still hovered over the food table.

Jake's face was alight, engaged in a conversation with Andy and a young woman. By the time Laila approached, they'd burst into laughter. Jake had probably told another of his amusing mess-hall stories about serving in Afghanistan.

Laila waved her hand to get their attention.

"Excuse me. I need to pull Jake away for a moment. Please forgive me." She led her husband to a far corner by a fake tree where no one could listen in. He wrapped one arm around her shoulders.

Her voice trembled, "That was Negar. Baba's in the hospital."

His grip shifted as he brought her into a hug. She pulled his shoulder down enough to whisper, "He's had a heart attack."

He looked at her as if studying every feature of her face. "Heart attack. I'm so sorry, Honey." He rubbed her back.

"Can we go? I'm not in the right mood to be here anymore."

He grimaced and sighed. "We just arrived. I haven't seen everyone in ages and I'd like to spend some more time with Andy. I haven't even said hi to General McDougall." A US Army friend of Jake's father.

Hot anger bubbled inside her, threatening to erupt. *What about me?* She'd had to survive for two years without him and in a matter of two days she risked losing her brother and her father. She lowered her gaze for a moment until she regained balance and buried the fury.

Andy and Jake were practically brothers, this community his extended family. It was no different. She understood his desire to spend more time with them. She wanted the very same thing with her family, only they lived half-way across the world. She waved her hand, helpless and in search of the words that could change his mind.

"I *can't* stay here."

"Just a bit longer."

"I'll leave; you find a ride back."

Jake hugged her tight and nodded into her hair whispering, "Thank you."

***

The next morning Jake entered the kitchen in a haze, before exchanging any greetings with his family, he poured himself a coffee, pulled out a chair at the table, and sank onto it. Laila sat next to him spreading jam on toast for Dillon who tilted his head to one side and squinted at his father.

Jake made a silly face and squinted back. Dillon laughed, the sound warming Jake's heart.

He took a few mouthfuls of the hot drink brewed with mocha beans. After a few minutes the caffeine made it to his brain: he felt energy course up his arms, legs, and through his chest—his mind finally got a good jolt too.

Laila placed a bowl of hot cereal cooked with soya milk in front of Megan, then turned to him.

"We have to talk."

Jake knew why. All night her tossing and turning robbed him of a good sleep—and that didn't usually happen. Her once light, happy eyes that had so easily stolen his heart, were now puffy and red. He'd rather not talk about it, but for the sake of his marriage he had to hear her out.

"Sure." He took another sip of coffee.

Laila picked up the last piece of bread and placed it in Dillon's mouth saying, "Okay, Daddy and I are going to have a talk. You play with Mini Automoblox."

She displaced Dillon from the chair to the floor in the living room and put the toy in front of him.

"Megan, you're doing well with your cereal. When you're done, you can watch TV or play with Dillon."

Laila tilted her head back to him, the sign to start talking. As was habit, they walked to the corner farthest from the children, maneuvering past the sofa in front of the TV to a sitting room on the far side by the bay window.

After sinking into the well-used wing chairs, Jake caressed his mug and said, "What's on your mind?"

"The only thing I *can* think about—what's happening to my family. Orie is in the custody of *Sepāh.*" She cupped her mouth with her hand to resist a cry. "And now my dad is sick. I should be there to give them support."

"Are you sure about the *Sepāh*?"

"Yes, Negar updated me on Orie when I got home last night."

"Those bastards." *Is she thinking clearly?* He didn't want her to be swept away by emotion. She had a tendency to ignore logic when it came to her family.

He leaned forward to prevent the children from hearing, "You realize you can't go, right?" The horror on her face said that nothing of the sort had crossed her mind. "There are two things you have to remember, Hon."

She wiped fresh tears from her cheeks. "What? Are you serious? You can't be serious."

Jake put a thumb up in the air, "First, we can't afford it."

"I can use the money I'm saving for my education." A few years ago her parents sent them a gift of four thousand dollars which they decided to put aside for her Master's degree. A year ago she enrolled in religious studies at the University of Texas in San Antonio; since then she'd been chipping away at this goal by taking one online course at a time.

"Are you sure you want to use that money for airfare and not your education?"

"You'll find a job soon. I know you will. You're resourceful. And now that you're home, I can get a part-time position somewhere."

Jake took another sip of the heavily roasted coffee. Swallowing it slowly he reflected, "And there's the second thing. What if you get arrested? They're crazy over there. I don't trust them and neither should you."

Laila dropped her head into her hands as her elbows rested on her knees. He could almost see her thoughts churning and fighting.

"Being arrested … I've thought about it. I have. I just need to make sure they won't. In other words, I'll give them no reason to arrest me. I'll travel from here to Istanbul. Once I'm there, I'll buy a ticket to Tehran using my Iranian passport. They'd have no reason to suspect I live in America, or that I'm married to an American."

"Honey, I'm worried. If the *Sepāh* have Orie your whole family's at risk, including you." He leaned forward and caressed her cheek with his hand. She leaned into it, cupping his with her own. He lowered his voice to the same place where he sang to Dillon at night, "Wait and see how your Dad is doing. If he shows signs of improvement there's no reason for you to go."

"Jake, my father might be *dying*. At the very least my family needs my support." She pulled away from his touch. "Look, Iranians travel in and out of the country all the time. They can't arrest everybody."

He examined her expression: two signature pink spots warmed high on her cheeks; she blinked relentlessly; and her fingers repeatedly wrapped her golden-brown hair around an ear. Three sure signs she'd reached an uncompromising state of mind.

"I don't know what to say."

"I've made my decision." Laila stood up and crossed her arms. "I need to be there."

Jake rotated one shoulder at a time to release the tightness around his neck and rubbed his forehead.

"Just like that, you're leaving? What can I say?" Concerns spun in his head like a circular wind. *Could I even take care of the kids properly? I'm only just getting to know Dillon. Dammit. I have to change her mind.*

***

Ali Mohmed stood in front of the cell where Orie sprawled, thrown by the guards the night before. He watched his assistant rap the iron gate. The cell's area was barely large enough to house a foam mattress and a toilet, the wall covered with old paint, marred by stains and scratches.

The rap had no effect. The boy lay motionless on the thin mattress. With a wave of his hand, Ali signaled the assistant to rap again. The rattle clanked loud enough to startle. With his eyes barely open and confusion written plainly over his face, Orie tried to move his battered body.

"Get up!" Ali barked.

Slowly the teen managed to lift his body. He sat on the mattress with his back against the wall. He tried to lick swollen lips. Puffy skin disfigured his face and disheveled hair gave him a beggar's look, like the scum he was.

Ali had ordered another round of torture the day before; this time it was singularly out of retribution for numerous failed attempts to have the child convert to Islam. Ali's assistants were given specific orders to inflict severe pain with the sole purpose of breaking the 16-year-old boy's spirit.

Ali stood facing his prisoner. In this part of Evin prison only prostitutes, those condemned to death, and political dissidents were housed—unwanted rabble.

Ali took another look at his subject and ground his teeth. Orie's resistance disturbed him to no end. In his career as an interrogator, this did not happen often.

In the Ayatollah regime, interrogators were granted enormous power bestowed upon them by the Supreme Spiritual Leader. To crush the unwanted was part of their job description; to earn the Ayatollah's trust, one had to deliver. Failure meant disgrace and severe punishment. The boy's friends had died for their resolve. Ali had done his best to retrain the dog before him, as was his duty, but to no avail.

Ali gave the assistant the sign. The man's hands pulled two straps from a bag. He wrapped one around the boy's body just below the shoulders. The other around his legs. Orie did not resist. His muscles were weak and he likely couldn't comprehend the action of the man in front of him.

From a metal container, Ali dug out a syringe and a vial containing potassium. He pierced the syringe into the rubber and watched the liquid fill the cylindrical tube. He then inserted the needle into the kid's arm muscle and injected the fluid. Ali knew that with such a high dosage of potassium flowing into his body, eventually reaching the heart, it would give this dog more than a wake-up call.

He pushed the filthy body away and strolled from the cell. It was the fault of the boy's family for raising such a stubborn, ignorant child and that would have to be rectified.

Chapter 4

Laila hurried towards the departure gate with Dillon perched on her hip, both gripped each other in a tight embrace. A few steps ahead of her, Jake pushed an airport cart with one hand and pulled Megan along with the other. Minutes earlier, Laila had checked in at the US Air counter on flight 1789 from San Antonio to New York, later connecting with a Turkish Airline plane to Istanbul.

Jake caught sight of Gate 34-55 and made a sudden stop two feet from the top of an isle where a security officer let passengers board after checking their tickets and passports one more time.

Laila passed Dillon over to Jake.

"Where did I put the boarding pass?" She dug into her hand bag, shifting through makeup, passports, and serviettes. Then she unzipped all the inside pockets.

"Where is it?" After a few seconds of frantic searching her breathing became labored. "Come on, Laila. Where did you put it?"

She pulled a zipper on the outside and there it was. Relief streamed through her. *Not enough sleep.*

Only between four and six this morning did she not watch the numbers on the digital clock by the bed tick away the hours. The exhaustion was hard to bear. Laila always pushed herself harder, refusing to let fatigue take over her life. Like taking care of Dillon when Jake was away on assignment, she'd had no choice but to raise the family single handedly. A heavy heart added another brick weighing down her mind and her mood.

Jake pulled the cart and children over to the side away from the security guard, to clear a passage for a dozen Asian tourists.

"Lalouska, don't leave. We can all just turn around and go home," His strong voice resonated but the crack at the end of his words nearly broke her heart.

Laila knelt and hugged her little blond boy closer, the spitting image of his father; she kissed Megan's cheek then turned away from Jake to look outside. She stayed that way for a long time. The last 72 hours she felt tied to three different ropes, being pulled mentally and emotionally in all directions.

One rope dragged her away from her children for fifteen days; she'd never been away from them. The second rope lifted with the thrill of being back with her family in Tehran; yet the last time Laila spoke with Maman, they did not know where Orie was and her father's health was stable but critical.

The third rope noosed her—the Iranian Revolutionary regime. What if they found out she lived in America? Worse yet, that she married someone who'd served in the US Air Force?

She prayed hard, "Please God, send me a sign that I should *not* go to Iran. Break my leg or make me sick. Anything that'll prevent me from leaving and not feeling guilty should anything worse happen to Orie and Baba."

Staring at the airplanes and crews outside, her mind refused to clear as she resigned herself to this destiny.

Turning back to Jake she fanned her face with the boarding pass and said, "I've never been so scared in my life."

"You don't have to go. We can get a refund on your ticket."

Laila locked gazes with her husband, the man she was only just starting to relearn how to be with. "Hon, I wish it was that easy. Thoughts have been churning in my head like a hurricane. I feel battered. I wish God would give me a clear sign. I haven't seen any so far."

"God isn't going to give you any answers. Be rational." Jake pulled her into his arms and held her as if he'd never let her go. Dillon clung to her leg and Megan hugged her waist. His words pleaded for a change of mind, something she couldn't give. He had the kids and they had him. That had to be enough. She slowly drew away from his arms as he moved to hold the kids' hands. Megan watched them closely as Dillon became distracted by another young boy with his family.

"Jake, Maman, Baba, and Negar are so helpless. What if something worse happens to Orie? How can I live with myself knowing I wasn't there to help?" She caught sight of the wall clock as it ticked to ten after four.

"Looks like nothing will stop you from leaving." His voice choked out and disappeared for a moment, then a veil passed over him and suddenly he was detached and business-like. "Remember, don't give any more information to any officials at the airport than they need to know. Understand?"

"I *know*. You've gone through this a zillion times already." She raised her voice to compensate for the growing commotion of passenger noise but he misinterpreted her tone.

"Don't get upset with me. You trust people a bit too much for my liking and act like an open book. There are some real crazies in Iran. You can't trust anyone."

"Don't you think I know? Say a prayer for me while I am gone."

He closed his now clouded blue eyes. "Did *you* say prayer?"

She nodded as he opened them again, "Yeah."

"You must be desperate. Where does a prayer from a non-believer like me go? Probably to a box office in Buffalo, never to be looked at." Relief swelled her heart. She loved him even more when he came up with crazy comebacks.

Managing a faint smile, she said, "Say it anyway."

He shrugged, "I'll look stupid but I'd do anything for you."

She pulled Dillon back to her and held him tight. He was just learning to string words together. There's so much she feared missing on both sides.

Then she pressed Megan against her leg. All three wrapped around each other, squeezing closer and closer until they were fused into one.

"Megan, Dillon, listen to Mommy. I'll be gone for few weeks but I'll be back as soon as I can."

Jake squeezed her shoulder. "You mentioned about preparing meals. Where did you put them?" Jake was always hungry.

Laila pulled away and looked up at the man who made this life everything she ever wanted. Her chest constricted but she swallowed the pain.

"In the fridge. All the meals are in plastics containers. There's enough to last fifteen days. No need to go to McDonalds."

"We'll see. You'll get a full report when you get back." His posture loosened and shoulders drooped—his own inner turmoil finally starting to settle. Laila felt fortified that he believed in her and was finally willing to support her. Too many others would've just said no, but that wasn't the man she married.

Laila passed Dillon back to Jake and then grabbed her baby boy's hand, not wanting to let go. Her heart heavy, she reached for the handle of her carry-on and stood it on its rollers. She wiped the tears pooling in the corner of her eyes as she turned to walk through the last security point. She kept sight of the three people she loved the most, then obeyed the guards request to place her bag, change, shoes and purse on the conveyer belt. Next, hands from another guard motioned her to go through the body scanner.

After passing through, she took another look at her family. Her body couldn't comprehend the volley of emotions rising and falling inside her. She knew she'd miss them but couldn't find the words to tell them how much. All she hoped was for the pain of separation to be bearable.

Not to break the flow at security check, she had to keep moving; her gaze rested on her family every step of the way. As she put her shoes back on, the sound of the speaker blared the announcement that passengers of US Air flight 1789 were about to board.

She couldn't wait any longer. She blew three kisses and disappeared.

***

At ten after nine in the morning the kitchen worker rapped the iron gate of Orie's cell. No movement from the detainee spurred him to try again. If the jarring metal-to-metal noise didn't wake the person inside, he couldn't care less. Amal unlocked the gate, walked closer and peered down at the kid. He had seen such an incident frequently—one or two every month and knew the routine.

The worker continued making deliveries to another twelve prisoners, then returned to the staff common area where he sat for his morning break with tea and flat bread loaded with goat's cheese. After swallowing the last sip of tea, he walked over to his supervisor's office and informed him of a death in cell 251.

The supervisor ordered Orie's body to be moved to a morgue within the compound. Being a non-Muslim, he was not given a prayer and a wash, as would warrant a follower of Islam. Amal filled out a few forms and handed them over to Ali Mohmed for final approval.

Ali ordered the body to be moved to Eyvaz Mehrad Hospital. This facility was not accessible to the public, only used by military and paramilitary.

When the body arrived, an autopsy would be ordered, likely taking over a week to complete. The coroner, after a routine examination of the heart would concluded death by severe cardiac arrest. When the kid's family would be informed of the death depended entirely on Ali Mohmed.

***

A voice amplified over the cabin speakers interrupted Laila's nap, "Passengers, this is your Captain speaking. We've been given clearance to land. Flight 237 from Istanbul to Tehran will land in about thirty minutes. Thank you for flying with Turkish Airlines."

Snapping back to awareness, Laila ran her fingers through her long hair. She unbuckled the seat belt and, like a loaded spring, jumped to her feet. Grabbing her purse, she moved along the narrow aisle towards the rear lavatory. On the way, she squeezed by two attendants collecting trash from passenger trays. Reaching the back of the plane, she found one of the two doors with a vacant sign and entered. The body of the airliner shuddered as it began the first stage of decent.

The face in the mirror reflected back paler than usual, caused by the fear coiling in her breast. She freshened up her makeup and tried to look cheerful, as much as she could muster. The extended journey from home had already taken its toll. Her heart ached at the thought of being so far from Jake, Megan, and Dillon—the three bright stars of her life. She consoled herself with knowing the two weeks away would quickly pass and they'd be back in her arms again.

She dug out from her purse a pair of heavy black tights and pulled them on over her sheerpantyhose before smoothing her dark green skirt-suit back over them. A heavy green scarf domed her head. She took another glance at her reflection and accepted the conservative look required for women by the society she was about to step into.

When she returned to her seat, an alert came on for passengers to buckle up, followed by another announcement.

A female voice said, "This is the Crew Captain. Please place your chairs in upright position in preparation for our final approach."

The entire plane shuddered again, but with more vigor as it took a quick decent. The fast dip was to avoid the mountains surrounding the city. After a few maneuvers the jetliner aligned with the runway as the landing gears whined into position. Moments after touchdown, the engines roared as their reverse thrust slowed the vehicle until it reached taxiing speed.

Laila stepped off into the fresh, spring air of Tehran. She walked across a stretch of tarmac from the plane to a waiting bus ready to transport passengers to the terminal. On the bus many joyful teenage memories crossed her mind. Thoughts of silly laughter, singing western songs, and pretending to be super stars as she and her friends prepared for college life at Texas U.

The memories uplifted her spirit. She'd been away from Tehran more than ten years. Now, a woman with two beautiful children and a remarkable guy, a lot had changed in her. Had Iran changed? *Probably not.*

When she stepped into the large airport reception area, an overpowering pain clutched at her stomach. *What'll happen at the passport check point? Will I be allowed to enter the country? Will they let me see my family?*

With the room jam-packed with passengers arriving on several different flights, every face showed fatigue as bodies moved shoulder to shoulder. Some impatient passengers even resorted to pushing and shoving. The chattering voices and screaming made Laila's ears ache.

Hundreds in the crowd formed a circle of some sort, packed tightly together forever inching towards six streams leading to the passport desk. With every move Laila examined the attire of other women. Hers was very conservative: a large, half-moon-shape chador entwined around the shoulders, forehead, and chin, showed only eyes, nose, and mouth.

In her teen years she rebelled against the dress codes imposed on women by men who devised such things through their own interpretations of the Quran. In her research, she found very little about the harsh regulations of female attire. Inside she hated it, but now she needed to blend in, show no trace of rebellion in her expression or demeanor.

Baby steps and partial shuffles towards the passport desk tortured her already strained patience. Half an hour passed before she finally found herself face-to-face with a scowling officer. At every turn of the passport page, he glanced at her. At no time did she make any eye contact, as it was considered to be an act of disrespect. This man who knew nothing about her would pass judgment on her life.

What is he going to do? Her body stiffened. She asked for help from above, from anybody who might hear her plea: an angel, an ancestor, whomever. Every moment, every glance, lasted a lifetime.

His hand grabbed the stamp and slammed it on a page. The noise shook her out of her frozen state. He waved her through. Relief washed over her.

She let escape, "*Merci,*" thank you in Persian, took her passport and walked away. Somewhere else she would've jumped with joy, but here she restrained herself.

Next she faced customs.

Laila made sure to hide all trace of the United States. To hide her American passport, Jake had slit an opening at the bottom of the carry-on, in the middle just inches away from the rollers. He added stitches to disguise the cut. After landing in Istanbul, Laila placed the American passport in the bag as planned, she hadn't checked it since.

The chatter grew louder at the luggage carousel. After a wait of another half hour, she picked up her luggage and move towards the next queue. Again, everyone gathered chaotically. The inspector went through every piece of luggage: makeup, tissues, gift items picked up in Istanbul. The female agent zipped Laila's suitcases and asked her to proceed.

When she stepped outside she heard, "Laila *joon, inja, inja.*" *Negar.*

Looking past a sea of heads Laila spotted her older sister's waving hands.

"Maman joon," Laila screamed then held her mother in a firm embrace, arms thrown over her shoulders as if to never let her go. Tears poured from both mother and child. After Manjula had smothered her daughter with enough kisses, Laila turned to Negar and hugged her tightly. Ten questions popped into her head at once. *No.* Baba and Orie were not there. She decided not to ask anything until they got in the car.

Chapter 5

Shortly after 8:00 pm Laila entered the family kitchen. With new appreciation for her childhood home, she scanned the dishes one-by-one on the table. Her mother held a plate of steaming basmati rice and inching towards the table said, "Laila, sit down."

Negar and Baba were already seated. When Maliheh joined, Laila showered praises on the family for a heartwarming dinner, the kind she remembered growing up. Maliheh had cooked Laila's favorite dishes—rice, vegetarian ghormeh sabzi, hummus, pita, lentil soup. Iranian spices filled the air and she realized how comforting it felt, a core part of her identify reclaimed.

After savoring a few mouthfuls of rice and the ghormeh sabzi, she said, "Maman, you are the best cook in the world. Oh how I wish Jake was here. He'd love it. That man can eat!" She enjoyed cooking for him; he'd try anything once and delighted in eating a well-cooked meal.

Nagar said, "Promise now. All of you, Jake, Megan, and Dillon will come to visit us next year."

"How I wish."

"What do you cook for him? Hamburgers?" Negar asked.

Laila frowned at her sister's biased comment. "No, no. Jake loves Iranian food. All food actually."

Negar jumped to her feet to clear the table just as the doorbell rang. They were expecting Neda and Mandana, two of Laila's old friends who'd returned home after finishing their studies.

The women exchanged hugs and kisses, then all three settled on the couches a few feet away from the kitchen table to get caught up.

Though tired from the travel and suffering from jet lag, Laila felt energized being surrounded by friends and family. Overflowing with excitement, all three exchanged news and reminisced about the past. Maman did the dishes and Negar brought tea in a pot and served everyone.

But the laughter and exuberant exchanges died when Negar gave an update on Abbas and the whereabouts of Orie when the guests asked after them. Maliheh pulled a chair from the table and joined the others for tea.

The doorbell echoed through the kitchen and hallway.

No one spoke.

Maliheh placed the half-full glass of tea down and whispered, "Who could that be?" Then silence. She stood, wrapped her head with the chador, and ran to the front.

Three men in dark green military uniforms forced their way inside. *Revolutionary Guards.* A gun swung up toward her mother's temple.

"Where is Abbas Dareini?" the guard yelled.

Eyes wide with surprise she said, "He's not here."

The men pushed past her, forcing their way to the kitchen. To clear a path, Maliheh stepped backward knocking a chair behind her.

The bearded one said, "Where is he?" His tone was loud and annoying.

Maliheh walked behind them, "In the hospital."

"Which hospital? Why?" He stared at her as if he did not believe her.

"At Arad General Hospital. He is recovering from a heart attack." A cloud of fear drained the last light of joy from her mother's face. Her tone changed and her eyes darkened.

Laila's heart sunk. She'd never seen her mother this scared before. Laila's heart pulled between love and sorrow at another harrowing moment her family, especially her mother, had to face. Maman didn't deserve this. Her life had been hard enough. At thirty she'd contracted tuberculosis, and now had a husband in the hospital. Of course, Orie's situation weighed equally as heavy but she never showed her anxiety. She was stoic.

The guard's piercing eyes studied the faces of Laila's family and friends one by one. As he scanned the room, he studied the walls, stove, cutlery covered counter, plates with leftovers, and almost empty pots.

"Stay here." The guard with the beard pointed his gun at them while two others searched the house.

Negar stood up. "Why are you here?" She demanded. "Why are you looking for my father? Where is my brother?" With a fiery look, she waved her right hand in the air. Laila's sister still had the hot-head she recalled when growing up, but Negar could make things worse. Laila moved to calm her down.

"Your brother is in Evin prison I'm very disappointed to say. Serious, very serious." He paused to examine his listeners' attention. "He confessed to being an Israeli spy. We are here to ask Abbas a few questions. We need to conduct a proper investigation."

"You accuse my son of being a spy! This is a lie. I know my son. He is a spy for nobody and of no country. He'd never do such a thing. He's only sixteen." She wiped tears from her face with her shawl.

He pulled a folded sheet of paper from the top pocket of his uniform and waved at her. "Here. He confessed and signed. If you don't believe me I can show you a video of his confession."

"Let me see." Negar pushed Laila aside and took the sheet. She burst out, "No. No. My brother would never sign his name to this. This isn't true. He was forced."

"You better believe what I say," the guard growled.

Laila put her hand on her sister's shoulder. "Please, Negar, don't argue." She stroked her back.

Negar's checks turned pink; her eyes now blood-shot with anger and hot tears. She shrugged off Laila's hand. "No, I don't believe you."

"You'd better. If not, you'll pay a dear price. I promise you." He raised his chin and yelled, "You are all dirty. Dirty dogs."

Laila's sister clenched her fists and took half a step forward.

"Negar, stop it," Maliheh said, pulling her daughter away from the man. Laila heard a squeak behind her and checked on her friends, holding one another on the sofa in the living room. She pursed her lips together and turned back just as Negar threw the confession at his face.

The guard bent down to pick up the paper. His eyes flashed. "Where is Orie's room?"

No answer.

He yelled, "Where is his room?"

"I'm not telling you," Negar said.

Maliheh pointed with her finger. "Over there, next to the washroom."

Laila watched everyone in that moment. Neda sat motionless, shock freezing her face as if she watched a horror movie. Mandana covered her mouth with her scarf, absorbing the guard's actions. The man's eyes opened wider showing extreme irritation at the disrespect Negar showed. Iranian women were supposed to be subdued, but Laila's parents taught her children to fight for justice. As usual, unfairness stirred her sister's consciousness, causing her to lash out. Laila's eyes shifted back and forth. She heard the strain of mattress springs and the opening of dresser drawers.

The two guards came back to the kitchen. One held three books in his hand. The bearded man said, "Stay here while I'll search his room."

Laila wondered what they could expect to find. She examined her mother's face for clues, but her blank stare reflected only the nightmare of this experience. *Will they fabricate false evidence?*

After ten minutes the guard came back and announced he was taking Orie's computer, all his school books, CDs and DVDs.

The man with the beard went out and returned with another sheet of paper. Laila could see a list scribbled on it. He started questioning.

"Who is Negar?" Pointing at Laila, "What is your name?"

"Laila."

"You don't live here. You live in the United States."

How does he know? Orie ... She shook her head. All the care she'd taken to hide her true residence came to nothing.

She looked at everyone. The weight to the silence pressed her to say something. But all she could say was, "Yes."

"Since Abbas is not here, you are coming with us for questioning."

"No. Don't take her. I'll go instead," Negar protested.

The guard pushed Negar, "Stay back or I'll shoot you."

Not Negar. Laila stepped forward, "I'll go."

Maman placed a hand over her mouth, so visibly shaken she couldn't speak. Laila went to her room and shoved a few clothes, toothbrush, and combs into a bag.

Negar asked, "Where are you taking her?"

The guard watched closely as Laila came out with her handbag. He pointed to the door with his gun as the other two fell into step behind her.

They brought her to a white Toyota Land cruiser waiting in front of the apartment. The bearded guard opened the door with a smirk. Laila stopped and turned her gaze towards her wailing family. For a moment she considered not climbing into the vehicle. *No, I have to or these men will brutally punish my whole family.*

"Get in! I don't have time to waste."

The air felt heavy as the odor of stale sweat clung to the inside of her nose. The vehicle pulled away. Her mother wiped tears from her cheeks as Negar clutched Laila's two friends tight. All four women stood helpless outside the front door.

After traveling for several minutes with these strangers, fear choked Laila's ability to breathe. *Where are they taking me?* The same question kept spinning in her head. The nervous patter of her feet did nothing to ease the pain inside. Laila found herself staring through the windshield at the passing world to help calm down. The vehicle sped towards the Albortz Mountains in the distance, an old familiar site. She tried to re-acquaint herself with the city, forcing her mind anywhere but her present circumstances.

The guards seemed more relaxed. They carried on a conversation about a wedding, to which she paid little attention. As she stared at the empty streets, except for a few cars, she was repeatedly drawn back to what brought her here.

Pain churned like a washing machine in her stomach as she spiraled into an abyss of despair, a place terribly unfamiliar to Laila. She tried to look at the brighter side of the situation, but there wasn't any. She was aware of too many stories of men and women taken to Evin never to come out alive. In the deepest corner of her mind she prayed for a quick release after minimal questioning.

Charging her brother with espionage was a well-known fabrication in Iran. She vaguely recalled two men and a woman charged when they accidently crossed the border between Iraq and Iran some years ago. These men would have her believe there were no *accidents.*

After half an hour into the journey, Laila caught sight of a wall zigzagging on a hill in the distance.

The guard sitting in the front-passenger seat turned to Laila and said, "We're almost there. One piece of advice you should never forget: whatever questions are asked, answer them truthfully. If you don't, they have ways of getting it out of you. You've been out of Iran for many years, you need to remember that."

What are they looking for? I haven't done anything illegal.

The vehicle entered a narrow lane and moved until it reached a red-brick wall—the notorious Evin prison. Floodlights swept past at regular intervals allowing no one to escape. Intense spotlights positioned at the top of the towers lit up the area; the prison was further fortified by armed guards below each tower. Laila trembled uncontrollably.

The vehicle stopped at a large metal gate, flanked by two walls covered with barbed wires. The driver got out. The guard sitting next to Laila threw her a white blindfold.

"Make sure it's tight around your eyes. If not, you'll face severe punishment."

The vehicle carried on for another few minutes before coming to a stop. When the door opened a woman told Laila to step out. The female guard handcuffed Laila's wrists behind her back, forcing her to follow until they entered a room. When the blindfold was removed, Laila blinked until her eyes adjusted to the light.

"Sit." She pointed to a chair. The growl made Laila lower her body until she faced yet another hard-faced woman, a table between them. With a stern look the new woman asked, "Is this a moral offense?"

Laila did not understand the question.

She repeated, "Is this a moral offense?" This time louder and with more force.

"I don't know what you mean."

"Listen, I am not joking or playing around. Be serious."

"I am serious. Three armed guards came into my mother's house and they brought me here. I have not committed any moral offense."

"Are you a prostitute or a drug addict?"

"No. None of those."

"Okay. Political offense." She wrote something on the paper.

"No. I never get involved in politics. It's against my religion."

"Yeah, yeah. I hear all kinds of excuses. Yours is a first. Take her to her cell." The woman waved to one of the other guards. "She's crazy. Get her out of my sight." Laila was re-blindfolded and dragged away.

A sharp, rank odor assailed her nose like a dagger strike. With every move forward the smell grew unbearable—a combination of sweat and musty air. With every cell she passed came moaning and harsh crying from the women trapped within. At that moment, though, Laila was more concerned with how she could breathe in such a place.

"Here's your cell. The best in the house."

The sarcasm did not amuse Laila, but she wondered about the condition of the space based on the never-ending stench of the prison. When the blindfold was removed, she blinked until her eyes adjusted to the flood of light.

She stared at the cell small as a closet. The guard pushed her arm. Laila walked inside with the small bag carrying her tooth brush, comb, and underwear, all they permitted her to keep from what she'd packed.

Laila covered her nose with one hand, and threw the bag to one end of the foam bed on the floor. Tired and defeated, she lowered herself down and curled into a fetal position with her head resting on the bag.

***

Jake locked the front door with one hand while holding Dillon on his hip with the other. Wanting to know where Megan was, he turned to see her walking towards his old beater. He jogged over to join her and opened the rear passenger door. He placed Dillon in the baby seat and buckled him up. By the time he walked around to slide into the driver side, Megan had climbed into the booster chair with the safety harness strapped around her as she worked on connecting the latch.

He put the key into the ignition and smiled, glancing at his daughter in the rearview mirror. For the first time he saw Laila's straight brown hair, creamy skin and round face on his daughter. She had his thin, pointed nose and other small imperfections, but at a glance she radiated her mother's aura.

His heart swelled with pride. Preparing two kids for this outing took longer than he realized, and his parents expected them ten minutes ago. He needed to drop the kids off before heading to the job placement office. After dealing with the work counselor, he planned to spend time with Andy to catch up on news at the base over lunch. They hadn't been able to talk much at the awards ceremony last week.

He felt surprisingly good. With Laila away, Jake discovered how much he enjoyed caring for the kids. To compensate for being an absentee father for two years, yesterday he took them to local baseball game where they had picnics in the park and then went for ice cream. He also appreciated having his parents, who loved spending time with their grandchildren, live only twenty minutes away.

Jake turned the ignition key. The car clock flashed 11:45 am. Just as he reached for the stick shift, his cell phone rang. He really didn't want to take this call as he was running late, but a closer look at the number indicated an international call from Tehran.

Must be Laila.

He picked up the phone, "Hello?"

Negar's sobbing voice came across.

"Whoa! Stop crying, Negar. Calm down."

The sobbing continued.

He kept repeating the words in an even and steady voice. *Iranian culture. Too emotional.* Laila had her moments, but she wasn't anything like her family.

"It's time to go, Daddy," Megan said, handing Dillon a car toy from the seat between them.

"Soon sweetie. Just a minute." Jake stared at the front of his house through the windshield until Negar finally got a hold of herself. It took several minutes.

"The guards have taken Laila," she said, trying to restrain her distress.

Jake went into a blinking frenzy. "Taken Laila?" He paused, wondering if he heard right, then lowered his voice, "What do you mean?"

"We were finishing dinner. There was a knock at the door and three guards came in. They told us to stay in the kitchen. They had guns. Two of them searched every room. When they finished they took Laila with them."

"Did they say why?"

"They claimed Orie's a spy. Maman doesn't agree. She told them, 'no', but they didn't believe us," she sobbed.

Jake didn't know what to say. He gripped the steering wheel so hard, his knuckles ached.

"We were afraid they'd kill us."

"Where did they take her? Did they say when she'll be released?"

"Didn't say where. But we think to Evin prison where they're keeping Orie. Jake, they knew Laila lived in America. We didn't tell them that!"

Looking straight through the windshield, Jake's brows formed high arches. "What kind of spy, Negar? What did they say about Orie?"

"For America and Israel."

"That's what they say every time." Negar's words sunk in. "Dammit!" He hit the wheel.

"What's wrong, Daddy?" Megan asked.

He waved his hand asking for another minute, making eye contact with her in the rear-view mirror.

"Jake, I'm so sorry. We didn't know what to do. They forced Laila to go with them." She gave in to another wail, "I wish I could've prevented it."

Jake felt the helplessness and anguish in her voice wrapped around his soul squeezing tighter and tighter with every breath.

"Negar, I have to go. As soon as you hear anything, let me know."

"Okay." She hung up.

Jake put the phone down beside him, eyes blind to the world on the other side of the windshield. He played every word back in his mind and hit the steering wheel again.

"Bastards." The news pierced his chest like a knife and shattered the hope of a life together with his wife in pieces. An image from the news flashed in his mind—the coffins of two Iranian-Americans arriving on American soil, citizens charged and executed for espionage. *Could that happen to my Laila?*

Jake threw the car into gear and pulled it out onto the road. With sweaty palms he turned the wheel as the car moved along Knoll Crest Street. When he halted at the stop sign he rolled down the window to let the breeze cool his body.

Megan said, "Daddy, how many more minutes?"

"What's that, Dumpling?"

In a louder voice, she replied, "How many more minutes to Gramma's?"

"Soon." He craned to the right to look behind him and found Dillon fast asleep.

When he stared at the road, anger erupted inside him, an anger he wasn't sure he could control. *Damn, damn, damn. They'll pay if anything happens to her.*

After being on the highway for five minutes, a car zipped by in the passing lane blaring the horn. The noise brought his attention back to the road.

With a dirty look at the other driver he yelled, "What's wrong with you?" A quick glance at the dashboard indicated he traveled twenty miles lower than the limit.

Ten minutes later, he stopped in front of his parent's house. His mother stood at the front door waiting. When he handed the kids over to her, he didn't mention anything about Laila's arrest. With a mumbled goodbye, Jake climbed back into the vehicle.

All he wanted to do was to crawl into a dark cave and work out his problems alone. The ache inside grew with every minute to the point where he could no longer drive. He parked the car at a nearby green space, rolled down the windows, reclined back in the seat, and closed his eyes.

His enthusiasm gone, he missed the employment officer's appointment. Instead he let the lava-like anger spew out in all directions—mostly abuse at himself for allowing his wife to get on that plane to Tehran. She could be hard-headed at times, but he *knew*. He should've been firm. He knew how people were treated when charged with espionage by the Iranian regime.

What if they hang her? He placed his hands over his eyes and let out a pent up shout. *I'll never see her again.*

Chapter 6

The next morning the clank of a meal tray against the cell gate broke Laila's sleep.

Someone shouted, "Breakfast," and pushed the tray through. It held a piece of bread, a small square of cheese, and tea. Still lying on the foam mattress, eyes wide, her vision danced around the tiny space: a filthy ceiling with cobwebs in the corners framed a cinder-block room. *Where am I? Is this a dream?*

A vague recollection of the events of the night before, the iron bars, and the mattress brought her back to reality. *Oh-my-God, I'm a prisoner.* Starring at the food, her stomach rebelled. All night she'd drifted in and out of consciousness.

Ten minutes later, a female guard appeared and rapped at the door.

"Get up. You're going to the office for check-in. Wear this." She tossed in a prison chador with the picture of the scale of justice. *Justice,* she thought, *was an irony in this hell hole.*

With little energy, Laila forced herself to place her weary and tired body on its feet. The cloth wreaking with sweat attacked her sensitive nose. It repulsed her so much she was afraid to hold it. After a moment's reflection, she obeyed her instruction and followed the guard.

This time as she passed through her wing of the prison, she saw the faces of the women occupying each cell. Their howling and piercing screams had lasted all night. On top of that, she still suffered from jet lag. As she walked along the narrow corridor with high ceilings, a young woman in her mid-twenties, arms holding the iron bars, lay crying. Her round face and slightly curly hair reminded her of Negar. Her moaning made Laila's heart ache to the point of making walking difficult. When she caught sight of the guard she yelled, "Tell me, please! Why I am here?" The guard ignored her.

Agonized by the woman's suffering, Laila knew she had to continue though she desperately wanted to ask the that very same question. Yet, knew better not to.

At the end of the hallway, she entered an office where the guard who brought her in took her finger prints, then hung a number tag around her neck and took her picture.

A second guard scrutinizing a sheet asked, "What do you play?"

Laila didn't understand. "I play nothing."

He barked, "Don't be stupid. I don't like games. I'll ask you again: What do you play?"

She recalled as a teenager she was attracted to Western music and knew playing or listening to music was forbidden in Iran. Later she discovered this prohibition was the Ayatollah's and not the teaching of Islam.

"I play no instrument. I have no such talent."

The guard who brought her in explained, "She's not an addict. Her brother was charged with espionage."

At that point it dawned on Laila that in Persia w*hat do you play* means w*hat's your drug?*

The office guard grimaced with tightened lips and a shake of her head, her expression laced with disgust. She dismissed Laila with a wave, indicating to the other guard to take her away.

On the way back to her cell, Laila saw another of the women groaning in agony. She had a puffy face, as if not having slept for days.

The woman yelled, "You bitch, get me out of here!" The guard ignored the insult, and continued walking with Laila.

This time Laila dared to ask the young guard, "Why are these women here?"

"They are drug addicts. They are brought here to quit their addiction."

"Do they get any help?"

"No."

"They're screaming for help."

"They're animals and must be treated as such."

Back at her cell, the guard slammed the door and left. Laila lay down on the mattress. She tried to erase from her mind the faces in the cells she'd seen. Desperately she directed her thoughts to good times with her family, but to no avail. The mental switch was too difficult; her experiences too fresh, raw. *Am I strong enough to endure this?*

***

Late that night, Laila jolted awake.

A woman's voice yelled, "Wake up! wake up!"

Laila managed to sit up. The woman, dressed like a prison guard, was already inside the cell beside her mattress. She threw a book, cloth, and chador on top of Laila's bag before tossing her another set of clothes. Laila raised her hand in front of her face for protection.

So far, she'd contained her anger. She'd hoped that whatever optimism she could muster might get her out of this hell without severe damage to her reputation, body, or spiritual wellbeing. She'd heard many stories of abused women in the Evin prison, and did not want to become part of that statistic.

Yet, as tired and weak as she was, she couldn't contain herself. "What's going on?"

The guard reacted with a sneer. "Moving to another area of the prison." The woman's onion laced breath attacked Laila's nostrils.

"Why?"

Silence.

Onion-breath laughed. Her large bosom bounced under her uniform. The fat of her belly gyrated vigorously. "The food is better there." She clapped her hands loudly. "We don't have much time. Move. Now." The green color of the uniform indicated her rank. This was a woman not to be trifled with.

After Laila gathered her belongings together, she looked at the floor and bed to make sure nothing got left behind. When she rose to her feet, the guard blindfolded her.

"I want to know why?" Laila pushed, even though she knew she shouldn't.

Onion-breath shoved her shoulder. "Walk."

A few minutes later, cool air hit Laila's face. She could hear an engine running. A hand pushed her into the vehicle. When the door closed, it sped away.

Never had she encountered a woman filled with such contempt and venom. *Bitch, I hope someone teaches her a lesson ... No.* She banished hideous thoughts as fast as they filled her head. Her parents would be proud of her for not harboring ill-thoughts of any one, including someone who treated her like filth.

She felt the injustice. Three days and no one had given her probable cause for incarceration. A prison was just a place filled with rude workers and sick people, justice a forgotten ideal.

The vehicle's sharp turn gave her nausea. To avoid constantly shifting from side to side, Laila extended her arm until she found the arm rest. Her fingers gripped it, giving her balance. Suddenly and unabashedly, she felt like singing, "Que sera, sera." She didn't know why it popped into her head. Maybe her unconscious mind was trying to comfort her as it waded through the dense insomnia-ridden neural pathways. She definitely wasn't thinking clearly.

A short ride later, the vehicle stopped. Someone got out and open the door nearest to her.

"Get out." It was Onion-breath again. She yanked Laila's arm. A shiver reverberated throughout Laila's body at the strength and malice contained in such a simple touch. After taking maybe a dozen steps, warm air indicated she was inside. Two sets of footsteps echoed off the walls.

"Here," said Onion-breath.

The woman removed Laila's blindfold. The light, though dim, hurt her eyes. "You're not allowed to talk to anyone. If you're found disobeying any order, the punishment will be severe." Her narrowed eyes and pursed lips indicated she meant every word. Onion-breath turned around, locked the iron-barred door, and walked away.

Laila examined her new surroundings. The mattress on the floor was lumpy and no better than the previous one. The toilet bowl was stained with a brown ring of some sort, the cell was windowless, and the floor carpeted with a grimy fabric that had never been washed.

But it was quiet.

An emptiness crawled inside her heart and chilled her body.

She noticed bumps on her arm. When she rubbed her neck, there were more. *What? Lice?* She sat on the bed and stared the wall, the vertical bars of the cell, the nothingness beyond. She was too tired to think or feel.

***

The next day, a vicious kick in the leg woke Laila. When she opened her eyes, a stout woman towered over her.

"Get ready to see the interrogator."

"You hit me. Why?" Laila asked, furious with the ill-begotten treatment from these guards. She was only half awake—the expectations of instantaneous reactions were ignored.

"Get. Up."

As Laila rose, the woman picked up the chador from the floor and held it between two fingers.

"You have no right to hit."

"You're the one who has no rights. You people have less value to me than a starved bitch." The guard shoved the blindfold in Laila's face and pushed her out of the cell.

Logic rattled some sense into Laila's head. She took a chance and asked, "What's your name?"

"Fatima."

Laila knew exactly where this woman's hatred stemmed from. Religious minorities had less value than the Muslims in Iran.

"Fatima *khanum*. Everyone should be treated with respect, regardless of one's belief." Since she was much older, Laila added *Khanum*, or madam, as a sign of respect.

Silence.

Both walked the corridor flanked by a dozen or more cells. After few minutes, Laila halted with the pressure on her arm. Fatima removed the blindfold. This time the flash of light did not bother her so much.

She stood in front of a man about five-foot-eight in height, in his forties. Fatima's shoulder was a few inches shorter than his. Dark, cold eyes stared at her as he twisted the ends of his thick mustache, twitching his lips.

Fatima turned, walked out and closed the door.

"My name is Ali Mohmed. Please, sit down."

Laila sat in a chair placed next to a dilapidated table which nearly occupied the entire room. She faced Ali. Beside him was a smaller table with a telephone. It held a plate of half eaten chole kabab, an Iranian meal with a heap of rice and grilled chicken on skewers. A wire extended down from a high ceiling ending at a lamp fixture.

"Do you know why you're here?"

"No. I would like to."

"It's your brother. He confessed to being a spy. This is a very serious offense. He's a danger to society. It's a crime punishable by death you know."

"No. I don't accept that. My brother is not a spy. That's a complete fabrication."

"I respect your opinion. Of course, it is an embarrassment for the family. I understand that. We found him working for an enemy country. It is a deep shame."

"Where is he?"

A long pause made the silence all the more deafening.

"He's in the hospital. When we told him about the charge, he acted very strange. When the doctor checked his condition, they found something wrong with his heart. Your father is also in the hospital with a heart problem?"

What are they doing? Are they bent on destroying my family, one by one? "We're innocent. We are good people. We mean no harm to anybody. This is not just."

"I understand what you are going through. But I have a duty to do. I have an offer for you. It's very reasonable and if you accept, you and your family can get out of this mess."

Silence.

"What is it?"

"All you have to do is accept Islam as your religion and you will be free."

"What if I don't?"

"I will take you to court. There's enough evidence to show that you, too, are a spy. You'll be found guilty. Even worse though, is that you are fighting against God. There is only one penalty for that: death by hanging."

"Me? A spy? No. I'm not a spy."

"You live in America."

"How does that make me spy? I'm the mother of two children. I know nothing of being a spy. This is a lie. This. Is. A. Lie." Tears crept on unaware. She fought back, not giving the interrogator the pleasure of her weakness. She lowered her head, covered her eyes and instead, allowed the emotional release to happen in her heart.

"Consider the proof before me; centers of your religion are in Israel and Chicago, *and* you are married to an American." He pauses. "What's his name?"

"Whose name?"

"Your husband."

Silence.

"I have ways of making you reveal this information. Your brother was most forthright when given the right opportunity."

What did they do to my Orie? If this man finds out Jake was in the US Air Force...

"No, I won't tell you." She had born two children *naturally*; she could handle the pain.

Ali stood and walked over to Laila. He leaned in close and stroked her check with a finger.

"You are a very pretty woman. When you are in your cell, think about what I said. The food here is terrible. It's hard to sleep, and you will *always* be alone."

His touch made her stomach turn. Anxiety attacked her body and mind.

"I'm married. According to the Quran, making lustful remarks towards a married woman is considered adultery."

Ali pulled away. "You know the Quran?" He glared at her. "Go back to your cell. We'll meet again soon." He left the room only to return with Fatima.

As Fatima wrapped the blindfold, Ali reiterated, "Think carefully about what I said. Here you have lots of time for that. The cells have no windows and there is only one exit. To go through it, you have to be accompanied by a prison guard. This is a fortress guarded by hundreds of loyal men and women who will not hesitate to shoot."

Back in her cell, Laila worried about what they could do to her. She directed her thoughts from herself to how her children would suffer without a mother. And Jake. Would he miss her? Two weeks had not been long enough after so many years apart.

But now she understood why she was there. Orie was not a spy; of course not. Very likely he did not agree to convert and as revenge, he was charged with espionage. *Am I doomed to suffer the same fate?*

Chapter 7

Jake sat by the kitchen table staring at the neighbor's roof through a large window next to the back yard. With the kids in the front he had a quiet moment. Jake had difficulty concentrating on anything else. He swallowed a mouthful of lemonade to cool down from the morning's heat. He couldn't afford to have the air-conditioning running.

They got her. He shook his head. *The Iranian Revolutionary Guard got my Laila.* Since he received the dreaded news, the same thought ran through his mind as a dull ache worked to engulf his head.

He berated himself yet again for allowing Laila to take such a risk. Life would never be the same without her. Knowing he'd be coming home to her after his tour in the Middle East made the horrors of war palpable. But now, she was trapped with no way out. That knowledge only served to bring back one of the most harrowing events he faced while serving in Afghanistan. The memory swallowed him whole.

Green triangles on a map of rugged terrain, winding roads, and mountains showed the position of every troop on the ground. As a member of the 802nd Mission Support Group, Jake's daily task consisted of being in a heightened state of awareness regarding every military activity taking place in the region. If anyone faced a threat, he deployed support as requested by the forces on the ground. Three computer screens and a wireless headset were his weapons on this battlefield.

One morning Jake monitored the increase in an alarm on one screen. Suddenly the message, “Ambushed by enemy. Request support immediately,” streamed across his central monitor. The one on the right showed helicopters and a drone, either of which he could deploy if requested. Then his sight shifted to the screen on the left displaying a map of the region studded with green markers. With every passing moment he scanned all three screens in their concave formation at his make-shift field station. The tech and the mind operating it were the value points here.

With a few more mouse clicks, a video feed came in showing the live the action.

“Oh no!”

His friend, John Dwyer, stood on an armoured Humvee with a machine gun mounted on it. The battle ground consisted of a dry river bed surrounded by boomerang-shaped farming terraces, dotted with huge boulders. Riffle fire came from behind the huge rocks where the enemies hid. John manned a .50-cal gun with five hundred rounds, far more firepower than the AK rifles. With such powerful ammunition John had a chance of surviving this ambush. His troop had been assigned to establish a peaceful relation with village elders in Ganjigal, not instigate a fire-fight.

The night before, John talked about the mission. He relished being assigned to the team as a tactician and gunner, in case the situation turned sour. He knew his weapon well and wanted to support the peace talks any way he could. However, the video feed signified a grave situation only made worse by the team’s positioning.

Jake watched as John’s vehicle made a sudden stop with a sharp turn before speeding off in the opposite direction in an area nearly as large as a football field. Jake hammered his fist on the table. Through the radio contact, the sound of incoming gun fire from all directions meant John and his troop faced multiple enemies.

A cloud of dust rose behind the Humvee as it swerved left and right trying to avoid the increase in gun fire.

Jake filled out the mandatory request form with lightning-fast keyboard strokes to deploy the Blackhawk and ten soldiers. He clicked the

Request button and waited for approval from a higher chain of command. After thirty seconds, surprised that the request hadn't gone through, he double-checked the mission profile—sure enough there were no helicopters in direct support of them, but one or more could be diverted if needed.

Megan walked over to her father and pulled his hand. "Daddy, I'm hungry. I want some food. How many times do I have tell you that?"

Jake snapped out of his dream-like state, but a deep sense of gloom lingered. Guilt haunted him since John's death. Knowing more could have been done but wasn't. *I did not save my friend's life.* Now, it was Laila who faced mortal danger. Instead of US troops under fire, her life rested in the hands of a different kind of enemy, one he didn't understand.

Megan pulled his arm again, harder this time.

"Come."

"Sorry, Dumpling." Jake got up and walked over the cupboard to pull out a box of Kellogg's Mini-Wheat. As he reached for a bowl, he jumped when his cell rang. *Negar?*

He pulled the device and looked at the screen—a local call.

"Hello?"

"Is this Mr. Hudley?"

"Yes."

"I'm Miss Abernathy, Megan's teacher. Where is your daughter, sir? We haven't received any message from either you or your wife as to Megan's whereabouts." She sounded annoyed and impatient.

"Oh. Yes. Sorry. Megan will be at school shortly."

He ended the call, grabbed a bowl, and poured some cereal and milk. He pulled Megan, who must've been waiting for her breakfast for over two hours now, by the hand to the table.

"Dumpling, we're late for school. Eat this as fast as you can. I'll go get your clothes and knapsack. Quick now."

He dashed up to her room, and returned with a pair jeans, t-shirt, and her backpack. While she ate, Jake peeled off her PJ top and replaced it with a shirt.

"Hurry, eat faster. When you finish, take off the bottom jammy and put these pants on. I'll get Dillon ready. Hurry, you're taking too long."

"Daddy, I can't eat any faster."

He went to an area in front of the TV where Dillon sat playing with his toys, also in his pyjamas; he too had not eaten yet.

"Megan, Honey, remove your jammy bottoms and put your pants on." Jake emphasized the last two words.

"Not finished yet."

"I know. You can eat in the car."

With Dillon in his arms, he went outside and buckled him in the car seat. Back in the kitchen, Jake saw Megan had her jeans on and was doing up the zipper.

"Good girl. You're so fast." He then lifted the knapsack with one hand and the half-full bowl of cereal with the other. "Out to the car now."

He secured his daughter into her booster chair and placed the remaining breakfast on her lap. Rushing around the car, he slid into the front seat and jammed the key into the ignition. After cranking the engine a few times, it finally turned over and roared to life.

Good. Damn thing started.

After parking in the drop-off lane at the school, he took the empty bowl off Megan's lap and let her out of the back. Inside at the office he signed her in and then gave her a hug by the main doors. Dillon sat in the car eating an old cracker left in his chair.

"Go to your class and I'll see you later."

"What about lunch?"

He hadn't thought of lunch. "I'll get you something."

"Not McDonalds. Mom'll get mad at you if you buy that."

"Okay. Go." He waved bye.

When he got back in the car Dillon was crying. His cracker gone, he had nothing to keep him quiet anymore. Jake combed his hair with his fingers and inhaled a deep sigh. *I'm falling apart.* He couldn't think of what to do next. *Dammit Laila, I need you.*

Jake whipped open the glovebox, found a stash of Goldfish Crackers, turned and passed them to his son. The boy's eyes lit up. Jake watched him dig into the bag and pop a Goldfish into his mouth. His round rosy checks, pointed nose and creamy-brown skin blended the perfect attributes from he and Laila, though Laila swore the boy looked exactly like Jake.

He started the car but didn't shift into gear. Dillon would be fast asleep in a few minutes. The motion of the car would be Jake's saving grace when the food ran out. Jake took his eyes off the rear-view mirror and looked at the field ahead, set up for soccer drills. The bright orange triangles dotting the green lawn morphed into green triangular icons on the screen—soldiers in peril.

Jake's eyes shot between the green triangles on the monitor and the heli request—back and forth, and back and forth. The battle of Ganjigi raged on as the status of the helicopter request still waited for official authorization. In a situation like this every second counted. Casualties were supposed to be avoided and yet every man out there needed cover from the RPG, a deadly weapon—one hit would blow up the Humvee.

He pressed a button and a commanding voice came on the speaker. In a non-committal way, the liaison explained his tardiness.

"Quite simply, there is no helicopter available right now."

Jake knew pleading with him wouldn't help. He disconnected the call and focused on the screen. Every second seemed like eternity. He watched everything unfold. John ducked down in the turret at an odd angle.

"You okay man? You hit?" the driver yelled in a strong Afghani accent. His com was still on.

"Yeah, yeah. Keep driving," yelled John.

Several minutes passed when John came on the speaker, “Fox Four-4. Lost contact with my team. Four marines are missing. Don’t have grid or radio contact with them.” His weak voice strained with pain.

“Four-4 this is White Horse,” a pilot said. “Roger. Give us your vector. We’ll stay with you.”

“White Horse, fire coming from schoolhouse, grid 977 611.”

“Four-4. Got it. Be right back,” the pilot responded.

It took nearly three minutes before a Kiowas appeared on the display, followed by a cloud from a village above the farm terraces. When Jake turned to look at the Humvee, John no longer manned the mounted gun. He must’ve been shot or bumped off the vehicle or both.

A honk blasted from behind the car. Jake lifted his head enough to glance at the rear view mirror. He started the engine and drove off to make room in the kiss-n-ride spot.

He couldn’t go back home. Not yet. He found himself headed for his parents’ place, hitting the steering wheel and blaming himself for his friend’s death—for Laila’s. That would undoubtedly be her fate stuck in that prison.

Jake parked in the driveway of his parents’ old colonial-style home and walked in holding a drowsy Dillon in his arms. The scent of fresh baked cinnamon muffins invaded his nostrils. After placing Dillon on the couch he walked into the kitchen. Jake appeared at the doorway just as his mother, Ruth, placed the hot pan on a cooling tray. He approached the counter.

“Mmm, these look good.” Pockets of blueberry on the bran muffin stimulated his appetite and he snatched two.

“That’s enough. These are for the afternoon snack at the seniors centre.”

“Speaking of afternoon, can you watch Dillon for few hours?”

“No. I have to get ready and leave in an hour. Where are *you* going?”

Jake shrugged his shoulders. “I don’t know. Somewhere.” He didn’t want to tell her about Laila, that her arrest weighed on him. He was still absorbing the reality of it and couldn't bring himself to share the tragedy with anyone.

With both hands in oven mittens and an apron wrapped around her waist, Ruth said, "What's wrong with you?"

"What do you mean?"

"You look like the homeless on Drummer Street who hasn't slept, shaved or washed for days. I think you need your wife. When is she coming back?"

Her response irked him. She'd asked the same question six times already in the past two days and Jake had given her the return date every time. He knew his mother had a mental block about Laila. Anything to do with her didn't register for long.

"I told you before, she's gone for two weeks." He paused. "But the plan has changed. Exactly when she's coming home now? Who knows."

She straightened up as if poised with enough ammunition for a fight. "Is she staying longer than two weeks? She shouldn't. She shouldn't stay away from her children for that long. It's called abandonment."

"Mom, don't exaggerate. Laila would never abandon her children." At that point an urge to unload his burden overwhelmed him. "Is Dad around?"

"Yes. In his office."

Jake heard the sound of footsteps coming down the stairs. "I think he's coming down, now. Yes, there he is."

His father's six-foot frame standing tall, straight, and slim appeared at the bottom step of the stairs. "I heard the raucous here and wanted to know what was going on."

Jake said, "I need to talk to both of you."

Well-dressed every morning as usual, he puckered, "Sounds serious. Let me pour myself a cup of coffee and then we'll talk. Ahh, fresh muffins."

"Chuck, lay off the coffee. That's your second cup this morning."

Jake was also concerned about his father's latest health issues. Charles Hudley, 66, a retired US General, only a month earlier was diagnosed with arrhythmia, caused by taking high blood pressure medication for too long. His doctor advised him that caffeine wasn't good for his abnormal heart rhythm. His mom's reminder to kick the habit was a nag. But Dad always fought back.

"When the right time comes, I'll be off my fix. For now, I'm enjoying it. I have only one life to live." Charles emptied the carafe into a mug, turned off the machine, picked up a muffin and walked through the sliding door onto the patio, where he spent most of his time.

Jake followed. The area, furnished with rattan chairs, a sofa and table, was protected from the Texas sun by a roof supported by four posts. He sat on the sofa next to his father.

"Mom, are you coming," he yelled.

"You go ahead without me. I have to clean up." His mother always left serious business to the men of the house.

Jake sunk into the seat. The man he faced was a proud one for many reasons. A well-admired person in military, political, and community circles, he was also a Rhodes scholar at the University of Oxford where he earned a degree in Philosophy, Politics and Economics. Later he graduated from the Command and General Staff College with a master's degree in military science. In the army he served in Vietnam and many other parts of the world. Jake's father carried all this in his bearing and wore it like a medal of honor.

"Son, what's on your mind? You looked haggard." He was dead-accurate on judging characters and moods, that's why he'd moved quickly up the ranks.

"The Revolutionary Guards went to Laila parent's place and took Laila for questioning."

"Questioning?" Charles froze. He was never one to react abruptly. His eyes narrowed as he absorbed the word. Placing the mug on the table, his father's face gave nothing away until his jaw tightened. With two fingers he caressed his moustache, then his chin. "Questioning for what?"

"All Negar said was that Orie, her brother, had been charged with espionage."

Charles had worked closely with military intelligence, a division that exchanged information and experience with the CIA and FBI.

"American?"

"American and Israeli."

"That's their typical charges. They aren't very creative over there."

Dillon's sobs floated out to the porch from the front living room. Jake went inside and held him.

Rubbing his son's back, he asked, "Mom, can you make some lunch? We kinda missed breakfast." Jake placed Dillon on a chair while the boy's grandmother brought over a lolly pop and placed it in his mouth, then rushed to make a sandwich for the boy.

Jake returned to the porch and sat down again. "I keep thinking the worst. I haven't been able to sleep. Both Megan and Dillon are missing their mother and I can't seem to keep up with what they need right now."

Charles looked up, deep thought. With fingers joined in a cathedral shape and arms resting on the chair, he said, "We know their behavioural pattern. They arrest a Westerner, charge her with espionage, put her through a fake trial, and then sentence her to death.

"Of course, the country of the accused would normally protest. Then a negotiation starts between that country and Iran and, if she's lucky she's released. Just a few days ago, an Iranian-Canadian was on death row but I think in Laila's case it'll be difficult if the Iranian authorities find out that you"—he pointed his finger at Jake—"the husband, have been in the US Air Force. For her release, the price will be high. Very high. They'll want the US government involved."

"I was thinking of going there."

"There? You mean Iran? No, no, no." He shook his head vigorously. "You don't want to do that. The minute you set your feet on that soil, you'll be arrested. I guarantee it."

"Dad, I can't stay here and do nothing. This isn't how I operate."

"I don't care how you operate, son. You're not going over there." His tone came like an order from General Hudley and not his father.

"But Dad, how would you handle it if mom was in Laila's situation?"

"Your mother wouldn't have gotten herself into a situation like this. She always listens to me. Besides you've served in the Air Force. Someone like you shouldn't even think of going to Iran. No, no, no." Charles waved his forefinger at his son.

Jake knew his father was a true military man who always followed the rules by the book. But Jake also knew his loyalty to his wife came before the US Air Force. He'd fallen in love with her first. Without his dad's blessing Jake was now more confused than ever.

***

Negar rushed to the front door. She faced three men dressed in the uniform of the Revolutionary Guard. After assuring the right address, the guard in the middle gave her the news. It took a moment for the thought to sink in.

"Orie's death … How did he die?"

"Heart attack."

"He was only sixteen!" She choked back a wail, robbing them of the pleasure of her distress. "No. *You* killed him."

"Here." His extended hand held a sheet of paper.

"What's this?"

"The medical expense. This has to be paid before the body can be released to the family."

She took the sheet and spat on his face, "Take this."

The other two guards lifted their rifles, ready to shoot. The one doing the talking calmed them with the movement of both arms. "Not now. Judgment Day is coming. On that *special* day, you will pay a dear price. And no one will be able to help you."

Negar seethed, "I have bad news for you too. Judgment Day is here now. For what you are doing to me, my family, and innocent people, you and the whole Iranian regime are going to hell. Mark my words."

They turned and left. Negar returned to the house. She couldn't believe her reaction. Sure, she was feisty and always fought for her rights but was never so rude as to spit on anybody. With so much injustice already piled on her, asking payment for the release of her brother's body was too much to bear. The anger choked her senses, making it difficult to walk, to breathe.

When she shuffled into the kitchen, Negar found her mother leaning over the sink washing dishes. She clutched Maman tight as an uncontrollable cry swept over her.

Maliheh clutched her daughter's back with a damp hand and in an impatient voice asked, "What happened?"

"They killed Orie."

Maliheh only nodded and said, "I had a dream last night. Saw him standing in very vast space. He looked like a toddler. Then he turned into a bird with feathers of beautiful colors. This morning I got a sense he was no longer with us." She held her daughter for long time. "Let us say some prayers for my son."

Both walked over to a table and said several prayers for the departed. At the end Maliheh whispered, "I give my son as a sacrifice and as a result of his blood, I hope this regime will collapse before it does more harm to innocent people."

Negar had been gradually falling apart after Orie's disappearance. But her mother's strength only dug deeper into sturdy roots she had never seen before.

Maliheh rose like a lioness. "We will fight and will not let them bully us. Get ready and we'll go to see Baba."

Later that afternoon, when both women left home and stepped out onto a busy street, Negar wondered how her father would react. After the arrest, Baba was upset with Orie for not heeding his warnings to stay close to home—not travel to the city. Every week brought more news of youth being targeted by the Revolutionary Guards. Negar knew how bored Orie was all the time, and being sixteen with a rebellious attitude to parental restrictions, one little mistake led to Orie's life being cut short.

***

Jake pressed the elevator button for the Colonade Center, a prestigious edifice housing politicians, corporate head offices, and lawyers. Then he turned to his dad, "It was lucky to get an appointment with Senator Quest with such short notice."

Charles nodded. "Ted owes me a few favors." He was wearing well-pleated dress pants and a button up short-sleeved dress shirt.

Ted Quest and Charles Hudley followed a similar military path, both achieving the rank of general. In his fifties, Ted joined state politics until his aspirations changed and the man was elected as a US Senator. Though Ted's
career kept him mostly in Washington and Charles was all over the US, both kept their friendship intact with frequent phone calls and the occasional lunch.

At the sound of a ding, father and son stepped inside. When the elevator rose to the ninth floor, they exited into the reception area. The walls were filled with Senator Quest's pictures: one when he was a boy scout, another as a US Army general, one with President George W. Bush in the year he was elected to the US Senate and many with his family. Charles headed to the receptionist who greeted him with a sweet voice.

"My name is Charles Hudley. We're here to see Senator Quest."

With perfect white teeth and a perfect smile, the thirty-something with natural blonde hair said, "Mr. Hudley, please take a seat. Senator Quest will see you soon."

Both sank into a leather sofa and silently absorbed their surroundings. The floor was decorated with Persian carpets. The tables were antiques. It had an atmosphere of comfort and elegance, and more importantly the air was a lot cooler than outside.

A man with a trim five-seven frame soon moved to stand in front of them. Father and son rose to their feet and the greeting ensued with vigorous handshakes. "Charles, so good to see you! It's been a while. A long while."

With a broad smile Charles responded, "Ted, thanks for seeing us on such short notice."

The Senator put his hand on Jake's shoulder. "Jake, good to see you. Let's go to my office and we can talk." Once inside, he closed the door, then gestured his guests toward a red leather wing back chair. Jake and Charles sat on the sofa facing the elite piece of furniture.

The Senator settled into the wing chair and crossed his legs, his freshly shined shoes pointing towards Charles. Rubbing his chin, he said, "So, what's the occasion for your visit?"

Charles got straight to the point. "Jake's wife, Laila, went to visit her ailing father in Iran and once she got there, was arrested and thrown into Evin Prison."

Senator Ted Quest was the chairman of the House Committee on Foreign Affairs. His grey eyebrows arched, erasing the smile on his face and replaced it with a concern. "When was Laila taken into custody?"

Jake reacted. "A day or two ago."

The Senator's face relaxed slightly. "Very likely I'll get a report on Laila today or tomorrow. Our agents in Iran will send me a message as soon as they find out. It's routine." Ted looked directly at Jake. "I am so sorry to hear this." His concern was genuine. He and his wife had attended Jake and Laila's wedding.

Charles took a deep breath which drew attention from the other two. "How can you help us to bring her home?"

"Charles, I'll be honest with you. It wouldn't be easy. There are many issues that'll complicate the situation. One is that the US government does not have a direct diplomatic tie with Iran. To deal with them we have to go through Switzerland's embassy which slows things down, and we have to follow certain international protocols. Secondly, Laila was born in Iran, therefore the government does not recognize her as an American citizen. Thirdly, we have a serious negotiation happening between us and Iran regarding nuclear armament. If we raise this as an issue they could use it as a bargaining chip."

Charles leaned forward. He jabbed the air with his index finger as he said, "You draw a gloomy picture. You mean to say, we can't do anything for her? She is an American citizen for crying out loud, and married to an American man." He took a short pause and shook his head. "Ted, you have to be able to twist some diplomatic arms to get her out of that awful place."

Jake was impressed by his father's commitment to helping Laila. At the same time, he was also irritated that the diplomatic doors were closed, at least according to the Senator.

"I honestly believe they'll kill her, sir. Her brother was taken to prison. I can't say whether he's alive or not. My father-in-law suffered a heart attack as a consequence of this atrocity. The authorities are targeting the whole family."

The Senator, soft spoken, took his time to answer, "Jake, I understand it's a grave situation." He stood up and walked to his desk, empty except for his business cards and a family picture with the dog. From a drawer he pulled out a box of chocolates, walked back and offered one to Jake, who accepted. Charles declined. Then he sat in the wing back chair. "I'll look into it and, who knows, I may find an answer."

Jake knew he was getting a political side-line, but he needed solid information. "Senator, you have great credentials. You've served in the US Army overseas with my dad and you have an influential position in foreign affairs circles. I need to know; please tell us if the US government can do anything to help Laila."

The Senator leaned forward and calculated his answer. Silence reigned for the longest moment. "The short reply is no. But I will not give up on looking for ways to get her out of Iran and back to the US with you." He took a glance at the wrist watch. "I have to catch a plane to Washington in an hour." He stood.

Jake and Charles got up too. All three stepped towards the door.

"Senator, what about a covert operation?" Jake knew a guy—ex-CIA. Knew these kinds of things happened more often than the brass wanted to admit.

Ted pulled his hand from the door knob, took a strong stance and gave Jake a teacher's disapproving stare. He wagged his forefinger. "Don't even think about it. Iran is a formidable place. Already we have our CIA agents there gathering information on their nuclear plant's progress and in no way can we afford to go there and put our missions at risk."

"Why not? I don't understand."

"One agent would never be able to pull off a clandestine operation and if he got caught, a red alert would go off, making it impossible to gather intel on the progress of the nuclear plants."

After exchanging goodbyes Jake and Charles left the building. His government refused to help his wife; his country was leaving her to a fate worse than death and expected him to simply accept that. He slammed into the door on the way out, shaking his father's hand from his shoulder.

***

Laila's sleep was broken by clanking and the approach of voices. She wondered at how this life made her look forward to meal time, not to eat but for a chance to hear a voice and have a little human interaction. In the last few days, she'd befriended a woman in her twenties, who always had a smile for her when passing out the food trays. This time was no different.

"*Merci*. Have a good day," came Laila's soft voice.

The girl smiled, "*Merci*. You have a good day, too." Then moved on to the next cell. A zing of appreciation tingled through her veins. Then Laila took three grains of rice from the plate, walked over the corner close to the gate, and placed them in a row next to seven other piles. Each heap represented a day living without her beloved family. One grain was for Jake and the other two for Megan and Dillon.

Returning to the food, Laila ate the rice and mixed vegetables, and left the horrible smelling mutton untouched. She searched for a refreshing memory but couldn't latch on to one. Though quiet, disgusting smells and a lack of nourishment hovered close to shroud her mind from clarity.

She slid the tray through the bottom of the gate to be collected later, just as Fatimeh's huge legs appeared on the other side of the iron bars. Laila lifted her gaze. The sight of the woman made the food in her stomach sour.

What now? She never displayed any malicious intent towards this guard even though her personability needed a lot of work. As usual, Fatimeh barged in after unlocking the door.

Without any exchange of greeting, she demanded, "Get ready. I'm taking you to brother Ali's office."

Laila put on the chador, allowed Fatimeh to wrap the blindfold, and both women walked down the hallway. With every step Laila silently recited the "Remover of Difficulties" prayer. She really needed that. Just the sight of Ali made the churning inside jump up several notches. She needed all the courage she could muster.

As she entered the room, Laila noticed the air wasn't as musty as her first *visit*. Fatimeh disappeared leaving Laila to stand by the desk while Ali concluding a phone conversation.

He placed the receiver on the holder, rubbed his thick hair and commanded, "Sit down."

Laila's self-worth diminished ten-fold at the sound of his voice. She avoided direct eye contact and lowered her head.

"I have bad news. Your brother died. The doctors tried their best to save him. But they could not." The words tore at her heart as the curve of her back deepened more than she thought possible.

Never again would she hug her free-spirited kid brother. What Laila would give now to burst out with her grief and sorrow. But by withholding her pain, and containing the aching pressure inside, she scraped a modicum of justice for Orie. *How did he die? Did he suffer?*

Laila fought too many conflicting emotions: love and sadness for Orie; anger and fear with Ali; confusion and stubbornness with Fatimeh. She couldn't take much more of this man and hoped she'd be dismissed soon. Still absorbing the terrible news, all her senses wanted to go into a freeze mode, but she refused the deep shock. He wanted her numb, malleable. But the explanation of her brother's death didn't make sense. Circumstances behind his treatment and passing were suspicious at best and she refused to believe anything this man said.

"I thought you would be screaming. Wailing your sorrow and grief to honor your brother. America has changed you."

Laila ignored him. Ali was used to women begging for mercy. With every ounce of power in her, she would deny him this pleasure.

"How exactly did he die?

"The doctor says cardiac arrest."

"He was only *sixteen*. How can that happen?"

Ali paused to calculate a response. "What I know is that he was charged with espionage. I'm not a doctor, but what I've noticed is that people charged with such a crime go through a severe shock. They think they will never get caught, then they are and are held accountable. Your brother's case is no different. In such a situation it's not unusual for someone like him to have a heart attack."

"I want to go to his funeral. Can I leave this prison now?"

"It's not up to me. It's up to the judge."

"I've been in this rotten place for over a week. I can't keep track of day and night. I haven't been charged with anything. This is inhumane. Where is the justice here?"

"I understand. I'll arrange a quick session for you in front of a judge. Here is what you can do for us. Give me your husband's name, and the names of the members of your religion in America and I'll expedite the process."

"That's not going to happen."

"We have ways of getting this information with or without your aid. I'm trying to help you. With this information I can quickly arrange for a court hearing, and if you are *not* found guilty you will be released. I understand this place is not like home. It's not meant to be comfortable."

Home. The feeling of Dillon in her arms. Megan, and Jake hugging her fiercely at the airport flashed through her mind. How sweet it would it be to go home? Home to her babies, all three of them.

She yearned for Jake's love and support. Except for a stranger's smile, every moment in this place wrung out her strength and will power. But she refused to show this to Ali. That's why he wanted to see her: to have her crawl like a wounded bird. And she was wounded.

"If you don't mind I like to go to my cell. I need to be alone right now."

"Think of what I said. I repeat, we have ways of getting the information we want."

Ali stood up, opened the door and signaled for Fatimeh to return Laila to her cell.

***

Maliheh Dareini stood in the cemetery along with her husband and daughter, about to bury her only son. At this funeral there were only three souls. Many wanted to attend but were strongly advised against it. At one in the afternoon, bright sunlight showered the ground, walls, trees and houses in the neighborhood. The vast land appeared empty with no head stones to mark the resting place of the deceased. Instead, groupings of flowers decorated the ground. If ever anyone disobeyed the order of this land by placing markings of remembrance, cemetery caretakers came with bulldozers and shovels to remove such *undeserved* ceremonials.

As Maliheh waited for the arrival of the body, she stood near her son's grave site holed up next to a wall sobbing and wailing, "Orie, my Orie. Why? Why? Why? How can a mother live without her son?"

Negar stood next to Maliheh rubbing her shoulder. The sorrow of her daughter had run its course, for now. The girl couldn't help but swim in an ocean of sadness.

Heart heavy, Maliheh blamed the Iranian government for taking such a young, innocent life. A life too precious to simply be snuffed out. Now she'd never see him grow to be a man, get his education, marry or have a life like billions of others.

Less than a foot away Abbas, her husband, stood in his own world completely oblivious to her grieving. With his hands down before him, arms joined, and head lowered towards the ground, he remained lost in his own thoughts.

Maliheh's passions kept her head lifted as their heat fueled her rage. Mostly her anger blasted the Iranian regime, the rest volleyed between herself, and her son for taking such an unnecessary trip into town.

Yet, there was no trace of vengeance in her heart. In fact, she'd never held ill-will towards anybody. When praised for her character, she would humbly tell the listener how many mistakes she herself had committed. But those who knew her, praised her for her purity.

The Khavaran cemetery sat in the South East of Tehran; a graveyard mainly for religious minorities, communists, political dissidents, atheists, and homosexuals. According to the religious orders of the land, these souls could not be buried alongside any Muslims, good or bad. The non-Muslims belonged in the "Accursed Land".

Silence fell.

The sobbing stopped as Maliheh tracked a black vehicle until it stopped on the lane in line with the hole in the ground, only a hundred feet away from Orie's final resting place. She stood still and watched as the driver and two caretakers got out, pulled up the body wrapped in cloth, and took it to the hole in a stretcher.

At his final resting place, only Orie's parents and one sister were present. Relatives, friends, and neighbors were asked not to participate. Instead they planned to meet in secret, in two days' time, for a service filled with prayers, remembering all of Orie's deeds in such a short life.

Abbas had been warned of watching eyes this day. Maliheh scanned the area and sure enough, she saw a pair of voyeurs in the car parked on the street next to the cemetery, and a few others who pretended to visit loved ones, watched and waited. It was well known that these government agents made visual or written notes of those who were present. Orie's family would become targets of harassment.

As the men lowered the body into the ground, all three loved ones chanted a prayer for the dead in unison. Then each said separately their private prayers for Orie.

Maliheh felt hot in her layered clothing but a gentle wind wafted over her, cooling her down. First Negar approached the white shroud folded around the boy's body. As she knelt to the earth, she let fall a single yellow rose, for remembrance. It landed just above the molded clasp of his hands, meant to do so much more in this life.

Then Abbas shuffled forward and used Negar's shoulder to bear his weight as he leaned over the grave of his son and let fall a single white rose for the purity of his child's soul. It came to rest next to Orie's mouth, where never a foul word passed such kind lips.

Lastly, as father and daughter slipped back from the graveside, Maliheh left her clutch of the nearby wall, dropped to all four limbs and placed a single red rose over his heart. Negar helped her mother back to her feet.

As the family stood in silence, Maliheh noticed a strange sensation pass through her body. An energy swept away her sorrow, and instead a tranquility and joy filled her inside—a serenity she'd never before experienced. Orie was next to her, telling her he was fine. That comforting thought accompanied a few more tears rolling silently down her checks. Her little boy was gone.

After a lingering moment, all three understood it was time to leave. Flanked on either side by his dearest family, Abbas slowly moved with the support from his wife and daughter. As Maliheh left the cemetery, her thoughts were on what to do next. Her only son dead, one daughter in the claws of the vultures, and an ill husband—she had to step up.

All her life, as was the Iranian tradition, she walked a few steps behind her men in the path of life. But she had to rescue Laila, even though it could mean giving up her own life. So far Negar had done her best to hold the family together. But the girl was a spitfire, headstrong, and naïve; her personality could get her into trouble. Maliheh was determined to protect her. To protect them all.

Chapter 8

Driving along Kenly Avenue, Jake slowed down at the sight of Lackland Air Force Base. After a quick turn, he pulled up to the gate. The male guard on duty immediately recognized him.

"Hi Jake."

The iron bar went up and within minutes he passed through rows of cars, eyes scanning the parking area for an empty spot. At the same time his mind danced around his father's and the Senator's warnings, his main reason for going to the base. *Am I doing the right thing?*

What his dad said made sense, but it didn't sit right with him. And knowing the government wasn't willing to help, even in the slightest, made his blood boil. He had to find another way. He had to talk to Andy, a security specialist at the Surveillance Support Center—the same place Jake's career started and flourished. Here, he too became a specialist in satellite surveillance. Then, duty called two months before Laila was due to give birth. He'd been forced to leave her when she needed him most. Never again.

The success of Jake's plan hinged on Andy Burke's full co-operation.

Beyond the sliding glass doors of the military building, he passed within a metal frame attached to scanners and monitors, similar to those found at airport security check points, but more precise. Next a guard scanned his body with a hand-held device; again no alarm went off. The guard signaled Jake to go ahead.

At the front desk Jake greeted Susan, a female officer with a broad smile, a woman he once dated for six months. That relationship ended abruptly when Jake met Laila. Susan had been upset, but not devastated.

"I hear your wife has gone to Iran." She never called Laila by her name; it was always *the wife*. The small-town rumor mill ran 24/7.

"Yes, Laila's in Iran. Can you please let Andy know I'm here?"

She picked up the phone, pushed a few buttons and gave the message to the listener. After hanging up, she said, "This Saturday, we're having a party at my place. Why don't you come? You must be lonely." She ended the sentence with a seductive smile.

Jake shot her a non-committal response. Not wanting to continue this conversation he pointed to a couch.

"I'll wait for him over there."

Sitting on a black leather chair he nervously watched the glass door Andy would walk through. His moist palm rubbed the arm rest, a way to ease the nervous tension filling his body. The occasional deep breath slightly eased the pain around his chest, until it clamped down again moments later with the flash of Laila's face as she glanced over her shoulder when boarding the plane.

Another sleepless night sapped his energy. As he'd tossed and turned he imagined Laila learning about Orie's death. The churning in his head never stopped. *Was she scared? Hopeless? Sad?*

The second Jake spotted Andy Burke he got up and moved to give his best bud a hug. After the jovial greeting they headed for lunch in the mess hall. At the end of the line, each of them pulled up an empty tray and moved through the entrees to the desert and drinks area. He got a soup and Andy got Sheppard's Pie.

Andy stared at the tray and said, "You're usually an eating machine, man. A soup? Just a soup?"

"Not hungry." Every passing day without Laila, Jake's appetite diminished.

Andy snagged a few extra items as they approached the cashier and paid for their meals. Jake found a private booth, where the noise was less and located far enough from the next table so no one could overhear their conversation.

After settling into the seat across from Andy, Jake reflected on his friend as both men attacked their food. When Jake's family moved to Lackland AFB, his father was given the task of heading the Space Surveillance System. After finishing Basic Military Training, followed by obtaining a degree in electronic engineering, both Jake and Andy joined the Space Surveillance System as electronic engineers. They were inseparable.

Both boys moved up the ranks from being engineers to becoming specialists. Andy took charge of the test program for the latest and greatest in technology. Jake became support staff in combat zones; unfortunately, that took him to Afghanistan. While they were apart physically, they were never far from each other. The friends managed to communicate weekly via email, Skype or phone call. Occasionally Laila would relay greetings if Jake couldn't spare the time for a 2nd communication.

Jake took another spoonful of beef barley soup. "What's wrong with this soup?" He took a bite of his whole wheat bun.

"What do you mean?" Andy asked. "You always liked the beef barley."

"Ugh, I can't eat. Too many things on my mind."

"Not hungry? Strange coming from you."

Jake didn't want to dwell on it. "What's new with the AH project?" Military personnel always talked in coded language. AH stood for Assignee Holiday, a code name for the most sophisticated surveillance system in the compound that Andy just happened to be working on. DARPA co-tasked the project; it was so cutting edge.

"Jake, man, I just got my hands on the latest version. Awesome, awesome, awesome."

"Tell me about it."

Andy put his fork down, chewed and swallowed as fast as he could. His eyes lit up as he smiled.

"Where do I begin?"

"Gimme the specs."

"Get this. It is lighter than a MacBook Pro but a hundred times faster. One of my guys. Actually a gal. She did a comparison test." He took a swig from his water bottle. "It connects directly to one of our main intelligence satellites, and has full GPS functionality. Get this, the *Street View* is so sophisticated that from a point on any road you get a 3-D view you can manipulate in real-time. Point to a building, and you can see anyone inside. I am not aware of the exact technology used, but what I do know is this device is top, top secret."

"What kind of land communication does it provide?"

"You can do a secure SkyTalk conversation anywhere in the world. Search the Internet from anywhere too. It's limitless using the interface with the satellite. But here's the kicker. You can view *anywhere* in the world. Live. Real time. Freakin' amazing, man."

The more Jake absorbed, the more he realized the importance of this device. This was what a guy would need to travel into dangerous territory *alone*.

"You're testing it, right? How robust is it?"

"The touch screen is the toughest military-grade polymer available. And it's fancier than any Apple product. Looks like a laptop. Agents can move country to country without being detected at airport security checks."

"What's SkyTalk?"

"It is like Skype. You can talk to anyone by internet phone uplink. 'SkyTalk-to-SkyTalk' is encrypted to 128-digits, best ever. Of course, we've integrated the best graphic card too, way beyond public standards."

"What if it gets into the wrong hands?"

"No one is capable of reverse-engineering it."

"Why?"

"It is so top secret. No one person or group knows how to build it. That's why DARPA has us in on the deal. It doesn't even use transistor-based technology. I think we're looking at the first wave in Quantum Computing or something similar, but don't quote me on that."

If the Defense Advanced Research Projects Agency, DARPA, was a key agency in the development of this amazing tech, Jake knew there was nothing else like it and no one would be able to hack it. *Perfect.*

"Can I have one?"

Andy burst out laughing, "Come on man, you're pulling my leg. You know how it is here. In this building alone, only three people have seen this baby. Once the test period is over, it'll be introduced to the military engineers for approval. From what I know, not only will they be wowed, they'll want it in the hands of their agents immediately—the ones on intel missions, like in Afghanistan. You know what I mean. You've been there."

"I think it's dangerous for an agent to carry something like this around. Usually you don't want to leave any footprint behind, including electronic signatures."

"I know. It's an age-old problem. You want your agents not to be vulnerable so they don't carry a cell phone. But at the same time you want home-base to be in touch with them as needed. With this device, they can stay in touch 24/7."

"What if an agent gets caught with it, what then?"

"You know, for security reasons I am not supposed to tell you anything, right? This is just between us."

"Of course." Jake zipped his lips with his fingers.

Andy paused, calculating his response, "All I can say is that a non-subscriber would be prevented from seeing what's inside."

Jake wasn't sure how that was possible but he'd get back around to that in a minute.

"Seriously, how can I get my hands on one of these?"

Andy looked puzzled. "What are you talking about? First of all, you're not in the military anymore and second, why would you need one?"

"I have to leave the country. Go to Pakistan."

"So? Americans go to Pakistan all the time. Why do you need this computer?"

"I'll be going to Pakistan, legally. From there, I'll cross the Pakistan/Iran border, *not* through customs."

Andy's face changed, showing more and more unease. "Should we be having this conversation?"

"I need you to hear me out. Let's talk somewhere else."

"No. What we should do is change the subject, right now."

Jake leaned forward and whispered, "Listen man, I'm in deep shit and I need your help."

Andy got up and left the mess hall.

Jake followed, placing his tray on top of Andy's on the collection station by the door. He caught up to his best friend.

"Look, Laila's been arrested by the Iranian Revolutionary Guard and her mother and sister haven't heard from her in days."

"They should just go there and find out."

"Andy, the justice system over there churns a different way. They're gonna kill her, just like they did her brother a few days ago."

"What are you planning to do? Rescue her?"

"Yes." The word ground from him with conviction.

"No, no. When did you turn stupid? You go there, you'll get killed. You've served in the Air Force; you know you can't do that."

"Maybe not, but Senator Quest assured me no one else would either. How secure is this device of yours?"

"You've crossed the line. Let it go."

Jake refrained from saying another word until they reached reception. He tried to be nonchalant but his words came out stiff and awkward. "Thanks for lunch. Talk to you soon."

***

The day after the disastrous lunch date, Jake sat behind the steering wheel of his dilapidated Ciera in mid-day traffic drumming his fingers, deep in thought. He'd called Andy that morning to patch things up, but detected a deep concern in Andy's voice.

Andy refused to meet again.

Jake, well aware of the strict military policies regarding top secret devices and ex-Air Force men going rogue, also knew that if he or Andy got caught, the price would be high treason. The military protected its technological advances and personal intelligence with a heavy cloak of secrecy.

To the few who were in the know, this super high-tech device was on the top of the most advanced product list, even above the stealth bombers and drones. For Jake to get his hand on this device, he had to push the boundaries of his and Andy's friendship …

Andy's mind was very much molded by the military culture. A loyal worker, he obeyed the rules and honored faithful dedication to the United States. Jake wasn't just asking his buddy to smoke pot in the high school bathroom, and yet he didn't know what else to do. Jake loved his country and was proud to have served but things were never that black and white for him. Hell, he'd married an Iranian transfer student!

It all came back to how he could possibly convince his best friend to betray his country. On the other hand, getting his hands on AH would increase his chance for safe passage into the unknown. If this was going to be a prison break, the software that allows him to see through buildings was invaluable just on its own.

As his mental battle waged, Jake tapped a different rhythm on the steering wheel to help maintain partial attention on the road. Weighing in on whether to travel to Iran or not exhausted him more than field-training ever did. His dad and the Senator had told him nothing could be done—that a one-man covert mission was impossible … but they didn't know about AH. The grave warnings dished out by these highly respected men gnawed at his stomach. The last time he felt like this was his wedding day.

He'd somehow managed to stain his suit and Andy had wiped feverously at the mark on his jacket pocket. Laila stood by the cake with the photographer in a glorious white-laced dress searching with her eyes alone to try and find him—exuding grace and poise even as her fingers nervously picked at the sleeve of her glove. Finally, though, Andy had taken his pale blue kerchief from the pocket of his jacket and casually stuffed it into Jake's, allowing the excess fabric to fall down and cover the stain. The second Jake had broken through his expectant family and friends, the smile on Laila's face lit the entire room and eased the ache in his gut.

How can I leave Laila to rot in prison? How can I not rescue her? If she's executed like Orie ...

He shook the unwanted thought from his head and tried to focus on the road. But Jake's recent research into Iranian news showed the government routinely executed prisoners after they were charged with espionage, insulting one of the Ayatollahs, or participating in a protest against the government. For any of these reasons, after an arrest, a quick false trial took place to expedite the removal of the unwanted. He'd even watched a YouTube video where two Americans were captured in Iran while hiking in Iraq and got lost. Both were accused of spying, but after a long negotiation with the Iranian government they were released. But for an Iranian by birth, death waited without exception.

Jake slowed down when trees became more prominent along the side of the road. After Jake's fourth call to Andy, his friend had finally agreed to meet again; a secluded place. They decided on Stillman Park, off Kenly Avenue. It wasn't too far from the base and relatively barren around two in the afternoon.

At the sight of the park sign, Jake pulled onto a road that led to a picnic area near Leon Creek. Andy had many qualities Jake admired, one of them was punctuality. He stopped under a shady spot on the grass, glad the heat kept picnickers away today.

Jake expected to see a sporty Vienna in mustard yellow approach. He used the intervening time to think about all the things he had to do before leaving. Mentally, he packed his suitcase and made a note to grab some cash for the journey as well as the phone numbers of contacts at home. Megan and Dillon would stay with his parents. He hated the thought of leaving them again so soon, but they'd understand when he made it back home with their mother.

Jake checked all three mirrors a second time. Instead of a car he saw someone riding a bicycle. The closer the person got, the more he looked like Andy. *Why's he riding a bike? This can't be good.*

Within minutes, Andy threw the bike to the ground, opened the front door of the Ciera and hopped in.

"What's with the bike?"

"Just don't know who's watching." Impatience laced his words.

Jake didn't understand the logic so just accepted it for what it was worth. He tapped Andy on the shoulder.

"Thanks for coming. Please, help me save my wife".

"Why exactly was she arrested again?"

"From the bits of information I've gathered, it's hard to get a clear picture. Negar, Laila's sister, doesn't give details. Maybe she's afraid her phone is bugged. This is what I do know. Her brother was arrested just over a week ago. He was charged with spying for America and Israel—something to do with their religion. Now he's dead and Laila's in jail. I'm not religious, but some religious groups like the one my wife and her family belongs to, are always targets for harassment by the government or government elites."

A long pause stalled the conversation. With eyes wide and fingers resting on his forehead, Jake knew his friend reflected on this desperate situation. Andy shifted his shoulders back and forth, then scratched his head.

"What can *I* do?"

At this critical moment Jake knew the thin ice he walked on. "I don't know. Whatever you can. I'm going to Pakistan. Don't mention this to anyone. Including you and me only four people know. Once I'm there I'll cross over to Iran via some covert route and then make my way to Tehran."

"As a friend, I am telling you you're crazy. Absolutely crazy for doing this."

Jake combed his fingers through his hair, took a deep breath and let it out slowly. He frowned. "Andy, this is damn hard. It's the hardest decision I've ever made. How can I not do it? This is my wife we're talking about. I *love* her. By sitting here and doing nothing, I may lose her forever."

"Now you're really not making any sense. What is this? Romeo and Juliet? It's not logical. You don't need to go. We can get the US government to look-"

"No. I tried. One week, Andy. One week and her brother died in there. I don't have time to wait another month to be heard by some politician who reports directly to the Senator anyway. I've heard it from the top. They won't risk a rescue mission; their nuclear talks are more important than one woman's life. I have to go. Now. Besides, I served in Afghanistan—I've seen action."

"From behind a computer monitor, Jake. Give your head a shake, man. Shit. Even in the field you were heavily guarded and worked remotely." Andy stopped ranting. He knew Jake was simply voicing his concerns, what he needed to hear in order to go through with this insane decision. "Okay. I get it. I do. You're beyond determined. I've known you long enough to know that much. We've been in a ton of strange situations; I know when there's nothing stopping you." Silence. Andy's face muscles relaxed slightly and then came the words he was looking for, "How can I help?"

"I need one of the new AH devices."

"Jake. No. No! No! I made it very clear to you."

"It'll be a tough journey. That device will allow me to make calls, find my way around, search the web, and look for strategic answers. You *know* what it can do."

"No."

"Just one. Set me up with test satellite and no one will know. There's no way anyone can track it to you. I understand the risk, but I'll make sure your secret is safe."

Andy slammed the door, picked up the bicycle and rode off. Jake sat in his car watching his best friend disappear.

***

Later that day around 5:00 pm Jake took another peek at the rear view mirror to ensure no one had followed him before slowing his Ciera on

West Nueva Street until he caught sight of Mexican Restaurant. He parked couple blocks away, as per the instructions given, in a nearby strip mall. Known as a cheap eatery, students from the nearby University of Texas frequented the place.

Jake reviewed the precise instructions he needed to follow then tucked them away in the glove box before shutting off the engine. The vehicle sputtered and coughed; his face burned hot as the old rusted tin can faked death throws and drew stares from passersby. But, the beat-up piece of crap car had been a faithful companion too often in troubled times. Though it whined and squeaked like an old man, it had taken him wherever he wanted to go and hopefully would return him safely home to his children later. He hopped out and walked the two blocks back to the restaurant.

After contacting a former CIA operative who used to liaise with his dad, Jake got relayed a number to call. The person at the other end gave instructions for how to receive this address and contact name. At the restaurant, he'd interact with a man who promised to help in his travels between Pakistan and Iran. Apparently this old, poorer part of San Antonio was safe to do clandestine business—no surveillance cameras. At least, none that worked.

Previous to this visit a surveillance expert, hired by Jake's CIA contact, had checked buildings, streets, shops, and lamp posts for any device that would record movement of any kind in the neighborhood. None were found. Jake was also asked not to take his cell with him since smart phones were easily traceable even if turned off.

As he walked through the front door, a nervous tension filled his whole body. The aroma pushed his stomach into a growl forgetting Jake had eaten just an hour ago. The restaurant held some resemblance to a Taco Bell, but without the corporate image and run by a Mexican family.

At the counter he ordered two enchiladas and a coke, then turned around to observe the sparsely filled dining area. The walls were decorated with pictures of Mexican heroes.

A man, who could be Pakistani, sat facing the counter devouring a taco.

Jake picked up his order and chose a seat facing him, but not directly. He never made eye contact with him. After taking the first bit of the enchilada, he sneezed and went over to the condiment's stand to grab a napkin. When he returned, a plain brown bag sat on his tray. The man had disappeared.

After taking the last bite of his meal, Jake picked up the small bag, and walked out with his soda in one hand and his prize in the other.

Jake walked around the back of the restaurant and pretended to be occupied with finishing his drink. Then, with cup in hand, he approached the trash bin—dumping the cup with one hand and dropping an envelope on the ground with the other. In it was $500.00 as payment for the help he'd receive, money borrowed from his credit card.

Walking back around to the front of the building, the same guy brushed past him. Jake never actually turned or slowed down, two things he was advised not to do, but managed to catch sight of the guy from the corner of his eye while he collected the drop.

Jake didn't even register having walked the two blocks back to his car but the feel of that old steering wheel yanked him back to the present before driving out of the lot and heading toward home.

When he got within a few miles of his place, Jake pulled over to the side of the road and opened the bag. He drew out a recording device taped with written instructions warning him the recording would erase as it is played. He had only one chance to listen and remember as much as possible.

The audio recording came with a plan. While listening, he scribbled down a few words not familiar to him. The post instructions demanded he destroy any notes, the contact paper, and the recording device. A knot tightened in his stomach as he wondered if everything would unfold as planned.

***

At ten after six that evening, an engine rumble drew Jake's attention. The kids were upstairs in Megan's room with her favorite Raffi CD playing in the background.

Jake went to the window and peeked through a crack in the curtain. *What the devil are you doing here?*

Andy drove a borrowed car up to the house. From the back seat, he slid out a carry-on luggage and rolled it up to the house.

Jake waved him in and closed the door. Compelled by a surge of euphoria, he smothered Andy in a bear hug. When the tight squeeze ended, Jake punched his friend in the shoulder and crossed his arms, "I never thought you'd actually do it, man." A frenzied joy pumped through his veins, then he clapped his hands together. "What do we do?"

Andy went to the kitchen, pulled a chair and said, "You sit here." Then he unzipped the bag and drew two machines out. One resembled an instrument found at a doctor's office for eye examination. He placed it on a tri-pod and adjusted the height until Jake's chin rested on a curved bar and his forehead against a flat metal one.

"Positioning is crucial in getting an accurate reading of the retina." Andy made several adjustments on the other side of the machine.

"Can you see bright red dots?"

"Yes."

"Don't move."

Andy pressed a button. A high-pitched sound resonated for three seconds. Then he pulled a USB memory stick from the base and placed it in AH *Assignee Holiday*. After several key strokes, the screen came alive. He spent the next five minutes typing at rapid speed setting things up for Jake's use.

"Done."

"What did you do? Set my username and password?"

"No. This baby needs neither."

"Okay. Tell me."

"I'll show you."

With a few more key strokes, Assignee went into a shutdown mode.

“I don’t believe how thin this thing is.” Jake set his nose nearly on the table top to look at the device closer.

“Here.” Andy handed the computer over. “Look at the scanner.” He pointed his finger at the top of the screen. “Looks like the hole of a camera.”

Jake shifted.

“A bit closer.”

Andy lifted his hand in the air to get his friend’s full attention. “According to specs, twenty-four inches is close enough. But we found a bug in the software that’ll be fixed in the next release. For now, six inches from the scanner is necessary to identify you.”

Jake moved forward a touch more. Assignee came alive.

“Wow.”

“It uses the eye pattern, such as iris size, optic nerves and pupil color to detect if you’re the right user.”

Jake examined the keyboard. “Where is the power button?”

“It has no power button. It’s on all the time. When the authentication program determines the right user, the OS comes alive and then you can use it. To turn it off just pull the flap down. It has an eye, and if it does not see you, it hibernates.”

“Excellent.”

“How do I charge the battery?”

“No need. Battery’ll last for ten years and at which time it’ll destroy itself.”

“James Bond, eat your heart out.” Jake’s face held the excitement of a five-year old on Christmas morning.

“Oh, one more thing. There’s no manual. The OS is so intuitive you don’t need one—not even a *for Dummies* book.” Some of the strain eased from Andy’s voice. Jake could tell he loved his work and enjoyed showing it off. But he also knew the acidic reality of their clandestine arrangement would eat away at his friend all too soon.

“It’s light and powerful.” He packed away the scanner and loaded up the carry-on. “Look, I have to go. Just play with it.”

At the door Jake gave Andy's shoulders a squeeze. "I hope I'll have a chance to pay you back for this."

"It was a test of our friendship. I know you're putting your life on the line for Laila. This wonder machine can definitely help you find her. Maybe it can even help rescue her too. Lives are on the line and knowing Assignee's computing capability could save those lives was the deciding factor. That and even if you do screw up, no one can hack it. You need to be alive for the retina scan to work. Don't lose it." After those last words, a dark shadow covered his face.

Jake knew exactly what his friend was concerned about but did not want to voice it. He squeezed Andy in a tight embrace. "Putting your life on the line is the meaning of a true friend."

Andy gave a grim smile and walked out the door, pulling the luggage behind.

***

The next evening Jake pushed a small airport cart loaded with one piece of carry-on luggage and a computer bag. Both looked very expensive, as intended. The son he'd only met in person for the first time two weeks ago sat perched on Jake's hip playing with the lapel of his jacket. Dressed to impress in a blue suit and white shirt with a crisp collar, he hadn't looked so put together since his wedding day. The non-prescription eye glasses added to the dignified, classic good looks persona—all of it felt uncomfortable. But everything was chosen to give the airport passport and customs officers the impression of an elite American business man.

After a glance at the boarding pass, the customs officer handed back Jake's passport and pointed.

"Gate 51 is over there." Perching Dillon on the handle of the cart helped alleviate the strain of the unaccustomed weight on his arm as he sunk the document in his coat pocket with his free hand. He headed over to towards the gate.

Makalla, Jake's sister, held Megan's hand and stepped out in front of the cart. "You have to stop. What the hell are you doing? I never wanted to be here but here I am. Jake, for the last time I'm telling you, don't do it. Don't go."

Jake stood there, yards away from destiny. Earlier that day he had managed to convince his younger sibling to take the kids to their grandparents after he left for Pakistan. But his folks wouldn't know the plan until they saw their grandchildren walking through the door with their aunt.

"I have to do this. No other choice." *Maybe she's thinking of bailing on me. Shit.* "What can I give you?"

Makalla had a good job with an expensive taste for clothes, shoes and jewelry. He'd already dropped a grand on her for 'helping'. More money he'd borrowed from the credit card.

"Look at you. You're friggin' dressed like a business mogul. This isn't you. You never dress like this. Better than at your wedding. Do you honestly think you can pull this off? You know all of your pie-in-sky projects have a way of failing."

She'd always been skeptical of his capacities and achievements. This was not the time or place to rehash old arguments and end up in a verbal brawl in front of the kids. This needed a resolution, now.

He motioned her to a corner, away from anyone over hearing. "I don't have a choice. If I stay here I know I'll lose her ..."

"For days I've been telling you. Talk to some government officials. They might be able to her get out of jail and back here."

"Lower your voice." Jake was desperate for her co-operation and he had to do everything to remain calm. "I *have* looked into it. I'm not a moron Makalla. Besides, you don't know the whole story. Laila has three things working against her. One is her religion, which the government is determined to suppress. The second is she's Iranian. If she were an American by birth, that would have been different. Third, if the officials find out she's married to an ex-US military officer, she's out. Killed."

She looked him straight in the eyes.

"What about your children, hmm? What if you don't come back?" He cringed. The words hit his heart like a dagger. His breathing accelerated.

Dillon pinched his nose as Megan twirled pirouettes under Makalla's arm. Yes, he'd thought about them. How could he not? But he had to stay positive. Stay focused.

"Look sis, don't worry. I'll be back. Of course, I'll be back."

Makalla was bright and argumentative. Their father always made it known that Jake would never be as good as her. After college, Makalla had claimed that Jake only joined the Army to gain their father's respect. Regardless of his intentions all those years ago, now he was on the mission of his life. He may not see his wife or his children again but he wasn't going to risk losing one to keep the others from worrying about him. If he couldn't live with himself, he'd never be the parent his kids needed him to be.

"I am *not* as stupid as you think. All the angles, possibilities, and risks have crossed my mind. If I die and Laila can't come back to the US, read my will. It is in the dresser drawer in my bedroom. Mom and Dad get custody of the children. They also take the house."

"What about me?"

"You get all my books."

"I don't want your books. All you read is sci-fi. I'm not into that."

"What do you want? My car?"

"Jake, your car is an embarrassment. It's noisy and runs more on luck than gas."

The bargaining was getting too hot. "You can use my house."

"Not a bad idea."

Makalla had a taste for the wild life. "No parties."

"You and I have never seen eye to eye." She pursed her lips and squinted at him like lasers might come out of her eyes. But she surprised him, "What you're doing is really cool. Going into the lion's den to save Laila. That's love."

With one arm around Makalla's shoulder he said, "True love can only be tested through sacrifice."

With teary eyes she hugged him. "I'll look after your two monkeys."

"Thanks. I have to go. This is too much."

Jake gave both Megan and Dillon a kiss on the forehead followed by hugs.

"Sis, you're the best."

Chapter 9

The tray noise from the delivery girl shattered Laila's restless slumber. She jumped to her feet and limped to the barred door. Severe stomach cramps spasmed in intensity with every step and shift of her body.

When the breakfast tray passed under the iron gate, Laila waved the girl closer. Leaning forward, she whispered, "I need pads."

The girl returned a puzzled look. "Pads?"

Laila moved another inch closer until her cheeks touch the cold iron. "Women's pads?"

The girl shook her head. "No one gets pads here."

Sharp pain sliced through Laila's lower abdomen. She moaned, "What do I do? I'm on my period."

The face of this young person lost color, empathizing with Laila's misery. "You're supposed to drink tea. If you ingest enough, you wouldn't need pads."

To ease the sting, Laila shifted her body weight to the other leg. The girl's explanation seemed so bizarre. "Why would that be?"

"The tea has Canfor in it and, according to the guards, is supposed to prevent menstruation."

"I don't drink that tea. It smells horrible."

She laughed, "I know." She muffled the sound with her hand.

"What's your name?

"Maryam."

Laila sensed she was not like other prison workers. “Are you a Muslim?”

“No, Christian.”

“I thought Christians weren’t allowed to work here?”

“I am not a worker. I am a prisoner.”

“Prisoner? Oh my God. You look so young. What happened?”

Maryam inhaled a deep breath and checked to either side in case anyone was within hearing distance. “I’m seventeen. At school I was sort of a rebel. In religious class I disagreed with the teacher regarding his interpretation of Jesus. When I expressed my opinion, he rebuked me in front of the class, then asked me to leave if I didn’t like it.”

Laila’s eyes opened wider in admiration for this teenager’s courage. “What did you do? Did you walk out?”

“Yes, I did. So did many others. Some were Muslims but others were Christians, Zoroastrians, even a few Jews.”

Like taking a shot of morphine Laila’s pain disappeared with her attention captivated. “Then what happened?”

“It’s a long story. I’ll tell you another time. People are watching; I have to continue with the meal delivery or else someone will complain. There are eyes everywhere.”

Laila nodded and watched the young prisoner push the trolley to the next cell. Her body aches resurfaced, but her mind remained consumed by the girl’s story. She couldn’t wait to hear the whole narration. Since being thrown in this hell hole, that was the longest and most intimate conversation she had with anyone.

As resentment brewed larger in her stomach, Laila tried to reign in her feelings of injustice. She put a lid on the negativity by transferring her thoughts homebound: Megan standing with her hands on her hips tattling on Dillon about chewing her toy, brought a smile to Laila’s lips. The absolute certainty on Megan’s face and Dillon’s innocent curiosity made her laugh and hug her children. She firmly believed that anger damaged the liver and she respected her body too much to dwell on the unpleasant nuances of life.

Laila picked up her tray and shifted her weight from one leg to the other when the cramps came roaring back. Holding tight to the platter with one hand, the other grasped the iron bars as she walked back to the corner of the cell. Still holding the tray, but now gaining support from the concrete wall, she limped to the mattress.

As she rested in the fetal position, the pain eased enough that she could reach the bread on the plate. Chewing on a piece of *Nan-e Barbari* she pushed bitter feelings aside by focusing instead on Maryam's ordeal. That simple exchange of words helped return some of her failing humanity. She reflected on friendship, love, and the basic need for human contact that people took for granted.

***

Negar Dareini stood still, letting her mother pass by as she locked the gate before stepping onto Khak-negar Street. Walking briskly, she pulled up her beige shawl to cover her forehead. The cloth lined just above the eyebrows and tightened around her chin. Eyes fixed on the road, she ignored the beggars, loud merchants, and noisy vehicles.

Negar avoided eye contact with anyone, desiring no one to notice her, especially the guard on whom she spat when she was given the bill for her brother's death. For days she had nightmares about him coming to the house to take her away.

It reminded her of another guard who'd harassed her father. In his younger days, during the time when Reza Shah Palavi ruled Iran, Abbas was a bounty hunter for the government. As part of his assignment he arrested a man and took him to the authorities for not paying taxes. Many years later, after the Iranian Revolution, the same man became a guard in the *new* regime and spotted Abbas one day. As revenge he targeted the Dareini family with threats. Many times Nagar reminded herself that spitting on that guard was a very bad idea.

She walked with Maliheh by picture after picture of the Ayatollahs with her eyes lowered towards the asphalt. She refused to spare even a glance at the spiritual leaders of Iran. Hateful slogans like "Death to

America", "Death to Israel", and "Death to communists" reminded her how the government filled the minds of Iranians with prejudices. She was against discrimination of any kind, and now her family was a victim of it.

Both women passed along Helal-e-Ahmar Street, a busy enough road where they had to weave a path among the people, occasionally bumping shoulders. This Tehran street was lined with stores, vendors, and ancient maple trees. The aroma of roasted sunflower and pumpkin seeds saturated the air.

After an hour's travel Negar and her mother got off a bus at Evin Prison's visitors parking lot. Negar turned around, looking from one end of the area to the other absorbing everything, until she completed a 360-degree rotation. Guards in grey uniforms, with helmets and eye protection, remained rigid in a combative position. Two men, each holding a machine gun, stood before the notorious building as a dozen others dotted the space around the walls next to barbed wire. However, the visitors gave these uniformed men little attention as their main focus was to visit family members and friends housed in the jail they were about to enter.

The night before, Negar finally received a call from the authorities informing her of the whereabouts of her sister. Since Laila's arrest she'd made many calls to the Ministry of Justice and police stations, even visited these places in search of her sister's fate. The questions were always the same: *Where is she? Is she alive or dead? What are the charges against her?* Every attempt was met with ignorance, delays, and apathy—in Iran, this was typical. She had many verbal bouts but after days and many fruitless attempts, she realized she had to stop. Any wrong move could make matters worse for her sister.

Standing in front of a building and looking up at the façade, black writing on a blue sign announced 'Evin House of Detention'. She also noticed two other signs: one was for visitors with a pass, the other without. Hundreds formed a line before the first sign where a guard used a loud speaker to blare out names. At the far end was another guard, to whom Negar inquired of the process.

Maliheh attentively listened while Negar learned of the information she needed. As they broke away from the guard she asked her daughter, "What? Where do we go?"

"The line without the pass."

Negar made her way over as Maliheh followed a few steps behind. It was a sunny day, but every face she passed looked drawn and pale with sadness and anxiety. And so, with every step her hope at seeing her sister diminished.

Both went inside. Three officers, each facing a line, stood behind a counter. Negar joined the shortest one and soon faced a man with a beard and bushy hair.

"Salam, I am here to visit my sister."

"What is her name?"

"Laila Dareini."

He ran the forefinger on a list. "*Khanum*, you cannot."

"Not see her? What do you mean? I am with Maman."

"I said, you cannot." His tone irritated her.

After a brief pause to pacify her feelings she said, "We want to see her. Is there anything we can do?"

"Yes." He handed her a page. "Fill out this form and come back in two days with $15,000."

Maliheh nudged her daughter to the side until she came face to face with the officer. "Please, we have traveled many hours to see my beloved daughter. Is there nothing you can do?"

He shook his head. "Before anyone is allowed to see a detainee, the form has to be filled out and money paid."

Negar knew well enough how the regime worked and there was no point pressing their request.

Sadder than ever, both returned home.

***

Ali Mohmed eased into the Minister of Justice's office for a meeting—right on time. According to Iranian customs that meant he was early.

Seeing a guest, the minister stood up and walked from the hand-crafted mahogany desk towards the door to receive him.

Head bowed, as a sign of respect, Ali said, "*Salam aleikom,*" then gave his host a kiss on both cheeks.

With arms open wide, the minister said, "*Be farma, be farma.*" *Please sit down, please sit down*, pointing to chairs. Both men stood on an expensive carpet whose arrival from England had caused tremendous buzz in the minister's circle of friends and supporters. At Christie's auction house the silk Isfahan rug fetched over four million dollars for its lineage, age, knot density, craftsmanship, and above all, status for the previous owner, Clarence Duke, the famed rug collector. The minister could easily afford this one or many others with similar price tag as he was the son of a rich oil billionaire.

The carpet spread out in the middle of a twelve by thirteen-foot room, two walls were adorned with the sacred image of each Ayatollah—one deceased, the other very much alive.

Ali placed his left arm across his chest and said, "*Ghorbaneh shoma,*" meaning *I sacrifice my life for you.* Then he took a seat after the minister sat down.

With arms spread wide the conversation flowed. "Ali, my brother, how is everything? Under control?" the minister asked.

Ali nodded his head assuring the minister of his sincere response, "Yes, yes, everything is going well."

Controlling the inhabitants of Evin prison was the key to keeping power in their hands. Anyone who opposed the Iranian Revolution was rounded up and sent to Evin. Both men understood all too well that as easily as power comes, it can also slip away.

In recent months the issue of Ali's security came up regularly. Someone wanted to usurp control of the prison from him. He did not dwell on this, as enemies came and went with the setting of the sun these days. Instead, Ali updated him on the inner workings of the prison, showing the minister how well everything was in hand. The minister nodded in agreement with the steady progress, showing himself to be an attentive listener to his guest.

Then he asked, “How is Maryam doing?”

He remembered her name—a cause for concern. Maryam Danesh had been scheduled for execution shortly after her arrest, but an interrogator named Reza saved her life. He found her to be attractive and since Reza needed a woman in the prison where he was ordered to spend most of his time, he got an injunction from the minister not to execute her. It was granted with the blessing of the Ayatollah. Maryam became his prison wife. Though a prisoner, she enjoyed some freedoms: not being confined to a cell all the time, serving meals to other inmates, and performing simple chores.

“She is fine.”

The conversation waned as a butler entered the room with a silver tray, holding a pot and three glasses. A rich and heady aroma filled the air when the servant lifted the top of the glass teapot. It had the perfect balance of flavor, color, and aroma with just a hint of cardamom.

When the butler left, both men picked up their glasses and expressed their satisfaction while sipping the fragrant tea. The small talk continued for some time until a knock came at the door. Judge Rouhani sporting a full, grey beard, a white turban, and long shirt arrived ten minutes late. In Iranian time that was perfectly acceptable. All three exchanged their courtly ‘affections’ for each other with the appropriate kisses and hugs.

Chest puffed with pride, Judge Rouhani spoke briefly about his daughter’s recent wedding. Then he jumped into details of the honeymoon: traveling to an exclusive Bell Mare resort in Mauritius, where one night’s stay came to over $10,000.

Ali had to show interest in this man’s daughter whether he cared or not, “Wonderful, wonderful! Where are they planning to live?”

A broad smile indicated the minister could not be more proud of his eldest child. “Switzerland.” Ali also knew that’s where many rich ministers stashed their money.

Every judge in the system first became a cleric of Islam and then gained appointment to the judicial post by the living Ayatollah. Clerics and judges played an important role in maintaining the power of the Islamic Republic.

Ali's father was a good friend of the Ayatollah. They went to same school and studied the Quran together. Ten years earlier, when Ali did not have a clear vision of his future, his father advised him to become a cleric, a step that could lead to securing a judicial position. But his interest in practicing religion was next to none.

After the small talk, the three men settled down on the luxurious Turkish sofa. Ali brought forth and examined a list. Without comment, all three understood it was time for business.

The names were sorted into three categories: eleven to be executed by hanging, three to be placed on trial, and finally, Laila Dareini. There were no issues with the first two categories. The judge approved the actions and the minister usually went along without complaint.

When Ali read the last name on the list, he paused. After a long moment of silence, he explained, "Laila Dareini was born in Iran but currently resides in the US under the name Hudley. She came to visit her parents in Tehran but the Guards arrested her in place of her ill father. She is currently at Evin."

Judge Rouhani asked, "Living in America?" He rubbed his long beard. "What's her … religion? If she's a Christian, then according to the law she could be executed after a fast trial. The same fate was given to a Muslim who became a Bishop in Europe, after his return to Iran."

"The international community, Amnesty International, and a few dissidents living outside Iran will make the usual noise," the minister remarked.

"That's true," Rouhani said. "But that rarely makes a difference in our judicial process."

The minister protested, "When it's an Iranian living outside Iran, if that person is executed it always draws the attention of the activists. Then shortly after other governments and the UN get involved. With our current negotiations with Europe and the US regarding our nuclear program, we can't afford the negative publicity."

Rouhani took a sip and cradled the warm glass. "So what should we do with her? Why not let her go?"

Ali stepped in quickly, "No, no. We can't do that. This family belongs to a dirty religion that needs to be rooted out of Iran. Her brother already signed a confession. We can use this to our advantage." His gazed darted between the two men before him. Ali knew both clearly understood his objections.

"What's your plan?" Rouhani asked, at ease with Ali and his capabilities.

"We post her arrest in the papers, here and abroad, giving information about her marriage to an American and living in the United States. Then the international news media, specifically the US networks, will pick it up and investigate and report who this American is. The more we find out about this enemy the better. It could be a bargaining chip against the Americans regarding their insistent nuclear restrictions."

Rouhani also happened to be a member of Intelligence and National Security, directly reporting to the Ayatollah. He endorsed Ali's plan without hesitation. The minister got up indicating the meeting had reached its conclusion.

Ali bade both men Khoda-Hafez, may God protect you, and walked out of the meeting. He was pleased how well he played his role. He knew all the kisses, hugs, and smiles had no real meaning. Every word and gesture made were rituals in personal engagements. None of these three deeply trusted each other.

Ali pulled a cell phone from his jacket and made a call to his body guards announcing his arrival at the front of the ministry building. Ali had been a target for assassination several times. Traveling in Tehran in a bullet-proof vehicle was of little comfort as his enemies were smart and could wage a war to take his life.

The threat came mostly from the Mujahidins, the main opposition to the Iranian Revolution. A good number of this religious faction were incarcerated at Evin and other prisons around the country. One of their operational goals was to target the powerful, ruthless prison interrogators. So far, Ali had been lucky.

Back at Evin, Ali's first task was to call his contact at *Enghelab-e Eslami*, the Islamic Revolution paper, an important organ of the regime to promote its side of change in the country. He made sure to dish-out all the information needed for an article to appear the next day.

***

Charles Hudley filled a mug with coffee, his second so far that morning and the last one for the day. Forever mindful of his wife's persistence, he knew ingesting too much caffeine wasn't good for his heart.

Sitting down in a chair next to the kitchen table he took a sip then turned to CNN on the 30-inch flat screen he got for half-price at Walmart on Black Friday last year. Coincidently CNN was hungry for news that day. The American audience, according to some survey, was exhausted from hearing about the European financial crisis and the primaries in the Republican Party. And with no sex scandals to report, the fodder needed to fill twenty hours of news was scarce.

Charles watched a segment on finance when BREAKING NEWS flashed on the screen. An anchor woman announced news from Iran, just received from an international agency.

Charles, holding the mug halfway to his lips, riveted his attention to the screen as the female anchor read, "According to a government newspaper, a woman named Laila Hudley, an Iranian by birth, traveling from the US to Iran has been arrested for questioning by authorities."

Now that the world knew about his daughter-in-law's plight, Charles wasn't sure whether this was a good or bad thing.

Then a scene in front of Lackland Air Force Base, in San Antonio appeared and a reporter announced, "According to our sources, the woman in question is married to an ex-US Air staffer named Jake Hudley who previously worked in the building behind me. Neither officials in

Washington or with the US Military have confirmed or denied the validity of the story as they need time to investigate this case."

Charles froze, something he rarely did having to constantly be prepared for any situation at the office—but he wasn't at the office any more. He was unprepared for this engagement. His heart dropped and he swallowed for air his lungs didn't want to provide.

He set his mug down. "Ruth, come here!"

No answer.

He got up and took few steps to the bottom of the stairs. "Ruth, where are you?"

This time the sound of his voice traveled farther. He heard water rush down the drain after a toilet flush and waited till the noise died down. He called again, "Ruth, come here quickly."

The door opened. "What's wrong with you? Stop yelling."

It wasn't unusual for her to ignore him, but this time it mattered. "Come quick. Laila's on the news."

He went back to the kitchen and flicked the channel to FOX 29 News, then bounced around to several local channels. Ruth appeared, face expectant.

"Laila is still in the hands of the Authorities. Where's Jake? If he is in Iran, he could be in big shit." He threw his hand up allowing them to crash onto the table. His coffee sloshed.

"Chuck, my goodness, watch your words. There are children around." Megan sat coloring at the dining table as Dillon snoozed away on the sofa not too far from his sister.

He ploughed ahead anyway, "I told him not to go. You know how the media is in this country. Now the news about Jake and Laila will be everywhere."

Ruth grabbed a cloth, wiped the spill and poured the rest of the coffee down the drain. Her tight lips and frown said she needed to absorb the situation before responding.

"You'll figure it out. Just don't get too stressed. I have to take the kids to school."

"Ruth. Don't tell anybody. I mean don't tell anybody that Jake is on his way to Iran. Is that clear? Makalla just said he left and needed us to watch the kids. Don't—"

"I have to go."

Her words worked like a sound slap up-side the head. He watched as she picked up Megan and Dillon and went out the door. For the next two hours he rotated through news channel looking for more information. No one gave any more details than CNN had.

The ringing of the phone startled Charles. He glanced at the call display before answering.

"Dad, have you watched the news?" Makalla asked.

"Yes. It's crazy. Both CNN and FOX are looking for Jake. It's nuts." He combed his gray hair with his fingers. "How did you heard about it?"

"Twitter and Facebook. A bunch of Jake's friends are posting tweets like crazy. That's not good. They're uploading his wedding pictures, and pictures of Jake, Laila, Megan and Dillon in the playground."

"Damn social networking. A modern online gossip venue. Yep, that's what it is. I don't know where Jake is and I don't want to ask anyone. That could lead to more questions. You know what I mean."

"He sent me a text message."

"And?"

"And he said he made it on board."

"If his picture is splashed all over the world, it could certainly be in papers, police stations, and public places in Iran. I don't believe he's done this to me."

"Dad, you're getting agitated over nothing. He's safe, for now."

Charles felt tension building around his neck, a sign his blood pressure could be rising. No one in his family seemed to understand the severity of the situation.

"What do you mean *nothing?* This is extremely serious. You're smart enough to know that. Why did you help him?"

"Help! No, I didn't. I didn't agree with him; I didn't finance his travel; I did nothing."

"You took him to the airport this morning and dropped off Megan and Dillon at my place; that's help."

"Dad. Dad, calm down. I know it *could* be serious. But we're not there yet."

The doorbell rang. Charles craned his neck to see if he could make out who was there. "Someone's at the door. I'll put you on hold and see who it is. Don't hang up."

He walked to the front hall and twitched the curtain beside the door. A woman in a business suit waited patiently. He opened the door.

"Mr. Hudley?"

He nodded.

"I'm a reporter from the San Antonio Express. Can I ask you a few questions?"

"Sorry, not right now."

"Your daughter-in-law." She paused to glance at her note book. "Laila Hudley, has been accused of espionage. Spying for America and Israel. Do you have anything to say about that?"

"No, no. She's no spy for anybody. She just went home to visit her parents. Her father was ill."

"So you're denying this allegation?"

"Absolutely."

The thirty-something blonde women wrote in her notepad and said, "Have you talked to your son lately?"

Charles didn't know how to answer. *Best to be vague.* "Ah. No. Not recently."

"When did you last see him?"

Charles was getting tired of all the questioning. "Last week I think." Just then a van with CNN in big letters slowed and stopped in front of the house. "Look, I told you I'm busy right now. I have to go. I have a call on hold."

"Here's my card. If you see Jake can you let me know? I'd like to clarify the charges against Laila. Why do you think she's been arrested?"

Charles slammed the door on her, locked it and took a peek through the living room curtain. The reporter was still scribbling and no one came out of the CNN van. He paced the hallway, then went back to the land-line in the kitchen. He picked up the receiver from the counter.

"Makalla, you still there?"

"Yes. Who was at the door?"

"You won't believe what's happening. A media circus is about to emerge on my front yard."

"Who was at the door!"

"A pushy reporter. I told you this was serious."

"Dad."

"Call me later." He ended the conversation and snuck another look outside.

Charles had been in many battles both on the ground and in military rank politics. Like a chess player, he was used to seeing seven moves beyond his opponent. This could very well be the battle he never wanted to face. At this point, he didn't even know who the opponents were.

***

A scream filled Laila's cell. *Another nightmare?* Loud voices jarred her the rest of the way awake. When she opened her eyes, she witnessed two female guards dragging a twenty-something year old down the hall.

"Don't do this!" The girl shrieked. "I don't want to die. I don't want to die!"

After the screaming faded Laila tried to go back to sleep, tried to ignore the woman's pleas, but she couldn't. Were they taking her someplace for execution? Why was that young woman so terrified? What had she done to deserve her fate?

The next morning when Maryam came with the breakfast tray, Laila mentioned what happened, "Last night a young woman was being hauled through here screaming."

She sighed, "That could be Sarah. Was her name written on her forehead?"

"I don't know. It was dark."

"Sometimes they take drug addicts to the doctors. Most of the time these addicts resist and are forced to go." She paused and brushed her long light brown hair. "But I think it was Sarah. She was taken to the execution pad."

Laila shook her head. "Execution pad? You mean she was taken to her death?"

"Yes."

"Why?"

"It is hard to tell why one isn't killed in here."

Laila was surprised by Maryam's reaction. Perhaps in a place like this, one gets used to the idea of seeing prisoner's dragged to their death.

"I see."

"I never see you do *Nemaz,* you are not a Muslim?"

"No."

"Christian?"

"No."

Maryam gave a puzzled look and said, "Sorry, it's not my place to ask."

Laila said, "Ahh. I respect all religions, including Christianity, Islam, Hinduism, Buddhism, Zoroastrianism, and Judaism."

Maryam sounded so innocent yet curious, "I didn't know there were that many."

Laila explained, "There are even more than that. What's important is that they all come from God."

"I wish I could believe in that. I couldn't sleep last night because I wanted so much to share my story with you. To have another woman to talk to."

Laila moved closer to the gate. "Please tell me."

"It'll take a long time. Later today, I'll arrange for you to have a hot shower. Have you had a shower yet?"

"No shower since I've been here."

"Oh my God, that's terrible. I'll see what I can do."

Laila watched Maryam's back as she pushed the trolley with trays to the next cell.

Chapter 10

Jake sat still with his eyes closed concentrating on lifting one butt cheek then shifting to another. A headache pounded relentlessly, like wind from a storm, caused by long hours on a plane, sleepless nights, and worrying about the journey ahead. With meditation, something Laila drilled into him, he tried to relax his brain. After ten seconds, he shifted focus to his arms, then neck, and then back to his ass. When he reached the torso, a voice from the cabin speaker broke his concentration.

A female voice with a light accent announced, "This is your captain again. Our flight has just received clearance from the control tower and we are moving into position for the final decent. In another twenty minutes, we'll be at the gate." *Female captain, Laila would be impressed.* The long flight from New York to Karachi had more than taken a toll on his body. *Time to get up.*

In the tiny washroom, he steadied himself with his left arm as the plane lowered to one side. When the aircraft leveled the roaring of the engines grew. Regaining his balance, Jake looked into the mirror and a stranger looked back.

He washed his face and puffy eyes, shaved. He combed his blond hair, parting it on the left, giving him a conservative look. After straightening his blue tie, the image reflected back had improved if only somewhat. He still wasn't sure if he could pull it off though. So many things about him screamed *liability*. As a tall white man he'd stand out amongst the Pakistanis and Iranians. *Damn, I should have dyed my hair darker.* But then, of late with the US involvement in Afghanistan, Pakistanis had become suspicious of *any* white person.

With another examination of his reflection he whispered, "Goodness knows I'll need the luck."

Heading back towards his seat, a flurry of activity arose from passengers and staff, indicators of an imminent landing. He squeezed by two stewardesses as they moved towards the rear of the plane.

On the ground, Jake found his carry-on in the luggage rack and placed it on the floor. Everyone left the plane and entered a large hall moving as one towards the booth with passport officers. He quickly texted Makalla about having landed safely, then pocketed his phone.

Jake inched forward in the foreign traveler's lane as hundreds jockeyed for position. The line moved steadily until it was his turn. A middle-age man with thick mustache, cap, khaki uniform, and a stern expression eyed him critically. Jake gave him his passport and the entry form, which he'd filled out in the air.

"What is the purpose of your visit to Pakistan?" The officer studied Jake.

"Business."

"What kind of business?" His tone was laced with doubts.

"I work for Pak-American Petroleum."

The officer wrote R12 on the form with a red marker and returned it to Jake along with his passport while pointing to another officer.

"He will ask you more questions."

Jake forced his face muscles to relax, hiding the fear of the unknown deep inside; an exercise Jake had practice many times as part of his military training.

He followed the officer with a mole on his cheek until they entered a private room. Waving his hand towards a chair he said, "Please, sit."

Jake took a seat across the metal table.

With a face totally devoid of emotion, the man flipped through the pages of the passport, examining each entry. "What is the purpose of your visit to Pakistan?"

Jake followed the advice given him by the ex-CIA officer. *Just answer the question with least number of words.*

"Business."

"What kind of business?" *Different officers ask the same question, over and over again, to find any inconsistency in the interrogator's reply.*

"I'm meeting with a colleague at Pak-American Petroleum."

He flipped more pages and stopped. "Your occupation?" he examined Jake's expression.

"Vice-president of operation at our plant in San Antonio."

"Who are you seeing in Pakistan?"

"Mr. Riaz Quereshi at the Hilton Hotel in Karachi, where I am staying, for breakfast in the morning."

"Mr. MacDougal, what are you doing after the meeting?"

"For lunch I'll eat with the supervisor and then in the evening I take a return flight home."

"Mr. MacDougal, how long have you been in the Petroleum business?"

He cleared his throat to further hide any trace of his Southern accent, "I'm originally from Alberta, Canada. My family's been in Oil business for many generations." He handed a business card to the man. "You can talk to Mr. Quereshi, if you'd like." Mr. Quereshi being a liaison of the Agent helping him. If he didn't come through, Jake was as good as dead.

"I think I will."

When the officer disappeared Jake quickly ran his hand over his moist forehead. He ran the tips given by the ex-CIA through his mind one more time. Staying calm and avoiding a rapid descent into an anxiety-ridden psychosis took all his focus and willpower.

When the officer reappeared five minutes later, he stamped Jake's passport. "Have a nice stay in Pakistan." Jake slowly emptied the air from his lungs and was thankful his contact came through for him.

The tension evaporated with the sound of the rubber stamp hitting the page. He thanked the officer and walked out of the room where he could just have easily been imprisoned until the authorities arrived. In the main hanger, he passed by several white passengers sitting in the waiting area. With the death of Bin Laden in May of last year, and the constant strife between the West and Pakistan, the general mood in the country towards westerners remained loaded with suspicion. *It's no wonder they all gravitate towards each other.* He found an escalator and pulled his carry-on behind him onto the moving stairs, straightening the shoulder bag with Assignee.

On the main floor, he sought out a men's room. In a stall, Jake opened the carry-on, pulled out a back pack stuffed with casual clothes and stripped to his underwear. Folding the rental suit, shirt, and tie as best as he could, he put them into the carry-on. Dressed like a back-packer ready to travel, he walked out in the open air of the large passenger waiting room. Squaring his shoulders for the next phase of his plan, he walked over to the Pakistan Intl Air counter where he bought a ticket on the next flight to Quetta, the closest local airport to the Iranian border.

***

Jake paid the fare with a generous tip and slid out of the back seat of the taxi. He pulled his luggage towards the entrance of an old building with a huge façade inscribed *Railway Station Quetta* almost one-hundred years ago. He dropped five rupees in the hands of each of the three beggars he passed by. That was Jake's way to attract good karma. Being generous was his cardinal belief. "What comes around, goes around." One of many principles shared by Laila. How he missed her so. Where ever she was, was it possible for her to feel what was happening inside him?

Jake left off his musings as he approached the ticket counter and scanned the space around him. His adviser warned him this place was a war zone. The chatty driver from the airport also warned him of the city being besieged by fighting groups. Just the day before, a bomb placed under a tea stall exploded, killing seven people, including one child and two women. Jake joined the line that led to the man with a thick, dark beard who sold tickets. Everyone wore somber expression as two policemen with riffles scanned the room, looking for attackers. But they didn't seem bothered by his presence and didn't approach him.

In a few seconds a mob of taxi drivers surrounded him, each yelling to attract customers, trying to coax and convince. He ignored them.

One kept saying, "Going to Zahedan, bus. I take you. Good."

But after a few minutes they left him alone and he continued the slow shuffle toward the counter for a ticket to Taftan on a train heading to Zahedan, Iran. To his disappointment, he could not get a sleeper, the service was withdrawn for security reasons. Taftan was the legal official border crossing to Iran.

Ticket in hand, he stepped outside for some fresh air. On this spring day, the hot, dry heat smothered him. He opened his mouth to breathe while taking in the barren hills in the not too far distance—familiar surroundings. The landscape reminded him of Afghanistan, which could be a hundred miles from where he stood.

The image of that Humvee without John behind the mounted gun and his voice relaying his separation from the team caused a spike of fear to fracture Jake's hard-sought calm. But this time the fear wasn't for his fallen friend, it was for his wife. Laila may have been raised here, but she'd never been incarcerated before.

Quetta had been an important strategic spot for almost a century. During the reign of the British Raj, over a hundred years ago, Britain kept an eye on Russian threats since they could advance into the Indian-subcontinent through Afghanistan. Now, the strategic thinking was different.

In Kandahar, part of Jake's job used to be monitoring Quetta via satellite. This old city was a key point from the Karachi harbor to US military bases in Kandahar and Kabul. The generals preached to the support staff often that protecting convoys loaded with food, ammunitions, and armored vehicles were crucial to the success of US troops fighting terrorism.

After soaking up the sun in the dry air, Jake remembered to buy food for his journey; he'd been warned that no meals were served aboard the train. He studied the tea, vegetables, and fruit stalls. In the Air Force, many lessons were given regarding terrorist attacks. One such lesson was that attackers wanted maximum impact and publicity. Therefore, he waited for the stalls to clear before approaching them to buy grapes, mangoes, bananas, and bread.

After shoving the food in his nap-sack, he headed back to the platform. Jake couldn't help but get a strange feeling; he stood out like a white tiger in the jungle among the waiting passengers. Jake's dress code of jeans, t-shirt, and a cap was noticeably different from the Pakistani national dress of shalwar kameez.

Most wore baggy pants hanging from the waist, over which a shirt came down. Some men sported a vest over their shirt and some donned turbans. Most men's clothing tended toward white, light grey, or blue. The porters, in their twenties, wore brown to clearly distinguish themselves. Women also wore shalwar kameez but with more variety and color.

The distant rumble of the train engine filled the air along with a rhythmic bell signaling its approach. As the train slowed into position, two policemen patrolled with machine guns between the platforms. All four eyes scanned the platform ready to shoot. From the opposite direction several arriving passengers walked on the track to get to the train, an act unheard of in the States.

Jake walked around until he found a bench relatively secluded from the others. He opened up Assignee and placed his eyes within few inches of the camera; it came alive. Expected icons, file folders, and browsers filled the screen, all restored to where he last left them. One icon caught his attention. It flashed 'LVC' – Live Voice Command. He clicked on it.

"Hi. My name is Maya."

Immediately Jake clicked to suppress the voice. He turned left and right looking around, no one payed him any mind. He dug into his pack to fetch a mike and earpiece. He up-linked the hands-free headset and then activated the LVC.

"Hi Jake, it's Maya."

"Maya." Pause. "You said Maya?"

"Yes. Maya is my name."

He laughed. "Okay. A computer has never talked to me before. Who are you? What's your function?"

"I am a virtual personal assistant. You can interface with Assignee through me rather than the keyboard."

"Okay, Maya, nice name. What does it mean?"

"It is a feminine name with multiple meanings. Do you want me to go through all of them?"

"Sure."

"In Hindu philosophy Maya means illusion. It is also the alternate name for Hindu goddess Durga. The mother of Buddha was called Queen Maya of Sakya. In Hebrew it means brook or spring, and in old Persian it means generous."

The lack of emotion in Maya's words irritated Jake slightly. "Okay, that's enough. Nice." Briefly, the whistle of the conductor summoning passengers disrupted his thoughts.

"Where am I, Maya?"

"You are on the train platform at Quetta Railway Station."

Jake was impressed. "Tell me about the weather."

"Sunny, with a light breeze of 10 miles per hour. Humidity fifteen percent. Temperature is 80 degrees Fahrenheit."

Very nice. "What else can you do?"

"Just give me a command. I will let you know if I can answer it or not."

"How can I call my father in San Antonio, Texas?"

"Give me his name and address."

"Charles Hudley, 102 Stony Brook Drive, San Antonio, Texas USA."

"I can make the call for you but they are asleep. Over there it 3:41 am."

Just then he noticed two boys approaching. "Bye Maya."

"Bye Jake."

The boys looked about five and twelve. The youngest brought back the image of Megan running to him as he got off the plane from his tour in Afghanistan. He'd scooped her up and hugged her so tight. Then Laila walked over with shy little Dillon and Jake kissed his son's forehead for the first time, squeezing Laila ever so tight.

At that moment he realized how exhausted he was. He felt emotionally and physically weak, just as he had that day at the airport. Tears dropped from his eyelashes as he tried to blink away the overwhelming emotion. His family needed him more than ever now. Laila needed him to find her and the kids needed him to bring their mother home again.

He picked two bananas from his purchases and extended them towards the boys. They were shy, just as Dillon had been. Jake smiled and beckoned them with a twist of the fruit in his hand. The older one, wearing a traditional cap, with baggy pants and shirt turned to his parents who were watching; they smiled. The older kid took the fruit, and his brother's hand, then ran back to his mother.

The train announced its arrival with an unbearably loud noise echoing throughout Zahedan as it finally chugged into the station. A commotion erupted. Mothers gathered children and men lifted luggage up onto shoulders. Many adults' eyes tracked the open doors of second class where seating was unreserved. Getting a spot for this long journey was like winning a prize as the trains are often over booked.

Jake watched for first class and stepped inside amidst pushing and shoving.

An hour into the travel, a screeching and grinding of wheels jolted Jake awake. When he opened his eyes, the train pulled into Spezand station.

The tea merchant standing on the platform yelled, "Chai, chai."

Conductors got off the car, chatted with the merchants and some passengers left and came aboard. So far the ride had been painful on his body, as every bump and turn of the car reverberated through his frame.

He'd hoped to get some badly needed rest, but it was an old train that showed its age frequently.

Jake recalled watching the activity of this train during digital surveillance sweeps while stationed in Kandahar. But his main focus had been the convoy traveling from Quetta to Kandahar, a 238 Kilometer distance. This vast, barren Baluchistan desert was inhabited by Talibans and bandits, both groups constantly challenging the US transport drivers. It was also widely suspected that Bin Laden, the master mind of the Al-Qaeda operation, escaped the wrath of the Coalition Forces in Kandahar. These lands had a history and a future marred by extreme conflict.

After a fifteen minute pause, a whistle filled the air seconds before the engines groaned again, spewing smoke towards the rear. It took a while to pick up speed. In the distance, Jake noticed hills with caves where locals, bandits, and the Taliban people lived.

He checked around the car he rode and found himself seated in a spot somewhat secluded from others. A boy of maybe ten sat next to him. Figuring the risk was minimal, he decided to continue his conversation with Maya.

"Hi Jake."

It seemed strange talking to a computer. "Hi Maya. Could you check something for me?"

"Of course, what would you like?"

"Can you calculate how long it'll take this train to reach Tafta?"

"Sure." Within seconds Maya replied, "At current speed it will take about twenty-five hours."

"Twenty-five hours! What's the speed?"

"About 25 Kilometers per hour."

"The distance?"

"Six hundred and thirty-two Kilometers."

Jake was disappointed with the answer but he couldn't do anything about it. Everything moved at a snail's pace in Pakistan. His anxiety put him in no mood to be a thankful traveler. Every day Laila spent incarcerated set her one day closer to death.

"Let's move on to something else. Find out how many people are staying at my father's house."

"Okay, let me see. It might take a few minutes." After a brief delay Maya said, "There are four persons inside the house."

Jake turned his head towards the window letting his eyes follow the valleys and peaks. "Great, how old are they?"

"Two adults and two children."

"Are they still asleep?"

"Yes, that is correct Jake." Maya's lack of emotions made Jake uneasy. He wasn't used to talking to a machine. When he got back home, he'd be sure to tell Andy to make Maya's voice more dynamic and intuitive. But he still wanted to explore all the functionality of this extraordinary computer and now was as good a time as any.

"Can you find out the whereabouts of a person called Laila Hudley? She could be in a Tehran prison."

"I can try. It might take a few days to gather intelligent information on that. Let me check something." Silence. "We have five undercover agents in Tehran right now. I'll find out if they are aware of anything."

"Maya, you're fantastic. I'm heading to Tehran, where my in-laws live. The address is 48 Rouhani Street. Can you tell me who's in the house right now?"

"Yes. There is one adult."

"Who lives in that house?"

"Three adults."

"I have to go. The conductor's coming."

"Bye Jake. I'll gather information about Laila Hudley and your journey."

After showing the conductor his ticket, Jake placed his backpack against the window, rested his head on it, and closed his eyes. Within minutes the swaying cabin lulled him to sleep. His nap was broken several times during the night but he stayed focused on getting some degree of rest.

Precisely at 7:01 pm the next evening, Jake walked off the train. It was over two hours late, though the tardiness was understandable as it had to crawl up the mountains in some areas. Just walking freely eased the joint pain in his knees.

Next to the platform stood a tired looking station building surrounded by empty space. When he entered the waiting hall, three taxi drivers approached him. He politely refused their service with a shake of his head and sat on a wooden bench close to the entrance, an area where there were few light bulbs.

The warm air smelled musty and old. Jake watched the ticket master lock and leave the booth for the day. The place was nearly empty but no matter how uncomfortable he felt, Jake knew he had to stay put. He tapped his fingers on his knee as he sat waiting. The next phase of the journey rested in the hands of his ex-CIA contact. He only hoped the money he'd spent on the intel meant more than duty to God and country to this guy. According to the plan, the man Jake waited for would take him across the border into Iran and then drive him to Tehran.

Thought after thought chased in endless circles in his mind. Would they cross without being detected? How would the travel to Tehran be? What if he was wrong about where Laila was being held? How reliable would this guy be?

When the clock on the wall struck quarter after seven, a man in his forties, with thick hair and a mustache, showed up wearing pants and a long-sleeved shirt in the Western style.

"Mister, you need a taxi?"

The timing was right, fifteen minutes after Jake got off the train, and his appearance was enough to tell Jake this was the right man.

"Yes, I do."

"My name is Riaz. Please follow me, sir."

Jake slung his knapsack over his shoulder and held the computer case with Assignee close to his chest as he stepped down slabs of marble to the street. He passed by a colorful bus loaded with passengers inside, the top filled with bags, furniture, luggage, and many other household items.

He slid into the front seat of the black and yellow Nissan, the vehicle looking just like any other taxi cab waiting in front of the station, but this one sat parked away from the building behind a cluster of rickshaws.

The ever-present knot in his stomach tightened, just to make sure Jake knew he was in over his head. Unless asked a direct question, he had to remind himself not to talk too much.

As Riaz pulled the vehicle onto the road he said, "Asallam-u-Alecom."

Jake replied, "*Alecom – Asalam.*" *Peace be upon you.* During his orientation sessions two years ago, he learned a few phrases, which happened to be very similar in all three neighboring countries.

The driver looked friendly enough.

"Good, you know Urdu."

Actually Asallam-u-Alecom was Arabic. Islam, the religion of this country, came from Arabia, so many Arabic words and customs had been interposed in Iran, Pakistan, and Afghanistan.

Jake didn't respond immediately as he held tight to the dashboard while the car negotiated several sharp turns.

"Where are we now?"

"This is the city of Taftan. We go through here and then take the road to the Iranian border."

He drove through narrow streets, passing lines of parked pickup trucks, pedestrians, commercial and residential buildings. Life in this place had quieted, to be expected as night fell. Nearly ten minutes later, they reached the border road out of Taftan and Riaz slowed the vehicle down in the near complete darkness. The landscape was barren. The man took several glances at his passenger.

"Are you American?"

Hesitation. "Yes."

A pregnant silence. "You Americans have done a lot of harm to Pakistan."

Jake knew very well the politics and tension between Pakistan and the US since 2001, when the coalition forces arrived in Afghanistan to quell the Taliban. It was a touchy subject and he wanted to avoid any such discussion.

Riaz continued, “You killed Bin Laden. Americans are in Afghanistan and that’s causing a lot of problems for us.”

Jake really wanted to change the subject and wondered why this guy was so obsessed with politics. He became suspicious of his driver’s motives. *Is he going to keep his side of the deal?*

Jake attempted to pacify Riaz. “Americans will leave Afghanistan in 2014 and hopefully things will calm down. By the way, how often do you do this kind of trip? Taking someone like me across the border.”

“May be once or twice a month. This job is very, very dangerous. If we get caught by the Iranians, both of us will be killed. Guards shoot to kill.”

Jake scratched the back of his neck. He hadn’t showered for days and the uneasiness a smelly, dirty body brought peaked during tense moments.

“How often does this happen?”

“At least once or twice a month. Iranians escape Iran and go to Pakistan. Depends on the driver.”

“Really?”

“Yes. Because Iranians are Shiites and they hate Sunnis or any other religious groups for that matter.”

“I heard fighting is going on in Quetta.”

“Yes, fighting in Quetta. Sunni and Shiite.” He shook his head. To show agreement. Pakistanis shook their head, unlike Americans who nodded.

“Why? What is the difference?” Jake asked.

“What’s the difference?” He paused calculating a reply. “They act like enemies. It’s a long history, my friend. Long history. It would take too long to explain. What is your religion?”

Jake scratched his head. “I was born into a Christian family. My parents aren’t religious. My wife is, but I’m not.”

Riaz turned to Jake, "Do you believe in God?"

"I'm not sure." He paused to reflect on the question. "What I do know is that I believe in goodness. I try to do good deeds for others and hope to attract positive vibes in return."

"One thing my friend. In Iran, don't tell anyone you don't believe in God. If the people find out, they'll think you're a communist and they'll call the Ayatollah's Revolutionary Guard. Very, very important."

"Okay. I'll remember. Thank you. Very kind of you."

"One thing I don't understand though. Why do you want to cross the Iranian border illegally? Usually, I go to Tehran and bring Iranians who want to escape *from* Iran. This is the opposite."

Jake sighed. "My wife is Iranian and Revolutionary Guards are holding her in prison. They've already killed her brother. I think they're gonna kill her too."

Ahmed laughed loudly. "You want to rescue her! Impossible. Impossible. I know one person who tried to rescue his parents from Evin prison and he was not successful. They were all executed. It looks like you are alone in this plan."

"Yes. I am alone."

"With great respect, you should not go to Iran. Go home."

"Not going home. I may get killed and never see my children again, but I'm not going home."

"We're coming up to the border. Get ready to jump."

"Jump? What do you mean jump?"

"You walk to Mirjaveh. The road is there. There. You can see it." He pointed out the windshield.

"You're supposed to take me to Tehran. That was the deal."

"I wish I could. But I can't take you. In Mirjaveh you'll find a taxi. Take it to Zahedan, then a bus to Tehran."

Jake yelled, "Why? Why are you breaking the deal?"

"I promised you nothing."

"Your co-worker did. What's his name? I saw him in San Antonio. He took $500.00 which I had borrowed to pay him."

The car slowed. "If you don't get out now, I have to take you back to Taftan. This is a very dangerous place. I can't be here for too long. Guards are watching all the time. Jump, jump now."

Jake opened the door and threw out the computer bag first then his pack. Recalling his training, he opened the door wide, then rolled out of the front seat with his shoulder forward and right arm tucked to his stomach. Wind whistled past his ears and he felt the body of the Nissan blast by. He landed on the ground, his body moving like a tumbling weed. The car sped off into the dark.

Brushing gravel and road dust from his clothes, he limped back a few yards to collect his pack and computer bag. He unzipped it and pulled Assignee out.

Maya asked, "Hi Jake. Are you hurt?"

"How can you know to ask if I'm hurt or not?"

"I heard your conversation in the car, and with the abrupt move I concluded what likely happened."

After a quick mental check of his body for any severe pain he said, "No, nothing serious. Just a sore back."

"I'm sorry Riaz did not take you to Tehran. I can help."

"Damn idiot. He stole my money." At a distance the tail light faded out entirely. "Asshole."

Jake fought off the overwhelming urge to yell and focused instead on the AI in his hands. "Okay, guide me to Tehran."

"Turn around and walk twenty-two feet. You will see a path, then turn right. Watch on the screen and I'll give you voice guidance."

"The border is close by here somewhere. I was told the guards take a break at each prayer call. The prayer only lasts about ten minutes but they extend their break for an hour. The next break will be at dawn."

"What I can do is put a 10 km radius canopy around you."

"What does that mean?"

"If there's any movement, in any direction for ten kilometers, I'll alert you and let you know what it is."

He sat on the ground by some sparse shrubs for cover. “Okay good. Give me a map of the ground around me, the border line, the road that goes to Zahedan, and the closest town. Um, ah …”

“Mirjaveh.”

“Yes, that’s the one. Glad you remember.”

“You are welcome.”

Jake was impressed with Maya’s polite responses. Monotone voice aside, interacting with her slowly help his anger subside.

“Can you give me the distance from here to the Pakistani/Iranian border?”

“3.54 km.”

“Maya, can you cut the kilometer shit and give it to me in miles?”

“2.2 miles.”

Her tone did not indicate any emotional hurt. *Better than a human, right now anyway*. “I’ll just rest here. Put a shield around me for any intruder. Wake me up thirty minutes before dawn.” He figured it’d take him about that long to walk the distance to the border.

“Requests noted. One more thing to consider. A sand storm is predicted to pass through this area around dawn. Should I wake you up one hour before dawn?” *Wow, she just saved my ass.*

“Yes, do that. Thanks for looking out for me. Goodness knows I need the help.” Andy really came through for him. Without Assignee and Maya, he’d be lost and alone walking unprepared into a firefight he didn’t stand a chance against. Jake owed him for life. Jake shifted his pack under his head, set Maya on the hard, packed ground beside him and lay down on his back under a bright canopy of stars and fell asleep to the quite hum of the computer.

The next morning, he crossed the border without incident, walked to the nearby highway and took a taxi to Zahedan.

Chapter 11

Laila stood waiting for Maryam to unlock the cell gate. Her friend arrived as expected, after her meal delivery came to end.

"Sister Laila, please put your chador on." The words were delivered with respect and infused Laila with warmth. "We'll go out of this building, walk through a lane outside and then enter the next building where the female showers are. At both entrances there are male guards."

"Yes." She understood that modesty rules must be strictly obeyed. The thought of fresh air and being outside made her giddy.

By now, she had lost track of the day of the week. The rats had eaten her rice piles, and when she forgot to add new ones every day she completely lost sense of time.

"I haven't been outside in weeks. I can't remember the last time. Will it be a long walk?"

"Very short, a few minutes."

"Please make it as long as possible." She gave Maryam a broad smile.

"Yes, of course." After a nod, Maryam placed the blindfold over Laila's eyes.

"Maryam, I must say I appreciate what you're doing. It's unbelievable. I don't think I could do enough to pay you back."

"Our balance is zero. You owe me nothing—I feel the same way. Our conversations and mutual respect have lifted me this past week. We share a sister spirit. After I entered this place, my life, future, dreams all shattered. Some nights it's so bad, I stop believing in them."

Laila stepped forward, guided by Maryam's hand around her arm. With every move her mind ran through questions, a list she'd prepared during the night and made a mental note to ask Maryam—the most pressing one when family visitations were allowed.

Five minutes into the labyrinthine walk, a man's voice said, "Salam Alaykum."

"Salam," Maryam replied.

A gentle wind wafted across Laila's face, hands, and feet. The warm, dry air set every cell dancing with renewed energy. She inhaled until her lungs overflowed and slowly exhaled with every step. The cycle of breathing and exhaling continued. *Oh clean fresh air!* The light wind flushed the scent of vomit and stale urine from her nose, and the oxygen pumping through her lungs made her light of heart and head.

She absorbed every whisper of the breeze passing through nearby leaves. Every moment was so precious, she lost all sense of time as the enjoyment of being in an open space overwhelmed her. The experience ended too soon when she heard another deep voice acknowledge Maryam in greeting.

Moments later a stale air hit her, back inside once more. After a dozen more steps, Maryam pulled her arm slightly. Laila stopped. Distant giggling echoed from down the hall.

"Turn right here. We're going to the shower stalls." Both walked side by side. "On the left is room 247."

"What kind of prisoners are held there?"

"Less dangerous offenders."

It was hard for Laila to digest Maryam's explanation. "I'm not dangerous."

"I know, sister. But the authorities don't." After a short pause Maryam continued, "247 is a big room, dorm-like with forty beds. But sixty stay there. Some get beds to sleep on and other get a piece of the floor. Sometimes I go there and other times to a solitary cell."

Laila leaned closer and whispered, "Why were you switched?"

"It's a long story. I'll tell you some other time."

Another question added to the list, increasing the intrigue surrounding Evin. If she ever got out, she promised herself to expose to the world the oppressive campaign of this prison. Her mind weighed in on the options. "Why am I in solitary confinement?"

"Because The Islamic Court has not made a decision on your future yet."

Maryam pulled Laila's blindfold off. Her vision adjusted to the light. The hallway was just wide enough for two people to walk shoulder to shoulder. Dimly lit bulbs hung exposed from the ceiling. Laila ventured with another question.

"When will they decide my case?"

"Really, I don't know your situation. But from what I understand, a lot of bargaining, haggling, and discussions go on behind the scenes, most of which is hidden from the prisoners."

"This is so confusing. It's not fair. They play God with people's lives."

Maryam paused for a while. "That's true." Her words, heavy with sadness, echoed Laila's own struggles.

A tug brought Laila to another stop. The moist air and irritating scent of cheap soap assailed her. Five shower stalls stood in a row.

Maryam turned and closed the main door behind them, setting the lock. "Now we can talk."

Laila couldn't wait to hear the girl's story. It boggled her mind to no end how someone so young could end up in such a terrible place.

"What happened to you after they brought you here?"

Maryam cleared her throat. "After I was arrested, the interrogator asked me very nicely and calmly to give the names of my friends and classmates who walked with me out of the Islamic class. That was in high school. I refused. I knew why he wanted them. When I refused a second time he beat me and tortured me."

"What did they do?" Since her arrest, Laila had lain awake many a night wondering about the indignities women endured at the hands of the authorities—waiting for something equally awful to happen to her. Alternating scenarios of torture, rape, and mind control circled her thoughts.

"I was forced to lie on a bed with each wrist handcuffed to the frame. Same for my legs. With an iron rod, he hit the bare soles of my feet. With every smack he asked for names. I still refused. At first, the bar was simply pressure on my feet, but hours later, for I can only imagine it took that long, the slightest tap sent spikes of pain up my shins and into my legs." Maryam held her mouth with hand, holding back a cry.

"When he realized I would not break, he untied me and made me stand on my feet. Oh the pain! Unbearable, unbearable! Like standing on fiery needles. He told me to walk. I couldn't. I clutched the frame of the bed, crying. He blindfolded me and dragged me into the open air. Removing the blindfold, he pointed to dead bodies with a flashlight. Each had a name written on its forehead; each executed earlier that night. The bodies of eight or ten women lay broken and haphazard over one another. It turned my stomach. I threw up until I passed out."

Laila looked at the innocent eyes as tears slid down Maryam's checks. She wrapped the poor girl in her arms and gave the tightest squeeze. It was therapy for both of them.

"I'm so sorry."

Maryam wiped her nose with the side of her hand. "Take your shower. We only have ten minutes."

Laila stripped, no longer self-conscious, stepped inside the closest stall and closed the curtain. A pipe ran up the wall from the faucets then curved to a tin shower head. Slowly she turned the warm water tap, letting the water run over her skin. The sensory touch was more heavenly than the fresh air had been.

"What about you?" Maryam asked, raising her voice to compensate for the noise of the running water.

"I was visiting my parents shortly after my brother was arrested by the Revolutionary Guards. They were in a panic when they didn't hear from him for days. Then, my father had a heart attack and was in the hospital. On my second night in Iran the Guards arrived at my parents' place, arrested me, and brought me here. A hell hole. A few days later I was informed of my brother's death."

"Where were you before?"

"In Texas."

"Oh, you're from America. My brother lives in Canada. He wanted me to go there after I finished my education. That'll never happen now. I'll never get out of here. Do you have any children?"

"Yes. Megan and Dillon. God, I miss them so much. I think about them day and night. And my husband too. Jake …"

"It is time to get out." An order came out from a loud authoritative voice Laila recognized. One she'd never forget.

Maryam said, "Sister Fatimeh wants us out of here."

Bitch. That voice irritated Laila to no end. At the same time, she was annoyed with herself for the negative thought. Suddenly, she realized how easily this place could turn a saint into a devil, unless one was very strong.

As guilt erupted inside her, she asked for God's forgiveness. This place tested all her virtues, finding how weak they were. Her mother used to say, "A baby is innocent, but an old woman is tried and true." She never understood what it meant, but she always remembered the phrase for its depth in wisdom. It felt right to apply it here.

Laila closed the tap. "I'm coming out." She dried herself, wrapped the scratchy cloth around her body and stepped out of the stall.

"Sorry, we have to go. We get warm water only once every two or three weeks, only two hours at a time for all the prisoners." Laila dressed as Maryam passed items of clothing to her.

"Maryam, I'm so thankful to you. You've been the answer to my prayers."

"I feel the same way about you. I hope we can get out of here alive."

"It's a deal, then." Laila gave Maryam another embrace.

Re-blindfolded Laila traced her steps back to the cell. Maryam hurried out as curfew neared. Laila hadn't gotten a chance to ask about family visitation. *Next time.*

In the cell, she lay down on the mattress and replayed every moment of her trip to and from the shower: thoughts, feelings, sensations came alive again. Before falling asleep she reflected on whether or not she could manage to get out of Evin alive.

***

Ali Mohmed shot a glance at the wall clock as the hands ticked past ten. With a quick move to his feet, he gathered papers from different piles and shoved them into a brief case. Grabbing the briefs, Ali left his office in the interrogation building. As he stepped outside, two guards bowed with a right hand over their chest.

Ali picked up the pace heading towards the courthouse, a ten-minute walk away. He passed by guards and employees, some of them dragging prisoners, to which he ignored as routine occurrences. His mind remained preoccupied on the court session he was about to attend. Being ten minutes late for Laila's Hudley's court trial was not his concern, rather his thoughts were taken by whether or not he'd have enough evidence to convince the judges to execute the woman without further delay.

He entered the courthouse, a two-story structure dotted with barred windows. Passing through a dark hallway, Ali arrived at chambers and knocked.

A deep voice said, "Come in."

When Ali stepped inside, three judges, each behind a desk stood and shook hands with the interrogator. These three Islamic jurors were Shiite clergymen and scholars, all appointed through a chain of authorities that led up to the Supreme Leader of Iran.

After everyone took their seats, the mullah in the middle, oldest of the three and with the most seniority and authority, spoke.

"In the name of God, the merciful and kind, this court of Islamic justice is now officially in session. We will hear Ali Mohmed present information against Laila Dareini. Brother Ali is an interrogator for this case, a man who has always protected Islam to the best of his abilities and, on many occasions, has shown a great deal of personal sacrifice while serving Islam."

Ali pulled a stack of paper from his brief case. Reverently he stared at a picture of the Supreme Leader hung on the wall behind the judges.

In a soft but firm voice, Ali said, "Accused's brother, Orang Dareini was arrested during a routine citizen inspection by our beloved Revolutionary Guards. He was found guilty of being an enemy of Islam and a spy. Before we were able to initiate his court proceedings he died of a heart attack." Ali lifted his eyes towards the three faces who watched his presentation with focused attention. He knew they understood the charges and the boy's fate. They were relaxed and unemotional with this background information.

He flipped to another page and continued, "The unexpected and sudden death of Orang led us to investigate his family and arrest Laila Dareini in the absence of her father." Ali paused to summon the judges' full interest and cleared his throat. "This detainee and her family belong to a dirty religion that poses a great danger to Islam." The three heads in front of him moved in agreement.

Then with far more vigor and passion Ali informed the three men, who listened attentively and occasionally took notes, of the latest and most crucial phase of the investigation. "Laila Dareini is Iranian born but was *never* a Muslim." A reprehensible sin. "She married Jake Hudley, a United States Air Force Officer previously stationed in Afghanistan as a flight controller for drones in the US Army."

Ali squared his shoulder and read his first request. "This court must declare Jake Hudley an enemy of Islam, an American complicit in killing Muslim brothers and sisters in Afghanistan. Also I ask the court to charge Laila Dareini with espionage—spying for the United States of America." He got up and placed in front of each judge a copy of newspapers clippings and TV news reports detailing Hudley's background and the Dareini woman's time abroad.

At the conclusion of the presentation, the judges thanked Ali's for his dedication and they all drank tea.

Ali walked out of the courtroom pleased with the strength of his case. He never held compassion or patience for anyone who did not conform.

Knowing exactly how to manipulate the system, his goal in having Laila executed before her case ever went to trial was now set in motion.

Later that afternoon Ali waved Fatimeh out of his office to accept an important call. It was the most senior judge from this morning's hearing.

"Balay, merci," Ali thanked the judge for his praises.

"Brother Ali, you'll be pleased to know that the court's decided to declare Jake Hudley an enemy of Islam and Laila Dareini a spy."

Ali did not smile but knew in his heart that justice was being served.

At the end of the conversation, Ali was given the task of notifying Laila's family of the court's decision and to make sure a lawyer was present at her future trial. When Ali replaced the receiver he lifted his chest with pride, adding one more credit to his flawless job performance.

***

Sometime after lunch Maryam slipped unexpectedly into Laila's cell.

"Sister Fatimeh told me you get a family visit today." Maryam clapped excitedly. "She wants me to take you because she doesn't like being around all those crying people."

"Is that the truth?"

With a faint smile she shook her head. "I'm sorry to say, she does not like you—good. I get to spend more time with you."

I wonder why. She ran a few possible reasons through her mind, settling on one she felt strongest about. But she wouldn't mention it to Maryam until Laila confirmed her suspicions.

Laila's legs wobbled as she stood and her head spun. She hadn't eaten a decent meal in weeks and found it difficult to do even the most mundane of tasks. She clung to the iron bars of her cell as Maryam wrapped the blindfold around her friend's eyes and tied it at the back of her head. Only then did it strike Laila that she'd be seeing her family. *Who would come? Maman? Baba? Negar?* Overwhelmed by the competing sadness of being a prisoner and the hope of hearing about her children and family, tears broke free. Realizing how weak and vulnerable she'd become, Laila waved off Maryam's sympathetic hug and reined in her emotions until the weeping slowed to occasional sniffles.

"How long will they allow?"

"Half an hour."

"After they locked you up, how long was it before you saw your parents?"

"Six weeks."

"Six weeks. Terrible. I've lost track of time. I don't know how long I have been here. Three? Four weeks?" Laila shrugged.

"Sister, I don't exactly, perhaps two or three weeks."

So few? It felt like a life time.

Maryam adjusted the blindfold. "Is this too tight?"

"No. Maryam, how did you escape execution?"

"As it is, if I had a choice, I would have chosen death over spending the rest of my life here."

Laila couldn't imagine being trapped here forever. As they walked, she reflected on her experiences back in Texas with the Iranian community. She'd never considered before how many stories of rounding up family members, trumped up charges, and quick trials denounced life imprisonment. "Why was your sentence changed?"

Maryam stayed quiet far longer than Laila expected. But her worry at offending her friend slipped away when she felt Maryam shift and rotate her body as if looking for anyone within hearing distance.

"Reza, an interrogator, contacted the Imam and had my sentence changed. Then he asked me to be his *Sigheh*. You know about it?"

Laila had studied the practice of *Sigheh*, the temporary marriage. "Yes, I am very familiar. What is the time limit?"

Maryam went silent again. After a moment, she said, "Time limit? I don't know."

"And you still don't have a space of your own?"

"No. Most of the time I live in 246 with other girls. Three to four evenings, I hear my name called in the loudspeaker which means spending the night with Reza in a private room." She felt shame. "Names of other girls are called this way as well."

Laila probed, "Do you like it?"

"What's to like? What choice do I have? It's nothing but a temporary arrangement."

"Did you leave someone special behind?"

"What do you mean?"

"Someone you cared for and wanted to spend your life with?"

Maryam sighed, "Oh, yes. Thomas. With every passing day I try to forget about him. I'm sure he'll want nothing to do with me when I'll get out of here. How could it be otherwise?"

Laila lowered her voice, "I have an idea. You and I should plan an escape. I saw a Hollywood movie called Alcatraz. It was supposed to be the United States' most inescapable prison but two men got out."

Maryam laughed. Something in the set of her jaw and the look of her eyes told Laila she wished she could believe in such things. "We should work on it." She guided Laila around a tight corner. "We've arrived at the waiting room now."

Laila hadn't registered other voices or noticed the presence of others at first, and yet now that Maryam pointed it out she couldn't believe it. *Who will I get to see?* The room felt large and sounded full though there were only a few whispers, mostly sobbing.

A man's voice called names at regular intervals. Finally, he spoke Laila's. She and the others in her group were instructed to follow the hand rail towards the waiting room and then remove their blindfold just before entering and not a moment before.

Maryam walked with her and then stopped to remove the blindfold. When Laila's sight was restored, a long rectangular space spread out in front of her with thick glass dividing the large room in half. Armed guards stood at every corner. On both sides of the glass men and women scanned bodies and eyes, searching for loved ones, some crying and some leaning their hands on the glass for even the remotest contact.

In a sea of faces, Laila finally spotted her mother, next to Abbas and Negar. Their gazes connected. All four ran towards the full-length glass wall and placed their palms on it in an effort to bridge the physical gap. All eyes filled with tears, even Abbas'.

Laila managed to read her mother's lips, "How are you?"

She nodded, holding back her own tears.

Negar uttered a few words but with no response from her sister she repeated the lip movement. She lifted both hands and looked up at the ceiling as if she was praying for her.

"What?" Laila said shaking her head, desperately trying to decode her words.

Her lips went into slow, exaggerated the movement. "We are looking for a lawyer."

Laila shook her head, "Thank you."

Maman wiped her eyes with her chador. "Be brave."

Laila mouthed, "Jake? Megan? Dillon?"

Maman shook her head.

Laila ran her forefinger on the wall spelling out her children's names.

Maman turned to Negar for an answer.

"Okay," Negar mouthed.

The separation from her family pained Laila's stomach and with each passing moment became more intense. The only cure would be an embrace by her family and never letting them go. Her father's face appeared thinner, though he managed to keep on his feet with the help of a cane.

"We'll get you out of here," he managed to convey.

Holding the tears back Laila prayed, *God willing*. "I am so happy to see you," she mouthed.

As Negar ran her finger over the glass, this time Laila followed it with hers.

"Orie?" Laila asked.

"Yes." Negar pointed her fingers up in the air, indicating he was gone to another world.

"Yes. I know." Laila examined her father's face. He wiped his eyes with a handkerchief. A shadow covered the aura of this broken man. It was just too hard to bear. She changed the conversation by writing, "Jake?"

Laila could not understand her family's reaction. They looked to one another and the ground, almost confused. *Where is he? Did he call to find out about his wife?*

"Time's up!" a guard yelled.

"Be brave, Laila." Abbas motioned, and stroked the glass as though tracing his daughter's face. "We'll get you out."

As the guards cleared the space for the next batch of visitors, Laila sent a kiss as the faces of her loved ones disappeared through the doorway.

Maryam reappeared and placed the blindfold over Laila's eyes once again. Holding her arm, she steered Laila back to her cell. Along the way, Laila's cries grew louder and then she whispered, "Why, why, why?"

When the sobbing diminished to an occasional sniffle, Laila said, "That was a lot harder than I imagined it would be."

Maryam squeezed Laila's arm with one hand and rubbed her friend's back with the other. "I know. I wish I knew what to say to ease the pain. Dark as it may look, we at least have each other."

"Thank you for your help. You are a God-send."

***

Later that afternoon, Maryam appeared for a second time in front of Laila's cell.

"I'm here to take you to Brother Ali."

Mind foggy, Laila mumbled, "Ali?"

"Ali Mohmed, the interrogator."

Laila's emotional wrenching from that morning had stripped her of any remaining strength. Dealing with Ali did nothing to bolster her will.

Blindfolded, Laila was led through the corridors to an adjoining building. Maryam freed Laila's vision from its shroud but never set foot in the man's office. Laila entered alone, mentally shoring up every weak wall she could find inside of her. Ali's eyes were cold and dark. A barren bed sat in the back corner of the room. The spiritual wall in her heart crumbled at the sight of it—thoughts of Maryam's story penetrating her thoughts. She forced her eyes to look elsewhere. A desk and two chairs blocked most of the room but her gaze was dragged back to the metal bed and the length of black cable hanging from the headboard.

Is today the day?

A huge poster beside the bed read, "If one permits an infidel to continue in his role as a corrupter of the earth, the infidel's moral suffering will be all the worse. If one kills the infidel, and this stops him from perpetrating his misdeeds, his death will be a blessing to him."

"Sit down."

With the verbal slap, Laila complied. Her capacity to think for herself slowly diminished. Under her breath, she murmured a prayer, "Is there any removal of difficulty, save God?"

A horrible feeling crawled under her skin. She watched the interrogator walk to the bed peppered by blood stains. Her eyes tracked the man before her, like a mantra she repeated her prayer until the racing of her heart slowed. He picked up the iron cable and walked toward her.

A tremble rippled through her frail body.

After many minutes, he broke the silence, "Your husband's name is Jake Hudley and he works for the United States Air Force. You said that you came to Iran to visit your parents. I don't believe you. What's the real reason you're here?"

"Visiting my parents is the only reason."

"Where's your husband?"

"In Lackland, Texas."

"A military base. No one seems to know where he actually is. Did you ask your mother or father where your beloved Jake is?"

"Yes."

"What did they tell?"

"Nothing. I wanted to know. But with a glass wall between us they could not communicate."

"Tell me the truth. That's not the truth."

"I swear to God, that's the truth."

With two steps he drew close and backhanded Laila across the face. Her ear rang as she collapsed forward onto herself.

"Don't ever say *God* again! You're unclean and unworthy to mention His name. I have to wash my hands now because I've touched you."

The abuse vibrated like electric pulses through Laila's body, numbing her senses. Ali fell silent as if waiting for a response. When she gave none, he continued, "See the stains." He pointed the cable towards the bed. "That one is fresh."

The cable went up into the air above Laila's head. She squeezed her eyes shut tight, hugging her quaking body.

The phone rang.

The blow did not come. Laila opened her eyes as Ali took a step back, lifted the receiver, and listened to the voice on the other end for several minutes.

"Yes, yes. I'll be there." He hung up the phone. "I have to go."

Maryam entered the room only after her interrogator disappeared. Both women walked in silence for some time. The pressure from Maryam's grip on Laila's arm felt like the only thing keeping her from collapsing on the spot.

Then, holding Laila's hand to her heart, Maryam whispered, "What happened?"

Limping in slow motion, drawing strength to her voice with difficulty, Laila managed to explain the red cheek mark.

"Ali does not need good reason to seriously hurt people. All interrogators gain pleasure from crushing a prisoner's spirit. Don't let him." She squeezed her friend's hand. "Don't let them, Laila."

Chapter 12

At ten-to-eleven Jake Hudley slipped his arms through his back pack one at a time. Standing beside a table in his hotel room, he grabbed the case with Maya, then swung a camera around his neck. He felt rested; his energy restored after days of travel. The way one day blended into the next made him lose all sense of time. Thank goodness for Maya.

The night Jake had arrived at the hotel, he had a fast shower, then fell into bed. The uneven mattress and squeaky frame did not prevent him from falling asleep within minutes; any place was good enough to recoup from the last few days. He felt secure in the room at the Abuzar Hotel, the least expensive place Maya could find in the neighborhood.

Jake surveyed his room at the Abuzar Hotel where he'd spent the last twenty-four hours. Grateful for the rest, Jake prepared for the next phase of his plan, now ready to leave behind the pastel green walls, worn floors, and smelly carpeting. He'd regained the strength needed to face the world outside.

But where to go from here? He had too many options and yet not enough all at the same time. He'd been so focused on just getting here, now that he'd arrived he had to accomplish the impossible.

Approaching the window overlooking Metri-e Kamarbandi Street, Jake studied the movements below. The car models looked unfamiliar, some men wore western clothes and others traditional garb. Some women were covered from head to toe, except for their faces, while others only wore a simple head scarf.

This quick glimpse into Iranian society made him realized how much better the American standard of living seemed, at least compared with his experiences in Afghanistan and Pakistan. The cars were noisy and at times reckless. In this bright sunny morning the street life unfolded with true regularity.

The memory of Megan's stoic little face pressed nose-to-nose with Jake as she inspected him moments after walking off his return flight home from active duty and Dillon's tiny hand slipping into his for the first time overwhelmed him. *What am I doing here?* To save his soul mate, the mother of his children, from the claws of tyranny. That thought brought him strength and the resolve to move forward. He was alone in his pursuit, but that didn't matter. Getting his questions answered became his first priority.

Jake turned from scene below and locked the door behind him. As he walked along a dimly lit hallway covered with the pungent carpeting, at every step the wood joints squealed under his feet. On the main floor he approached a man behind the front desk. The words Abuzar Hotel were printed in bold letters on the wall. When Jake place the key on the desk, the clerk immediately went to a filing cabinet and pulled out some paperwork. He glanced it over then waved his right hand. Jake took that as the signal to say he owed nothing more for the night's stay.

Stepping onto the sidewalk of Mir Hoseini Street, Jake scanned the busy road. Two guards of the Guardians of the Islamic Revolution, commonly known as the Ayatollah's Boys, approached him. Jake vaguely recalled the night manager making a call immediately after he'd checked in, but he'd been too tired to think about it at the time. Now that he was on high alert, he cursed himself for not asking Maya about the nature of the call before falling asleep.

The older guard wore a green khaki uniform and carried a machine gun over his shoulder, "Good morning. Can I speak with you for a few minutes?" He was in his thirties with a dark beard and full head of hair.

His serious expression alarmed Jake, who wasn't sure if the demeanor was normal for the routine interrogation of foreigners. Usually they were after smugglers from Pakistan. Maya had informed Jake of rampant drug trafficking along the border towns.

With a brief mental note he remembered to drop the Texan accent. "Yes. Certainly." His military training kept him in check about not divulging more than the situation warranted.

"Can I see your passport?" His voice was deep and authoritative.

"Sure."

Jake dug the passport from his front pants pocket. A few pedestrians stopped to watch. The intense street noise of car horns, motorcycle engines, and the resonance of daily life bombarded him even as the heat elevated the stench of the city.

"Here." Jake handed over the document.

The guard stared for a long moment at the front cover, then thumbed to the photo page which he examined carefully, lifting his eyebrows slightly as he read. He flipped pages until he reached the one with the "Iranian Border Security – Zahedan" stamp, which Jake had applied earlier, after getting up. The guard spent a minute or more analyzing this page.

"You came last night."

"Yes." Jake was brief but friendly.

The guard returned to front page.

"Canadian?" Suspicion was written all over his face. "Where do you live in Canada?" He shook his head, an Iranian habit when asking a question.

Jake's mind blanked. He didn't have adequate knowledge of Canada. He should've built a stronger background with the help of Maya, a task suggested by his ex-CIA contact back in San Antonio. He'd just been too preoccupied to think past getting here. Very few city names ran through his mind.

He blurted out, "Toronto." Jake made a mental note to educate himself soon as possible about the main streets, landmarks, and neighborhoods of that city. This wasn't likely to be an isolated incident.

The Guard lifted his head and stared at Jake's face, this time absorbing every detail with intensity. "Mr. MacDougal, what is your profession?"

Relieved of the shift to his occupation, he said, "Photo journalist." The response was loaded with confidence.

The interrogating guard turned his attention to the Canon Rebel 3TI hanging from Jake's shoulder. "Photo journalist. Which magazine?"

The younger guard hadn't uttered a word so far, but Jake noticed his undivided attention during the interaction.

"I work for National Geographic. I'm doing an article on beautiful Iranian historical sites."

"Where is your next destination in Iran?"

"To Isfahan."

The guard grimaced but his attention remained fixed on Jake's facial expressions. "Any place specifically?"

Time to impress the guard. Muslims were always astonished when a white man talked positively about Islamic places, something he learned when interacting with Afghanis.

"There are many beautiful historic landmarks. What I admire the most is the architecture, with its sweeping boulevards, covered bridges, palaces, mosques and minarets."

The guard gave no hint of an impression, as was likely his training. He further examined the passport from the front cover, picture page, and border stamp as if he was not too certain of what to make of the stranger standing before him.

"How long you will be here in Iran?"

"Not exactly sure. Could be one or two weeks."

"Are you able to show me any of your work?"

"Sure." He pulled out a copy of National Geographic and flipped through the pages until a picture of the Taj Mahal appeared. He showed the page to the guard. "I did this article."

Jake had rehearsed this scenario many times, but was not sure how well the man was buying his story. The name on the article matched his and there was no image of the actual journalist in this copy of the magazine. Still, the guard took an inordinately long time to weigh the truth of Jake's words. The man had wicked poker face.

The guard clamped his chin with his fingers, taking a moment to reflect before handing over the passport, "Welcome to Iran."

I made it? The officer's words rang like a bell of joy, releasing the tension on his shoulders.

"Thank you. That's kind of you." The words came without any effort. Jake just stood there watching the guards move away. He paused for the longest moment as he took stock of what had happened.

An American, pretending to be a Canadian had made a clandestine crossing of an international border. *I am free.* Senator Quest said one person couldn't do it alone and he'd just accomplished phase one. The tension from every muscle in his body eased making him feel light.

But just as fast the knot in his stomach returned. Here he was, standing in the middle of an Iranian street with curious bystanders watching his every move with phase two: finding Laila and phase three: rescuing her still to figure out.

Jake crossed the street, making his way between cars and avoiding motorcycles. J-walking was not a pedestrian sin in Iran. The scent of shish kabob drew him toward a local eatery. He dropped a dollar in the hand of a beggar who sat next to a billboard plastered with the pictures of both Ayatollahs.

He felt thankful as he mentally examined the list of those who'd helped him so far. He hoped the universe, or some force up there, would be kind enough to bring good people his way during this time of need. No man was an island but one American could save the love of his life with a little local assistance.

When he entered the eatery, the place was empty except for one man preparing lunch and another by the cash ready to receive customers. Both stood behind the main counter.

"Salam."

"Salam, what would you like to eat?"

With a renewed appetite, Jake lifted his hand toward the picture menu of the plate piled with rice, salad, and two skewers of meat. “Chole Kabob.”

“Drink? Zam Zam cola. Good Iranian drink.” His English was good and the man was clearly comfortable dealing with foreigners.

Jake paid for his meal.

“Please, take a seat,” the cashier pointed to a restaurant full of empty chairs.

At a table closer to the back, Jake pulled the computer out and opened the screen before putting the ear bud in and starting a conversation with Maya. Right now, he had to find out more about Toronto. He scolded himself again for neglecting this task. One mistake could easily derail Laila’s rescue, and even worse could cost many lives.

He did a thorough search as his food cooked and was about to shut the super computer down when he decided to send a quick message to Makalla.

He simply typed, “Made it across,” and tapped the send button. Jake knew his sister was smart enough to understand what he meant.

He acknowledged the waiter bringing his plate. As the steam rose and the aroma hit his nostrils, Jake’s stomach growled. Moving the computer aside, he made room for the plate and drink. The smell of basmati rice reminded him even more of Laila.

The first time Laila invited Jake to a dinner party at her tiny apartment, she’d set out a sumptuous spread of rice and other dishes he’d never seen before. That night he fell in love with her cooking, specifically the Iranian style rice. The look on her face as he managed to eat the last traces from every dish had been priceless. His chest burned at the thought of her, worse now than when he’d been on assignment. Just when he thought they’d finally be together forever, the world found a way to tear them apart again. *I can do this. I can save you my little Lalouska.*

His body commanded he eat, so Jake dug the spoon into the heap of rice and shoveled food into his mouth. When finished, the plate was clean and the two men behind the counter stood bemused by his appetite.

Back to Maya, he searched for more information about Toronto. Different sections of the city arose: North York, East York, Scarborough and Etobicoke. Special neighborhoods: Kensington Market, Jewish, Italian, Indian, Chinese, and Greek. The most notable landmark one talked about was the CN Tower. Maya impressed him with the dazzlingly speed of Assignee, while fetching information. After a few more searches, his eyes ached and his head throbbed—*that's enough for now.*

After closing Maya, he raised his sight to the men behind the counter. He felt comfortable with Iranians. They were a nice people and not to be confused with the government who had mistreated his wife.

From what he had seen, Jake had a good feeling about Zahedan. He felt a connection with this old, rugged city. In Afghanistan, some of his mates only criticized the Afghani ways, but he was always different—wanted to be appreciative of local culture, behavior, and the alternate tempo of life. Laila always saw the best in people, her kind spirit and gentle smile always managed to reassure him that good things were just around the corner, all you had to do was look for them.

After their whirlwind affair on campus he focused on exactly those positive thoughts when he asked her to marry him. At first her parents wouldn't give consent. Among Iranians, marrying a doctor, lawyer, or engineer was held in the highest esteem. If that failed, the fourth preferable choice was marrying rich—Jake was none of those. They'd waited four long months before she finally gained their permission. He'd swept her up in his arms and kissed every inch of her face, saving her lips for last.

He got up, collected his bags and headed towards the exit.

The cashier asked, "American?"

"Canadian. How do I find the bus station?"

After giving Jake directions, the cashier said, "Be careful, be careful."

Jake waved his hand, "Salam."

When Jake turned in the direction of the bus station he noticed a man standing next to the hotel across the street. A face he was certain he'd seen before. *But where?*

Chapter 13

Holding the remote control, Charles Hudley watched Ruth pace toward the front door carrying Dillon in her arms.

"Be careful. Don't be out for too long." *Will she listen? Probably not.*

"Chuck, shake it off. You haven't been out of the house for days." Ruth's sharp words confirmed his concerns.

In the last twenty-four hours the race to find Jake had intensified among the big four: CNN, FOX News, ABC and NBC. The reporters were getting more aggressive. Hudley's landline had been ringing off the hook. Charles never answered his cell phone without checking the call display; if he didn't recognize the incoming call, he just let it ring and waited for a message, if any.

"I can't go out. Reporters will pounce on me like a hungry lion looking for a juicy meal."

Ruth had a different approach, as usual. "Juicy meal. Nothing juicy about me. When I go out that door, they better not come after me. I'll show them the good side of my face when they point their camera at me. Then my ugly side when they ask about Jake. I told one to shove off just yesterday."

Ruth carried Dillon to the door, took Megan's hand and walked out. His granddaughter closed the door behind her. Charles worried what Ruth might reveal about the family. Then he walked to the front window, opened the curtain slightly and watched a swarm of reporters and camera men approach his wife. With her head down, Ruth created a path for herself as huge camera lenses and mics surrounded her head. At one point, she even pushed the equipment right out of her face.

After Charles watched her load the kids safely in her car, he walked back to the sofa facing the TV and dropped onto the cushions. When he retired from the military, he was diagnosed with a heart problem. The worry of an illness led him into a mild depression. He thought often of dropping dead unexpectedly, but his long-time physician comforted him with the idea that a heart illness was easily treatable. Today most men his age would get them sooner or later.

Now this problem with Jake brought the world to his door step, digging into his past to get to his son in Iran. A fact the world did not know. If things kept up, eventually they would know, including the Iranians, and then Jake would really be in trouble. Charles tried to rub the tight feeling from his chest.

He went back to channel surfing; he'd been doing that since the breaking news earlier this morning. He liked Ashley Maslin. Pretty and in her thirties; he'd noticed with passage of time that anchor women were getting nicer looking on every news channel.

Jake was still the first news item. *Now they're drilling into his military career. Everything.*

Charles watched strangers parade pictures of Jake with colleagues and friends from military school across the screen. At the end of the news brief Ashley mentioned that Charles Hudley, a retired US General, had denied comment and remained hunkered down.

"And there's a picture of my house. Now the whole world knows where I live."

***

David Scott tiptoed late into the meeting, holding his laptop like a platter. The man's size was anything but subtle and everyone's attention focused on him as he sheepishly crossed the room towards an empty seat. This gathering happened in an extremely important room specially designed and secured for his boss, Tom Delany, whose office was next door.

The space could comfortably fit ten. With no windows and the walls covered with a copper wiring mesh behind the drywall, discussions were protected by military engineering blocking any incoming or outgoing signals.

David was always late but the boss tolerated his tardiness. Not that he didn't care about being on time for a meeting, he was so buried in his screen that sometimes he lost all sense of time. His other team members understood. His genius programming skill and knowledge of databases outweighed most of his short comings.

Hours after the breakout news of Laila Hudley's arrest by News TV in Tehran, followed by her husband's detailed life as ex-Air Force, Tom Delany, director of NSA, got a call from the US State Department. The message was clear: drop-everything-urgent.

According to a mandate from the President and Congress, David's department was charged with surveilling the Internet, Social Media, and all calls regarding this sensitive matter. David headed up a team with Raj Patel and Rick Chow—the next best in the field. Both of David's co-workers were present at the meeting. Raj and Rick were hand-picked by David for their academic achievements as doctoral students at MIT, but that wasn't the main reason.

Together, they had invented the most proficient search algorithms mankind had ever seen. They were discovered, contracted, and signed before Google had a chance to even consider them. Now, Google was sorry that Raj and Rick were working for NSA and not them. Their analytical capacity for mathematics and physics opened the door. What sealed the deal were their linguistic capabilities.

Both were experts. Raj spoke fluent English, Hindi, Urdu, and Punjabi. Lately he'd been learning Arabic at Dave's request. Linguistic skills were paramount in the global reach of their work. Similarly, Rick's expertise lay in Cantonese and Mandarin; the bosses demanded he study Hebrew as well. Both followed orders instantly with an exact measure. In the department they were known as human robots.

Moments after that White House request was thrown in Delaney's lap, David was immediately told to query the databases as a way to locate Jake Hundley's whereabouts. This meeting was to report on those initial findings.

David surveyed all the faces and then directed his comments to Tom, "Ahh … the team and I haven't found anything on Jake Hudley."

Disappointed, Tom's eyebrows arched.

"I searched every database available." In Dave's fingertips he held the data of every user on the top five sites: Google, Facebook, YouTube, Yahoo, and Baidu. "In the last three days there's been no sign of him. We checked his email and all his online accounts."

Tom got up and paced. The others followed his progress in silence. He stopped and turned around.

"What about days or weeks before his disappearance?"

"Lots of buzz." David shook his head and inhaled a deep breath, "Before disappearing into a black hole he called his sister, parents, and multiple friends. One number shows up several times. Andrew Burke. Looks like they're close friends."

Tom rubbed his chin. "I don't like this. No American should be able to disappear from our sight. We need every moment of every living person accounted for. At least that's our goal. Where is this character, Hudley? Did he escape into the wilderness and abandon modern living? Why would he do that after learning his wife is held captive by these Iranian idiots? No, even if he is far from civilization, with our satellite capabilities, we can track the movement of anybody, anywhere, including the Amazon. You *will* find him."

The boss' lecture irritated Dave.

"We're trying."

"I have to respond to the State Department. They're up my ass hounding me day and night. We have to locate Hudley before the media gets hold of him. He is an ex-Military man. You understand."

To ease Tom's strife, Dave finished delivering his findings. "Ruth Hudley, the mother, doesn't seem to have email or Facebook accounts, but pictures of her at bingo and bake-sale events in Lackland, Texas show up."

"What kind of fund raising events?"

Dave scrutinized his notes on the laptop, then let out an amused laugh. "Never mind that, according to news tweets, she hit a reporter in the groin with her purse. In another tweet, he warns others not to get too close to her. Another one calls her *the abusive mama*." He laughed out loud. Raj and Rick hid their smiles.

Tom was not amused. "What else did you find out?"

David lowered his head again towards the screen, "Charles Hudley, the father, is a retired US Military General. Has a heart problem. Made a few phone calls to his daughter, ex-colleagues. None to Jake."

Tom's eyes perked up and his face muscles relaxed slightly, "It's a military family. I'll make a few calls and hopefully find out where Jake is before the White House conference call. His father's hiding something. He would've called his son by now."

David continued, "Makalla Hudley, the sister, made local calls, was in Facebook, sent a few emails … nothing strange or suspicious incoming or outgoing. A message was texted to her but I couldn't pinpoint the sender."

"We have to do better." Tom looked frazzled. "We have to find out who called her."

Dave wanted to find out where that call came from too. When the meeting ended with a dismissive gesture from Tom, the team filed out of the director's secured meeting room.

David Scott held the door marked "Black Chamber" about one hour after his meeting with Delany. He let Raj and Rick in before assuring himself the door was securely locked. Only the very elite software analysts, architects, and programmers could enter this inner sanctum. Located in the middle of the seventh floor, it sat surrounded by a layer of offices, populated with staff in supporting roles for the those working on the most advanced, top secret projects for the NSA.

David sat in front of a 30-inch computer monitor next to Raj, who was beside Rick, all sharing a ten-foot long desk against the wall. In this room, obedience to rules set by the Director of the NSA was of paramount importance. Any breach of any rule was met with severe consequences. Each man had been offered an individual office, but they refused for the sake of conforming to a new agile methodology in the workplace. Older IT professionals didn't care much for this new way, rejected it as a fad soon to die out.

David took a bite of his Mars bar, placed it next to the mouse, and scrutinized a task list. His mind absorbed the items as he took a sip of coke to wash down the chocolate. "We have to prioritize the list."

Raj clicked away on the keyboard; getting his attention away from the screen was never an easy task. Rick tapped the floor with his foot while making changes to a program. Neither of them paid any attention to Dave.

"Okay, guys. We have to work on this list," said Dave with a burning tone.

Raj obediently peeled his gaze from the monitor and turned his swivel chair towards Dave. Rick did the same seconds later. The three twenty-somethings went over the scope of this urgent task. The first critical issue was the mountain of data they had to churn through. The NSA intercepted around 1.7 billion emails daily, from major U.S. internet-based communication service providers: Microsoft, Yahoo, Google, Facebook, PalTalk, AOL, Skype, YouTube and Apple. The data gathered included email, video and voice chat, videos, photos, voice-over-IP chats such as Skype, and file transfers—all stored in a vault at the Utah Data Centre.

Although they'd gone through the same data once already, they had to do something different this time to find what Tom needed. Making and keeping the boss happy was their highest priority.

They spent nearly twelve hours a day at work, only going home if they were totally exhausted or had a bad enough case of BO that could only disappear with a shower. Often they showed up for work on the weekend. This level of dedication was expected.

After an hour of vigorous discussion, with occasional sips of caffeine and bites of chocolate, they decided to load the daily data onto one server, going back seven days and changing the search criteria in incremental ways.

This time they chose two different approaches. David moved his face closer to the screen until his nose was only a few inches away. With a few mouse clicks he activated seven instances of IBM's Blue Gene, a supercomputer also known as *super server* among techies. This was *the* most powerful computing machine of 2012. It used Linux software and system-on-a-chip technology. In 2004, Blue Gene became the most technologically advanced computer and IBM was honored with the National Medal of Technology and Innovation.

The other and most crucial step decided by the team was to unleash *Boundless* on each of the seven servers, the most powerful search engine in existence. First Dave selected the transfer option to copy of all 1.7 billion pieces of information from the data vault at the Utah Data Center in the server. Next, he added the search criteria such as names, date of birth, addresses, phone numbers, vehicle numbers, and credit card numbers.

Dave's hunch was that the source of that one unknown text to Makalla Hudley could lead to Jake. He clicked on the run button.

I'm comin' to get you, Hudley.

***

At ten-after-twelve when Charles' favorite anchorwoman, Ashley Maslin, ended the noon hour news, he turned off the TV. So far there were no reports of Jake's whereabouts. The media frenzy continued, regardless. Charles was getting fed up with all the allegations, suppositions, and unrealistic scenarios they were cooking up to feed their audience's appetite. He'd told that first reporter the truth … but no one covers the truth in the news any more.

He got up from the couch and limped towards the kitchen. As he walked across the floor he growled about his leg pain. According to his cardiologist the cholesterol medication caused muscle pain. At the counter he opened a bag of bread and placed two slices in the toaster. He took account of his health as the toaster cooked the bread. Based on the doctor's advice and his wife's nagging, coffee was now out.

Just then the doorbell interrupted his thoughts. He shook his head. *Damn reporters.* The repeated request for Jake's whereabouts by the media had finally exhausted his energy, making him more stressed than he had been commanding a unit or during his time in politics.

His first reaction was to ignore the bell. A minute later it rang again. Limping along he approached the front window and moved the curtain slightly to take a peek outside. Three men: one in military dress and two others in suits. A visit from the military was expected, though neither he or Jake were officially part of the Air Force anymore.

Charles opened the door, let them in, and gave each a vigorous *army* handshake. Chuck's ex-colleague Tony Palladini smiled. With a wave of his arm, Charles ushered them towards the living room. The two in dark suites sat on a sofa, Tony took the other sofa, and Charles sunk into his wing chair.

"A surprise visit calls for nice drink. I would offer you Vodka but it looks like this is official." Charles put on a fake smile to hide his nervousness.

Tony said, "Thanks Chuck. We're not planning to stay long." He indicated his colleagues with a slight hand wave, "Linda Moore and Chris Welter are with the NSA." Both nodded at their names.

Charles knew a lot about the NSA as part of his role providing hardware and software surveillance. He knew a lot of people over there but never saw these two before.

"From ..."

Moore replied, "A special project."

Charles noticed that Linda Moore kept her answers vague, and from his experience in the military it was best not to probe. That didn't mean he had to like the answer.

"You must be looking for Jake."

Moore said, "You got it. The media's been going crazy trying to locate him. With Laila in custody in Tehran, the President wants to be informed of all details, in case he has to make a statement." She paused. "Where's Jake?"

Charles twiddled his thumbs. "I wish I knew ..."

"When did you see him last?" The woman persisted.

Charles thought saying the least possible was for the best. "He came here to talk to me about the arrest of his wife shortly after it happened."

"Did he say what he was going to do about it?"

"No. Just that he was stressed about the situation."

Moore got up, agitated, "Did he say anything else or mention where was he going?"

Charles wasn't about to give her what she wanted. If he mentioned their little jaunt to see Senator Quest, he risked burning a bridge with the man. In fact, he was telling the truth—to a point. "He kept shaking his head and feeling guilty for agreeing to let his wife go to Iran."

The other two men watched Moore's intense questioning.

"Why did she go there?"

"I asked that question too. Apparently, his father-in-law had a heart attack."

"Heart attack." Moore scratched her forehead as if reflecting on something.

"Is my son under surveillance?"

Moore took a long moment before speaking, "We have to locate him. In this situation his military expertise could be a liability for the US government."

What if Ruth walked through the front door with kids? He could only imagine the interaction between her and these three. She'd never been a compliant, supporting wife as other officers enjoyed. He put that thought aside for a moment.

Charles realized that if Jake was under surveillance, his whole family would be too. He absolutely could not reveal that Jake had left the country. While it was true that Chuck knew of his son's intentions, he didn't have personal confirmation on his exact whereabouts. Hearsay from his daughter didn't count. The moment the government realized where Jake was, the hawks in Washington would want his boy back on US soil.

Once the head of the Satellite Surveillance System, Charles knew the kinds of clandestine and underhanded schemes the NSA could engage in. He knew it all.

"*Is* Jake under surveillance?"

"We have to get a hold of him before any Iranian undercover agents do." The vagueness of this woman was infinite.

The probing continued for another ten minutes. Charles kept his answers as vague as he could.

Moore's face grew redder and redder, her frustration becoming obvious in her tone the longer she went not getting what she wanted.

Finally, Moore got up and said, "This is a national security issue *General* Hudley. The second you learn anything, call us." She dropped her card on the coffee table and headed for the door. Tony and the other agent followed with only a nod and a grim smile.

Chapter 14

It was lunch time when Maryam appeared for her usual meal run. Her face glowed as she unlocked the cell and entered. Normally she'd slide the tray under the iron gate and rushed to the next delivery.

This time, Maryam placed a tray with *Barberi* bread, cheese and tea *without* camphor, especially made for Laila, on her lap. Maryam had noted Laila's deteriorating form, specifically her gaunt cheeks and thin lips. She'd talked Laila into abandoning her vegan diet. After much resistance, Laila finally agreed to add cheese to it.

Bouncing on her feet Maryam said, "I have good news! My sentence has been reduced to two years."

"That *is* good news. What happened?" Laila managed to show a faint smile.

"One night when I was with Reza, he was in a good mood. For a long time, I've been wanting to ask if my sentence could be reduced. But I was afraid. Usually when I ask something he yells at me. That night I felt I could take a chance and made my request. He thought about it and said he'd work on it, but it would be easier if I accepted Islam. I did and he presented my case to one of the Imams. The Imams run this place you know." Maryam pointed to the floor with her finger, meaning Evin prison.

Laila nodded.

"My case went to a court and it was reduced to two years. I have been here eight months already."

Laila placed the tray on the floor and slowly got up on her feet. She staggered, feeling top-heavy for some reason, but managed to wrap her arms around Maryam and hold her tight for the longest moment.

“We have sister souls. I am so happy for you.”

Maryam’s face brightened for a few seconds, then it changed to a darker color, suggesting concern. “One problem. Do you think Jesus will forgive me?”

“Maryam, forgive you for what?”

“Becoming a Muslim.”

“Oh.”

Laila’s energy was so low that her mind was fogged and thinking became painful. She tried to put her thoughts into words.

“I can’t speak for Jesus. In fact, I would never speak for Jesus or any of God’s prophets. But what I do believe is that Jesus, like God, is all-forgiving.”

Maryam’s eyes went wide.

“All-forgiving. That’s a lot. Are you sure?”

“I’ll tell a story about a naughty young man and the Master of Palestine.

This young man asked, ‘Master, does God forgive our sins?’

The Master replied, ‘Yes, He does. He is all-forgiving.”

‘All-forgiving. He would forgive anything?’

‘That’s what all-forgiving means’

‘How about the criminals who rob and kill innocent people, dictators who murder their subjects by millions?”

‘Yes, all of it can be forgiven by God, if He wishes.’

‘I can do anything and I’ll be totally pardoned?”

‘No, all except for someone like you, who asks too many questions.’”

Maryam lightened up again. “Trust me, I’ll never ask God a silly question like that young man.” She giggled.

Laila gave a full laugh as well, then, not to draw any attention from staff, she muffled the joy with her palm. A much needed comic relief ran through her veins as Laila watched the young woman slip back out the way she came.

***

Later that afternoon, Laila stumbled as the imposing presence behind her compelled her through a door at a formal appearance in an office facing Mullah Said, one of the judges of the court. Next to the man sat Ali. The room was small, housing a simple table and three sturdy chairs. Behind the Mullah, the wall was decorated with photos in wooden frames of the Mullah with the Ayatollah. The door closed behind her with a click.

Said pointed to the empty chair and said, "*Be farma, be farma.*"

Laila's weak body was not prepared to face these men. She tucked the edge of her chador to cover her forehead and avoided eye contact with both of them. She lowered herself into the chair facing Said, separated only by the desk—bare except for a file before him.

The proceedings started with praise for Allah, the Islamic Republic of Iran, and Ali, followed by quotations from the Quran. The words rolled out from Said's lips in a monotone and hurried fashion. Then he nodded to Ali.

Ali bowed his head facing the judge. The Mullah's white turban with matching shirt and pants, covered by a black overdress, signified this man in his fifties held a high position in the judicial and clerical order of Iran.

"The United States government knows about this case. In the US the media is doing its best to learn every aspect of your situation." Ali had been following the news: CNN, Fox News and ABC, NBC and San Antonio media as they all looked for Jake Hudley. "In the last session the court pronounced Jake Hudley an enemy of Islam and Laila Dareini a spy, praised be Allah. I informed the family of the accused of the court's decision."

The Mullah said, "By the power invested in us by the Ayatollah, our Supreme Leader, this Islamic court is now informing *you*, Laila Dareini, that you have been accused of espionage—spying for the United States and Israel and are now deemed an enemy of Islam. As Mr. Ali mentioned, your family has been informed."

"Why are you accusing me of this? I don't understand." Laila raised her head, not looking directly at Mullah Said, but high enough to see his chin. "Why? Under what authority do you have to charge me of these crimes? I have done nothing harmful to the faith of Islam. What gives you the right to make that judgment? You are *not* God." Her body shook. The frailty of it exasperated her all the more.

"From what I understand only the prophet Mohammad, may peace be upon Him, can declare anyone an enemy. In my judgment, He would look at me with eyes of understanding and forgiveness. These charges are for your own benefits."

Laila was surprised how fiercely she defended herself before these two men. She felt like prey to the court system of Evin. This proceeding was just another formality before her eventual execution.

An injustice was being thrown at her; no, not so much at *her* but at her children, husband, and extended family. She had nothing left to lose. Her last emotional release would be to give these men a piece of her mind. Her head lowered but she took a quick glance at Ali. His mouth was half open and terror clouded his eyes.

Said broke the silence that seem to last eternity. "Your mind has clearly been contaminated by your time in America. You have no respect for authority." He paused again. "The only remedy is for you to accept Islam into your heart."

"I accept Islam, but not the way you want me to." This time Laila's words were softer but still spoken with conviction. "In my heart I know you killed my Orie, my only brother—he was an innocent." Physically tired and emotionally exhausted she did not search for mercy, rather justice. She held back the tears, though few came anymore due to severe dehydration.

The Mullah, upset, threatened her, "You should think of your children in America. You need to make things easier for yourself, in order to get back to them. What kind of a mother abandons her young?"

Laila nearly looked at the man, but knew the act would end her immediately. "I know reams of killing go on in this place. In the dark of night, I hear gun fire. I *know* women are raped and tortured. You call yourself a Muslim? Honestly, are you really a faithful follower of Islam? How can that be if you permit these atrocities?" A sob escaped. Laila raised her hand to cover her mouth as the sob grew louder and more erratic.

Leaning forward, the Mullah starred at Laila as his fingers touched his grey beard. With every word spoken, his face became darker, muscles tighter.

"What do *you* know of Islam?"

Laila swallowed her sorrow, smoothed her chador and said, "This year alone, I know the Islamic nation is engulfed by violence throughout the world: Egypt, Libya, Lebanon, Pakistan, Turkey, Iraq, Afghanistan. Are you are waging war against your own brothers and sisters? Is that what Allah wants? Declaring someone an enemy, following this decree with violence, this is not what *my* Islam is all about."

"You people are dogs," he spat. "What do you believe in? You are *not* Muslim."

"According to my Allah, I don't have an enemy. According to your Allah you have enemies. We worship two different Allahs. I prefer mine to yours." Laila's eyes burned for want of tears that could not come.

The Mullah got up and left the room in anger.

Ali jumped to his feet as a sign of courtesy; his face puzzled by the exchange.

He just mumbled, "This has never happened."

When Said was out of sight he rounded on Laila, "You should not have done this!" He threw his arms high in the air. "This is not America. You can't say anything you want here."

"I believe in freedom of expression, my God-given right."

"You don't have this right here!"

"I was polite and honest. Please, allow me to return to my cell."

Ali took one step closer to Laila and whispered, "Where do you get the strength? How is it you know so much about the Quran and yet you're not a Muslim. *Why?*"

"There are many Holy Books in this world, they are chapters of the same Big Book of God. The Quran is just such a treasured book. I simply happen to follow the most current one."

Ali's rage swept away his wonder. "From Mullah Said's expression, he was very angry. He'll likely arrange for your execution immediately."

Silence ensured as Ali calculated how to respond. Eyeballs bulging, he said, "Leave. Now." His authoritative voice vibrated throughout Laila's body like a shock wave. He went outside and brought Maryam, who tied the blindfold and helped Laila stand. With an arm still supporting her soul sister, Maryam guided Laila through the door.

Outside the building, once they had passed the guards, Maryam demanded an explanation.

"What happened?"

The short walk and fresh air cleared Laila's mind but still she could not talk.

"Sister, what did they do to you?" Maryam tugged her arm several times.

Laila lost her balance and stepped on Maryam foot. "Sorry." She stopped as her limbs could not carry her any more.

After a few minutes standing in the open air, Laila said, "Later." She was not in the mood to talk, though her companion kept asking probing questions.

Laila was in fear of being executed and never seeing Jake, Megan, or Dillon again. She felt a sense of betrayal run through her heart and said a prayer she had learned as a child. *O God, guide me, protect me. O God, guide me, protect me.*

She should have listened to Jake. She never should have returned home. The ache in her chest made it difficult to breathe. She drew a tight, stuttering breath. *Jake* ... She patted the arm around her and found only Maryam's thin, child-like limb.

Her leg muscles weakened with every step, she pulled on that arm to stop the momentum. After a moment's rest, she adjusted the blindfold slipping from her eyes.

She remembered Fatimeh's sharp words, "Don't forget; never raise the blindfold—not even a little. If I see anyone peeping around, they'll pay a dear price."

The knot in her stomach tightened along with the pain in her heart. Laila kept reminding herself that she had to face these monsters. With a sigh of relief, she collapsed in her cell without having thrown up.

***

At dinner time, Maryam appeared again and entered Laila's cell with a meal of rice, vegetables, bread and cheese. Placing the tray on the floor next to the mattress she said, "Laila *joon*, I have some news."

This time, the girl did not bounce nor did her eyes show any kind of light.

Laila struggled to push her body until she was up on her feet. Her weakened legs muscles ached and her joints cracked and snapped from bearing even her slight weight.

"What is it, Maryam?" The girl's tone worried her.

"Reza is dead."

Laila paused a second, trying to recall who this person was. "Reza, your interrogator?"

"Fatimeh just told me he died about an hour ago in the hospital."

"Died of what?" Laila leaned against the bars and reached for Maryam's hands; they were colder than usual. Maryam didn't squeeze back but she didn't pull away either.

"When he left his house for work, two men on motorcycles sped towards him and opened fire."

"What? Who are they? Why?"

"Mujahidin's."

Laila shook her head, "Why Mujahidin's?"

"The Ayatollah has declared them enemies of Iran. So now, whenever the Guardians locate any Mujahidins they're rounded up and brought to Evin. In retaliation, the Mujahidins are targeting the interrogators."

As the explanation slipped past Maryam's lips, the fogginess in Laila's mind lifted enough to recall Maryam's relationship with the guard. He was the one who saved her from execution and engaged with her in a *sigheh* relationship. She put her hand in her mouth.

"Oh my God, you spent nights with him."

"I'm relieved I'm not his sex slave anymore."

"How else do you feel?"

"I feel a lot of things, Laila: Angry for being stubborn and ending up here; Gratitude that he saved my life … because of him my sentence has been reduced; Guilty—I can't explain why. Yet, I also feel robbed."

"I know what you mean."

"He forced himself into me."

For many women, it was hard to talk about rape.

"I understand. Completely." Laila shifted her frail hands up Maryam's arms.

"I just can't take this place anymore." This courageous girl had shown the traits of an invincible Super Woman—wanting to burst free from prison taking as many of the girls with her as possible. They had both shared this dream, but now a dark void engulfed the young woman's soul. Laila gently wrapped her shaking arms around Maryam and finally the girl squeezed her back.

"I know you dream about being a hero, but don't even think about escaping from here," Laila advised. Pulling back from the embrace, she grabbed Maryam's arms with an unexpected force and pulled her closer until their faces were only an inch apart. "I repeat, don't try to escape. If you get caught, they'll shoot to kill. Reza is not here to save you anymore."

"I know about the rebel in me. I can keep her under control now."

Laila knew how true that admission was; it's what got her into this trouble in the first place.

"If you encourage others to do the same, they could get killed too if your plan fails. And who would you blame for their deaths? You have sixteen months left. I know you can survive this."

"I have prayed long and hard. I had to beg God to get me out of here … I know he's trying to, but with Reza gone I'm afraid again. Laila, this place is driving me crazy. The emotional churning—the death. If I can't get out of here, I'm afraid I'll kill myself."

Laila hugged her again and squeezed, wishing this simple act was enough to pull the pain from this dear girl. She pulled back a few inches and cupped Maryam's face with her hands. Maryam broke out into tears. Laila smoothed the hair on her head and swayed with her as she used to when Megan woke from nightmares.

"You are beautiful and noble and the best part is, you are my sister." She laughed. "Repeat after me: I am beautiful and noble. Laila is my sister."

Sobbing, Maryam repeated the words.

"Say it again."

This continued until the darkness around Maryam's eyes lightened.

"What should I do? This is so hard."

"I don't know yet, but killing yourself is not the answer. I love you. God loves you. We'll get through this together."

Chapter 15

David Scott barged into his boss' office. Dave did not need an appointment to see the director; everyone else had to go through his executive assistant. The express lane Dave enjoyed had to do with his expertise. In an advanced age this techie commanded Tom's attention more than any other, except for the President, Tom's boss.

Tom Delaney waved Dave in, the telephone pressed to his ear. By the time Dave sank into the chair facing the 5-Star General, Tom was done his call.

He demanded, "Better give me good news, the a-holes at the White House aren't happy I haven't located Jake.

Dave shifted under Tom's stare. He'd never been stumped like this before. "I'm getting closer. Jake sent a message from a device with a 909 extension. When I checked with all the US carriers, I found that it doesn't belong to any commercial company."

Tom frowned and shifted his lips to the left, adjusting the glasses perched on his nose. "Give me the juicy part."

Though Dave knew the boss needed him, he was careful not to push beyond the limit of the General's tolerance. He reflected on a response as his eye flitted to a huge picture of Tom in military dress replete with medals hanging from his chest pocket.

"After digging farther, the extension and the number associated with it belong to the *US military*. Such a number is only used by a select group of people—very few I might add—among them are the President and top military brass."

Tom leaned closer. His face turned red.

"Impossible. How did he get use of it? Jake was in the military but left after his term was over. What's he up to?"

"I found the ten-digit phone number from where the text message originated. It ended with 'Love Jake'. But I don't have the privilege to access the recordings of the number, the way I do public lines."

"I know what you're getting at." Delaney tapped the desk with his hand. "Just give me the number and I'll find the device. It could be military too. I did some checking up on Jake. He started as a technician then became support staff in combat, taking him to Afghanistan for two years. I bet this guy knows a lot about communications, satellites, whatever. If he's done something illegal, I'll make sure he spends the rest of his life in jail. I swear I'll make it happen."

Dave examined Tom's cheeks as they turned a brighter red with every word. "All I need is clearance to dig deeper and locate the device Jake used to send this text message. This is the most crucial piece of information we have."

"Okay, I'll get right on that. Check with me in five."

Dave walked out concerned about the boss's reaction. *How does someone jump from searching for a missing person to life in jail?*

***

Ten minutes into the walk from the restaurant, Jake's attention turned to a large building with arches. In the parking area a group of singers and a drummer played. Above them rose a huge sign for the Zahedan Bus Terminal. Jake strode past a group of men in Pakistani garb, then slowed down as he neared the open front door to the terminal. Before walking through he turned and scanned the road.

Since leaving the kabob place, he'd noticed a particular pair of eyes paying close attention to him. He'd hurried away at the time, but wondered who might be watching him, if any one? The idea of calling on Maya for help crossed his mind; maybe he'd grab an opportunity later at the station or on the bus.

Jake went inside and purchased a ticket to Tehran. He checked the huge board on the wall for the listing of platforms and bus departure times. He had an hour to kill. Maneuvering over to a secluded seat in the waiting hall, Jake passed by families in small groups, all chatting in loud voices. A heavy rosewater perfume lingered in the air. Not surprising since Iranians in America wore strong scented fragrances too.

Sinking into a seat, Jake fired up the computer. Within seconds Maya's subservient voice came over the earpiece, ready to receive commands. With no time to waste, he queried if he was being followed. According to Andy, this function was available but not fully operational. He'd used Maya's ability to cloak an area but this was different.

Maya hardly hesitated before responding, "The answer is negative." Jake noticed a level of humanity to her voice now that he'd spoken with her several times, even though it remained monotone. If she could walk, she'd outstrip C3P0 any day.

Jake's vision idled over the computer screen, past the crowd, and up to the ceiling. He wasn't satisfied with the answer and reflected on the algorithm of the app.

Okay, what makes you tick Maya?

From any point where the computer was positioned, the GPS from space gathered information on any mobile device within a thousand feet of Maya. If a device pinged, the program tracked it for half an hour or longer. *What would happen if someone wasn't carrying any tech? Someone could still be following me*. He decided to stick with his gut and kept a wary eye out for anything unusual. Maya continued to instruct him on the geography and history of Toronto.

Occasionally he shifted his vision to examine the faces in the vast hall. On his fourth such sweep, he took notice of one. A man in his forties came through the front door, stood there for a several moments scanning the room, then with slow, deliberate steps moved towards Jake. He looked like a passenger searching for a seat. Jake followed the guy right to the empty chair beside him.

The man dropped a bag from his shoulder before placing it on the floor. He fingered a page for a minute or two. He fanned his face with the pamphlet and then turned to Jake.

"American?" A wide grin spread across his face.

"No, Canadian."

"Oh, Canadian. My name is Ira Kohan." He extended his hand.

After a handshake, "My name is, uhh, Dave, Dave MacDougall." He almost blurred out Jake Hudley.

In that part of the world it wasn't unusual for someone to start a conversation with a foreigner. Some looked for tips on how to escape the hard life of the Middle East and others simply want to practice their English. Of course drugs dealers were always looking for clients, but that happened everywhere.

"Happy to meet you." His English was fairly good. "First time in Iran?"

"Yes."

"Tourist?"

"Yes."

"Going to Tehran?"

"Yes." Jake's short answers did not discourage the man from asking more.

"Me too. Me too. I lived in Canada for five years. In Toronto. Near the Bathurst and Steeles area. Jewish area."

The response immediately peaked Jake's interest. This would be a good opportunity to put into practice what Maya had been teaching him. He considered Ira closely: fair skin, dark wavy hair. "Are you Jewish?" A man who spoke English well could be a valuable asset. Jake hadn't realized how isolating it was not being able to properly communicate with those around him.

"Yes, born and raised."

It was a bit puzzling to Jake why this guy was in Zahedan. "Are you here visiting?"

"Kind of. My parents lived in Tehran and once in a while I come to visit their house. After all, this is the country where I was born. It's in the DNA. Why did you choose Iran?"

"Photo journalist. I'm fascinated with the Iranian culture and history."

"Are you visiting Isfahan? Some great historical buildings there."

Jake recalled what he'd said to the Guard earlier. Ira could be a spy, so he had to watch his words. "Right now I'm on my way to Tehran. Later I'll go to Isfahan."

Ira nodded. "Looks like we're on the same bus."

Jake didn't know what to make of this guy. With a glance at the clock on the wall, Jake put Maya away and headed to the platform. He caught the 1:15 bus. It was full so a child sat next to him. He watched the scenery go by until the vehicle's vibration lulled him to sleep.

***

Dave Scott yanked open the door to Tom's office and froze. Tom was in the middle of a meeting with three suits: one woman and two men. He retreated.

"Sorry, I'll come back later."

"No, no." Tom waved his hand motioning Dave in. He addressed his guests, "Can we take a ten minute break?"

Briskly, they collected their papers from the top of a round table and filed out of the room, the woman gave Dave the hairy-eyeball or at least the adult equivalent. Dave approached his boss who sat perched on the edge of a chair, anxiously awaiting the news.

"Sorry to barge in." Dave was rarely apologetic. Why should he be? He was always right. But this time he watched his manners.

"Next time knock." Tom's face looked worn out. His eyebrows arched and he shook his head with mild disappointment. "At times I have confidential discussions going on, which could be off limits to your ears. Understand?"

"Again, I am sorry boss." Dave took another glance at the screen of the laptop resting on his palm. "I found the source of the text Jake sent to his
sister. From an unknown device, the message went to an exchange server in a military base somewhere. From the IP address I can tell it's military and not a commercial site. I'll dig up which one later."

"Just make sure you find out the location of the server. Jake's not officially working for the US Air Force anymore and if what he's doing is illegal, I want to know about it. He could be a terrorist." Tom's lips puckered.

Terrorist? Dave had heard this random accusation cropping up far too often, especially in this department. In the sixties it was the FBI and CIA making accusations of communism. The same mentality had spread into the law enforcement circles: *terrorist* was the new enemy.

"Yah, yah, I'll find the location." He paused for a moment to check his notes. "Two things. One. The device he used is not a regular handset, like an iPhone. And two, the positioning of the device was in Iran."

"No, no, no." Tom's naturally ruddy face paled. Shaking his head, he said, "Don't tell me he is in Iran. Are you sure?"

"Numbers don't lie boss. Based on the latitude, longitude and attitude of GPS positioning, the latest message was sent from Zahedan, an Iranian city near the Pakistan border."

"If this bastard's in Iran that's terrible news. I had my boys check all the airlines departing from US airports in the last week and his name never came up. What happened?" He scratched his head and rubbed his eyebrows. "Don't tell me we have a hole in our surveillance system."

A wave of guilt struck Dave's heart as he contemplated how his findings could potentially get Tom fired.

"What's the next step?" Dave asked.

"We have to get our advanced satellite surveillance people involved and our agents in Iran engaged. Let me make a few calls and I'll get back to you."

***

Nearly four hours later, an announcement over the sound system woke Jake from a deep sleep. It took him half a minute to come to full awareness and realize the bus had stopped.

Passengers got up to unload onto the platform, but he waited. The last passenger to leave the bus, Jake watched the crowd as he lined up with the others in the coffee house and got himself Persian tea, some desserts, and a lamb sandwich.

After finishing the sandwich, he took a bite of the dessert. It was rice with yellow coloring, sweet, rosewater and almond—very familiar, something Laila must have made and served back home. He washed it down with a sip of hot tea. Again an invisible knife dug into his heart at the thought of his family.

Just days before he left for Afghanistan, he recalled Megan spilling tea on the kitchen table. When asked about the mess, she said, "Daddy, the mug is too hot." In fact, it was cold. Jake and Laila smiled at each other and when his wife handed him a paper towel he recalled the feel of her delicate hand grazing his.

Day by day this trip sapped his physical and emotional strength. What kept him going was the hope of sacrifice. *Sacrifice is a sign of love.* The first time Laila ever mentioned this quote, it stuck with him.

When Jake's eyes refocused, there was Ira at the door scanning faces again. He wished he knew who the guy really was: a curious friendly traveler or a spy? He had an unusual background that didn't help him determine one way or the other. After spotting Jake, Ira rushed towards him.

"I have to talk to you. Can we go outside?"

"Why?"

He grabbed the tea with one hand and Jake's arm with the other. "Come, come."

Jake didn't know what to make of it. He took the cake and followed the man.

"Are you carrying a cell phone or smart phone?"

Jake was puzzled. "No, why? What's happening?"

Pointing to Maya, he said, "What's in the bag?"

"A computer."

"Computer." He paused. "Is that device connected to a GPS?"

Jake wasn't about to give out any more information. "Why? I don't understand. Who are you?"

"I'll tell you who I am later. Right now, you're in trouble."

"Trouble. What trouble?" Jake raised his voice.

"Listen to me carefully. I know who you are. I've been following you for some time now, but that's neither here nor there. Someone is tracking you. They'll be here any moment. Once they locate you …" The stranger made a kill sign with his hand across his neck.

"Who are they? Iranians?"

"No, Americans."

Jake frowned.

Ira smiled and continued, "Of course they are Iranians. Or Afghanis—just working for the other side."

Jake's body twitched. *Can I trust this guy? I don't even know who he is, why he's telling me this.*

"What should I do?"

"Put the bag in a hidden spot. If they locate it through GPS, they'll go there to pick it up, and not find you attached to it. If they find you, they'll grab you and take you." Ira's body vibrated showing urgency.

Jake was well aware of a lot of intelligence activity going on in Iran. "Americans? NSA?"

"When I say I don't know, *I don't know*. They are locals hired by the CIA or NSA." Ira's explanation has some traces of validity.

"Okay." *I think.*

Ira weaved a path through the bus platform filled with travelers, Jake close behind. As both men passed through a waiting hall, occasionally Ira would turn to motion his hand for Jake to hurry up.

Outside the station they crossed the car park surrounded by trees and stopped by a cluster of them. Ira pulled the bag from Jake's shoulder.

"Hey!" Seeing Maya dropped next to a bush made his insides clench.

"Shh." Ira's hand felt like a vice on his arm as he yanked Jake back across Kavey Street, a main Isfahan artery.

Shit! It's a set up! Jake's brain calculated every possible avenue of escape, but the streets were full of merchants—raising a fuss would only draw undue attention to him. He had to make Ira think he was complacent. Jake forced his arms to loosen as the man led him over to the sidewalk filled with pedestrians and people hailing cabs. The nearby rickshaw booth could act as cover once he slipped out of Ira's grip. He'd circle around, and disappear in that large group about to pass. Both squatted on the concrete ground between beggars and the nut merchant.

Things were happening so fast Jake didn't have time to think through it all. *This is ridiculous. I can't trust this man.* Jake made a fist, preparing to yank his arm free from Ira's grip. *I need Maya to survive out here. I can't just abandon her because some stranger says so.*

"Look!"

Jake snapped his head away from the man to see what was happening with Maya. Nothing. Then the cold pressure of steel clamping around his wrist made him jolt. Ira gripped Jake's arm to keep him from falling over.

"What the hell are you doing?" Jake shook the handcuff attached to both him and the stranger. Betrayal and anger erupted inside Jake's mind and heart. His instinct of *fight or flight* spiked. His leg muscles were primed to raise him up as Jake shored himself to punch the man next to him in the face.

Ira lifted his free, "Trust me. Don't move or everything you've done to get this far will be for nothing."

Listen to him, his gut suddenly said. As the pent up confusion and fear was about to erupt, it suddenly halted. "Why?"

"I might be wrong and no one will come to take that computer from you. But there *is* a slight chance they will. Do you really want to risk everything by making a scene?" Ira motioned Jake to lower himself again.

“Slight chance, like hell. Right now I want kill you.”

“The cuffs are for your protection. In case you ignore me and claim the bag or from making an irrational choice when your tech is taken. You don’t want either situation to happen.”

Jake wiped the sweat from his forehead and tried to calm down. *What the hell have I gotten myself into?*

***

Twenty minutes later Dave walked into his boss’s office for the latest update. Tom pointed to a chair.

“Sit,” he said, clamping his forehead with his fingers. “What do you have?” he asked as Dave lowered himself onto a chair.

“Through our satellite capabilities we are tracking the IP address you gave me for Jake’s device. Also, listen to this.” He emphasized his point with animated hands. “Agents have been dispatched to locate the device from which the call was made.”

Dave noticed the tension diminish from his boss’ face. “That’s great,” Tom said, as his shoulders relaxed and he shook out his arms.

Dave was relieved, knowing his work contributed to finding Jake’s whereabouts.

Tom pointed his forefinger directly at Dave’s head. “Monitor that IP address and the phone number associated with it carefully.” He snapped his fingers. “Sooner or later we’ll nail him and bring him back to US soil. You understand? You’ve got two jobs to do right now.” He stuck a thumb in the air. Dave sighed inwardly, knowing what was coming. “One: monitor our agents tracking the position of the device Jake is carrying. And two: screen any messages or calls coming to the US from that device.”

“Yes boss, will do.” He closed his laptop, stood up and walked out of the office, knowing it would be his commendation when they finally brought Jake home.

***

Jake took advantage of a momentary commotion between a cyclist and motorist to find out more about the strange man cuffed to him. The confrontation was minor but still drew onlookers. Jake squatted next to Ira. Eyes still fixed on his prized possession, he ventured with, "I get a sense that you and many others are tracking that computer."

"Perhaps."

Jake's interest peaked as Ira avoided answering his question.

"Perhaps? What kind of a response is that? I'm wearing a handcuff, crouching next to a smelly person I only recently met, on the sidewalk of a strange city and this is all I get? I want to know, now."

Ira said, "I knew you were coming to Iran." He cracked a smile. "You are an American named Jake Hudley."

Jake opened the top button of his shirt. It was hot and muggy but it was the man's words that raised the temperature. "You're really pissing me off. You know that? Who the hell are you?"

Ira remained calm, "Let me put it this way. I'm a freelancer in the intelligence business. I collect information and sell it to the highest bidder."

"You're disgusting, making money from my misery." He turned away from the man, not quite sure what to believe. "How do you know I'm being watched and why do you care?"

Ira leaned towards Jake. "One of my informants got interested in you when your profile appeared on CNN. Their curiosity peaked after learning you worked at Lackland. He tracked you from San Antonio Airport to Karachi. Then within a day or two a white man showed up at Abuzar Hotel and I took over from there."

Jake shook his head, his mind numb. "Who do you work for?"

Ira turned his head back and forth, scanning faces. "As I said, I'm a freelance mercenary."

"Mercenary, my ass. Why me? Do you know why I'm here?"

"Your wife Laila is in Evin prison. Correct?"

"Yes."

"Interesting cover story. So tell me, what's ex-US Air Force personnel doing in enemy territory?" Ira looked Jake straight in the eye, as if asking him to be straight with his reply. "Why are *you* really here?"

Ira's questions irked Jake. It also made his guilt rise, not being a loyal American. But when loyalty came at the price of human life—his wife's no less … "I want to rescue her. I want justice for her. Ira. I'm a humanitarian not a military conformist. Let it be clear I am *not* with the United States Air Force anymore."

Ira nodded with a smirk. "You're a romantic guy, on your journey to rescue your beloved; like the story of Laila and Majnun—Romeo and Juliet." The sarcasm in his tone irked Jake.

Now that he had opened up, it was time to turn Ira into a strategic ally, a step the US Military often took to enlist local help in Afghanistan. "Can you help?"

Ira shrugged his shoulder. "Help? What? You don't know what you're doing? If nothing else, you're putting yourself and your wife in incredible danger."

Jake didn't like this mercenary's assessment. His anger, frustration and confusion ate him up inside. He really wanted to lash out with choice words, instead he said, "I think you need a shower." The man had obviously not taken a break to wash himself while following Jake.

"Shower? You need a new head."

"I take it your informant wants me alive. Why?"

"We'll have lots of time to talk about that." Ira tapped Jake on the shoulder and pointed his head to the road. "A Ford cruiser. Check it out."

"Shit."

Two men got out, pulled the bag from the behind the bush, looked around and then took off with it.

There goes Maya and my only chance at finding Laila.

Chapter 16

Tom Delany could smell a crisis coming. Only three months ago, after his appointment as the director of the NSA, the President confided in him that counter-terrorism would be part of his 2012 reelection platform.

With his vast expertise in tracking people down, now, he struggled to locate this *nobody* Jake Hudley. He called a meeting with his staff for an update before a scheduled phone conference with the President.

The trivial conversation with the NSA agents Moore and Welter was swept aside with a knock and the arrival of Dave Scott, five minutes late again. Tom waved him in, passing judgment on this techie holding a laptop like a plate, wearing an oversized short sleeve shirt to hide the bulge of his gut over his khaki pants. His fat ass did not hang out. *Small miracles.*

While Tom waited for Dave to settle himself, he reflected on the changes in the NSA over the last few decades. When he'd started as a fresh agent, often he was hiding behind a tree with binoculars watching targets. Now, old-fashioned surveillance tools and techniques were replaced by computers sifting through data collected from social media and Internet service providers. That's why he needed techies like Dave Scott, and put up with the shit that clung to them. His eyes tracked the man as he sank into a chair.

"Linda Moore and Chris Welter have been working the Hudley case." Tom was aware that veterans in his department, such as these two, were not fond of young techies either. "Dave tracked the text message Hudley sent to his sister and found the whereabouts of the device he used. I want him in the loop," he said to the two agents. With a nod, Delany signaled Welter to resume.

Welter shifted his weight in the chair and cleared his throat. "As of now we don't know where Hudley is. From the IP address we got from Dave," he pointed at the techie, "We placed a track and hold status on the device in the satellite surveillance system. Our agents located this device in Isfahan under a bush by the bus terminal. But, *big* but, we could not associate a person with it. How this bag and the device got there we don't know. If there were cameras at the terminal, we don't have access to the recordings. Needless to say, it's difficult at any time getting intelligent information from Iran. Is this a wild goose chase?"

Scott objected, "No, no. It is not a wild goose chase. The phone call to Hudley's sister was made from Zahedan and you located the device in Isfahan. Someone carried it from one place to another. Likely it was Hudley."

Delany intervened, "Two things. First, what kind of a device is it? An iPhone, Blackberry, what other kind do we have? Oh yeah, Android?"

Welter shook his head. "None of those. It looks like an Apple iBook but our agent in Iran hasn't been able to start this particular computer."

Delaney noticed puzzled stares from all three subordinates, a reaction he didn't want to see. He expected his workers to have all the answers at any given time. He tapped the table.

"In half an hour I have to talk to the President and I don't know where this guy is or what kind of device he was using. If it were Hudley carrying this *whatever* device, he was tipped off. He *knows* we were going after him."

An impatience rang in his voice as the old-style clock on his desk ticked precious seconds away. Still no one was inclined to give him any solutions.

"Where is this device now? How soon it will reach our soil?"

Moore, the woman leading the team, said, "An agent is heading to Iran from Afghanistan. He'll take it back to Afghanistan where it'll be placed on the next cargo plane to the US. I have instructed our agents in Iran to locate Hudley. Should we get the CIA and FBI involved?"

"No, no, no." Delaney shook his head vigorously. "We want to keep them far, far away. They'd love to take the glory and credit at our expense. We started this job and we're going to finish it by giving Hudley's head on a platter to the President." He turned to Dave Scott, who'd raised his hand like a school boy.

"I did check the IP address and phone number of the device in question. Both belong to the US Military Data Exchange Center. When I started to dig deeper I got a huge run around. The analyst at the center refused to find out who owns this information. Said she was too busy and unless we got the okay from *her* boss there was no point in me calling her back. I don't like her. She called me an ass."

Delany noticed a faint smile on Moore's face. "What's the big deal?" he asked.

"She said that one IP address is the same as thousands of others. When I asked her what she meant, she gave me a long convoluted story. The short version goes like this: Her mother is a nurse and she likes giving injections to patients on the ass. Her mother often says, 'Having seen one ass, I've seen them all.'"

Delaney understood his staff were always under a lot of pressure, and overworked. At times their nerves became raw and sensitive. "She did *not* call you an ass, Dave. Send me the name of her boss."

"Whatever." Scott made few keyboard clicks. "Email sent."

Tom turned to Chris Welter. "Update on the surveillance of Hudley's parents."

"Everyone is being watched. Father, mother, sister *and* friends. Especially his friend Andy Burke, who he saw at the Lackland Air Force Base just days before his disappearance. We'll interview each of them."

Delany took another peek at the clock and dismissed the meeting. "That's all the time I have. Thanks for your help."

Everyone stood up and filed out, dissatisfaction written over their faces and ingrained in their stances. After closing the door, Tom returned to his chair. A wave of despair washed over him. *What am I going tell the President?*

***

Thirty minutes after Maya's computer-napping, Jake followed Ira into a local safe house. As Ira securely locked the door, he watched Jake rip off the head portion of the burka covering his face. Jake tossed it to the floor then lifted the rest of the fabric until it passed over his head and dumped it too.

"Piece of shit." He surveyed the area. "Where the hell are we?"

"You make a fine woman Jake: tall, slender and with blue eyes?" Ira bat his eyelashes at him.

Jake stomped his feet. "I shouldn't have listened to you. Get serious, would ya."

Ira insisted on his guest disguising himself as a woman or he wasn't going to take Jake to the safe house. With his pale, white skin, and blonde hair, Jake knew he would've stuck out like a sore thumb, but that didn't mean he had to like it. He checked the place out as Ira fiddled with some kind of hand-held device, sweeping it around the room.

On the second floor of the building, the apartment was bare except for a couch, small table, and two chairs. The walls were covered with old beige paint and the only window, completely draped, let in a sliver of evening sunlight. Jake scanned the layout looking for a door that could possibly lead to the crapper.

Ira finished sweeping the apartment for bugs, then he came back from the kitchen with food. He placed *Barberi*, feta cheese, humus, two bottles of an Iranian drink, and plates on the table.

"Help yourself. You must be hungry."

"Famished, actually." Jake wanted to swallow all the food in front of him, but slowed his impulses for fear of being piggish. He placed a bit of everything on his plate then grabbed the drink and chugged it down. Food had a naturally calming effect on his nerves. His mother's muffins and home-baked goods worked miracles whenever school or moving got overwhelming.

Ira perched on the arm of a worn-out couch and Jake leaned against the wall. Both were silent as they devoured the food. Jake dipped a piece of bread into the humus and watched Ira in his peripheral vision. If this freelancer had a deliberate plan and their meeting at the bus station in Zahedan wasn't a coincidence, he had to figure out this guy's endgame before he could even consider trusting him. He'd already admitted that his "employer" had showed interest in Jake—whatever that meant. Ira had dodged Jake's questions as they waited for Maya to be snatched but he was going to answer them now.

"How did you find out that I was being followed?"

"One of my sources had been following you from Texas to Iran."

"Why?"

"Why. That's a good question. You have some information he wants."

"Is that so? How can I believe anything you say? These people who took my Maya, are they your friends? Is this a setup?"

"I told you the truth, Jake. The guys who took your computer work for American agents and they wanted to take you alive with the device. Don't doubt that. They are not my people."

"Why should I believe you?"

"In my line of business, trust is the most important factor to staying alive."

Jake couldn't help but think of Andy—his sacrifices. Jake ran a hand over his head and mussed his hair. "I really couldn't afford to lose my computer. It's vital in helping me complete my mission."

Ira paused a moment as he examined the plate in front of him. "What kind of a device was it?"

"Sort of a smart phone."

"How smart?"

"I don't have all the details but I have to get it back. No two ways about it." Not just for Andy's sake, but Maya was the key to freeing Laila and reuniting his family.

"I can probably get it back for you."

"What? You're shittin' me. Why didn't you say so sooner?" Jake narrowed his eyes. *Did Ira plan to have Assignee taken away from me?*

When Ira stopped chewing, he calmly said, "It *can* be done, but nothing's easy in this line of work." *What is he up to? What kind of power does he have?*

"Really?"

"Yeah."

"Yeah. Well, if you could, that would save my ass.

"I understand. I'll see what I can do."

"Thanks, I think."

Ira washed down the food with a gulp of his drink. "Now, tell me why you're really here."

"I *did.* I have to save my wife Laila from Evin Prison." The ever-present knot in Jake's stomach tightened even as he held everything he could back from this man.

"Evin … how did she get there?"

"She came to Iran to support her family after her brother was arrested by Revolutionary Army Guards. Her father had also suffered a heart attack. One night after her arrival they arrested her too."

"Do you know that the US media is trying to locate you? They know you're ex-military. One report in particular talked about the US government looking for you, which you know. They've figured out you're in Iran."

A shadow of doubt cast across his heart. "The US media and government are after me? It's worse than I thought. At the same time, I know I couldn't have stayed home and done nothing. No one was going to anything, so I had to step up." He rubbed a hand across his chest. A net encircled him. *Will I get out of here alive? Did I jeopardize Laila's life? Should I have tried more extensive diplomatic options? Was that even possible after what the Senator told me? I just don't know anymore.*

"I understand. Once the Iranian authorities know that you, the husband, were part of the US military, they'll make a case for executing your wife. In other words, she's doomed, regardless of where you are, here or in the USA. The worst part is that once the Iranians know you're here they'll go after you too, just like the Americans are. You're in deep shit man."

Jake nodded. *Deep shit all right*. "How about you? Why exactly were you tracking me? You seem to know a lot about what's going on."

Ira hooked a piece of the bread with some cheese and placed it into his mouth. "I told you. I'm a freelancer, a mercenary."

"No, who are your clients? Americans? A local group? Israelis?"

"Why are we going over this again, Jake? I'm in the business of trading information. Look, I make a margin on each trade. It's like corn. Buy a bushel for a $1.00 and sell it for $1.25.

"Lately Israel's been very nervous about Iran's nuclear program and in the last six years as many as five top nuclear scientist have been murdered. Israel's been accused but it denies the accusation."

Jake rubbed his fore head. "I know you're Jewish. Are you a Mossad agent?"

Ira paused. "All I can say is that I am *not* a Mossad agent. I got a tip from my sources that you worked at Lackland Air Force Base in the Space Surveillance System. It's no secret they develop some of the top surveillance devices. Can you tell me something about them?"

Now Ira's motive was clear. "We'll talk about that later. Why are you in Iran?"

"For the thrill of it."

Jake saw a dark shadow around his eyes as if a deep, deep secret lay hidden inside him.

I'll get to the bottom of this yet, he promised himself. "How soon can you get Maya back for me?"

"Maya? You name your computer like a car?"

"No. I call it Maya because the interface program that takes voice activated commands calls herself that."

"Okay. It is hard to believe a simple computer is so important to you."

Jake thought of Andy who'd trusted him with this most guarded secret. A chill ran up his back. He should never have put Andy in danger. "It is. I want it back."

After wiping the last piece of humus from the plate with a piece of pita, Ira got up. "I'll go find it."

"I want to come."

"No." Ira's reply was short but firm. "It is a risk not worth taking."

But Jake knew the real reason; being an agent, Ira wouldn't want to share any secrets.

"I understand." Jake didn't know what to make of this guy. His sixth sense told him to be reserved but not to abandon him. Jake could use his expertise to his advantage—he just had to figure out how.

"Stay put." Ira's tone emphasized just how deep down the rabbit hole Jake had gone.

***

Charles Hudley jumped to his feet, placed the TV remote on the coffee table and walked to the front door. The echo of the ring faded as he peeked through the curtains and confirmed it was only Andrew Burke. With his forefinger positioned across his lips, he stepped out and waved the boy to follow him.

Andy followed Chuck across the front lawn and around to the backyard. When the two men reached the edge of the tomato patch, Charles lifted a hose and watered the plants. He leaned towards the young man and whispered, "Our house is bugged."

"Mr. Hudley those tomatoes look terrible."

Charles was surprised by Andy's reaction—that being under surveillance was less important. He knew his gardening skills were inadequate but seriously, his tomatoes?

"I've never been into growing vegetables. It was my doctor's idea, gardening, hoped it could help with my hypertension."

"No, no. Don't get me wrong." Remorse oozed from Andy's tone. "I'm not here to criticize, sir. Have you heard from Jake? The media's going crazy. Reporters have been after me and I keep brushing them off but like a bad rash it only gets worse." Andy's robust Texan accent didn't match his pale face and worried eyes. His voice lacked energy though and Chuck wondered if this had been a long day at the office or an on-going trend.

"I wouldn't be surprised if you're under NSA surveillance, too. Be careful son."

"Have you heard from Jake?"

At this point he couldn't trust anyone. "No, not lately. You two are good friends. What did he tell you?"

"He told me he was going to Iran and talked me into giving him a unit of Assignee Holiday."

Charles knew exactly what tech Andy referred to. In the last ten years of his military service Chuck been the head of the Space Surveillance System at Lackland Air Force Base. He took a long pause.

"Why did you do that? You breached military code. And—"

"Mr. Hudley, I know I screwed up royally. Now that Jake's disappearance has been become a national security issue every reporter in America is looking for him. I can only hope no one in my department notices a copy of Assignee is missing."

"*And* the NSA agents. Son, this is treason. High treason." He took a deep breath and slowly let it go, trying to put the pieces of this mess together. "The device is with my son, and you are his best friend. Can it be traced back to you? This is terrible." He looked up towards the sky with the hose in his hand.

"Mr. Hudley, I know it's terrible." His tone suggested the cry of a helpless child. "I can't sleep at night and I've been going through every thought and counter-thought to his request. I *had* to help him. He's my best friend. Laila always included me in their activities and made me feel like part of the family. No one was going to help him—not even the government."

Chuck reflected on the reality of helping others. "You can get drowned while trying to save someone." The pain hit him hard in the stomach since the drowning man here was his son. He'd hoped their talk with Senator Quest would have set things straight with Jake, but it had only made the boy more blockheaded about the whole ordeal.

"Jake's always been a good friend, the brother I never had. After my father died, Mom couldn't afford much and some days I skipped lunch. When Jake found out, he brought lunch for me. God bless him."

"Ruth and I wondered why he always took extra food," Chuck gave a nervous laugh, shaking his head.

"When he said he needed my help to save his wife, I tried to say no but I couldn't. Just couldn't. Simple as that. It never once dawned on me that the government would go looking for him." He paused, then whispered, "Now, I have to live with it. It was a big mistake. Stupid, stupid, stupid."

A facility, created by a special order of the President of the United States and Charles Hudley, providing the most sophisticated surveillance hardware and software mankind had ever seen, had been compromised for the love of a woman. He shook his head and continued hosing down the sickly tomato plants.

"My gut says we have to tell NSA about your side of the story. They came to see me, you know. At the time, I didn't know Jake had a copy of AH-302. An engineering marvel that. Should never have left US soil."

Another long silence. Charles continued holding the hose but his mind worked at lightning speed calculating a strategy which would result in as little collateral damage as possible.

Head lowered Andy walked away.

"Ah … Andy." Charles waved him back. "According to *my* sources, no one is looking for the AH-302 that you gave Jake. All the NSA wants is to know where Jake is hiding. Who else knows about this?"

"No one. Just three of us."

"Okay, good. Don't mention this to anyone. No one, you understand? If someone with any kind of authority, like your boss or an NSA agent asks you point blank 'did you give this unit to Jake', then you have to tell the truth. But don't go around offering it up on a whim."

He nodded. "I understand." His face muscles relaxed slightly, but the boy still looked pale in the evening sunlight.

Charles extended a hand to the boy's shoulder. "Son, this is the most technologically advanced computer in the world and right now it's in enemy territory. In the military brass' mind it would be …" He was about to say treason again but instead used, "serious".

"Mr. Hudley, I fully understand and I'm grateful for your advice."

"Another thing. You're under just as much surveillance as I am. At least, I'd be surprised if you weren't. Strange. Isn't it? You're working for the Space Surveillance System, I helped build this division, and here we are both are being watched by the same authorities. What irony!"

"Yes sir,"

"If they question you, without mentioning the device, tell them about Jake's concerns but make no speculations. The truth is you don't *know* where Jake is right now. Do you? Only what he said he wanted to achieve."

"No, I don't. He could still be in the USA."

"Yes. Remember what I'm saying."

Andy's body straightened at the tone in the ex-General's voice. Placing a hand to his forehead, he gave Chuck a military salute.

"Yes, sir." He made as if to leave, but hesitated and turned back. "Tomorrow, I can come over and give a hand with your tomatoes. The bed needs top soil. I'll bring some. Kristina is the real green thumb but I've picked up a few things from her."

Charles was slightly embarrassed with the meager appearance of his tomatoes. "No, no. You don't need to go to the trouble."

"Mr. Hudley, I think it *will* help with your blood pressure. As for me, I could use some time away from my anxieties and it'll add credence to our chat here today."

"It's a deal then."

With that, Andy left.

Charles put away the hose and went inside. He missed his son. He recalled some of the differences between them over the years. All he wanted was to get the job done. He'd been frustrated by Jake's laissez-fair attitude. Charles was a true New Yorker, a loyal fan of the Yankees, while Jake spent the majority of his teen years here, a supporter of the Texas Rangers. Charles was also known for his value system and no-nonsense approach. His reputation was at risk.

What a good bloody mess ...

***

Jake lay on the couch with his eyes closed reviewing the day's events. He weighed the positive and negative points of meeting Ira. Of course, losing Maya was a disaster, which might actually have been planned by Ira—an idea that haunted him for some time now. Footsteps climbed up the stairs. He sat up and waited. After the door creaked, Ira's face appeared.

Maya's not with him. He wanted to crumble, instead he said, "What happened? Did you locate Maya?"

"I located the agent, working for the NSA or CIA, not quite sure. It doesn't matter. She has it in her possession but wants five-grand."

Can she be trusted? "Is she good? Can she actually make this happen?"

"She's very good; one of the best. In fact, women make the best undercover agents, if you can recruit one."

"Why's that?"

"They have good people skills, controlled ego, are better listeners. She says she can keep Maya for about a day or two, that's all, no more. If I pay the price, we get her back. She is your second love, yes? Otherwise it has to be shipped to the US in 48 hours."

"How much did you say she's asking?"

"Five-thousand US dollars."

Jake wondered how they priced this transaction and the fairness of it. "I can't afford it. Besides it's *my* property. I think you planned all of this."

Ira ignored him. "This device has some strange features." He scratched his head. "It's completely sealed; the casement is in one piece. No screws. seamless. It looks like a MacBook Pro but it's lighter and thinner. The material is very different. She couldn't locate the battery to shut off the beacon emitter." He puckered and then his eyes opened wide. "It's an amazing machine. Where did you get it?" Ira's eyes danced with interest and enthusiasm.

Jake's response was as dull as he could muster. "A friend."

"She said the Chinese and Russians would pay a hundred-thousand for it. Five-Gs is more than reasonable."

"I have to pay five-thousand dollars to get my own computer back. Crazy."

"I know what you mean."

Jake did not believe what he was hearing. Now he had to save Laila and Maya. "I really need it back. But I don't have the money."

Ira walked to the window to check outside, a habit he had. "They don't take credit cards. I also realize it'll be hard to come up with cash."

Jake's frustration reached its exploding point. "You're damn right!"

"I made a deal with her. She's a MEK. She wants one of her fellow agents rescued from Evin prison. He was bagged for a scientist's assignation he did not do. The Iranian authorities know that too, and also know that it was not a Mossad agent. But, knowing it'll be difficult to find the real killer, they've kept him captive. So far they haven't found the killers of the five scientists. Therefore, for the benefit of the general Iranians population, they're obliged to put the blame on anyone."

"What is MEK?"

"Mujahidin-e-Khalq. A group that's at war with the Ayatollah."

Jake needed more clarifications. "We've been talking about a woman. Only men picked up the bag at the station."

"She's the boss and others are helpers."

Jake remembered Ira was a broker. "What are you playing at? From what I've gathered, this prison is a fortress. It's one thing to break Laila out but devising a way to find and save— No. Impossible."

"He's a valuable asset to her group and worth a lot of money. It would be worth getting him out of jail."

"Laila comes first."

Ira waved his hand in frustration. "I know. But she's been charged with spying for Israel and the US."

Jake was confused. He got off the couch and ran a hand over his face. "I don't understand the math of this transaction. It looks like just a trade for your expertise, not mine. I was going to use— Never mind."

Ira rubbed his head again. "I know someone else who wants that computer and is willing to pay a lot, I mean *a lot* of money for it."

Knowing this would betray Andy, Jake said, "I can't do that."

"Look at it this way. If we are in Evin Prison getting this other guy, we might get your wife out at the same time. If I owe you your computer, as you claim, then by helping me save the scientist you'll get Maya back and I'll get my bonus."

Jake shook his head while running through the long list of betrayals: his country, his father, his friend—all to get his wife back.

Ira's must have sensed Jake's hesitation and said, "We'll talk about it later."

Jake couldn't believe how excited Ira was about this idea. The burden he felt dropped him back down onto the couch where he laid his arm over his eyes. *What am I going to do?*

Chapter 17

Linda Moore applied pressure to the brakes. The Chevy Cruz obeyed, gliding to a smooth stop in a parking spot fronting Walmart. Her partner, Chris Welter, sat in the passenger seat. Together they observed Charles Hudley as he stepped from his GMC Terrain.

As the target headed towards the main entrance of the super store, Linda pulled the viser down to prevent the morning sun from hitting her eyes.

"Did you talk to Tom?" Chris asked, agitated.

Linda shook her head. After the conference call with the President, who was not happy with the Hudley case, the boss wanted an update every morning at 7:30 am, just as he arrived in his office.

"He was pissed. He was so mad, if I were in front of him he'd have thrown something at me."

"The problem is that the NSA has given too much power to the techies. Based on a frigging IP address, whatever the hell that means, we're supposed to track a suspect?" He hit the dashboard. "Our surveillance procedures have gone to the dogs. Linda, honestly, I'm so frustrated with my job. I'm seriously thinking of quitting to become a fireman." Linda had known Chris for a decade and he was always thinking of quitting. Last time it was to join the police force.

For another twenty minutes both puzzled over Jake's mysterious disappearance, occasionally letting out steam regarding NSA procedures and over-reliance on modern tech. Linda did not trust Dave's explanation of Jake Hudley's whereabouts.

Noticing Charles exit the building, he had a plastic bag hanging from his hand while limping towards his car.

When the senior Hudley was about ten feet from his vehicle, he focused on the car remote as Linda slid from the front seat of the Chevy. She and Chris closed in on the target.

"Mr. Hudley, good morning," Linda said. She saw the flash of recognition, and maybe something more, in his eyes. "Can we talk for a few minutes?"

"Sure, what's up?" His six-foot frame straightened to its full height.

Linda pointed to the SUV. "We can sit in your car or we can go to mine. It's up to you. It shouldn't take too long."

"Hop in." After placing the bag in the extended cab, Hudley Senior sunk into the leather seat behind the wheel.

Linda went to the front passenger side and slid in. The new-vehicle scent was so strong the SUV could have rolled out of the dealership the day before. Chris settled in the back.

Linda turned to face Charles. She shouldered a pressure to find Jake's exact location before Super-Dave techie could. "We need to know where Jake is. I think you know. Don't make this any harder than it has to be. I need your help."

Charles started the engine and turned on the air conditioning. A strong sun and warm ambient temperature made the air hot inside.

"Come on, now. Don't tell me you haven't found him yet? I thought nothing escaped the eyes and ears of the NSA."

Linda recalled the previous conversation with this General ending on a sour note. *Make no mistake, we'll find him.* Instead she said, "You know, someone is trying to reopen the scandal case in your division before you retired? Tom could put a lid on it. You know what I mean."

"Tom Delany, huh? Say hi for me, will you. I don't know if he remembers me." He locked eyes with Linda. "What do you want from me?"

"Do you know where your son is right now? We know he's in Iran. But what's he up to?"

"All I know is he planned to leave the country. Honestly, where he is now, I have no clue. Jake talked about going to Iran and I vehemently opposed the idea. The boy usually listens to me."

Linda pause to glance at a shopper opening the door of her car directly in front of the GMX. "I see."

Charles rubbed his graying hair. "What did you find out from others?"

"Others? What do you mean?"

"Other member of my family, his friends."

Linda recognized the ex-General was fishing for information. "Oh, we did interview a few." She shrugged.

Someone must know. "Have you heard from Jake at all? A phone call, email or text? Wherever he is, he must be worried about his children. I see you and your wife are taking care of them."

Charles shook his head. "Nope. Heard nothing."

"What kind of device was he carrying?"

"What kind of device?" Charles gave her the classic puzzled look. The problem was, it appeared genuine but that didn't mean this old military hound wasn't well practiced.

"Was he carrying an iPad, iPhone, a computer?"

"Linda, sorry. I can't say." The tone of his voice gave away the hint of a hidden story. If she pressed too hard, he'd shut down and she'd never get another chance to crack him.

"That's all for now. Thank y—"

"Wait. I have a question for *you,* Linda." The tension in his voice was obvious.

"Sure, Mr. Hudley. What is it?" Linda counter-balanced the General's demeanor with a polite tone.

"Why are you looking for Jake? He hasn't done anything wrong. I know my son; he's probably holed up somewhere fighting off demons and knows he won't be able to take care of the kids properly so he left them with us. You know he only just got back from a tour, right? He lost a friend over there and now he stands to lose his wife. The government should be more occupied in freeing Laila, an *American* citizen, than following some fool-hardy whim to find Jake."

"That's a good question." She paused to reflect how to give an appropriate response without giving away more information than necessary. "Because Jake was an Air Force Officer and employed at Lackland AFB, there's no need to tell you that whatever he knows in terms of previous work is highly classified—"

"So what?"

"It's imperative we talk to him. If his wife is in custody over in Iran and if there was any kind of pillow talk … well, Jake would need to tell us everything she *might* say if coerced." She paused again. "We have to find out what Laila knows. Tom and the President consider this situation to be *very* serious. If he's in the hands of the Iranians, too, they'll try to get as many of our secrets as possible."

Charles' face blanched. He shook his head. "No, no. I taught my son to be a loyal American. He left the military to be with his family—get to know his little boy. You should erase those ridiculous ideas from your head. He'd never betray his country, nor would he ever put his wife in danger like that."

"I understand your concern Mr. Hudley. But we have to consider *every* risk. Risk to the country that is."

Linda extended her hand to Charles, instead he grabbed the steering wheel and watched the car in front of him back out and drive off. She and Chris also departed.

Heading towards the highway, Linda braked hard at a stop sign. "Dammit, Chris. All signs point to Jake being in Iran. This is a crisis for the White House and we need to get on top of it now."

Her cell phone rang. She glanced at the screen, "I have to take this." Routing it through the Bluetooth to her earbud, she answered. It was an agent from head office who informed her that they could trace when Jake left the airport, disguised as a businessman, all the way to the Karachi airport in Pakistan. After that, the trail went cold.

Hanging up, Linda was convinced more than ever that Jake was in Iran. "Chris, send a message to authorize more resources, including agents and funding to find this guy."

Delany will not be happy.

***

Later that day Charles stared at the glass patio door with a lemonade in his hand. Exhausted from nursing the tomato plants, he'd taken a break in the rattan chair on the patio. By now he'd given up hope of Andy showing to help with the plants or just for company.

Ruth appeared from the sliding frame. She'd dyed her hair again. "I'm taking the kids to the park. They're just too restless today." She stood still to examine her husband's face. "You look as if you've seen a ghost. Chuck, are you okay?"

Charles motioned with two fingers to have her close the door behind her. "Door, close the door," he whispered.

After a pull on the handle she took a few steps closer to him. "What's going on?"

"Just didn't want anyone to listen to what I'm going to say."

Ruth's forehead furrowed. "Yeah. The surveillance. I forgot."

"I saw *two* ghosts this morning at the Walmart parking lot. They were waiting for me."

"Chuck. I can't read your mind. Who are *they*?"

"NSA. They came here a day or two ago."

"Hurry up then and tell me what they said."

"They're desperate to talk to Jake. Think he might be selling secrets. You don't seem to be worried about anything that's going on."

"Not really."

"What? Why not?"

"For one thing, I'm enjoying the time with my grandchildren. Their parents wouldn't let me get close to them when they were around. Thought

I was going to poison their minds or something. Especially, Laila. Very protective. Modern women think they know everything. And they don't. They think they don't need us, that we're too old. But older people have more experience, knowledge, and advice."

This really didn't come as a surprise to Chuck. Even married for forty years, communication between him and Ruth had always been an issue. As a military man, his call of duty obliged him to be away from home often, sometimes for almost a year. She was a mother and housewife. He understood her having a connection to the grandkids even if he didn't understand the connection itself.

It didn't help that having only finished high school, Ruth often felt inferior and couldn't engage with her husband at an intellectual level—and when she tried, she gave up. Jake was likely following Laila's lead but Ruth saw their boy as a younger and lesser version of his father. To her, Chuck would always be a soldier and gentleman, which he wore like a badge of honor.

"Come. Sit down for a moment."

She sank into the chair and extended her hand until it reached his. "I know it sounds like I don't care about Laila and Jake. I *do*. I trust my son. He's always gotten out of any serious situation."

That's the problem. Maybe it was good that she wasn't completely aware of what Jake was into—the weight of his decisions on more than just his family life.

"Let's hope for the best. He's always thought outside the box."

"I know you're worried about him. I can tell. But you have to consider your health." She gave his hand a squeeze then got up.

"Ruth, your hair looks lovely. Did you color it recently?"

She brushed the side of her head with her hand. "No. I haven't colored for weeks. That's strange, you commenting on my hair. You haven't done that since we were first married." Her lips broke into a smile. "Whatever medication you're on. Keep taking it."

She always depended on Charles to be the caretaker. He squeezed her hand.

"I hope you're right about Jake. I have to get back to work. Tomatoes are harder to deal with than an army."

***

Tom Delany sunk into the swivel chair with his head buried in a report on a cyber-attack at JP Morgan, Citi Bank, and Bank of America—three pillars of the financial institution.

With a knock and a turn of the knob, his train of thought was disturbed. Dave Scott appeared. Something didn't feel right. This time the techie entered with a white Apple computer and not his usual black Dell.

Tom stood. Something had gone terribly wrong.

"I don't understand. This pisses me off." It was not in Dave's character to use expressive language. He looked haggard, as if he hadn't slept all night.

"What's wrong?"

"This is the device we got from Iran." He dangled the computer like a soiled diaper from two fingers and emptied his lungs with deep sigh. "It's an Apple MacBook Pro, something I could easily buy at any store. After receiving it, my team and I tore it apart and checked everything inside." He chucked it onto the nearest chair and grabbed the hair on either side of his head. "*That* device was not used to send two texts from Jake to his sister."

Modern technology had made Tom's work extremely difficult. He wasn't trained to be a techie but a soldier. Pictures with army troops, generals, and presidents covering the walls behind him were the proof of his military prowess.

"What the hell happened? If they sent us this computer, this must be it."

"It's another screw up. They delivered the wrong device."

"Did you check everything? Programs or whatever?"

"We pulled it apart. We examined CPU, memory, hard drives, all the apps, deleted content. There's nothing here that could communicate with a military satellite and no trace of anything that sophisticated having been erased. Nothing, nothing. For that kind of communication, it has to be authenticated; the flow of data must be encrypted and secure. None of that is here. A piece of shit." He kicked the leg of the chair it rested on.

Tom scratched his head again. "Let me call Linda Moore." He picked up the receiver, punched few numbers, and asked the person at the other end to come pronto.

Tom and Dave went back and forth for another ten minutes trying to figure out what could have happed, until Moore arrived. Tom in his own non-technical lingo repeated what Dave told him. Linda listened carefully. Her blue eyes focused on the Apple lying on the chair.

"This *is* the device. My people are very reliable, professional agents. They don't make mistakes. It doesn't matter though. The device is irrelevant."

Dave's chest puffed up. "I wouldn't say that."

Moore countered the techie, "I'm convinced more than ever that Jake is in Iran. We have agents combing the streets, interviewing merchants, talking to taxi drivers, and reviewing any surveillance we can get our hands on."

Tom was impatient. "Have you located him?"

"No." Linda's voice echoed forcefully. "But we will. We always get our man."

With a scan, Tom studied the expressions of the two people in front of him. "When you have him, come to me first. The President wants us to talk to Hudley before the Iranians get to him. We're into a deep negotiation regarding the US easing the embargo on Iran in return for Iran ceasing nuclear armament. If the Iranians get this idiot Hudley, then he'll become a bargaining chip for them. You understand? We can't let that happen."

"Once we find him, what do we do with him?"

Tom paced back and forth for long while. "First, put him in an artificial coma. Then take him across the border to Afghanistan and load him in a carrier and send his ass home."

***

Jake Hudley scrolled down the data on Evin Prison spit out by Google's search engine as he did what research he could from Ira's computer. A creaking noise from the door startled him. He jumped to his feet as a slender hand pulled the top from a brown burqa, before peeling off the rest of the garment and exposing dark blue jeans and a top. He took in every inch of this woman from her head to her toes: slim, in her thirties, shoulder-length shiny hair hanging loose. Then their eyes connected.

The contact lasted just a moment, but long enough for Jake to become dazzled by her light brown eyes. So similar to Laila's.

He finally broke the silence. "Who the hell are you?" He was confused and groggy, having stared at the computer screen for the past eight hours or more.

"I'm Meena. A friend of Ira's." She extended her hand.

He closed the distance between them. "Jake."

She smiled. "Ira told me about you."

"He's not here right now. Don't know when he'll be back. Can I offer you something?" He wondered why he felt compelled to say that. It wasn't his place. What was she doing here? A nervous tension re-awakened when he surmised Ira must not have gotten in touch with MEK on time.

"No, thanks."

"So, are you an agent or a mercenary?"

She blushed. "Ah … I'm just supposed to meet Ira. Has he been gone long?"

Again Jake felt awkward. A shyness fell upon her as was the way of Iranian women in the presence of strange men. Jake guessed that old habits were hard to break, even for a woman in her line of work—whatever that happened to be.

Meena slipped over to the window and took a peek through an opening in the curtain. She jumped back, her eyes suddenly fierce, the line of her jaw hard. Racing back to the door, she slid shut the thinner, inner door and engaged two latches. Next, she pulled an iron gate from one side of the frame to the other and locked one pad-lock at the top and another at the bottom. Dashing into the bathroom and kitchen, she checked the windows, pulled the drapes and strode back to Jake in the near complete blackness of the safe house.

"Grab your stuff, we have to get out of here."

Footsteps approached accompanied by voices. "*Goh, goh, goh.*" The swear words were followed by a kick to the door.

Meena grabbed Jake's hand and pulled him towards the kitchen. He grabbed his backpack from behind the couch.

At the door of the room, she leaned close to his ear and whispered, "We have to take the escape route."

They tiptoed into the dark space. Faint light filtered through the cracks in the curtains. A hammering sound echoed through the place.

"Actually, we have to move the fridge. Underneath is an escape hatch."

Jake felt trapped. The enemy was mere feet away. He gasped for air and managed a faint, "Okay."

The smashing of a sledge hammer continued, accompanied by the clank of pry bars as the outside door peeled open. Meena yanked a wire off the wall connected to the fridge. "Come on."

Both gripped the back of the appliance and with a fierce push, forced it to slide forward until a hatch appeared. She pulled the door and a hole roughly 2' x 2' appeared. She dropped down then lifted her head through.

"I need the burqa."

Jake flew back to the main room. The outside wooden door was breached and they were cutting the lock with a saw. Thankful for the dark shadows, he grabbed both burqas and slipped back into the kitchen.

"Put it on."

He obeyed.

She took hers and went down a steep flight of stairs until a light came on. Jake followed her, scraping his arms against the wood frame and into the tight space and down the steps until they were both crawling through a small tunnel, no more than his shoulder width in diameter.

A few minutes in, the light behind them fainted away. In the absolute darkness a horrible smell assailed Jake. It must have been a mixture of sewage and dead animals. Jake slid along the dirt ground on his knees, his jeans starting to soak through from the damp earth.

Meena was fast but he managed to keep up. At a distance, a faint light appeared. The air was so damp and filthy that Jake's lungs ached, threatening to make him cough or worse. He focused all his energy into keeping pace with the woman in front of him. He knew whatever enemy had breached the house couldn't be too far behind.

Meena stopped. She stood and pulled a cover. It was stuck. She placed her head and both hands below the hatch and exerted a grunt, still unable to lift it.

Jake instinctively grabbed her legs to raise her up but they still couldn't move the lid. Instead he placed his head behind her buttocks and his palms under her elbow.

"One, two, three, push."

Both grunted.

Nothing.

"Again."

They pushed until they lost their breath.

On the third try, light penetrated. After two more times, the obstruction gave way enough that Meena could slide her hand out. With another shove, the lid came free.

Jake pushed Meena up until her waist was level with the ground. She climbed out. He shoved her fallen burqa up to her. She quickly put it on, then locked her right hand with his and pulled him out.

On his feet, he adjusted his own garment over his soiled knees and straightened the headpiece so he could see better. They stood in a court yard. Meena shoved the steel lid back over the hole before kicking rock and dirt over it.

They stood in a completely different place, filled with daylight and surrounded by concrete walls. The ground was covered with piles of garbage, soil, and patches of grass. After regaining his bearings, he followed Meena to a gate. With a squeal of its hinges, it gave way. Both stepped out onto a busy street and mingled with the crowd. Jake drew closer to Meena.

"Where are we going?"

"Don't know. Just follow me."

Chapter 18

When Negar Dareini entered the lawyer's office the air felt stuffy and thick. The place was packed. She maneuvered towards the receptionist, who was on the phone, and waited. Maliheh followed close behind. After the receptionist put down the receiver, Negar requested to see Nousheen Sabet. Negar's name was added to the list and then she found an empty seat which her mother sank into.

Maliheh's face grew paler with every passing day. To sooth the nervousness churning in her body and mind, Negar dug her teeth deeper into the nail on her thumb.

She surveyed the compact room crowded with sad-faced women. The harrowed look in their eyes made Negar's heart sink ever lower, allowing fear to over-take her mind. That moment encapsulated how women were worth half what society and the government valued of men. A list of causes flashed through Negar's mind. Probably they were victims of abuse, unfair distribution of inheritance, or even worse, violence. They needed legal help.

By now, Sabet had become the symbol of justice throughout Iranian society, known for taking on cases of human rights violation. Lately, Sabet's story was on all the local and national news. She even got international attention from CNN for challenging the court on Pari's mother's case.

Pari was killed by her step brother and the accused was found guilty, punishable by hanging. According to Iranian law the victim's mother had to pay the cost of the punishment. After Nousheen argued in court that such a law was not just, the judge asked the treasury to pay for the execution. All the liberal media hailed the young lawyer as a protector of the oppressed.

What were the chances Sabet would accept Laila as a client? With every passing moment Negar became more and more wary of their chances. For the last seven days she had hopped from office to office in search of a lawyer, but to no avail. Each had an excuse—they were busy, overworked, or lacked experience in defense against the government.

But Negar knew the *real* reason.

Taking on a non-Muslim client charged with espionage was a risk no one wanted to take. In the past such lawyers had been harassed by clerics and government officials, not to mention pro-Ayatollah newspapers.

When the woman called Negar's name, Maliheh jumped to her feet, picked up her purse from the floor and rearranged her head scarf. Both followed the receptionist into a conference room barely big enough for one table and four well-used chairs. After taking a seat, Maliheh mumbled under her breath with her eyes half closed. Negar thought she must be saying her Remover of Difficulties prayer.

The lawyer entered the room with a folder in her hand and closed the door.

"Salam." She placed the folder on the table and sat with one guest to either side.

"What can I do for you?" Her voice was soft yet clear and powerful.

Negar related to the lawyer Laila's arrival in Tehran from the US for a family visit, then her arrest by the Revolutionary Guards, being taken to Evin prison, and now facing an upcoming trial. She also added how Orie died at the same prison. Negar's focus was interrupted by her mother's lament as she wiped her tears with the loose end of her chador. Negar resisted her tears and continued.

"My family and I are afraid we might not be able to defend Laila's innocence." Negar chose her words with care, not being critical of the

Iranian regime as many citizens have some degree of loyalty towards the current Ayatollah government.

Sabet wrote on a sheet of paper. She interrupted Negar's story to ask many questions: why Laila lived in the US; had she ever been involved in politics; and what the charges against her were. The exchange continued for another twenty minutes and then the lawyer put her pen down.

Opening her hands to the two women she said, "There are several such cases in the court right now. I'll be honest with you. It's not that the accused is guilty or innocent. Whether it is your sister or the Iranian priest who came to visit his family, the story is the same. This has nothing to do with justice. Always the Iranian government has an agenda. Exactly what that is in Laila's case, I have no idea."

Maliheh, who'd done her best to stifle her tears during the interview, knelt down in front of Sabet.

"You have to take this case. We've knocked on fives doors and all were shut in our face. They were all afraid of what will happen to them if they defend my Laila. With your reputation, they would not touch you. You are the one who can save my baby from hungry lions." She lifted her hands up in the air, "She is not a spy. How can she be? I *know* her."

Negar had never seen her mother so desperate. Maman said, "We'll pay your fee, whatever it is." But Negar was acutely aware they were running low on cash. How would they come up with more money?

"It's not about the money. The judicial system is not fair to women or religious minorities."

Maliheh placed both hands on her right arm. "I believe in Allah. I trust you do too. The divine hand always helps us when we do good deeds."

Silence filled the room for long time, the air pregnant with expectation.

"I am not saying yes *or* no. I have to do more research on similar cases." She took a deep breath and let it out slowly.

A bright smile lit up Maliheh's face. "Merci, merci, merci." She kissed Sabet's hand.

Negar, slightly embarrassed with her mother's behavior, was relieved by the possibility of Sabet defending her sister. Negar locked eyes with the lawyer, "I know you will take this case."

Sabet got up and picked up the folder. "On the way out, make an appointment to see me tomorrow."

Negar stood, but staggered as though suddenly bearing the force of thundering skies. *How are we going to pay for all these expenses?*

***

The next morning, Nousheen Sabet accepted Laila's case. On their way home, mother and daughter were consumed with how to pay for all the upcoming expenses. Sabet discussed the legal costs with them, and it was far more than they could afford. Negar pointed out that all their funds had already been exhausted paying Orie's hospital and funeral bills. To pay for visiting Evin prison, they'd borrowed from relatives, later paying the debt by selling the family jewelry. Abbas' pension had been cut off. The burden of survival now rested on Negar.

By the time they reached home, selling a kidney became the only viable option. But the question remained, whose organ?

Negar went to the kitchen to make tea. When it was ready, she invited her mother to join her. Maliheh sat at the head of the table, staring out the window in a daze. Negar poured two glasses and lowered herself into a chair. She gazed at her mother's eyes clouded in sorrow, and stroked her hand.

Maliheh broke the silence, "My baby, you are young and have your whole life ahead of you. I've already lived most of my life. *My* kidney should be sold." She held both her daughter's hands. "You don't understand this sacrifice."

Negar stood straight, pulling her hands away, "No, *you* don't understand, Maman. How many times do I have to tell you that your body part will not fetch much money? We can easily get 12 million rials for my twenty-two-year-old organ." She pointed to her abdomen. "Yours is worth only half that."

"Sit down. Let's talk."

"No. You are so stupid and stubborn."

Maliheh's face flushed; anger filled her eyes and her sour mood let out a wail Negar had never heard before.

What is happening to my family? Negar collapsed onto the couch and pleaded, "I am sorry, I should not have said that." Calling her mother stupid touched a very raw nerve. Growing up, Maliheh had only gained a grade five education. Maman's father did not think she needed more. This gave her an inferiority complex.

Maliheh was quiet just before exploding with, "You should keep your mouth shut! You are not aware that words can be as sharp as a knife—sharper! The hurt from a weapon can last a month or year. But one from the tongue can last a lifetime—"

"I apologize. What else can I do?" Negar got up and yelled, "I'm selling my kidney and not you!" Maliheh's mood of late had been swinging like a wild monkey on branches. After consulting with her aunt, Negar was informed of menopause—something women experienced in middle age. She still had no clue what it was though.

Abbas hobbled in with his cane.

"You two stop. Stop arguing." He lifted one hand. "Please God, give me a big heart attack so I can leave this house." He raised his head towards the ceiling. "Just let me go. The constant bickering is driving me crazy."

Negar jumped to her feet. Holding one of her father's arms she helped him ease into a chair.

"Baba, calm down. You don't need any excitement."

He pointed to his wife. "*You* are giving away your kidney. That's final."

"What? Baba, you don't understand. We won't get enough to pay all our expenses."

"What I say is final."

Negar walked from the room drained; she needed time to herself.

***

In the end, the doctor announced that Maliheh was not fit to donate an organ and all of their arguing was for nothing. After selling her kidney, Negar had returned home after staying only one night at the hospital. With rest and Tylenol 4 pills every four hours, the sore areas became bearable.

In the guest room, lying on the couch, turning an inch at a time, Negar extended her hand toward the telephone. With every slight movement the pain in her back intensified, but she insisted on doing this herself. She grabbed the phone and brought it to her lap, closing her eyes as the pain deepened before slowly subsiding.

Negar dialed Jake's number in Lackland, Texas. Laila's recorded voice message came at the other end. Oh, she missed her sister so much. She listened to the very last word, left a message for Jake, and then hung up.

Placing her head on the pillow, images of being in the operating room flooded back … The IV drip moved from a plastic bag into a tube and then into her view, filling her blood with sedation. Drowsiness came upon her, as her eyes wanted to close. A nurse rolled in the recipient. He was in his thirties, face in a cloud of fear. But there was a twinkle in his eyes. He looked at Negar and whispered, "Merci, merci." She sank into a deep sleep …

Staring at the living room ceiling, Negar's body filled with satisfaction though the ache around her stitches blazed red-hot. She was happy to have donated her kidney to that man. Yet, she felt uncomfortable that a person she'd never met, and perhaps would never see again, had a part of her body.

Immediately Negar banished the thought, focusing only on her sacrifice for Laila. She finally understood the meaning of *ghorban-e-shoma*, "I sacrifice for you". An expression so common in daily Iranian conversations she'd begun to feel nauseated hearing the phrase. It was overused and had long lost its real meaning.

The home-coming treatment she got was delightful. Aash-e Aab Leemoo, kabob and rice. Baghlava, Koloocheh and faloodeh. Visits from aunts, uncles, and cousins with gifts. Everyone showered their sympathy on her.

Days later she tried to call her brother-in-law again. No answer. They were going to visit Laila at the prison, soon. She wanted to know how Jake, Megan, and Dillon were doing. How could she face Laila without news of her family?

Chapter 19

Dave Scott pressed the badge into the scanner positioned just below the sign *Black Chamber*, the wing of his division. The door opened with a click. Raj Patel and Rick Chow registered their entry to this priviledged area immediately after.

The three colleagues walked side-by-side, silent. At the conference room Dave sighted the green light above the door. He chose this room for its secure environment, yet, at the NSA everyone was suspicious of everyone else, including this room. An old motto "trust with verification" was the unspoken guideline of operation in this department.

Once inside, Dave sunk into the head chair and placed a half empty bottle of diet Coke in front of him along with his laptop. Rick sat to his right and Raj to his left. Both munched on a snack from the cafeteria, five floors below.

"Bitch," Dave had been brooding over what Linda Moore had told him earlier as they'd left Tom's office after an emergency meeting. "I can't believe what she said."

Raj was the essence of calm.

"Dave, stop it. Don't let her words eat you alive. We'll fix her. We'll give her a taste of what we can do." He sat up tall, face beaming with confidence.

Rick said, "The device is a fake. The real device Hudley used is being hidden from us. Why? It could be could be anywhere. Off site, in this building ..."

"That's it. Linda has it and she doesn't want us to have it." Dave clapped his hands.

"Maybe." Raj wasn't so sure.

Rick tapped a finger on the table. "If the device is still out there, sooner or later it'll be used. What we have to do is put an alert on it. If it's activated, we can track it down again. I don't think Jake, or whoever has taken it, will be able to resist using it."

Dave's anger dissipated. "That's good Rick. Raj, find out more about the mail exchange server. We need to know who built this device. It must be military and someone over there must know about it."

"What if I can't get the information through the proper channels?"

"Just hack it," Dave said. He knew the policy that NSA employees were not allowed to hack their own system, but Dave was impatient. It was a risk he was prepared to take to save his name and his team's reputation in the eyes of the director. He wouldn't let ignorant NSA agents dictate what to do.

"No, no, Dave. If we get caught, we could end up in jail," Raj objected.

Dave cleared his throat. "We *have* to get that information. They're playing hard ball politics. How else are we gonna do it?"

After another five minutes of discussion, they decided to find out all the information they could about this peculiar device. They walked out of the room heads lowered, brains revving in high gear.

Roughly an hour later, back in their work area, Dave got up, walked to the wall, and gently hit it with his head. On the sixth bump, Raj yelled, "Stop it, already!" Dave sat back in his chair, his co-workers only a few inches from their screens buried in code.

Dave placed his hands on the table and rested his head on them. There were too many office politics. All he wanted was to do his job well and satisfy his boss.

The tug of war between his team and Linda's reminded him of a bully in grade nine who teased him for being overweight. Dave needed to pull a trick on the guy before he'd stop bothering him.

He didn't necessarily see Linda as a bully, rather a territorial fighter between the old and the new in terms of technology and procedure. She likely thought her authority, experience, and seniority were being threatened. *She must be looking to retire soon and doesn't want to jeopardize her future.*

Dave decided it was too risky to break into the military database, instead he picked up the phone to call Wendy.

"Wendy, it's Dave. How are ya?" His said, as gentle as possible. "Are you having a great day so far? Did ya receive my gift?"

"Oh, yes, Dave. Thanks for the flowers."

"I'm sorry for being an ass last time we talked."

"I admire a man who admits his faults."

His ego physically pained him. "Honestly, it's my greatest strength, Wendy," *Lie, lie, and lie.*

"Okay, Dave, cut the bull. What do you want?"

"I need the IP address and phone number assignments. Please, please, pretty please?"

"Dave, you actually managed to get me in the right mood. Your dozen roses did touch my heart. Let me see what I can do. What were they again?"

After Dave gave the IP address and phone number, the phone went silent for several long minutes while she put him on hold.

Dave tapped his fingers watching the digital clock on his laptop tick away the seconds until Wendy clicked back on, "Both belong to the Surveillance Research Centre in Nevada, an arm of the Surveillance Support Center in Lackland, TX. Let me check … it's highly classified."

Dave felt his lucky stars shining. "Can you tell me the name of the device to which this IP address and phone number were attached to?"

"What's your clearance?"

Dave knew women loved to hear their names, “Wendy, I have NSA clearance level 3.”

“Let me check.” The keystroke noise came clearly through the phone line. “What is your full name?”

“David Dalton Scott.”

“Gosh, there are five David Dalton Scott’s at the NSA. Is this you? Top Secret security clearance. You report directly to the director.” Wendy was clicking with the mouse on the software tabs as her words rolled across the line.

Dave felt confident he’d hit a home run with Wendy. “You got it.”

“I have you on voice recognition verifying this is, in fact, you. Okay. What I can tell you is that this device interfaces with our SteathSat.”

“I’ve heard of that initiative.”

Wendy was silent as she searched. “SteathSat belongs to the Surveillance Research Center.”

“What can you tell me about the SteathSat system?”

“Not much. My eyes don’t have enough privileges to see that information.”

“I understand. Sweet heaven, Wendy, you’ve given me more than I expected. When I’m in your area next, lunch is on me.”

“I’ll remember that cowboy.”

Dave hung up and shouted, “Yes!” His co-workers gave annoying looks.

Dave knew the research center in Nevada developed the most sophisticated computers and surveillances devices. For Hudley to make a call from Iran, he must have used a computer with Internet and a satellite-capable phone. Someone at Lackland gave him this device before he left. *Now, how can I prove it? There are more moats built around initiatives for advance projects than fire ants protecting their queen ...*

Chapter 20

Ira Kohan absorbed another view of the street before running up the stairs leading to a particularly *safe* house. A few steps behind, his partner Meena followed. Ira unlocked the door and entered a dim room.

As expected his boss, Ephraim, was inside. The powerful man stood by the curtains watching Azadi Square through a two-inch gap—a busy place where most Iranian tourists, officials, and international tourists stayed at Esteghlal Grand Hotel. The hustle and bustle of an ethnically mixed crowd in this neighborhood made it a perfect spot for a safe house.

When Ephraim turned around, Ira said, "*Shalom, ma nishma.*"

Though this man only came up to Ira's chin, he was the king and knight of the chess-board of life.

Ira responded, "*Shalom.*" Ephraim was not known for words—just stares. A dark patch above his right eyebrow was his signature birthmark.

"It is rare for me to come to Iran," said the Mossad chief. This face-to-face urgent encounter with the two agents was warranted to fulfill a pressing need.

Ephraim's appearance hadn't changed since the last time Ira saw him in Paris, a year ago on his way to Iran from Canada. For security reasons, the man only went by his first name.

"Good to see you, Ephraim," Ira said.

"Only the two of you know I'm here. I can't stay long." He took a peek through the curtain again. The dim light penetrated the even darker room.

"We understand," Meena said as she removed the white hijab and fanned her face with her hand.

All three understood it was extremely risky for him to come to Iran. Ira could only imagine what would happen if Ephraim was caught by the Army of the Guardians. Likely, they'd parade him in the streets in front of crowds with media cameras recording every scene, and eventually hang him after long speeches by clerics spelling out death to Israel.

"Where's Jake Hudley?" The words came out with a strong Hebrew accent.

"In a safe house in Isfahan," said Meena.

"His instrument?"

Ira replied, "With an American agent."

"American agent? I wanted *both* transported to Israel."

Ira's jaw dropped. He turned to Meena to assess her reaction and said, "My understanding was that you *only* wanted the device he was carrying—that's all."

Meena ran her fingers through her hair. "We can get the device for five-thousand dollars."

Ephraim nodded. "*Ken*." He approved with a "yes" in Hebrew.

"Do you want to take it with you?" Ira examined the man's features looking for unspoken answers.

"No, no."

Meena was in charge of transportation.

"How then?"

"Jake and instrument go together to Israel. Meena, see that it happens."

No one spoke against the Chief but Ira couldn't contain himself, "I only agreed to be an *information* broker. It was made clear that I would not have to deal with targets. Only 'blue and white' operatives are given such assignments."

Assassination, kidnapping, or sabotage was done by Mossad agents belonging to the inner circle. Ira was an outsider and his loyalty to Mossad was of the lowest grade. Meena was in training to join the elite group and as an agent unquestionable reliability was expected of her.

With the flip of a switch Ephraim turned on the bulb hanging from the ceiling. Pointing to a veneer-topped table, he took a seat in one of three chairs. The other two followed suit.

Ephraim turned to Meena, “What you don’t know wouldn’t hurt you.” He ignored Ira.

Decoding his words, Ira understood that instructions to transport Jake and the computer would come later. Too much knowledge given to an agent could jeopardize Mossad’s plans in case the agent ended up in the hands of the enemy and information was extracted through torture.

“We don’t have experience in this kind of assignment,” Ira tried again.

“All my agents are tied up. To us, Hudley is a prized asset. And he came to our attention unexpectedly. I have confidence in both of you.”

Meena was a capable agent, trained at the Mossad head office in Tel-Aviv, unlike Ira. He’d have to rely on her experience and intellectual judgment.

“What’s the next step?” Ira’s words were loaded with compliance.

Ephraim waved his finger at both of them. “You take the instrument and Jake to Tabriz. There I’ll have more information for you.”

Meena said, “We’ll need more than five-grand.”

“*Ken*. When both are transported to Israel, successfully, each of you gets a hundred-thousand dollars.” He got up, approached the door, opened it and said, “Don’t lose him.”

Meena and Ira stood in awe and watched as Ephraim closed the door. Ira took five steps then glanced out the window to observe the boss disappear into the street below.

“Why him, Meena? Why him? Why do they want Hudley?”

***

Jake Hudley sank into the chair in front of the computer screen and emptied half a glass of water. As he fought the heat and drowsiness, he searched for prison escape movies and wrote down five of them: Escape from Alcatraz, The Shawshank Redemption, The Great Escape, Escape Plan, and Papillion.

A noise broke his attention, but he wasn't sure where it came from. When he turned around, the door opened and two people came into focus. Meena and Ira stared at him sitting on the floor, naked except for boxers. The tattoo on his arm with J and L intertwined drew Meena's eyes. Then she lifted something in the air.

"Maya."

Jake scrambled up, grabbed the bag, pulled the computer out, dropped back to his mat on the floor, and placed it on his crossed legs. He raised the monitor and moved his eyes closer to the camera on top of the screen. Sure enough, Maya responded with greetings. The last access was shown on the bottom left corner near the digital clock.

Thank goodness, no one broke into it.

Jake fired off a text message to his sister.

My dearest Makalla. I miss you guys so much. How are my darlings? Tell them I love them and miss them. Have you heard from Laila or her sister? I am in Isfahan, a city in Iran. I'm very tired but fine.

Love Jake.

After pressing the send button, he sat still to gather his thoughts. He missed his children and the comforts of home. To him it seemed like a dream that Maya was back, maybe now he could save Laila and reunite everyone. Only a few minutes had passed when he heard a ring, a message had arrived.

He looked at the screen: a reply from Makalla. Given the time zone different between Isfahan and Lackland, Texas, he was surprised to get an answer so soon.

Don't text me again. Hide. Run.

Jake's first thought was to get out of the safe house. He gathered his pad and pen, and stuffed them in the knapsack with his cameras. After placing Maya in the bag, he went to the bathroom and dressed. He stuffed his tooth paste and tooth brush in the bag too. When he returned to the kitchen, Meena washed dishes as Ira arranged food on the table.

Jake said, “Where’s my cap?”

Ira stared at Jake with the computer hanging from his neck and a knapsack on his back.

“Where are you going?”

“I have to get out of here. This frigging place is driving me crazy.”

Ira met him at the door. “I understand this is a nutty situation, but you’re safe here. I have four eyes on the streets in case anyone comes.” Ira watched Jake’s every move.

“You don’t understand. The NSA knows I have the computer. This is top secret hardware.” He also knew very well what the NSA was capable of. Andy and his family would only stay safe as long as Maya stayed with him. The words *treason* and *espionage* slammed around in his mind.

Jake found the cap on the floor next to a chair, put it on and headed to the door—to run or hide anywhere. But Ira blocked his way.

“Jake, Jake, listen to me. We know they’re after you. You’ve already been saved twice.”

“Not a third time.”

“Meena and I are working on a plan to leave for Tehran.”

Jake moved closer.

Ira leaned against the door knob.

“This place is driving me mad. I have to go, now.”

Meena appeared and placed her hand on Jake’s shoulder.

“Let’s sit down and share a meal. I know you’re hungry and angry. The food is already on the table. We’ll talk. We’ll leave Isfahan as soon as possible. We have to be very careful. Here, you have us; outside, you have nobody.”

Meena’s soft words reminded Jake of his mother’s calm rationale from when he was a kid. An emotional decision was not the wisest move. He dropped his pack and cap, placed Maya’s case on the couch, and let Meena lead him to the table. As they ate, they made plans on how to leave Isfahan.

Half way through his meal, Jake realized how dangerous it was to have texted his sister. Maya was a *liability* not an asset. Every move of this device could be tracked via GPS. He plucked Maya from the couch and fired it up. “What is the password for your SDE?”

Maya responded, “The password for Software Development Environment is A1VbFBaZm.”

With few keyboard strokes, he activated her SDE and the words “Welcome Jake” appeared on the mid-section of the screen. The program then painted an array of choices on the menu bar at the top.

“Maya, what module activates the GPS function?”

“GPSU289”

“Bring it up.”

At the top of the program was the documentation for the functions. Scrolling down, Jake found the code for activating the GPS. He then added ‘**’ at the beginning of about twenty lines of code to render this portion of software ineffective.

“Maya, compile this program and generate an executable file for making this new version of the code active.”

Green and red lights flashed just above the keyboard, as the hard drive whined. “Jake, the task is done.” Now maybe his digital footprint would disappear and he could finally put Maya to use saving his wife.

***

At 3:00 am Ira Kohan locked the safe house after Jake and Meena stepped outside. Ira wore a t-shirt, cap, and sun glasses. A bag with Maya hung on his front and a knapsack on the back. Meena and Jake traveled in the safety of a burka.

At the bottom of the stairs, an alley lined up with a cement wall that led to a street. With little light to see by, Ira walked in front, followed by the other two.

When they got to Asemi Street, Ira expected to see a green van parked at the mouth of the alley; it wasn’t. He told the other two to wait there and searched down the way a bit. He found the van. The engine idled with the driver inside. When he opened the passenger door to talk to him, Ira heard the unmistakable screech of tires. A white van whipped by.

Slamming the door, Ira raced back towards his companions—only one petite burqa approached him. *No, no, no.* The worse scenario ran through his mind.

"They got Jake!" Meena cried.

"Get in!"

The green van backed up to meet them. Ira jumped in the front passenger seat and Meena in the rear.

"Follow that white van," Ira ordered the MEK driver.

"No, no chase. I don't want my van damaged."

"How much does it cost?"

"Five thousand Tumas."

"I'll give you ten. Let's go."

The driver shook his head.

Already precious minutes had been lost. Ira got out of the vehicle, went around and opened the driver's-side door. With lightning-fast moves he grabbed the guy's throat, his thumb and forefinger forming a claw. Meena shifted forward, jammed her right hand under his thigh and shoved with her left hand, lifting the MEK's body towards Ira.

Meena's throw came with such power Ira had only to guide the driver across the empty road with his grip. He threw the man's body on the concrete and rushed back to the van. Jumping in, he stomped on the gas pedal. The vehicle rocketed forward. Meena sunk into the front passenger seat.

Approaching Meraj Street, he said, "I'll check right, you left." He slowed the vehicle slightly, craned his head forward and right and, from the corner of his eye, he made sure no one was in front.

Meena yelled, "Negative!"

Ira saw two bright tail lights in the distance. He stepped on the gas and made a sharp right, hoping the van wouldn't tip. Tires squealing, the back end swayed in response to the motion. The gyration pulled Meena's upper body toward Ira; she grabbed the dashboard to gain balance.

"Be careful!" She screamed as the vehicle stabilized and raced forward.

A silence prevailed while Ira regained control of the van and gave more gas to the engine. His eyes rested on two tail lights in the distance. The road was clear of pedestrians but both sides were filled with parked vehicles. He swerved past a slow car and took the Aghababayi Express Way. Still following the white van, they exited onto Route 62. He gave it more gas, pushing the speedometer over 130 km/hour. Ira hit the steering wheel.

"We were double crossed. Do you think someone followed us after picking up the computer?"

"I'm sure someone followed us. Karim did not keep his word. Go faster."

Ira looked at the speedometer running at 135 km/hr. "Don't want to go *too* fast. We could attract attention."

"Ira, *faster*. If there are any police ahead, the white van'll get stopped first."

"Good point." He flattened the gas pedal and the whole frame shook. He didn't want to lose control but couldn't afford to let that van get away either.

They drove for nearly an hour before the white van careened onto the Na'im Ring Express.

"As I suspected, they're heading to Zahedan to cross into Afghanistan and air-lift Jake back to the US."

As recognized Mossad agents, he and Meena were not allowed to openly cross the border into Afghanistan. "Okay. We're losing precious time. Let's turn around and go to Karim, instead. We need answers."

Ira slowed the vehicle, got off the highway at the next exit, and backtracked to Isfahan as the road remained shrouded in early morning darkness.

When they arrived at their destination, the gate to the mosque was locked—as expected. Ira parked and they approached on foot. He scanned the quiet neighborhood. They had to jump over the wall. Ira laced his hands together and Meena slipped her right foot into position. Ira lifted her up, but with difficulty.

"Have you gained weight?"

"Shut up. Just lift."

He gave another heave, elevating her body to a point where she grabbed the top bar of the gate. He pushed both her feet up until she perched on top of the gate and then jumped down. Ira sprang up and climbed over after her.

Standing at the door, he pressed the bell to the courtyard of the mosque and waited. He expected a long wait, but only a few minutes later the door opened. Karim appeared in full religious attire and his mullah headdress.

Karim looked puzzled. He waved Ira closer. "What are you doing here?"

"We got ambushed," Meena said. "They took the American and his device. We trusted you. Who did you tell? Somebody knew our exact moves."

"No. No. No. Not me." He stammered. "I didn't do it. I have to go to *Namaz*." He pointed to the community mosque where he served as a mullah; it was time for him to lead the dawn prayer for Mujahedins, a Muslim sect hated by Shiites, the major religious division in Iran.

Ira boiled with anger, "Karim, I followed the van to the Na'im Ring. They're heading to Afghanistan. This can't happen."

"You have to leave. If the neighbors find out I am talking to Jews, we'll all be in trouble."

Meena was impatient. "This is serious. We're staying. You'll talk to us after the prayers."

Karim closed the door and they all stepped onto the road. Ira rubbed his forehead. So many questions swirled in his head with Ephraim's words, "Don't lose him," ringing the loudest.

***

Tom Delany was on the phone when Dave walked in for a meeting. Tom looked at the wall clock; Dave was on time for a change. Tom waved him to the table.

Minutes later Linda arrived and Tom hung up, grabbing a file from the top of his cluttered dusk he moved over to the conference table.

"Linda, close the door, would you?" Tom sat at the head of the table, as usual. "Just got off the phone with the State Department. Give me some good news. Too many things are going wrong today."

Dave perked. A broad smile plastered his face.

"I've got exactly what you need, sir. We foreshadowed this happening." By *we,* he always meant the trio: he, Raj and Rick. "We put a software alert out for any message coming from the number attached to the device." His chest puffed up. "We knew all along that Apple iBook was *not* what Jake had in his possession."

"We can't make that determination yet." Linda's face turned slightly red.

"*I* have."

"Okay. Good. So, your team was able to track a message coming from Jake. Was that information used in pinpointing his location in Isfahan?" he asked Linda.

Linda did not acknowledge Dave's effort. Instead, she jumped straight to *her* accomplishments.

"Our team did an excellent job in gathering on-site intel on him. With due caution we were able to track his movements and finally nab him."

Tom was getting impatient as the credit-grabbing continued. He tapped his finger on the table. "Where is he now then? That's all I care about."

Linda flipped to a page in her own file. "As we speak, he's in a van, heading to Zahedan. From there Jake will be brought to the Iran/Afghanistan border." She glanced at her watch. "They may even have crossed the border by now and be driving to Kandahar where a transport plane is waiting."

Dave pounced, “Last time we got a fake computer. Where is the device Hudley used in Iran?”

“We’re doing a professional job here. I don’t like your snarly remarks. This time it won’t be lost. The computer’s in a travel bag wrapped around Hudley’s chest. He’s sedated for transport.”

Tom felt good. “Excellent job, Linda. Hope we can wrap this up soon.”

Dave said, “First, how exactly is he getting to the US? Second, can I get that computer—”

“My team is coordinating arrangements as we speak. The van will drive directly into the belly of the plane. The agents will be moved out of the van. Jake and the computer will be handed over to military personnel on board that plane, and we’ll see him here soon.”

Tom approved, “Sounds like a done deal. Here’s what else we’re dealing with. According to Pentagon intelligence, an NSA contractor has defected to the Russians. It’s not confirmed yet. If this *is* true, we’ll have to deal with massive damage control. Apparently he has access to top secret files, especially related to online projects. He could tell the Russians, and the world, how exactly we’re collecting meta data from phone calls, emails, chats and so on. Dave, you’re the expert. I need you to be ready for this.”

Dave nodded.

Linda said, “Once Hudley gets here, what do we do with him?”

“Find out everything we can about the device in his possession, starting with how he got it. We’ll have to build a case against him and charge him with treason. More importantly, we need to know who he talked to in Iran. Someone or some group was helping him. He had valuable information to share.” She looked at her file. “He was a specialist at Lackland AFB at the Surveillance Support Centre. Served in Afghanistan as communication support staff. His father is a retired General. The President, Pentagon, and State department would like an assessment report done asap to see what kind of top secret information has been leaked.”

Dave broke in, "I've learned a fair amount about this device already. It's one of the most sophisticated pieces of hardware ever made."

Linda looked at him with disgust, "I don't think we'll need his help, sir."

"I want to know *everything* about him. I don't care if the report is two thousand pages. Now, before we finish here remember: no leaks. As far as we can tell, Iranian intel says they're still looking for him and they don't know his whereabouts. We might just have contained a media grenade with this one."

***

Ira and Meena slipped into Karim's office, tucked into a corner of the Mosque courtyard, only known to a select few involved in activities against the Iran Regime.

After a ten-minute wait, Karim appeared. He closed the door behind him.

"I can't talk for long."

Ira's skin itched and crawled with anger. "What did you find out?"

Karim's eyes widened and his white turban moved as his eyebrows arched. "No. My team has nothing to do with the kidnapping of the American. Ira, you have to believe me."

Meena squeezed closer to Ira. This place wasn't big enough for three people and a desk.

"Did you find out who?" she asked.

"I don't have that information."

Ira doubted Karim. In the spy business trust was as precious as gold. "You were given the initial contract to capture him by the Americans."

"Yes. After we failed to capture him—thanks to you—at the bus station, the contract was cancelled. They gave us a lot of shit for it, too."

"Don't blame me for that. You made five-grand. That was a lot more than you would have, had you actually captured him. We paid you a huge premium to get that computer back."

Meena, as always, remained cool-headed, "Fighting will get us nowhere. What's our next move?"

Ira pounded the desk and scowled, "You have to send a team to Afghanistan to rescue Hudley. Bring him back."

"What are you willing to pay?"

"We already gave you five-thousand dollars."

"That was just for the instrument."

"That's *a lot* of money. You know that. I can't give you any more."

"No. If I ask a team to rescue someone from the jaws of the American military, which is risky to say the least, they'll want to be paid for their work."

"We haven't spoken with the boss. We can't promise you anything. Besides, we've given you plenty of business for the assassination of those nuclear scientists." Meena knew if the boss was aware of this situation, both she and Ira would be sent home with shame.

Ira said, "Karim, it's a waste of time talking about it. We have to move fast."

"Working for nothing ..." He raised his hand in the air. "You people are cheap. I have to barter far too often with you."

Ira was not offended by Karim's allusion. He was always a hard bargainer. In Iran everyone was.

"You have to rescue the American. Meena and I can't do it ourselves. It's too risky. If you don't do this, we'll be sent out of Iran. Finished. We won't be able to give you any more contracts."

"Ira." He rubbed his beard and sighed. "I'll do the best I can. This is a very risky proposition."

Relief ran down Ira's spine. He took a deep breath and let it out slowly. "*Merci.*"

As he and Meena slipped through a back door leading out to an alley, Ira wasn't certain Karim would actually come through for them, but it was better than nothing. As they walked, the pair brainstormed how to get another team in play for Jake's rescue.

Chapter 21

When Laila opened her eyes, Maryam stood before her without a food tray. *Why is she here?* Maryam picked up the blindfold and the chador from the floor.

"Sister Laila, it's time for your shower." She extended her hand and pulled Laila to her feet. For a moment, she wasn't sure if it was her turn for a shower or not. Has it been another two weeks already? Lately, with each passing day her memory became foggier and she couldn't remember when her last visit to the shower happened. Water running down her body would definitely benefit her weary body and crumbling spirit.

With the blindfold firmly in place, Laila gave the chador a quick pull to tuck her face in with extra caution. Both women walked hand in hand in the quiet corridor. Laila used Maryam for support as her legs refused to work properly. The mid-afternoon heat put prisoners to sleep; they passed by cells that were quiet in the heavy air.

Back in Texas air conditioning had been everywhere: cars, hospitals, shopping malls, and at home. Cool, dry air was a luxury here inside this prison.

A wall of fresh, warm air hit Laila's face. Open space. *It feels so good.* The moment filled her heart.

A male voice greeted Maryam, to which she reciprocated in kind. Maryam guided Laila over a gravel path. Both were silent except for the crunch of the stones under their feet.

Laila heard, "*Salam Alaykum, Khanum*" in a deep, strong voice all too soon. This time the tone indicated great respect, especially when *Khanum* was added to the greeting. Perhaps the respect was prompted by the fact Maryam had recently converted to Islam.

Maryam responded, "*Salam.*"

With the guard's presence Laila remembered they were about to enter another building. Once inside she could hear giggling in the distance. At the end of the hallway they turned to the right. The moist air hit her senses. In another twenty steps Maryam pushed the edge of the blindfold up past Laila's eyebrows, until it slid from her head. With several involuntary blinks, Laila adjusted to the light.

After Maryam closed the door, she wrapped her arms around Laila's neck and squeezed tight. Then Maryam exploded in a burst of tears.

Laila put her hand on the back of Maryam's head and pulled her closer, unsure if she had the strength for such a feat but trying anyway.

"What's wrong?"

The deep sob continued.

"What's happened?"

"This morning Sima did not come back."

Laila did not know what she was talking about. "What do you mean she did not come back?"

"She did not come; she did not come." The crying turned into uncontrollable wailing.

"Maryam." Laila soothed and pressed the girl's head harder to her chest. The pressure helped reassure Maryam just as holding a child close will bring safety and comfort. Laila ignored the sharp pain in her collar bone from the pressure of her soul sister's temple. "Just let it out."

Laila also knew guards occasionally visited the stalls. With her ears attuned, she listened for any approaching steps. After a minute, the wailing faded to a whimpering sob.

"What do you mean? What happened to Sima?"

"Last evening Sima and five other girls were called to the office over the loudspeaker. Something in my gut knew my friend was going to her death. All night I did not sleep. I lay there waiting and listening." She wiped her nose. “The gun shots rang—” her body shook. Laila rocked her back and forth. Now her own tears leaked out.

“Maryam, I’m so sorry.” Laila pushed past her own pain to the very real loss Maryam struggled to understand.

“God did not answer Sima’s prayer. Why? Now *my* faith in God is shaken.” She sniffled and tried to squeeze back the tears. “Laila, tell me. Is there a God up there? Please answer. I don’t know. I really don’t know. I’m losing my faith.”

Laila had no words of comfort for this broken-winged soul. Her mind went blank. She wished she could read God’s mind.

Maryam peeled her body from Laila’s. She held a shaky hand over her face. Her eyes were red as she pushed aside tears that broke over the dried skin again and again.

“All night I was thinking of something worse than being executed. I have been there, very close to it.”

“What’s that?”

“Sima wanted to die with dignity, without being raped. Raped women don’t go to heaven. Sima told me she’d heard that before executing girls, guards raped them, because they believe virgins go to heaven when they die.”

Fear tore at Laila’s heart, shredding it nearly to ribbons. This could happen to any female prisoner.

“That’s not true.”

Maryam wiped her nose. “What’s not true? They executed her. I asked sister Fatimeh and she confirmed it.”

“I mean, raped women going to hell. I don’t believe that.”

“I knew Sima was sentenced to death. One night I asked Reza if he could do for Sima what he did for me. Ask for a lesser punishment. He got upset. Now she’s gone. Both are gone.”

“I wish I could tell you something to help you feel better. Just know I love you very much.” Laila started to cry, not knowing what her own fate would be. Would she come out alive or face a firing squad? “This life is full of mysteries.”

"Laila, *joon*. Sorry to bother you with my problems. The last few days I have been going through hell. Now I wish death. It would've been better than this."

"Don't say that. I need you."

"Although I knew all that happened the night of my scheduled execution was real, I'd dealt with my memories as if they were a nightmare. I'm going crazy. Reza dead; now Sima."

A dark shadow crossed Laila's face. "You have a chance to get out and taste freedom mere months away now instead of years. You've done everything within your power to get this far—don't lose hope now."

Maryam bowed her head. "I'm too tired to think. I feel exhausted, like falling asleep and slipping into a dream ..."

"You're not alone. Come, take a shower. You'll feel better."

***

Ali Mohmed knocked at the door with *Iranian Court of Justice* written on it in gold. Seconds later he heard, "Come in."

He entered the room with head bobbing, showing respect to the three men he faced. As he approached these magistrates he placed his hand on his chest, another sign of reverence.

They stood up and greeted Ali, "*Salam.*"

"*Salam.*"

All four men took a seat. As Ali placed a folder on the desk he noticed how tired his mind was. Lowering his head, he placed his hand on his stomach in a bow. Mullah Said, dressed in a black turban, indicative of being a descendant of the prophet Mohammad, started with praises for the Ayatollah and Ali. The ritual continued with a reading from the Quran by the chief judge.

Within minutes of the chanting, Ali's mind drifted away from the court room and replayed what happened just hours earlier. Prosecutor Ladjervardi accused Ali of doing his job improperly—a terrible blow to his personal integrity, especially for someone so dedicated to the Iranian

Revolution. Ali's commitment to the regime took him to the battle field of the Iran/Iraq war where a shot in his leg caused permanent damage.

Ali fought back against the thoughts of gossip started by the prosecutor, now running rampant throughout the Evin prison administration going to his father and beyond to the Ayatollah.

Said stopped the recital, paused for a moment and in a deep, loud voice started the proceeding, "Brother Ali, *be-farma*." The interrogator was thus invited to present his case.

Ali pulled a thick stack of paper from the brown folder. After shifting through various sheets, he said, "I am here to bring your attention to new information obtained regarding Laila Dareini. In my previous visit, praise be to Allah, this honored court saw fit to charge this person with espionage, spying for America and Israel. Her American husband has also been declared an enemy of Islam by this same court. Through the diligent work and great dedication of our office, we have uncovered important information I'd like to present to you." He stopped to let the judge think on his words. It was the polite thing to do.

Said said, "I recommend that you not bring the accused to any more hearings." Ali shook his head in agreement, recalling what happened when Laila came last time. Women in Iran were expected to be submissive and *never* talk back to men, especially to Mullah Said, whose stature was revered as a minor prophet. Laila's confrontational attitude was unacceptable, so much so that Said now told him that he didn't want to see her again.

Ali handed over photocopies of BBC, CNN, and Fox News reports to the chief judge. "Jake Hudley's whereabouts is currently unknown. However, according to these reports he could be in Iran with an army of men ready to rescue Laila Dareini. This poses a security risk for our beloved country. Our investigation has shown that this man,"—he gave a picture of Jake to the judge—"has been sighted by our Guards in Zahedan. The Ministry of Justice has been informed.

"In agreement with prosecutor Ladjervardi, I propose to the court that Laila Dareini be declared an enemy of Iran, posing a threat to the security of this fine country, and therefore be
charged with treason." Ali made a point of adding the prosecutor's co-operation as he wasn't certain Ladjervardi's complaints had reached the judge's ears yet. He knew that being branded a dissident was deadly. And Laila Dareini had to die.

Mullah Said put his glasses on. He studied the CNN report listing Jake's assignments in the US Air Force, a wedding picture of Jake and Laila, and the fact that the US Air Force had been looking for him. Then the report went on to speculate that Jake could be in Iran. The Fox News clipping was similar but at the end it went on and on about the Iranian regime being an enemy of America. The BBC assessment of the situation just stated facts without any speculation of Jake's whereabouts.

Said went back and forth between original copies and the translated version. After a five minute study, he passed the file to the judge on his right. Over the rim of his glasses he said, "Treason is a very serious offense. According to the Iranian Islamic law, such a crime is immediately punishable by death."

Ali's spirit lifted, "The Dareini's *Mofsed fel-arz*." He sighed. "They should be dealt with accordingly." Ali referred to the corrupt conditions caused by unbelievers and unjust people who threaten social and political well-being.

All three judges nodded.

"We need more evidence of the husband being in Iran with an army."

Ali was surprised. If Laila was an Iranian *without* international attention, the judge would've rubber stamped this request immediately.

"As we speak, we have agents scouring all the hotels in Zahedan and interviewing Revolutionary Guards. As a tall, white man, Jake Hudley should be easy to spot and remember."

Said received the reports back from the judge on his right and passed them over to the judge on the left. He took his glasses off and placed them on the desk.

"Brother Ali, you're a dedicated servant to our country and a capable man from a reputable family. I am confident that you will be able to back your accusation of Laila Dareini and Jake Hudley with more proof."

Ali realized that the Mullah might need to be reminded of the words of the Supreme Leader. He said, "If one permits an infidel to continue in his role as a corrupter of the earth, the infidel's moral suffering will be all the worse. If one kills the infidel, and this stops him from perpetrating his misdeeds, his death will be a blessing to him."

"You are right."

Ali saw a smile pull at Said's lips, assuring him he was on the interrogator's side. "I will do my best," Ali said.

"This session is terminated." Said pointed his palm towards a door to the back room. "Let's have *chai*."

Ali responded, "No." It was *taraf,* an Iranian tradition to always refuse an offer. Then the giver would insist and the receiver capitulate. In fact, Ali really did not want to linger as he needed to get back to the office to check in on any new developments after the confrontational exchange with the prosecutor earlier.

After Said insisted, Ali accepted to join them for tea.

They moved to the back room where they carried on their conversation. Ali could not ask directly if Ladjervardi had been backbiting about him, but at the same time could not decode anything in the judges' conversation to suggest one way or the other.

***

Negar grabbed a chador, wrapped it around her head, and ran down the steps to answer the doorbell. Upon opening the door, a man in brown pants and white shirt stood before her. *Who is this?* He was accompanied by two Revolutionary Guards wearing khaki uniforms and holding guns.

"*Salam,*" the man said. He had an unfriendly demeanor.

"*Salam.*" Negar clenched the chador and wondered about the purpose of the visit.

After a pause, he said, "My name is Ali Mohmed."

"What … what can I do for you?"

"I am Laila Dareini's Interrogator. I work for the Sixth Division of the Courts of the Islamic Revolution."

Negar's chest tightened as fear ran cold inside her. Avoiding eye contact with the man, she said, "Is Laila okay?"

"Can I come in?"

There was no possible way she could refuse his request.

"Maman, Mr. Mohmed is here to see us. Put your chador on."

"Thank you." He passed through the door following Negar's steps into her home. The guards stayed outside.

Negar went past the kitchen table and invited the guest to sit on a sofa. "Can I get you tea?"

"No. No." *Taraf.*

She went by the sink and poured some tea in a glass and placed it in front of him on a table. "How is Laila?"

"She is in Evin prison. Of course, it's not like living at home. Given her situation, we want to help her."

Negar tried hard to hide her true feelings. *Help her?* "Is her health okay?"

"She is doing her best. What I want to find out from you is if you have talked to her husband. Before the court can make a final decision on her case, it is necessary for us to make some routine checks."

"No, we haven't heard from him."

Ali looked straight at Negar. "Did you not call him in America? Has he not tried to get in touch with you, knowing that his wife is in custody?"

She was careful answering his questions. "Yes, I called many times. No one answered the phone. I haven't been able to connect with him."

Negar's mother and father approached.

"Mr. Mohmed works at Evin prison. He has questions about Laila and Jake."

"How is my Laila? I have not slept many a night after she was snatched away from me."

"She is doing her best."

"Son, you should listen to this broken-winged bird. My heart aches day and night. If you could give us some relief, Allah will bless you."

"If you can tell me where Jake Hudley is we might be able to help."

Maman could not hold herself together, her body trembled. Negar was worried her sugar level might be too high as she couldn't sleep, except for short naps on the couch. "Please, I beg you," Maliheh wailed.

Negar went to her and held her hand. "Maman, please go to your room. Baba you too."

Negar noticed a sharp pain in her side where the surgery was done. Stress did that. So far the conversation with Ali only made her angry, but she had to control herself; any slip of the tongue could be disastrous.

"When was the last time you talked to him?" Ali asked.

Negar tried to recall. So much had happened since her last conversation with her brother-in-law. "I can't remember exactly. It was over a month ago."

"You remember well enough. I believe you're lying."

A fire threatened to erupt from her mouth, but she controlled her emotions. "I'm telling you the truth. Allah is my witness."

He made a clicking sound with his mouth, indicating disapproval. "Don't mention Allah again. You don't deserve the mention of His elevated name." His eyes grew bigger, like a fierce dog.

She subdued her emotion. "I can call Jake now for you."

"Okay. Call."

She dialed and after three rings she forwarded the handset to Ali to let him hear the remainder. Laila's greeting came on. It was hard to listen to even without this man sitting in her home. He hung up and passed the phone back to her.

"Do you think he is in Iran?"

She was surprised by his assumptions. "I don't know."

"I came here to help you but you are not helping. I'm a patient person. I always get what I want. I could order the Guards to search every corner of this place, but, no. I'm a nice person. I would not order them to do that. I'm leaving now. If you hear *anything* let me know." He handed her a card.

"Has Laila been charged yet? We were informed that a court date for her trial is coming soon."

"Yes, she has been charged. I want to save her from a very grave consequence. It is important that you find out where Jake Hudley is and let me know."

Save her. Negar's confusion about Ali's visit and request reached a new height. She cradled the warm glass of tea while her face turned to the window. *What is he really up to?* She replied, "Okay, I will. Could we visit her sometime soon?"

"Tomorrow afternoon at 3:00 pm."

***

Negar held the gate open while her parents stepped onto the street. She locked it behind her and all three headed towards the main road. Negar's uneasiness continued—Maliheh and Abbas insisted on visiting Laila too. But after their last journey to Evin, Abbas' blood pressure reached a dangerously high level, staying elevated for days until it was brought down with red beet juice, prayers, and meditation. Lately Baba had been constantly brooding over his government pension being cut off, another way for the state to torture them. Maliheh's mental condition only worsened with lack of sleep. Dizziness, depression, and despair persisted.

Negar said, "Are you sure you want to travel to the prison?"

Abbas limped along with the help of his cane. "Negar, why do you keep asking? Of course we want to see Laila."

Maliheh said, "Abbas, you don't need to be so loud."

All three walked without saying a word until they reached Ferdozi Street, busy with pedestrians and cars. Standing on the side of the road were merchants selling nuts, dates, and rosewater. Negar's attention was on the yellow cabs headed to downtown Tehran. After many hails, one came to a halt with room for three.

When the vehicle stopped, another passenger got out and helped Abbas and Maliheh climb in. Negar and her parents sat together and the young Samaritan took a seat behind. Now that the cab was full, the driver focused on how fast he could reach downtown.

Once downtown, they took another cab to the prison. Negar sat by the window. Her eyes followed the pedestrians, bicycles, and cars but her thoughts battled the calamities around her life.

The vehicle stopped at a gate. The guard peeked at the passengers, then signaled the driver to proceed. In another few minutes, everyone emptied into the parking lot. They went in to confirm Laila was scheduled to receive visitors before taking a place in the "Visitors" line.

After a long wait in the heat and sun, a loud speaker announced for Negar's group to move into the visitor's hall. As the line inched forward, Negar felt butterflies in her stomach.

There were five women on the other side of the glass wall. She examined each face. She went by two detainees who had already found their families, and two with waving hands. Upon close consideration, none appeared to be Laila. Cramps chased the butterflies from her stomach.

Agitation filled her voice as she said, "Maman, where is Laila?"

She shook her mother's arm, hoping her mother had seen her sister. She moved farther to the other end of the waiting room, going around family members until she reach the wall.

After examining all the faces a second time, none looked like Laila. *Are they playing a joke? It would be very cruel for Ali to deceive her in such a way.* She looked again and discovered one face without a family. The one in the middle. When she got closer, the woman waived furiously, asking her to come closer. *Laila?*

"Oh, my God."

She placed her hand on the glass where Laila had placed hers. Her sister had lost so much weight she was unrecognizable. Negar waived her parents in. Guilt ate at her conscience.

"What have they done to you?"

Her sister's eyes were sunken, showing bones around them. Her skin was dry and yellowish, indicating lack of nutrition, and her clothes hung loose on her body.

Laila's eyes lit as she purposely took a deep look at her father, sister, and mother. Slowly she said, "I am so happy to see you."

Maliheh covered her mouth with her palm, tears streaming down her cheeks; she choked on a burst of wailing. In shock, Abbas stared at his daughter, shook his head and whispered, "It's not possible."

Negar made an eating gesture. "Eat more food. Food. Food."

Laila came closer to the glass, with exaggerated lips movement, she said, "They will kill me soon. Look after Jake, Megan, and Dillon."

"No, no. Have hope." Negar vigorously shook her head.

"I don't want you to go," Maliheh burst into a wail, clawing at the glass separating her from Laila.

"I had a dream. I was flying like a free bird. I will see you on the other side." Laila lifted her hand above her head and her gaze towards the ceiling.

"You are my sister. How can I live without you?"

The guard interrupted the conversation with a shout for everyone to leave. It was hard, harder than last time, knowing that poor Laila was disappearing into herself. No one wanted to leave but the prisoners were ushered to a door where they filed out of the space. Negar's heart ached seeing her sister struggle to walk, her face having aged fifty years in mere weeks. She lifted her head towards the ceiling. *Please God, how is she going to survive?*

The guard yelled again. The family members, all in tears, emptied the visitor's hall. Negar squeezed her parents' hands and assured them that she would double her effort to get her sister freed from this awful jail.

The Dareini's were the last to leave. They caught a taxi for the return trip home.

When they arrived at Khak-Negar Street and got out of the cab, a man walking toward them stopped and blocked their way.

Negar remembered having seen his face before, but could not recall where.

"*Salam,*" he said

"*Salam,*" Negar replied tentatively. Her memory came back suddenly, sharp and clear: He was the guard who came with Orie's bill of death—the one she'd spat on. *What's going on?*

"I just happened to pass by your house and noticed five guards stationed there waiting for you."

A headache pounded Negar like a sledge hammer. All she wanted was to be in her home, alone.

"Waiting … waiting for what?" she blurted.

The man lowered his head, a sigh of humility. "They want to arrest you."

"You're a guard. Why are you warning us?"

The man stepped closer. "I *was* a guard. Not anymore. I quit because the Iranian regime is not just. I am a Muslim, but I know now that the Ayatollah is using Islam to protect himself."

Negar's suspicion was running high. "You quit? How do you know the guards are waiting for us?"

"I know one of them and he told me so. This is quite a coincidence that I've run into you."

So far Abbas studied the conversation from a few feet away. He limped toward the small group.

"Maybe it's not a coincidence." He raised up his hands and his eyes towards the sky. "Maybe somebody is finally trying to help us."

After thanking the man, they headed to Maliheh's sister's place instead.

***

Laila entered Ali's office blindfolded, Maryam following close behind. After removing the hated material, Maryam disappeared and Ali bade Laila to sit.

"I saw your parents yesterday."

Laila shook her head slightly so as not to show the man her disgust with his actions. *Now what is he up to? Has he not done enough damage to an innocent family?*

"Where did you see them?"

"At their home." Ali's words commanded power.

"How are they?" Her brief and harried time with them at the viewing earlier had relayed nothing but their sorrow.

"They looked fine to me. Negar, your sister, asked permission to see you. You saw them earlier today, did you not? How did it go?"

It disgusted her that he asked. Was he truly so oblivious to the pain he was caused? "Gut wrenching. They didn't even recognize me. I saw only a profound sadness in my parents' spirit. I don't know how much you care about the depth of our suffering, but they were far from *fine*."

"I want to help. I do."

She was weak, but she could use her last once of energy to fight back. This man wanted only to help himself.

"I think we have a different meaning of *help*. To me, inflicting pain is not helping."

"I have already shown you the way out of this situation."

"And what would that be?"

"Become a Muslim and you will be free."

"For me becoming a Muslim is *not* freedom. Here I am in a physical jail. Changing my religion without true conviction is like going to another kind of prison."

"I don't understand why it's so hard. Most people in your situation embrace the faith and are shown leniency. But it's up to you. I *am* trying to help you. The court wants to raise your accusation to treason, for which the penalty is certain death. If you convert, I can convince them to spare your life."

Laila blinked her eyes, fighting back tears. "Why treason? What have I done?"

"It is your husband. He's in Iran with an army to rescue you."

Jake's in Iran? She didn't know what to think. Was it another fabrication of the Ayatollah's regime?

"That's not true. He wouldn't do that. Why would he take such a risk? No. He's not here."

Ali looked and acted different than he had the last time she'd seen him. He now sported a beard and an unnamed shadow passed over his face. He'd never spoken so softly with her before, never shown a thread of kindness—and his eyes lacked the hatred from before.

"I am seriously thinking of quitting my job. There's a lot of pressure for interrogators to convert non-Muslims to Islam. When I am gone, whoever replaces me will be lot harder on you. They will succeed where I have not." He got up. A restlessness seemed to brew in him. "I see Orie in you. I desperately wanted to see him live; he was a smart, kind boy. Don't give them a reason to kill you, Laila."

His conscience was bothering him but his concern was misplaced. He truly believed that saying the words to convert also meant the spirit was willing and all would be forgiven. But Allah already knew her heart and she had nothing to be forgiven for.

"When did this change happen?"

"What do you mean?"

"The decision to quit?

He took a few steps towards the door and then back. "It's crossed my mind a lot lately. Often after a session with you."

"All the allegations against me are false, truly false. I'm telling you the truth. My religion has nothing to do with the love of my home country. Perhaps *you* can help me get out of this prison?" Laila pleaded as tears slipped down her cheeks.

"That would be impossible. If the prosecutor, the judges, or the ministry of Justice find out I helpped you in any way, other than advising you of converting to Islam, then *my* life would be worth nothing in their eyes. Don't you see?"

With too many important pieces of information to process, Laila didn't know where to start. *Jake in Iran is the most unbelievable idea I've ever heard.*

Politely Laila responded, "I understand." Her insides trembled as they tumbled and turned upside down. *But what if he is?* What could that possibly mean? "Thank you for the advice." *Did I really say that aloud?* "I will think on it."

Chapter 22

Jake cracked his eyes open as he wavered on the edge of consciousness. With a faint awareness he tried to figure out where he was, but couldn't, and drifted back to sleep.

When he woke again, this time he tried harder to concentrate—feeling vibrations and occasional shaking. For certain he lay in a moving vehicle. With a determined willpower he managed to hold his eyelids open long enough to see clouds in the sky through a window above him.

He went back and forth between awareness and sleep, struggling against whatever they'd drugged him with. He internalized that the driver spoke in Farsi to another person in the front seat. But, with his hands and legs tied, he lay trapped in the fetal position in the back of a van—unable to do anything about it.

Pain coursed through one leg, probably from some wound. The soreness in his neck likely came from being in an awkward position for too long. The drowsiness was hard to fight. When he saw a bag taped to his chest, he felt better knowing Maya was with him. He wasn't certain at what point he realized he'd been kidnapped, but mental fatigue meant he couldn't understand the whole situation. However, with every passing moment, his thought power improved—still, he fell asleep again.

Loud voices shouting in broken English at the front of the stationary vehicle, forced him awake. With an American accent, someone said, "You can't go inside."

The driver said, "Jake Hudley, American. American, inside."

"No, no. Park over there. You can't go inside."

"We work for Americans. We kidnapped Jake Hudley. We take him inside the base."

"How many times do I have to tell you? This vehicle is not authorized to enter the base. Back out of here immediately and park at the verification spot. I'll get an officer to check the van and he'll give you more information."

Where the hell am I? With his foot, Jake pushed his body towards the side of the van until his head rose enough to see two guards with guns out the open window. The view looked familiar. He was at the entrance of the US Military base in Kandahar.

No, no, no. How did this happen? He shook his head, not trusting his eyes. Then adrenaline rushed through him like a shot of morphine and all his joint pain and wooziness evaporated.

The van backed up into a new parking area a couple hundred yards away from the gate. He could see a long stretch of desert between him and the mountains in the distance. Jake tried to trace his memory backward, desperately wanting to know what had happened to him. But his mind failed him.

Just then, the thundering roar of a transport plane filled the sky. The driver of the van got out. Perhaps he went to explain to the duty guard why he needed to drive inside. Jake's only conclusion was that he'd been captured by American agents in Iran, and brought to this base to be loaded onto a transport plane back to US soil.

Jake struggled against his bonds, but with hands and legs tied up, he felt defeated. He thought back to the moment they'd left the safe house. Between then and now, the events remained foggy. He must have been drugged. *But by who and when?*

Ten minutes later Jake heard the crunch of boots on gravel, a sound he was wellused to during his time in Afghanistan. When the footsteps came close to the vehicle, a feverish voice said, "I am telling you the truth. Please, listen to me."

The American male said, "Where is he?" Jake slumped down, closed his eyes and pretended to be passed out as the visitor peeked through the rear window. Then the footsteps walked back to the front.

"Where did you find him?"

"In Isfahan."

"You captured him in Isfahan, Iran?" The tone was loaded with puzzlement.

"Yes."

"What's his name?"

"Jake Hudley."

"I don't have any information about him. Why is he here? Who ordered you to do this?"

"NSA. National Security Agency."

Ira was right. The NSA was after him as soon as he entered Iran. How were they tracking him? *Damn, damn, damn.* Filaments of memory wavered just out of reach until one became startlingly clear. Ira told him the device, AH-304, carried some form of GPS beacon—one he'd thought he'd rendered inoperable. *Another of Andy's glitches. Shit.* He was certain he'd turned it off, but after texting Makalla, Maya must have inadvertently sent positioning coordinates to a satellite and they'd found him again. The NSA likely got involved after Laila's detention in Iran because *he* used to work at the Space Surveillance System. And now, he was about to be sent back to the US, certain to face treason charges.

With a southern US accent, the American said, "What's your name?"

"Firooz."

"What's the name of the NSA contact in Isfahan?"

"Kamali."

"I'll check with the NSA agents at the base." He walked around several times, probably checking for bombs attached to the van before yelling, "Move back another hundred yards and wait."

Too many attempts had been made by Al Qaeda to get into the base to permit any non-US military vehicle within several hundred yards of the gate. In 2006, a man pretending to be a food supplier got inside and, during lunch time, entered the cafeteria, opened fire, and killed twenty-two Americans. Since then, extra procedures had been put in place.

The van moved again. Several times the driver went to the gate and returned until it got dark. Jake couldn't sleep like this, not only was it awkward and painful, but his thoughts circled around his future, his children, and Laila.

A loud crack woke Jake. The driver yelled, "Wake up! Wake *up*." Two gun shots rang out, followed by the vehicle shaking on its axels. Then three more shots echoed.

The back door flung open. Two men appeared: one hooked his hands under Jake's arms, the other grabbed his legs—both pulled his body from the van. As they moved him, Jake saw a face by the side of the van and another hand holding a gun pointing at him. The man had difficulty keeping his hand steady as if badly wounded. He managed his stance with one hand leaning against the van.

Jake vigorously shook his head knowing the man was aiming to shoot at them. With mouth taped he made a whining sound to alert the two carrying him. A gunshot rang through the air.

Jake slammed to the ground. Pain flared in his back. One of his rescuers rushed to the van, pumped out a few bullets and then returned to Jake. A sharp, hot pain shot through his leg. He was hit. The two men shoved him in the back seat of a car and sped off.

***

Tom sat in his office with special agent Hans Schilder engaged in small talk—baseball, kids, vacation—when Tom glanced at the wall clock before picking up his cell phone and made a couple of calls.

"They're on their way," he said. Then both men changed the subject to the latest public outrage on the NSA daily collection of phone and email records.

Hans flew from Houston on an Air Force plane to attend this meeting on an urgent request made by the NSA director.

Linda Moore, dressed in navy slacks and a blue jacket, hurried in carrying a folder. Dave Scott, looking more haggard and unkempt than usual, entered the office with his laptop and week old BO overlaid with fresh deodorant. Tom closed the door.

"Thank you all for coming on such short notice. My appreciation to Hans Schilder." Tom waved a hand towards him, then pulled a chair out and sunk into it. "As you know, the Hudley case has been lifted to a national risk concern. Homeland is in it now. We need all the big guns we can get to take care of this issue."

Tom watched the quiet assassin. Hans, born in Langenhain, Germany, was a sought-after agent for his unique skill set, intelligence, and diligent work ethic. In his native land, he played a key role in a foiled attempt to murder a German Chancellor. His credentials were impressive, even Mossad hired him during a rash of bus bombing in Jerusalem. In 2007 the NSA put him on payroll when tensions between Iran, the US, and Israel reached a critical point.

"Dave, how about you start?"

With a few clicks on the remote, the Samsun Smart TV came alive. Dave tapped on a few keys to project a broadcast from his laptop.

"In a hurry, we whipped up a program to track the device's GPS echo as it infrequently interfaces with the StealthSat showing us Hudley's—"

"Hans, FYI, Hudley has in his possession the world's most sophisticated computing device, which he had no authorization to remove from the country, let alone bring to Iran. Serious shit." Tom's checks turned red.

Dave continued, "On this map of Iran, Pakistan, and Afghanistan, the red, blinking dot indicates the travel of this hardware from Isfahan to within proximity of the US Base in Kandahar. At the front of the base Jake remained for almost six hours before the device turned around, traveled another 20 miles and disappeared."

"What do you mean disappeared? What kind of a device is it?" Hans shot a critical look at Dave.

"The signal disintegrated and we lost contact. As for the device, all I can tell you is it's a powerful computer, satellite phone, smart phone, and internet browser all in one. If it's GPS is tampered with it activates a transponder which sends a signal to our SteathSat, which is then relayed to a ground station, and the information goes to a military database. Something's happened to prevent the back-up signal from being transmitted."

"What could that be?" Hans pondered the situation.

"It could be many things. Once the transponder is activated it transmits regardless of the device being turned on or off. Therefore, one possible scenario could be that the battery was yanked out."

The boss read Dave's blank face, indicting his presentation was over. "Thanks Dave. Linda?"

"Here the most important issue is what happened in the vicinity of the Base's entrance." She was very good at outplaying the techie. "Two of our contacts were shot and Hudley fled the scene. When we talked to the military police, one reported that Hudley had his hands and legs tied up lying at the back of a van with his mouth taped. Clearly, he was incapacitated. What this tells me is that an army came to Hudley's rescue. Before this escape, he avoided two other such captures by our agents in Iran. This. Is. Serious." Linda's words rolled with her eyes toward Tom.

Tom nodded his head. "I agree."

Every gaze in the room turned to the expert. During the two presentations Hans thumbed through the pages of a background report he received on arrival. He was in Iran in 2008-2009 as part of a US and Israeli mission to plant software bugs in the network controlling the nuclear program, hyper-activating the centrifugal systems until the parts flew out of control and prevented the further killing of scientists.

"Iranians are hungry for our technology. They'll do anything to get their hands on it. Once, they captured a drone and reverse-engineered it to collect technical knowledge. The Iranians knew that Hudley was being followed by the US Intelligence agents. This is my assumption. He's getting the protection he needs to have this computer delivered to the right place."

Linda said, "Have you seen anything like this before?"

"No. We cannot underestimate the Iranians. It must be the job of a very intelligent army. This is better than what the CIA or NSA are capable of."

Tom did not like Hans' comment. He cleared his throat. "We have to do our homework. Dave, find out everything you can about this product."

"I know that the test site for the device, whose code is Assignee Holiday, is the Space Surveillance System in Lackland, Texas, where Hudley was an employee."

Tom nodded, "Get out there, then. Linda, do another check on Hudley: his family members, friends, co-workers. Dig into his past, especially his *Iranian* wife. They're in on this together. It's the only thing that makes any sense. Go back over his hobbies, phone calls, Facebook page—"

"We've done most of that already, Tom. I'll be preparing a report for you soon."

"Give a copy to Hans and Dave. We have to work as a team to bring this guy to justice. With all the evidence piling up on him, this has become more than a possible case of treason. Going into enemy territory with a highly-classified instrument is *not* what the president wants to hear about. This is making us look very bad indeed."

"Should we get the CIA and FBI involved?"

Hans said, "There's a potential for a criminal act here, which dictates their involvment. In any case, we'll need warrants to do searches and the proper authorities to handle them."

Tom said, "This is good. We've got a plan. Let's meet again tomorrow afternoon. I'll inform the White House and State Department. In fact, the President is meeting with his security advisor as we speak."

***

Charles sat in his wing-backed chair flipping channels again. In fact, he'd been surfing local and national stations all day, except for washroom breaks or food. Even the tomatoes, which had started to perk up, wilted with neglect. Nights were no better as he couldn't turn off his mind. He'd left Ruth in a cold bed more and more often as the heat of his anger smashed the TV remote, even in the early hours of the morning.

It was already late in the evening, time for the "Situation Room," a news journal hosted by Wolf Platt. The host started the show with a report on a persistently poor US economy, followed by flooding in Nice, France. Halfway into this weather-related segment, "Breaking News" flashed on the screen.

Moments later, a picture of Jake appeared in the upper right hand corner. Chuck straightened his back and moved his body closer to the edge of the seat.

With a grave tone, Wolf read, "This just in. Two agents killed in Jake Hudley's escape from the Kandahar US Military Base."

Chuck shook his head. All along he thought Jake was in Iran. "What's he doing in Afghanistan?"

Wolf's face covered the entire screen when he said, "It is reported that a classified computer, developed by the US Military in Nevada, being tested at Space Surveillance System in Lackland, Texas, is in Jake's Hudley's possession." A picture of the Base's entrance came into full view.

Wolf introduced Rick Ramos, a retired US Air Force intelligence officer and CNN military analyst. "Two dead in front of a US military base in Kandahar and the suspect flees the scene. What can you tell us about this Rick?"

"Yes. Especially in Kandahar, local Afghanis are not allowed close proximity to the Base; there have been too many incidents of suicide bombing. From what I know of these types of situations, Hudley was likely captured and being brought in for his journey back home to face justice. It appears that he managed to free himself and kill these two officers."

Then the camera turned to John Brook, sitting next to Wolf. "John, you've been following the story since Hudley's wife was *supposedly* arrested in Iran."

John turned to the camera, "Wolf, according to a reliable report, a highly-classified device built by the military, *with* leading technologies, has gone missing. Also, there's a speculation—I repeat it is a *speculation* at this time—that Hudley's wife is not actually under arrest by Iranian authorities. In other words, the Iranians are likely pretending to have made this arrest, giving Hudley reason to travel to Iran with this device."

Wolf said, "Rick, you've been in the intelligence business for some time. Have you ever seen anything like this?"

"No. This is the most sophisticated effort as yet for Iranians to gain access to our technologies." He shook his head with every word.

The program broke for a commercial. Charles wiped sweat from his forehead. He couldn't believe what he'd just heard; Laila's imprisonment fabricated to allow Jake sell tech to the Iranian government?

Lies, lies, lies.

***

Linda pulled the car out of the La Quinta Inn parking lot and veered toward Military Drive West when her cell phone chimed. She pushed the "talk" icon on the phone perched on a Bluetooth device. It was an FBI detective wanting to inform her that he was in front of the Burke residence. Linda was well aware that Andrew Burke was still under surveillance.

"What's up?"

"We had to go inside Burke's house." He sighed, "You won't believe it."

"Now what?" She heard sirens sound in the distance over the phone.

"He tried to take his own life. He's still warm, but I have my doubts. EMS should be here any second."

Linda assumed they decided to go in after not sighting him for a certain period of time.

"I'll be there shortly."

After terminating the call, her eyes teared up. She stopped her vehicle at the mouth of the parking area. To acknowledge a honk behind, Linda opened the window and waved the driver past.

Her son had been in rehab for drug abuse—had attempted suicide several times. *What drove him to it? This can only be proof-positive he knew something crucial and could no longer live with it ... I hope whatever it is, he didn't take it to the grave.* It took her several minutes to compose herself.

Before the Detective's tragic call, she'd been on her way to see the Chief Information Officer at the Space Surveillance System in Lackland, Texas, within whose department Andrew Burke was an employee. This meeting would now have to wait. She wiped her cheeks with the back of her hand and headed to the scene.

Chapter 23

Jake placed his right arm on his leg where the raw bullet wound pulsated with pain, his mind still foggy from the drugs his kidnappers injected him with. On this journey, every bump or turn of the vehicle made his misery worsen. He wished the piercing ache would go away, but it never did. The only thing that helped minimize the agony was muscle relaxation techniques, as he focused on pleasant memories back in Texas.

After a long time traveling, the car finally stopped. The two men in the front jumped out of the vehicle and opened the back doors. On one side, a man lifted Jake's shoulders and from the other side his partner grabbed Jake's leg.

"No! No! It hurts."

"Sorry, my friend." Leaning forward, holding a shoe with one hand and lifting his thigh with the other, the man pulled Jake's body out inch by excruciating inch until he stood on the road, less than two feet away from an elaborate front entrance. The driver pressed the doorbell. Jake didn't know where he was and he didn't care to ask. Violent streaks of pain consumed his mind as they splinted through his leg.

Minutes later a man with a long grey beard appeared at the door framed into the concrete wall of a mosque. With helping hands, Jake was shuffled into a narrow hallway. The bearded man, wearing the traditional garb of an Imam, led the group to a courtyard, then into a room with chairs, sofas, and a table. Limping along with support under his arms, Jake tried to endure the least discomfort before falling onto a wooden chair.

"My name is Karim. I am very happy to see you come back to our city, Isfahan, again." His eyes were big, and a broad smile spread across his face. He spoke English well with only a slight accent. The Imam placed a chair in front of Jake then lifted his wounded leg on it. After salutations and a bow, the other two men disappeared.

With eyes half closed, Jake managed to say, "Th- thank you for recuing me." He adjusted his buttocks to ease the pain but it didn't help. "Otherwise, I'd be on a plane back to the US right now." Jake pulled the wet, blood-stained hem up his leg. On his lower calf a dark brown blob appeared. "Damn, damn."

Karim said with a grin, "The wound looks terrible. But swear words close to a mosque might make Allah angry."

Jake appreciated this man's sense of humor. "Sorry, we don't want to offend anyone, especially Allah."

"I'll be back to take care of your leg." He disappeared and returned with a medical kit that he spread on the table. "I'm trained as a surgeon."

"Where?"

"Chicago Medical School."

"You're also a priest. No, no. I mean a Muslim priest." Jake examined the fresh bandage, cream, needle, and disinfecting liquid. He raised his head.

"Imam, that's my title." The voice was firm.

"What are you doing here? Why are you not in the US?"

"In 2004 I came to fight the Iranian regime. Since it came into power, the government has been slaughtering our people, the Mujahidins. When I arrived, I couldn't practice medicine because I'm educated in America. The government made sure I did not practice my craft, and I found out quickly that this policy also makes Iranians hate America. In order to serve my people, I decided to become an Imam."

Jake was interested but confused at the same time. Karim tied a new tourniquet before removing the old one and the blood-soaked temporary bandage. Needle-fire shredded his veins as he grit his teeth to keep from calling out. Jake, light-headed from loss of blood, turned away from his wounds.

Five minutes after the doctor administered the anesthetic injection, the pain became bearable. Slowly it lifted the brain fog. Jake fumbled with a sense of gratitude and helplessness at the same time. "Thanks for helping me."

"Let me know when the pain is totally gone."

"Okay. Can I ask you a question?"

"Of course."

"How did I get here?"

"Two men brought you."

"I know that. But the last twenty-four hours seem like a puzzle where not all the pieces are fitting together."

"What do you remember?"

He wasn't sure how open he could be with this person. "I was on my way to Tehran when I got ambushed by two or three men. The next thing I remember is waking up in Afghanistan with my hands and legs tied, lying in the back of a van. Those two men who brought me here also rescued me from being transported back to the US. There was a gun fight between them. I got shot and here I am."

"Those two men are my people. You are here because Ira asked me to help."

Now the picture grew clearer. "You know why I'm here in Iran then?"

"Yes. You are a romantic guy. In Iranian literature we have our own Romeo and Juliet story called Laila and Majnu. You are after your Laila. I think you should change your name to Majnu." He laughed.

Jake's leg muscles had relaxed enough to allow him a laugh without consequence. Inside he was still very worried. "How can I get my wife out of Evin Prison and escape from Iran?"

"Dozens of Mujahidins are already in that awful place. I wish they could taste freedom before they are executed. But I can't help them. If you can find a way, let me know." He lifted his hands up in the air and raised his head towards the ceiling, a gesture of begging for Allah's assistance.

That wasn't the answer Jake was looking for. "Is it that difficult?"

Karim made a clicking sound with tongue while shifting his head back and forth. "Difficult? No. *Impossible*."

Karim's fingers gripped Jake's foot like a vice; his other hand jabbed a forked tool into the open flesh.

Jake turned away again. Ira appeared at the door.

"Jake, good to see you."

"Thanks for your help, man." He noticed something missing. "Where's Meena?"

"She's on assignment." He came closer and watched the doctor dig out a bullet. "Thank goodness we have a doctor here." Ira looked around. "Where's your computer?"

"Got rid of it. Couldn't travel with it. NSA was tracking me."

The glow in Ira's face flickered out. "What did you do exactly?" He blinked rapidly, clearly distressed.

"Threw it out."

"Threw it out, where?" The muscles in Ira's face tightened.

"Out of the car."

"Out of the window of the car? I need more details."

Jake didn't really want to talk about abandoning the only thing capable of helping him save Laila, and Ira's reaction was pissing him off.

"What's the problem?"

"Jake, I spent five thousand friggin' dollars to get it back for you, and now I find you just threw it out like an empty can."

"Ira, calm down. I had to destroy it. Yes, I owe you five-grand."

"Destroy? Why? How?"

"As we were traveling on the highway, I rolled down the window and just threw it out."

"Where did it land!"

"I don't know. I don't remember much; I was kind of in a lot of pain at the time. For all I know it was run over by a truck."

Ira's hands flew into the air. The color of his face changed from red to near purple. He ran his fingers into his hair making it stand straight up. "Jake, Jake. What the hell did you do that for?"

Jake could not understand his reaction.

Ira took a deep breath and exhaled it slowly. "Karim, we have to get out of here as fast as possible. I'm sure US agents are out there looking for him as we speak."

"Right after I put this bandage on, you can leave."

"Not so fast; I'm starving."

***

Later that day, shortly after sunset, Jake managed to hobble on one foot and walk with the help of crutches. Ira walked beside him in case he needed help. Once outside the mosque, Jake saw a young man holding open the back door of a hearse.

With a few more hops, Jake stood on one foot, handed the crutches to Ira, turned around and sat on the back bumper. With the help of Ira and the young man, he maneuvered his highly-medicated body inside until he sat on a foam mattress with his back resting against the side of the vehicle.

Once Ira was inside, the man closed the door and they left for Tehran. This was the strangest situation he'd ever been in. Ira lay next to him on the foam. The air hung humid and hot. Being in this position for hours, next to a man who he really didn't know if he should trust, was not a trip he looked forward to.

According to Iranian custom, full respect was given to a dead person and the family could refuse a police or Revolutionary Guard's request to check inside the hearse. Karim also had two cars with armed men behind and before the hearse as an extra safety precaution.

Once the vehicle sped up and stopped turning corners, Jake knew he was on the highway to Tehran. *I've made it.* It was the mantra Jake repeated to himself with closed eyes—his way of praying to the Universe for help.

Jake took a moment to appreciate what had happened to him, and was thankful for the courage and strength to have made it so far. Knowing that agents were after him, he could've been in a different place other than a hearse traveling to see his beloved.

"Ira, I can't thank you enough for everything." There was something different in the air between them now. The hesitation was almost gone; instead Jake found it replaced with a congenial sense of camaraderie.

"You're welcome."

He still wasn't entirely sure what to make of this rogue Mossad *helper*, but he needed to talk to someone.

"I miss Laila and the kids so much. It was hard being in Afghanistan for two years without them. I had their pictures everywhere. My workstation, wallet, the wall next my bed." He recalled how he used to talk for hours with his wife as he sipped coffee and she cooked. He pushed down the collar of his shirt over his left shoulder where letters 'J' and 'L' were intertwined in a heart. He rubbed the tattoo. Jake continued, "How about you? Are you married?"

Ira was silent for long moment. "I was once." The words came with lot of effort.

"Where is she now? Why aren't you with her?"

There was a softness in Ira's eyes he hadn't let show before. The man blinked; one moment he was lying beside Jake in a stuffy hearse and the next he was a million miles away and ten years in the past, reliving for Jake a life he tried to forget.

Chapter 24

During his time in Canada, years before moving back to Iran, Ira Kohan found himself on a flight from Toronto to a sunnier, much warmer place for a well-earned vacation. When he walked through the sliding doors of Nadi International Airport, a wall of hot air hit his face. The warmth made the travel tension shed from his body. Leaving winter behind was worth the two-day travel to the Fiji Island.

Behind other vacationers, Ira pulled his rolling suitcase until the driver of the mini bus placed it at the back. The vibration of the vehicle lulled Ira to sleep even though he tried to keep awake; he looked forward to an all-inclusive Tanoa Waterfront Hotel.

During the first two days of his stay, Ira just explored the paradise resort. The food, beaches, bars, pools, evening entertainment, all made him wish he could stay longer.

On the third day Ira slid into the passenger seat of a taxi, showed the driver an address gifted him by an islander, and they were off. They veered to the right after passing through the resort gate, then soon swung to the left onto Kings Road, surrounded by great palms, banana trees, and other lush vegetation native to the tropical paradise.

About ten minutes later, the driver took a right turn onto a road with sugar cane fields on both sides shortly before he stopped at Kruepa Restaurant. Ira paid the driver then went in and followed a host to a seat on an outdoor patio overlooking a pond. He took a deep breath of fresh air and the warmth refreshed every cell of his body. *Perfect.*

When Ira turned away from the water to face approaching footsteps, his eyes grew wide. A goddess of stunning beauty, dropped from the blue heavens, greeted him and held out a menu.

"Can I get you a drink?"

With mumbles and hums he managed, "Beer … ah … please."

As she moved away, he watched her long black hair sweep across her back tied in a ponytail. The aroma of Indian spice filled the air. As Ira read the list of appetizers, entrées, and main courses, all with local names and English description, his mind kept drifting toward the server's lips, slim face, and chiseled beauty.

Occasionally peeking over the menu to see where she was, he noticed something happening inside him, but couldn't figure out what.

When he saw her coming in his direction again, he absorbed every move she made. After depositing the glass on the table she asked, "Are you ready to order?" She had the sweetest, gentlest voice he'd ever heard.

"Not yet."

"Take your time. I'll come back in a few minutes."

He took a serious look at her sharp features and dark skin. Her large eyes swallowed him—he couldn't look away. *Is this love?* It had never happened to him before.

As she turned, he watched her go to another table where she interacted with the patrons and scribbled on a notepad. When she passed by a second time, Ira waved her over. He ordered curried lamb instead of sea food. She was of Indian decent and he wanted to impress her with his culinary preferences.

Sipping the drink, Ira witnessed many more patrons coming in groups of two and four being seated around the tables closest to him. His contact had been right. This was a highly sought after location and within ten minutes, the restaurant was full. As he watched the activities, Ira's attention kept returning to the dark skinned, slim server with the bright eyes. Every glance at her, made his insides quiver.

After she delivered the plate with lamb, salad, naan, and rice, Ira felt emboldened to ask, "What's your name?"

"Devi."

"Nice name, never heard of one like it. Does it have a meaning?"

She smiled. The teeth between her lips glistened like white marble. "It's a Hindu name. It means goddess." Shyness filled her face. "But at school the kids called me 'naughty girl'."

"No, you're not a naughty girl."

Devi turned around and walked to the next table. His eyes tracked her every move. He ate slowly. Around ten that evening he left the restaurant, returning to the resort.

That night he couldn't sleep thinking about Devi's long hair, and mahogany hued face. The way her simple dress clung to her body, and that impish twinkle in her eyes made his mind run like an endless waterfall as he thought of spending the rest of his life with her.

On the fourth day, he went back to the same restaurant but didn't see Devi. He asked after her at the bar and was told she only came to work there occasionally. Her main job was nursing at Lautoka Hospital.

By the fifth day Ira arrived at the big hospital. Standing at the front, with a bouquet of flowers in his hand, he wondered if he was actually going to see her again. He only had her first name. Probable Devi in Fiji was like Susan in Canada.

For ten minutes, he watched every person unload from the bus. Then, suddenly, there she was. Her glowing face and jet black hair forever imprinted on his mind.

"Good morning, Devi. These are for you."

She gave him a grave stare and walked away.

On the sixth day, Ira stood at the entrance of the hospital again watching the faces of the people arriving.

"Devi can I talk to you? I'm in love with you. I want to marry you."

She took the flowers and shook them at him, "Crazy white man! You bring me day old flowers and speak of love?" To Ira, English, Swedish or French were *white* people. He was Jewish!

She walked to a garbage bin, shoved them in and hurried away.

"Devi, please." But she disappeared inside.

On the seventh day Ira stood by the hospital with fresh flowers. When Devi appeared, he stepped over to her.

"Fresh flowers this time."

She smiled but accepted the bouquet.

"I haven't slept for three nights. I have to talk to you before I go crazy."

She looked at the flowers.

"Don't throw them away, please."

Devi shook her head. "Crazy, crazy, crazy. I feel sorry for you. I'll be at the Kruepa Restaurant at six tomorrow tonight. We can talk then."

On the eighth day Ira arrived at the restaurant with fresh flowers and took a seat in a corner of the patio, away from other patrons.

Again that night, he asked her to marry him.

"What is wrong with you? I don't know you. And if my brothers find out you're harassing me, they'll kill you."

"Can I talk to your family? Convince them that I'm not crazy?"

She walked away and came back with an invitation to meet her family.

On the ninth day, when Ira met Devi's parents, brothers, sisters, nieces, nephews, aunts, and uncles—twenty-six of them—the family enthusiastically gave their consent for marriage.

On the twelve day, after a Hindu ceremony, Ira and Devi were pronounced husband and wife. He also found out that because of her strong personality and need to micro-manage everybody's lives, the family was happy to see Devi travel to faraway Canada

***

Still in the hearse, Jake examined Ira's face for clues. His eyes brightened slightly and a shadow of sadness hovered over his features, both barely discernable by the highway light coming through the tinted window above Ira's head.

"What an amazing story. From what I know about you, which is little, I'd never have imagined you as such a romantic guy."

Those words put a sad smile on Ira's face. "Glorious times they were. I wish I could bury the feelings deep in my heart." He fingered the button on a walkie-talkie.

One side of Jake's ass was going numb, so he shifted his weight, stifling a groan. "What happened? Where is she now? Divorced?"

Ira's lips closed tight and his head shook vigorously. "Another time perhaps. Tell me more about your Laila. The fact that you are here, on your way to rescue your beloved tells me it should be the most romantic story I've ever heard."

Jake's heart filled with joy as he recalled the first moment he met Laila. "Unforgettable for me, yeah." Jake smiled. "It was the first day of spring. I was taking a few courses at San Antonio related to my military training. My friend Andy asked me to be his wing-man at an event on campus—something to do with World Religions. I wasn't interested but he insisted I go with him because he needed me to distract this girl Kristina's friends. You know, normal shit. The next day I had to take an exam about security procedures in the Afghanistan war. Passing the exam was extremely important and I wanted to be as fresh as I could. A night out wasn't on my schedule."

"But you went."

Jake paused to shift his body. "Reluctantly. But yes, I did. The event was held in an old building, probably built during the Spanish settlement." He cleared his throat and turned toward Ira. "I entered the main hall and when I scanned the rows upon rows of chairs and saw only a few dozen faces socializing, one hit me like a lightning bolt.

"The instant I saw her, I was mesmerized. Beautiful light-brown eyes and long golden-brown hair flowing past her shoulders. I was only ten feet away from her but her face glowed like a full moon. She was animated in her conversation with someone. I didn't stay long; I did my duty as a friend and knew I'd need my sleep for the next day. But when I left, I had an uncontrollable urge to look back. With her bright face, everyone else around her dimmed in existence."

Ira took another glance at the walkie-talkie. He'd been obsessed with this device since the journey started. Jake had wondered who he was signaling with Morse code, but there was no discernable pattern.

"Then what happened?"

"Like you, I couldn't sleep all night. Instead I tossed and turned in bed thinking about her."

"What about the exam the next day?"

"I was so tired, I barely passed."

Jake remembered the days after that first encounter, "That inner fire burned away all reasoning. I couldn't get her out of my mind—off the back of my eyelids when I shut them. I was going crazy … So, I enlisted my friend Andy's help and found a way to see her again."

"I had that same fire of love once. It burned me away." Ira's voice wavered. He cleared his throat and took a deep breath. Jake knew that sharing Devi's story had brought up more than love; there was a heavy sense of loss there too. *Maybe Ira gets it more than I think.*

The vehicle suddenly stopped. Ira pushed a button on the unit in his hand and spoke to the driver, who assured him that the way ahead was still safe.

When the quiet stretched unbearably long, Jake tried again, "So, what happened then?"

"What happened when?"

"Between you and Devi?"

***

Ira shook his head; the memories still hurt to touch. "When I lost her, it was my first time dealing with the death of someone so close to me. Devastating. I'll never forget how sad, desperate, and confused I was when she was diagnosed with a deadly disease." He sighed and closed his eyes.

"What happened to her?"

He continued playing with the communication device, an absent-minded habit, as the memories threatened to overwhelm him. He opened his eyes and said, "It's hard. Very hard for me to go there."

"Leaving it buried inside isn't the right approach. I can see there's a lot pain in you. By sharing it, you can release the pain, at least to some extent."

"Some other time, perhaps." But Jake wouldn't leave it alone.

"No, no. You have to tell me now, buddy. We have lots of time. What else is there to do here in the dark for hours?"

"It is hard to talk about. You don't know how painful it is. It tears my heart to pieces."

"Consider what I'm going through, man. I understand. Come on, take a deep breath. Relax."

Ira followed Jake's instruction and recalled the dinner he and Devi had at Bombay Palace on Jarvis Street. "It was the first month anniversary of her job at Mount Sinai Hospital in Toronto. After a tasty but slightly spicy meal, we left the restaurant, arms wrapped around each other and walked towards home." During the slow walk, Ira had radiated joy and he knew Devi felt the same way. It had been a perfect moment. "When we got home, we had a lovely evening." He skipped the intimate moments, lying hot and naked in bed. His groin responded to the memory of her perfect body but he shoved the image away. "Then we fell asleep."

Jake lowered his body until his side stretched out on the mattress, relieving the aching throb of his injured leg.

Ira took a few seconds to phrase his next thought. "The next morning, she couldn't get out of bed. She was nauseated and all her bones ached. So, I took her to the ER at Mount Sinai."

"What happened?"

Ira's heart was heavy. "Two days later, we were in an oncologist's office." He took a sniff through moist nostrils. "He placed films from the CAT scan and then the diagnostic X-ray next to a low overhead light. I could see clusters of dark spots inside her. I knew he was about to give us bad news. Instinctively, I turned to Devi to examine her reaction." There was a long pause.

Jake broke the silence. "What did the doctor say?"

"He went on and on with medical jargon like metastasis, emergency radiation, focusing on 'quality of life,' but not a cure."

"How did she take the diagnosis?"

"Not well. She was silent. I was silent. I asked how long she had. He said at best, six months. The doctor had no gentle approach, eliminating layers of euphemism, he delivered the simple truth. He filled in answers to unspoken questions." Ira recalled his words, "Things like, 'There's a lot we can do. This is manageable. You might have many years.' Then he circled back to, 'It's too far along to be eradicated. Our goal now is to slow down the cancer and give you as much quality life as we can.' To Devi it meant only impending death."

Ira bit his lip. He turned away from Jake, pointing towards the ceiling. "The specialist advised sending Devi to the Magna Cancer Centre at Southlake Hospital." The words rolled out with the saddest tone. Ira fell silent and closed his eyes again, clicking the walkie to fill the silence.

Jake reached for a container from his front pant pocket, pulled two Tylenol 4 out and popped them in his mouth. "I hope to hear the whole story someday." Ira simply nodded.

Chapter 25

As the vehicle rolled along the highway, Jake couldn't help but become absorbed by Ira's sad love story. *Will I save the love of my life from the cancer that is this government?* After roughly three hours of travel, the hearse stopped and the grating noise of an industrial door on rollers fractured the air. After a short motion forward, the back door opened. A man extended a hand to Jake.

To minimize the pain, Jake slid his back towards the open air. Ira placed his hand under Jake's armss and gave him a push. Jake and Ira climbed a ladder into the back of a transport truck for the last leg of their journey. Both got on the 10-wheel truck owned by Hakim Transports in a warehouse close to the city of Qom. For their safe journey, the Hakim family provided Ira with two vans, both with men carrying weaponry, in case they were stopped by authorities or thieves. One man traveled in front and the other at the back of the truck.

Close to one in the morning, Jake and Ira arrived at a huge warehouse, inside which there was a comfortable apartment with a kitchen, bath, and two bedrooms. The living area was on the main floor, surround by trucks, vans, and forklifts. Not what Jake would consider an ideal "safe" house, but at least it hadn't been breached like some of the last ones.

During breakfast, Ira quietly ripped apart and ate pieces of bread and goat-cheese. Jake grew tired of the silence, "I am deeply sorry about Devi. Thank you for sharing your story with me."

Ira's face shadowed, his breathing quickened.

"Damnit, I shouldn't have told you. I promised myself not to tell it again. It's just too painful."

"Ira, no. You're like the brother I never had, man. You did the right thing. Don't kid yourself. You need to let even the darker places of your heart see the light. And now that we're in Tehran, the light says it's time to save Laila."

"Yes, we are in Tehran, but first I have to take care of some business. A promise I made to my boss."

"I can't thank you enough for all your help. When I set my foot on this land, many questions ran through my mind, 'What am I doing?' 'Why did I come here?' 'What can I possibly do on my own?' Please, tell me. Do you have any idea how to get my Laila out of the prison? With Maya gone, I don't even know where to begin."

He was silent. "I don't know. But before we start planning, I need your help."

"No. problem. What?"

"I'm waiting for someone to give the signal to go to Tabriz, a border town with Turkey. I want you to come with me."

"Why? What's happening in Tabriz?"

***

Ira sat in the front passenger seat of the taxi holding a piece of paper with the address for his meeting. At every turn his anger increased; he was running late. The driver careened around an old Tabriz neighborhood with narrow streets occasionally stopping to ask pedestrians for directions. Sometimes drivers pretend not knowing an address for the sake of driving the fare higher. Ira couldn't call him on the tactic because that would be rude and he'd likely lose his ride.

Finally, at twenty after six, the car stopped before an iron gate. Ira gave the man a couple of bills and slid out of the vehicle. After unhooking a latch, he pushed the heavy door with both hands, entering the perimeter of an old mosque surrounded by a nine-foot tall stone wall.

He headed to the corner room. When he entered, Meena stood near two men. Her silhouette was not as he remembered it; she was altogether more round than she had been a week ago. One of the men standing with her had a thick beard and turban, the other wore a pants and shirt set; both played cards.

Meena's eyes were slightly red, an indication of frustration. "Where the hell have you been?"

"Sorry, I got lost. Can we talk outside, privately?"

When they went to the courtyard of the Mujahedin mosque, there were two men washing the floor in preparation for sunset prayer. The two colleagues kept walking until they were far enough away to speak freely.

"What's with the belly?"

"The plan is that we load up an unconscious Jake in the back of the van. On top of him we put lots of luggage, baskets of food, and a goat. I'll travel with those two guys. One is the driver and the other is my pretend husband. Both of them speak Farsi and Turkish. When we go through border security, I'll scream of pain and go into labor." She pointed to her pregnant-looking stomach. "It explains this …"

"You're going with *those* two guys?"

"They are Mossad agents," her tone imbued certainty.

Ira had never seen them before and wanted to know their ranking. "Blue and white?"

"Yes, blue and white. Both have been trained at the Mossad head office."

Ira watched as two women approached. After a nudge he said, "Let's go over there." He trusted no one.

Meena's face projected confidence as usual. "We'll cross the border around two in the morning, when one of our guys will be on duty. If asked, my husband will tell them I'm in labor and we are going to the border town of Van, where my parents live. You understand the plan?" Iranian men avoided witnessing the birthing processes; it made perfect sense.

Both stopped walking. Ira turned to her, "Sounds like a good plan."

The twinkle in Meena's eyes got brighter as she explained the rest, "Of course, we don't stop at Van. We keep going to Ankara, where a military transport plane will be waiting for us. It'll take Jake and the device to Israel."

The noise of a procession with drums, singing, and trumpet music drowned out their conversation. They paused until the sounds subsided.

Ira said, "Are *you* going to Israel?"

"No, no. I'm not going to Israel but I am taking Jake and the computer to Ankara before coming back to Iran. Let's get going. We're running out of time. We need to load up Jake and his computer. Have you given him the tranquilizer?"

"Meena … I have something to tell you." Ira rubbed a calloused hand over his face and hair, stalling. "I don't know how to say this. I've practiced the words many times but …" He threw his hands in the air and let them fall to his sides in frustration. "I'm just going to say it, hope you don't take it personally."

"Spit it out, Ira."

"I didn't bring Jake."

A shadow of anger or maybe confusion appeared on her face. "Where is he?" Her eyes opened as wide as they could. "Why isn't he here? What's the problem?"

"He's in Tehran at Karim's warehouse. I don't want him to go to Israel."

Meena looked puzzled. "Ira. What are you talking about? I've taken an oath of compliance with the Mossad. Ephraim's order is to take Jake and the computer to Ankara. What will Ephraim think? What are you doing?" Her voice changed, "Are you a double agent?"

It hurt him to experience her disappointment. "I want to help him rescue his wife."

Meena shook her head vigorously. "No. You've got it wrong. Your allegiance is to Mossad, not this hopeless romantic." She waved both hands in the air. "You're about to lose a hundred-thousand dollars *and* your reputation over this American. I've known you for years. I don't believe what I'm hearing."

She looked like she wanted to him to say something more …

"What happened? I should have stayed with you in Isfahan, not left you two alone. What did he say to make you change your mind?"

"It doesn't matter. I can't turn him in."

"Ira, listen to me. It's not too late. We can go to Tehran and get him. What about his computer?"

"Gone."

"What? What do you mean *gone*? Ira, are you losing your mind?" The deep breath Meena took made her chest protrude. "I went through so much trouble to get that device back and now it is gone!"

Ira snatched her wild arms, placed her hands in his, and started walking. "When he was kidnapped and taken to Afghanistan, he realized he was being tracked by the NSA through the computer. It comes with a GPS tracker."

"Whatever."

"He was in pain, confused, I don't know what. He just threw the device out the window on the way back to Iran from Afghanistan."

"Ira, you can't be serious …" She shook his hands away.

"Meena, without the computer Jake is worthless. I have to go back to Tehran."

"This isn't right. You're betraying your commitment to the Mossad and to Israel."

Ira knew she was playing the emotion card. "What I do or don't do is not going to make a big difference to Mossad's objectives in Iran." He shrugged his shoulders. "But it could make a big difference in Jake's life."

"What do I tell Ephraim?"

"Just tell him that the plan had to be aborted due to unforeseen circumstances. Tell him the truth. The device is gone. He'll understand … I hope."

"No, you know him better than that, Ira. He'll find a way to get *all* the details from me. And when he learns that you messed up and lost Jake to the Americans, he'll come after you. You owe him now."

"I've given a lot of thought to what I'm doing. I inherited one of my father's character traits that I admire. As a Rabbi he wanted to help everyone in his neighborhood. He treated Muslims, Jews, Christians, Zoroastrians, poor, rich the same way. With respect and compassion. He was focusing on good karma, hoping the Messiah would come to Tehran someday. I had no control over the tracking device in the computer. I *do* have control over how I interact with my fellow human beings."

Meena sighed. "If you change your mind, let me know. By the way, the Messiah is coming to Israel, *not* Iran."

"Frankly, I don't care where the Messiah comes. I'm not religious."

"I have to get rid of this fake belly. It's so uncomfortable."

He smiled, half-laughing and half-sorrowful. He wanted to reach out and grasp her hands again, but he didn't.

"Be careful."

She nodded and they parted.

I wonder if I'll ever see her again.

Chapter 26

Charles Hudley drove along Backcock Road past a couple of buildings when CHRISTUS Santa Rosa Hospital Medical Center appeared in white on an entrance façade. He took the turn indicated toward a public parking lot. Media vehicles lined both sides of the road next to the entrance. The circus was ready for action.

Reporters and technicians moved about testing equipment in and around CNN vans with different types of antennas on their roofs. Fox News staff did the same several yards away. In between these two media heavyweights were the local TV stations. A reporter from the San Antonio Express, seated in the front seat with the door to his Ford Taurus open, busily typing something on a laptop. The neighborhood looked like a foreign invasion had hit.

Charles stepped into the reception area of the hospital. He went past a flower shop, a religious group in a booth, and the information desk; he pulled a piece of paper from his jacket with the room number written on it. The elevator brought him directly to the second-floor corridor down from room 2043.

Andy's relatives and friends sat in chairs arranged in a semi-circle. After greeting each one of them, Charles stepped into an area separating Andy from the others by a curtain. The boy lay motionless. A mask attached to a tank with a tube covered his nose. Another tube ran into his mouth. Wires attached to his arm, stomach, legs, monitored his vital signs via a screen displaying graphs and numbers.

Charles stood still with his eyes fixed on his son's best friend. The boy who took Jake under his wing and helped him find focus in his life. Spontaneously he said a prayer.

"Andy, son, I hope you get better soon. I need your help with my tomatoes." He stood there for another moment and walked out of the curtained area to Andy's parents to convey his sorrow. His father had a blank look, as though unable to explain why he should be at his son's hospital bed. His mother, so overwhelmed, simply couldn't talk. Kristina, Andy's girlfriend since university, sat trembling. Her red eyes showed she hadn't stopped crying since she heard the news.

Charles sat next to her, "I'm so sorry." He did his best to convey compassion as she tried to curb her sobs; a river of tears flowed unchecked over her cheeks.

"I might lose him because of your son." She squeezed her thin, pointed nose with a tissue. Her summer tan had long faded, leaving white skin contrasting with a black blouse on an overly thin body.

Kristina's words struck like arrows. Charles reflected carefully on the best response. "No one knows the whole story. But I'm very sad that Andy tried to take his own life. I really don't know where Jake is or how he's involved, but I do understand the situation is tragic and painful."

"He should never have taken a classified computer out of the country. It's a betrayal to our beloved country."

How does she know? In a moment of distress Andy must have confided in her. "Before passing any judgment, I'll wait till all the facts are known," Charles couldn't help but reason.

She got up. "I don't have that luxury." She walked away, down the hall.

Charles sat by himself and noticed no one wanted to talk to him. He didn't want to intrude on their grief, so he left the building and went straight to a CNN caravan. "Can I talk to a reporter?" He asked a technician running wires.

The techi dropped the line, went to the front of the van and came back with a young woman holding a microphone and a man with a huge camera perched on his shoulder.

After introductions, the reporter straightened her upper body, and ran her hand to ensure her hair was in place. Looking at the camera man, she said, "We're going live."

Charles tucked his tummy in and buttoned up his jacket. He wanted to project the image of the general that he was.

The reporter eyed the camera, "Ashley, we have Mr. Hudley, father of Jake Hudley here with us now. Mr. Hudley, could you tell us where your son is at this moment?"

Charles moved his mouth closer to the mike. "First, I want to say hi to Ashley Maslin. I like her show." The reporter smiled and motioned him to continue. "What I'm here to talk about is Andrew Burke. He is like a son to me. He loved his job and his country. Before he's accused of anything untoward, I want to ask that you wait till all the facts come out ..."

"Mr. Hudley, is your son an Iranian spy?"

At that moment Charles saw the reporter as his enemy. "One more thing about Andy. He's loyal to the US Military. He would never intentionally betray his superiors or country. I want to be very clear about that."

"Have you heard from Jake?" She was frustrated.

By now Charles was surrounded by more reporters with mikes pointing at him and cameras recording his words. He'd had enough of the insanity and wild speculation that ignored the truth for sensationalist TV. From the first moment, the news had botched the reporting of this situation and likely put Jake at risk. The ignorance and self-serving nature of these people sickened him. But now was his chance to set the record straight.

Charles directed his attention to the CNN audience. "No. I have not heard from Jake since he left the US. No. He is not an enemy of the United States. No. He is not a spy. No. He is not working for the Iranians. Yes. He will come home as an honorable man."

"Mr. Hudley, is your son's wife an undercover Iranian spy?"

Charles boiled inside. "No. She is not a spy. In fact, she is being persecuted by the Iranian Regime. Jake wanted to go there to secure her release. That's all I know. It's the truth, and that's all I'm going to say." As he walked away, several reporters followed him, shouting questions. He ignored them all.

***

Tom ended the phone conversation and placed the receiver on the desk before staring at the two people in front of him.

Shaking his head, he said, "She's like a bull dog." The call had consumed his mind so much that he failed to refresh his thoughts back to why Linda Moore and Hans Schilder were in his office. "Where were we?"

Linda shifted her weight on the chair and cleared her throat. "The media, especially Fox News, are spinning the story in such a way as to show the administration as *incompetent*. How irresponsible the US military was letting an ex-service man become an Iranian spy."

Tom's stomach growled as the requests by the Secretary of State still churned in his head. "Secretary Mary Jackson wants Hudley captured before an American and Iranian delegation meet in Geneva, where they'll negotiate a deal regarding the Iranian nuclear arms program."

Hans chimed in, "There *is* another piece to consider in this puzzle. I know the Israelis. They wouldn't want this meeting to be successful. They could use the Hudley affair to coax the American public opinion into how Iranians can't be trusted and push for the president to opt for military action sooner than later."

Tom turned his swivel chair around, snatched up his lunch bag, and emptied its content on the desk.

"I'm starving. Have you eaten?"

He got a positive response.

A glance on the wall clock indicated ten after two. Of course these two had lunch.

Hans continued with his theory. "The Israelis want us to bomb Iran and do the dirty work for them.

Tom took a bite of his peanut butter and jam sandwich. For the last twenty years, his wife made the same lunch every day.

Tom really wasn't interested in a speculation of what the Israelis wanted or not. He was more concerned about Madame Secretary's wishes. He turned to Linda. "What do we know so far?"

Linda's expression showed extreme disappointment. "We know he escaped from a van stationed at a base in Afghanistan and killed two men in the process."

The conversation stopped while Tom finished chewing and took a sip of juice. "We don't have much time. If the Iranians get Jake, they'll use him as a negotiation chip at this upcoming meeting."

Linda's eyes shifted towards Hans. "Tom, we understand …"

"When the President asks for something, there's only one option. 'Yes Mr. President, whatever it takes, we'll do it.' What's our next move?"

Hans took another glance at the report. "I've spoken with our CIA agents here and in Iran. The consensus is that we increase the number of agents working on this case to twenty-five. Then, we'll make an extra effort to infiltrate Iranian intel."

"Hans, Linda, success is the mantra. There's no room for error. Every morning at ten we'll meet here for five minutes for a quick briefing."

With that, Tom ended the meeting. As he watched them leave, his stomach churned, an indication of too much acid from job stress. He pulled out a drawer, fetched a Rolaids and swallowed it.

***

The morning after the hospital visit, Charles sat at the kitchen table contemplating Andy's fate. After chewing a bit of whole grain bread with cream cheese and strawberry jam, he took a sip of hibiscus tea to wash it down. He'd finally kicked the coffee addiction. The herbal drink helped him reduce hypertension, a condition he believed was caused by the turmoil surrounding Jake's disappearance.

If the media had bothered to report fact instead of speculation, the pressure on Andy's conscience about what he did to help save a life might not have pushed him past reason. Reporters these days were more concerned

about ratings than finding the truth. *Does Jake know about Andy? How could he? Maybe with the AH-302 he could watch the news in America.* Charles knew his son would be devastated if he found out his best friend tried to take his own life, an action caused by Jake's decision to go to Iran.

The doorbell interrupted his string of thoughts. *Who could it be this early? Must be another reporter.*

When he approached the front door to peek through the curtain, Makalla stood there clenching and unclenching her hands.

When she walked in, she grabbed her father in a hug. The tight squeeze reminded Charles of her reaction on the day she was teased at school about her braided hair.

"Where's Mom?" These were the exact words uttered after his little girl returned home that long-ago day, too.

"Upstairs, she should be getting ready for her senior's event."

"Dad, I am being harassed on Facebook and Twitter. I was on my way to work but couldn't do it—couldn't show up. I decided to come here. I can't face the world right now. Everywhere people are against Jake." Her blue eyes teared up.

Charles took a few steps towards the bottom of the stairs and yelled. "Ruth, Makalla's here."

"I'll be there in a minute," she yelled back, clearly puzzled.

"Someone created a Twitter account called #KillJake. Can you believe that? There are thousands and thousands of messages flying around like a tornado."

"What are they saying?"

"Most of them call him a traitor. I tried to tell them he's not, that his wife has been imprisoned by the Iranian government. The cynics think there's a conspiracy going on."

Father and daughter spoke as Ruth came down the stairs. Makalla lowered her six-foot frame to give her mom a hug. Both embraced in a tight squeeze.

"What's happening, sweetheart?"

"Mom, the world is going crazy."

Ruth looked at her daughter's face, stray strands of blonde hair hung limp around her face. The poor girl had come undone.

"Damn media. No one is trying to investigate the truth independently."

Charles shook his head, unconvinced. "Are you still going to that seniors' event?"

Ruth's face lost a shade of color. "Not going to the event. I'll only end up having a fight with several members … lots of arguing … I can't win. Better for me not to go."

"Dad, go to the NSA. Ask them to stop harassing Jake, us … Maybe they know where he is."

Charles said, "Should we try calling Laila's parents?"

Makalla's eyes glanced over the kitchen counter, like Jake she was always on the lookout for something to eat. "I checked Jake's phone; Negar left about three messages. When I called the number back, I didn't get anything."

"We have to keep trying."

"I need a coffee. I'll make a pot."

"I need to figure out how to stop this circus."

Chapter 27

Jake picked up the phone and dialed again. Just as he hit the last digit, the door opened and Ira walked in.

"What are you doing? Who are you calling?" Ira's eyes popped wide open as if his own death was imminent.

On the second ring, Jake sheepishly placed the receiver back on the cradle. Startled by Ira's reaction, he felt guilty.

"Why?"

"Firstly, every day this place has to be sanitized." He deposited a few plastic bags on the floor, then rushed over to a wooden desk and pulled open the drawer. He waved a device. "This baby is the best in the business. MCD-22H. It quickly detects both analog and digital taps, room bugs, concealed cameras and GPS tracking devices, *and* the devastating infinity devices." He handed it to Jake. "Just run it through all the rooms. Now, if some's listening to our conversation, they'll know we're as serious they are."

Jake went through two bedrooms, the kitchen, and the common room. As he scanned the ceilings, floors, and corners of each area, he paid attention to the four LED lights—indicators of hidden surveillance tech. When he returned to the common room, Ira sat in front of his computer.

"It's all done. Now we can talk. Where the hell have you been? I've been going crazy for the last twenty-four hours stuck in this place."

"Jake, I'm in the business of spying, surveillance, and counter terrorism. This is not a nine-to-five job." After a pause and equally pointed stare, Ira continued, "In this rotten business, do you know what the most important quality needed for success is? Patience. The ability to wait. Waiting for days, months, even years."

Jake was tired of Ira's lecture and wanted to change the subject. "Where were you? Did you at least get some food?"

Ira shook his head. "You've been hungry since the moment we met. What happened? Your mother not feed you as a child?"

"Lay off, will you." Jake sensed the room filling with tension. "Sorry. All this is driving me crazy. Waiting and waiting. I can't get in touch with Laila's family. Ira, this is fringin' important!"

"Go ahead, make the call while I get the food on the table."

Jake went back to the wooden desk, sat in a folding chair, and dialed the number. It rang ten times. This was the fifth call. *Are they in prison too*?

After hanging up, he headed to the kitchen. His stomach growled as he thought of JJ Burgers in San Antonio: a large bun loaded with two juicy Angus beef patties, pickles, and BBQ sauce would've satisfied his cravings perfectly. With a side order of double-down fries and a large glass of root beer, he could taste heaven.

As Jake's mouth salivated, he reached for a plate, grabbed the largest nan and snagged two skewers of kabob before heading to the common room to sit on an old, worn out sofa lining one of the walls. Ira flopped onto a smaller sofa in the middle of the room.

Jake stared at him. "What's our next move?" Chewing muffled the sounds of his words.

"This place is going to be our mission control. This is *my* safe house. Just to be clear it has nothing to do with Mossad. We are Karim's guests. I can only hope the Mossad agents don't know about this place." He held a plate with his left hand and waved the other one as he spoke, "Of course, I want to make sure they don't know about this place. Spy business is also information business. But if they did know about this place, it wouldn't be a total surprise to me either. We have to be very careful. One mistake could mean the death of one or both of us. Once the Mossad find out I'm not with them anymore, they'll be tracking my activity. Understand? I'll be under suspicion just like everyone else."

Jake nodded and made a mental note of caution. In fact, during his military training and deployments in Afghanistan, he was reminded of risk assessment at every step. But Jake's curiosity wasn't satisfied.

"How can you afford such a place?"

"By the good grace of Habib *joon*."

"Habibjoon? Is that his name?"

Ira picked up on the misunderstanding. "No. No. His name is Habib. You should know, you're married to an Iranian; *joon* is a term of endearment, usually suffixed with a name."

Ira's lecture bothered Jake's ego. "I know. I know. I have a mental block when it comes to learning Farsi."

"You Americans think you don't need to learn any foreign languages."

By now they felt comfortable expressing themselves openly, a good sign of trust in their relationship, but that didn't mean Jake had to put up with Ira's nonsense.

"Quit bashing Americans. Why would Habib let you use this place? I need to know."

"Habib runs a transport business. He and the government of Iran are at odds but—as intelligent people do—they've learned to live with each other. I did a favor for Habib and he's been very generous with me. As you know, this is a huge warehouse, big as two football fields—offices, truck parking, storage, and maintenance. Living quarters too. We have security—human eyes, cameras, motion detectors—everywhere. Again, we don't take any chances. I'm sure people out there are watching this place."

"What are you working on? Do you need any help? What should our next move be?"

"Jake, I understand your impatience. As I mentioned earlier, this is a flaw when it comes to this line of work. Just so you know. I don't report to the Mossad; I'm not taking any more assignments from them. I'm devoting all my time to helping you free your Laila."

It came as a surprise, but not totally. "From what I understand, you were never a real Mossad agent anyway."

"True. The Mossad structure has three tiers. I was in the third tier, brokering information. Meena is in the second tier, and a full Mossad operative is in the first tier. The last group is trained to be fiercely loyal to Israel and the agency. In fact, when each one is recruited, before being sent on an assignment, he or she pays a visit to the prime minister of Israel. I didn't … as far as I am concerned, I came here to fill a void after Devi's death."

"Where's Meena, then?"

Her name drained the color from Ira's face. "I wish she were here. But she has other commitments." He rubbed his forehead.

"Is she okay?"

"We'll get to Meena later. First, you'll have to stay here as the commander-in-chief. If you go outside, a six-foot tall, white man will stand out like a sore thumb."

Jake was getting tired of remarks about how white he looked and about his height as being some kind of disease. "I don't want to wear that goddamn burka again."

Ira pointed a finger to Jake. "You won't have to. You'll be staying here, running things. You've been in the military, in Afghanistan no less. What we're about to do is our version of 'Mission Impossible.' You watched that show, right?"

Jake took the last bite of bread. While chewing, he placed his hand over his mouth. "I've seen the movie with Tom Cruise."

"Let me remind you, In the US, there's a media frenzy surrounding you. CNN, Fox News, ABC, and NBC are all reporting that you're an Iranian spy. But I don't know exactly what the Iranians think about this craziness. I'll find out. Since they haven't spotted you yet, my guess is they might think this is just the usual US propaganda."

Jake froze. "What did you say?"

"There's a media frenzy surrounding your disappearance."

"No." He shook his head. Jake poked his chest. "The media think I'm an Iranian spy. That's what they think?"

"Yes."

"This is crazy. Godamn crazy. No." He felt a noose around his neck tightening. He threw the almost empty plate on floor. "Oh man, what about my family? What do they think? My dad? He's a retired general for god's sake." *What about Andy?* "What else haven't I been told?"

"Let's focus on the job at hand—save the girl, and then we get out of the country. Alive. Not an easy job by any stretch of the imagination."

Jake felt a quiver in his heart. "You're right. It's a miracle I'm still here."

"One more thing. You've pissed everybody off. From the media reports I've seen, the Defense Department and State Department are getting desperate. Three failed attempt to capture you … I'm sure they're tripling their efforts now. Iranians likely want a piece of you. Who knows who else wants you caught dead or alive."

Jake ran his hands over his face and sighed, resigned. "How did I become so important?"

A flashing red light above the entrance to the room stole their attention.

"What's that?"

Ira leaned towards Jake. Shaking his head, he whispered, "Motion detector."

"Are you expecting any one?"

When Ira's reply was negative, Jake's jaw dropped and his heartbeat tripled.

Next to the flashing alarm, a TV screen hanging from the ceiling came alive; Meena approached the only door leading to the apartment.

Ira jumped to his feet and moved to greeted her with the strangest mix of expressions—hope and questioning. The door opened.

"I didn't expect you."

She tore her hijab from her head and shoulders and threw it on a chair next to the sofa. She was silent, not sure know how to respond.

"I thought you might need some help."

Ira's face lit up with the broadest smile. "I do need your help. We're just finishing lunch, breakfast, whatever. Can I get you something?"

"Thanks. I'm not hungry."

Jake was happy to see her too. She'd be a valuable asset in the planning stages of the rescue. She was meticulous, able to multi-task, and her ego never got in the way.

"Good to see you, Meena. We're planning the rescue. Please, join us."

Meena pulled the chair in the middle of the room to confer with the guys. "What have you done so far?"

Jake picked his plate up from the floor and set it on the table in front of him. "Not much."

"Meena, would you agree that Jake should be the commander-in-chief of the operation?"

"Yes. Without a doubt. His strengths would be best used that way."

Jake laughed. "Then I guess I need to get my butt in gear. The first order of business is to find where Laila's parents are."

Ira said, "I'll take that."

Jake's body vibrated with joy. Two well-trained Mossad agents wanting to help was the greatest news he'd gotten since Andy came through for him with Maya. Since he could no longer rely on the super computer to help him do this alone, Jake knew Ira and Meena were the answer. His emotion was tempered, realizing he had witnessed many military operations, but saving his wife would be the most unique and unpredictable to date.

***

Ira parked his car on Khak-Negar Street under a shady Chinar tree. From the driver's seat, he commanded a direct, clear view of the Dareini home. Through the rear-view and side mirrors he took occasional glances of the surroundings in case anyone watched him. After nearly ten minutes of scrutiny, the street got busier with vehicles and pedestrians on the sidewalks. Children rushed to school, some adults to work, and a few merchants pushed carriages of goods.

At 9:10 am, he stepped out of the car, crossed the street, went to the gate marked 24, then rang the bell. He scanned the area; everyone seemed to be minding their own business. He pressed the buzzer again and waited. With no sign of any movement in the two-storey apartment, he returned to his Toyota Aurion.

His mind drifted to Meena's return. He'd thought about whether she might join him, but could only hope for a miracle since she was second-tier Mossad after all.

Then his reflection turned to Jake. He didn't like having to feed the man all the time, but he understood this tall, pale westerner should not be in the market shopping. Somehow, he became sympathetic to his plight, even if he did have a bottomless pit for a stomach.

A man from the Dareini's neighboring house appeared at the iron gate. When he stepped onto the pavement, Ira slid out of the car and headed towards him.

"*Bebakhshid*, excuse me, can I talked to you for a minute?" Ira placed his left hand on his chest simultaneously bowing. Respect of your elders was of paramount importance in Iranian culture.

The man in his sixties turned to Ira, acknowledging his request. "Yes."

"Have you seen the Dareini's lately?"

Suspicions gathered on his complexion. "What's the reason?"

"I'm not a Revolutionary Guard or anything like that. Someone has come from abroad and I'm here to deliver a message."

"Are you a relative?"

"No. But I was sent by a relative."

"I haven't seen them for a while, may be a week or two. I can't remember exactly. They are very private people; I didn't interact with them much."

"*Merci, koorbani shoma.*"

After another bow of the head, he returned to the car, rolled up the windows and drove off. When he turned right on Helal-e-Ahmar Street, the mid-morning traffic crawled as usual. The sun was bright. He unbuttoned his shirt to help his body catch the slight breeze as a rank odor attacked his nose. He turned the air conditioning on full blast instead—the only commodity that hadn't risen with the rate of inflation was the price of gas. It was like air and water, Iranians consumed as much as they wanted making the car one of the few places to beat the heat.

When Ira arrived at his destination, he walked down a busy street covertly examining others, a task he was well trained in and which happened to be one of his strongest assets. His brisk steps slowed as he made a sharp turn into an alley between two buildings before coming to a stop by a door in the wall. Checking both directions, he unlocked the door and went in. When he entered their head office, Jake was on the computer.

"Whatever you do, don't contact any one by email, Facebook, or Skype."

Jake jumped to his feet. "Did you meet Laila's family?"

"They've left their home. The Revolutionary Guards must have been harassing them, which happens often when a member is in jail."

A shadow covered Jake's complexion "We have to think of our next move."

"Any ideas? Do you know who might know about their whereabouts?"

Jake wrote something on a piece of paper. "Here. Contact them."

Upon reading, Ira said, "I know this group. My father might have contact with some of their prominent members."

Ira left with a nod.

Chapter 28

Jake scrolled down the results from his latest search on the computer when the door opened and Meena appeared. Her face was pale and clearly exhausted. Usually her tone of voice or facial expressions *never* gave away what was going on inside.

Jake turned his total attention to Meena as she closed the door and went to the fridge for a cola before wandering back to the common room.

"How did it go?"

Still standing in the middle of the room, she took a mouthful of the cold drink. "Damn, an Israeli expert on Evin prison just left Iran. Two days ago."

Jake did not understand her concern. "Okay, is there a way of getting in touch with him?"

"No. No. He's a Mossad operative and on another assignment."

Jake's interest peaked. "Meena, what do you mean an expert? How can a Mossad operative be an Evin prison expert?"

"The Mossad have been here long before the Iranian revolution, in 1979. They helped the Shah maintain his power, and they had access to everything—including the structure of the prison."

"I'm still not getting the whole picture. Why was he here and why did he leave?"

"About a week ago, Ali Azizi, who provided intelligence about nuclear facilities to the Mossad, was caught by Iranian authorities and placed at Evin. So this expert was brought in as part of the plan to rescue Ali. Just few days ago, Ali was executed." The waving of Meena's hands as she spoke, and her accent, reminded him of Laila.

Jake got up and rubbed his hand. "You've just made my day."

"Oh? How's that?"

"I've been running searches for hours, trying to find out as much information as possible about this prison. You said it yourself, Mossad is our greatest asset. I need you to poke around and get every bit of information you can. The more we know the better. Okay? You need to become our *new* expert."

The operative shook her head. "I don't know. I get frustrated when I miss an opportunity." She stepped back slowly until she rested against the wall.

Jake was an ultimate optimist. "Among the three of us, you have the best capacity to learn valuable information regarding where Laila is located in the prison—to find every detail about everything. You will become an encyclopedia on every person working there, the kind of weapons the guards carry, who they are and what shift they're on. Find out details about the buildings: how many rooms, cells, offices, interrogators, judges, storage lockers, shower stalls, kitchens—"

"Yes boss."

"Were you trained in arms handling, documentation, observation, explosives?"

"All of them. Why?"

"I've been wondering what prompted you to join our team. There's no pay and lots of risk, maybe even death—especially if we get caught."

She turned her gaze towards the ceiling as if it hid a deep secret. "I don't want to go there right now."

"Okay. I understand."

Meena chugged the rest of her cola, nodded to Jake, grabbed her hijab and walked right back out the door. He couldn't actually say there was a spring in her step but the determined set to her shoulders told Jake he'd given her the right assignment.

***

When Ira entered the control center for operation “Save Laila”, he yelled, “Good news, Jake! I found them.” With the Religious denomination Jake had given him, Ira searched through a hundred and twenty-two names all living in Tehran which, in turn, led to thirteen leads of which five were fruitful.

Jake picked Ira up and swung him around. “Best news ever. Tell me more.”

When Jake let go, Ira landed on his feet and leaned into the wall to regain his footing.

“Man, you’re dangerous. You attack when I give you good news,” he chuckled.

“Tell me what happened.”

“It took me fourteen hours, a non-stop effort, but I managed to find them. The leads to the whereabouts of the Dareini’s helped me discover that they’re in hiding in a “Unity Circle”. It’s a sanctuary for families whose members have been imprisoned by the Iranian regime; a way to protect them from harassment. I managed to talk to several key people.” Ira paused to breathe. “They were stunned when I told them you were here. Negar and Maliheh started to cry. But the father didn’t think you being here was a good idea. He’s certain that if the Iranian government finds out, which they will sooner or later, it could jeopardize Laila’s chances of release.”

“I don’t care about him—”

“You should. He’s your father-in-law.”

Jake ignored the remark, clearly impatient to hear news of his wife. “How’s Laila doing? Have they gone to see her? How’s she coping?”

Ira collapsed onto the sofa. “They’ve seen her a few times. She’s frail and has lost a lot of weight.”

“Frail ...” Jake recalled her weak constitution. Stress wreaked havoc on her health, making her sick for days. “How will that affect the rescue mission?”

"Don't know. It has to be factored into the plan though."

Reflecting on the issue, Jake rubbed his hair, sighed and walked over to the wall. He hit the concrete with his fist, calling out then shaking his hand to release the pain. He turned around.

"At least now I know where her parents are, in hiding and not incarcerated or dead.

"They suspect the Guardians are looking for them. It makes sense for them to remain in the Unity Circle. It's a human fortress, something I've never heard of or seen. It's lucky someone trusted me enough so I could find them."

Jake's emotions ran the gamut: excited, apprehensive, and worried. Ira saw all that and more flash over his face multiple times. Then, the American's confidence and hope came roaring back. He was ready for action.

"I have a plan. When Meena comes back, I'll go over it with both of you, get your opinion."

"Sounds good. I need to sleep more than anything else right now." Ira left the room and curled up on a cot until Meena arrived back seven hours later.

Chapter 29

Ali Mohmed surveyed a sea of footwear by the mosque door. As he slipped his shoes on, an uncomfortable idea, born while reciting the Quran verses of the Friday prayers, haunted him again. His heart sunk lower. The thought of quitting his post as the chief interrogator at Evin Prison had entered his mind many times, but became more pronounced early that morning.

As he left the mosque and journeyed towards the court for his next appointment, he weighed both sides of this dilemma. With every crunch of his footsteps on the gravel path, he tried to chase the thoughts away as ridiculous—with no success. Ali, a long-time staunch supporter of the Iranian regime, one who entertained deep devotion to the Ayatollah, who held a loyalty recognized among the government elites which allowed him to move up the ladder of seniority at Evin was actually contemplating leaving.

Of all his considerations thus far, two things weighed in the most: his failure to change Laila's mind when it came to her beliefs, and the assassination of Reza by the MEK. But quitting didn't just mean getting out of harm's way, it also meant falling out of grace.

The guards at the doorway interrupted his reflection with salutations, to which Ali responded in kind. After stepping inside the building, he walked to the court room and knocked on the door.

"Enter."

He approached the three Islamic judges, exchanged greetings, and took a seat. Then, the ritualistic prayers, citing praises for the Ayatollahs, and mentioning the purpose of this meeting followed.

Every Friday after the congregational prayer, Ali attended this particular gathering in which he received judgments on cases he dealt with.

Mullah Said proclaimed, "In the name of Allah, the merciful, this court pronounces the verdict on the following cases. First on this list is the case of Sarah Vahdat and Gita Omari. This court finds them guilty of conducts contrary to Islamic law, punishable to the maximum extent."

The judge scribbled something on a sheet. These two prisoners were found having homosexual relations in ward 246. As punishment, all the prisoners of the ward would gather outside to bear witness as the two girls were lashed and humiliated.

Ali stood up. Reverently he stared at a picture of the Supreme Leader hung on the wall behind the judges. Then he took the judgment sheet from Mullah Said and sunk to his seat again. Though the interrogator felt it was the right decision, a verbal comment was not permissible regarding a verdict.

The second docket item was about two brothers accused of insulting a cleric at a mosque, resulting in a heated argument ending in both men hitting the cleric.

To this case, the judge said, "They should be hanged in public." Said's face muscles tightened as the words rolled past his lips.

Ali thought the punishment far too severe for the inappropriate action of these two brothers. He wondered how many other extreme consequences had been meted out since the new regime came into power—something that had never crossed his mind before. He refrained from questioning the judgment.

The third item was about a group of seven people belonging to a religious minority. Two months earlier they were found guilty of spying for Israel, insulting religious sanctities, and propaganda against the system. They appealed the judgment.

Said read the new judgment, "Their sentence is reduced to 10 ten years and they'll be transferred to Raja'i Shahr Prison in Karaj."

Ali rose, perturbed with what he heard. The over-sized image of the Ayatollah caught his vision. It occupied one third of the wall, next to the door leading to the tea room. Other walls were bare except for spots where paint peeled off. His curiosity peaked about the change.

After receiving the judgment sheet, he said, "Mullah Said, I respect wholeheartedly the pronouncement of the court. I have a question regarding this case."

The middle judge, face covered with a bushy beard, nodded. His forefinger pointed to the ceiling.

"Go ahead. What is your question?"

The eyes of the other two judges widened, as if the session became a bit more interesting.

"Why the reduction in punishment for this particular group?"

Said rubbed his long beard. "As this case was getting too much international attention, I consulted with the Ministry of Justice and was advised that the family and friends of this group have become very vocal in their protests. This case has reached the ears of many, including the U.N. High Commissioner for Human Rights and many human rights associations in Iran, America, and Europe. The honorable minister suggested it was in the best interest of the international reputation of our beloved Iran to reduce the sentence." His face lit up with a broad smile. "Keep in mind that sending them to Shahr Prison is not like going to a resort by the Caspian Sea. In fact, in this prison, the conditions are harsher than in Evin." He gave a hearty laugh.

Ali nodded. "It is a good decision."

"On the last item," Imam Said said, "the court finds Laila Dareini guilty of treason. According to our records she has pleaded guilty on all charges including espionage. The appropriate punishment in this case is death by hanging."

Ali knew this verdict was coming as the judges were pressured into rendering the decision to satisfy the Ministry of Justice's request to move Laila's case to a conclusion. Her cell was needed for another inmate. Ali also reflected on Orie—a stubborn lad who was given a chance but did not take it. Ali had wanted to save the boy, but ultimately never felt guilty for the way Orie's life ended—it was his job was to protect Islam at all cost. The same for his sister; though he had tried everything within reason to get her to renounce her dirty faith, she refused.

At that moment one consistent character trait held by both family members hit him hard. Unlike other detainees, they never hurled insults at him, though they remained firm and passionate in the expression of their opinions.

He recalled how it wasn't uncommon for a prisoner to insult his mother or yell that Ali was a bastard. On one occasion, despite several warnings, a particular woman's ranting continued until it reached such a height that Ali slapped her so hard, she fell and hit her head. Often, in the middle of interrogation, Ali was spat on by prisoners. These incidents were the norm.

After the court session ended and all four men walked towards the tea room, Ali couldn't help but question his own resolve. *Am I loyal enough to Islam? Would quitting really mean I love the regime any less? Must I remain as steadfast as Laila and her brother Orie or is that a trait to be despised in the face of truth, of reason?*

***

Ira's grip on the steering wheel tightened at the distant sight of Evin Prison's Main Gate. The Albortz Mountains stood beyond the buildings only a mile away from the windshield. A queasy feeling never failed to form in his stomach at its sight, regardless of how detailed the preparation was; the tension-induced pain was predictable. For a final check, Ira exited the Chamran Highway and parked the car at a golf course.

He lifted a mirror to his face and was pleased with the overall image. Next, he examined the detailing of the mask he wore. Running his fingers along it, he felt a few wrinkles on the faked sixty-year old appearance and aging lines in all the appropriate places. With no blisters anywhere, he was assured that the silicone mask was placed firmly on his own skin. He pressed on the brow, chin, and below the eyes as an added precaution. Then, he turned to Negar sitting next to him in the passenger seat. She burst out laughing and through the rearview mirror he watched Maliheh choking a giggle with her hand over her mouth.

"Tell me, how do I look?"

"Very believable," Negar smiled.

In fact, when Ira met Negar about a week ago, he noticed how burdened she was with worries about her family, making her look ten years older. "It's nice to see that this facade of Abbas' helps you laugh."

The sparkle from her eyes disappeared. "Mr. Ira, I hope your plan will work."

"As do I."

Ira pulled a device from his jacket pocket. When he pressed the record button, a picture appeared on a screen not much bigger than an iPhone 6. A fiber optic tube ran from this machine through the underlining of his jacket to the camera attached to the front of the turban on his head. The headgear was similar in size and shape to what the Ayatollah wore, except it was green. This particular shade was an indication of the lineage of the holy family beginning from Abraham, a highly respected sign regardless of where you went in Iran.

The camera was of the size and appearance of a ten-carat diamond. It was most the powerful miniature recording device ever built, with over one thousand optical magnifications. Developed by NASA and used by the FBI and CIA, it detected images of people behind walls, producing a high definition video, sending the signal at the speed of light to the digital recorder in Ira's pocket. Problem was, it could only see through one wall at a time, not like the capabilities Jake told him Maya had possessed. It was finally dawning on him why that computer was so valuable to the guy.

"Mr. Kohan. Sorry to say this, but what if we get caught?"

"We'll all be dead. That's how it goes." Ira was a straight shooter, no sugar-coating in his words. He firmly pressed down the black and grey mustache once more. "Are you ready to go?"

He waited for a few seconds and when no response came from the two women he drove the rest of the way to the main gate, located beyond a wall zigzagging on the hill in the distance.

The vehicle entered a narrow lane and moved until it reached a red brick wall signaling the perimeter of the notorious Evin prison. Many floodlights, all paced at regular distances atop the towers, lit up the area with a high-intensity—clearly visible in the afternoon. The place was further fortified with armed guards everywhere.

Ira stopped at a large metal gate, flanked by two walls covered with barbed wires. A soldier with a gun in his hand scrutinized the faces in the vehicle.

"What is the purpose of your visit?"

"To visit my daughter, Laila Dareini." He answered with a sad voice touched with a growl.

The soldier checked a sheet and then waved him in.

At the visitor's parking lot, he scoped the entire area as he slowly exited the car; the camera absorbed everything until a complete 360-degree span was achieved.

Guards in grey uniforms with helmets and protective eye-wear stood combat-ready in nearly every nook and cranny. Two men, each holding a machine gun, were stationed in the front of the building as a dozen or more dotted the space around the wall. However, the visitors gave these uniformed men little attention as their main focus was to see family members and friends.

Raising his head, Ira saw a blue-backed facade announcing "Evin House of Detention" in bold black lettering. They went inside the admission office to confirm Laila was scheduled to receive visitors. Then they took a place in line. After a long wait in the heat and sun, a loud speaker announced for their group to move into the visitor's hall. As the line inched forward, Ira kept moving his head around to capture everything in sight *and* beyond.

Once inside, Nagar scanned the faces of the five women on the other side of the glass wall. Ira stayed next to her as she shuffled through the crowd. She placed her left hand on the glass and waved the other as a frail woman with sunken cheeks and dark eyes waved back. Both women had their hands facing each other with the glass in between, their eyes within an inch of each other. Tears flowed from Laila as she sent kisses to Negar and Maliheh, both standing next to Ira. He saw traces of the stubborn but beautiful woman she had been, and wondered how much longer this delicate flower might last. Time was running out.

Maliheh wiped at her eyes with the chador. She lifted her hand up towards the ceiling. "We are praying for you."

Using her lips in an exaggerated way Laila responded. "*Merci*. Me too." She wiped her nose. "Jake, Megan, Dillon?"

Negar nodded, holding back tears. "Good."

Laila ran her forefinger on the wall.

Negar uttered a few words but with no response from her sister. She repeated the lip movement and again lifted both hands and looked up at the ceiling as if she was praying for her.

"What?" Laila said with her head shaking, desperately trying to decode her every word.

"We hope to see you at home." Her lips went into a slow, exaggerated movement.

Laila shook her head. "Nice. Thank you."

"Okay," Negar said.

Laila wrote on the wall. "So happy to see you."

As Negar ran her finger on the glass this time, Laila followed it with hers. "God willing."

While the three tried their best to communicate with hands, lips, and signs, Ira slowly turned around, pointing his head towards the guards and other visitors.

After thirty minutes a guard shouted that everyone had to leave. They ignored the call; conversations continued. The guard yelled again. The prisoners were ushered out through a door at a slower pace, with heads lowered and tears flowing, until the room emptied.

Back in the car, Ira turned off the recorder and drove away with the female passengers in silence—only wet checks voiced their sorrow.

Ira was also silent, trying to replay what he had just witnessed.

Maliheh spoke, "Mr. Ira, please save Laila from this hell."

Ira reflected on a response as he navigated through Tehran's traffic, a challenging task as best of times. He was well aware that not all projects were successful; not all missions attainable. Skill, but also luck, played an important role in reaching a rewarding conclusion.

He also wondered for the hundredth time why he got involved with this project. Jake's character—sincere but naïve, that's all he could think of. But Ira was also sincere and naïve when he decided to marry Devi. He connected with this poor American on those two traits. The forces of the universe had a way of protecting the innocent. *Was it coincidence?* Perhaps synchronicity played a role in assembling the right people at the right time to try and save Laila.

"Mrs. Dareini, we'll di our best." He was the kind of man who under-promised and over-delivered.

The journey continued until the vehicle stopped at the entrance of the house where they were staying. Hesitation wafted from Negar as she leaned forward to open the passenger door.

"I wish you success. Every time I have seen my sister at that prison, I have nightmares for days. I'm afraid to go out, afraid to live. Life has been very difficult for all of us. We have no choice but to manage."

Ira nodded. "I understand. You're doing the best you can under the circumstances. I couldn't ask for more from you, your mother, or father."

Maliheh leaned forward from the back seat. "Can we meet my son-in-law?"

"He's a white man with blond hair, and happens to be six-feet tall. If he goes out in public, he could get caught and killed. If I give him a disguise, you will not be meeting the same man."

She did not say anything. She opened and the door and stepped out.

Same with Negar.

Engine still running, Ira watched these two women walk towards the gate. A sense of compassion engulfed his whole body, a feeling he'd never experienced before. Both were desperate. He knew then, this mission had a deeper purpose than anything else he'd done in Iran with the Mossad. It would be more satisfying. *But will I succeed?*

Chapter 30

"Shit! Why's this taking so long?" Jake yelled. Then he watched the small circle twirl around as SkyDome waited the arrival of data from the StealthSat he'd just hacked. When the software finished the task, the groaning of the disk on a six Intel Core i7-4500U CPUs computer went away. To complete this massive undertaking, Jake noticed all the computing power of the laptop was exhausted, like Samson flexing all his muscles to move a huge boulder up a mountain.

He wished he had the Soarias D20, an *ultra*-super computer he once used on assignment. Actually, what he wanted was *Maya*—but that wound still festered. That machine had a mainframe capability only available with the United States Military. But Jake was grateful to Ira for having used his connections to smuggle in so many sophisticated devices to populate his headquarters. And Jake wasn't about to question how hot they were.

When SkyDome painted a high definition photo of Evin Prison on the screen, Jake was impressed. *Even better presentation than what Google Earth can produce.* He clicked on a button to zoom.

"Damn. Damn!"

He pounded the desk with his fist. It didn't show the profile of humans inside the buildings. In Afghanistan, before troops were sent on a mission, his task was to scan the building in the battle zone with a software similar to SkyDome.

Once, his scan of a war-torn school revealed every living body inside, including five US soldiers taken hostage by the Taliban. Jake had been able to present to his superior where each soldier was held, in separate rooms, surrounded by children as human shields and guarded by men with guns.

Jake was looking for similar information about Evin. The tech was out there, he just had to find it.

Ira and Meena entered the room, back from separate assignments. He took a glance at them then continued scouring for clues in the log-file for the failure to get the human profiles. He probably overlooked a hidden internal file somewhere.

Ira came closer. "Jake, I have to show you—"

"I can't right now. This is important."

Ira made clicking sound with his tongue. "Nothing is more important than this."

"Ira, just leave me alone. Will you? I've been trying to get this stupid profile scanner to work for the last eight hours. I'm so close."

"Take a rest." Ira peered at Jake's face. "Your eyes are red and you look dehydrated."

"If you were in my position, you would be too." Jake pinched his fingers to show how close he was. "It took me five hours just to crack the password on the low altitude StealthSat and position it on Evin with a code running fake data on a loop based on its last known target."

"What I have to show you is more important. Trust me. You're not listening. Food. Food, man." He dangled a plastic bag in front of Jake.

Food did the trick.

"Okay. I should take a break. My brain is fried."

Ira walked over to the kitchen, "Come on. Get away from that screen."

Jake and Meena followed. Ira left the food on the table then slipped back into the common room as Meena promptly distributed the meals. Many Iranian women enjoyed serving, something Jake had noticed in Laila, unlike his own family. Often Jake's father had to fend for himself at dinner time, since Ruth was out at some social event. In fact, when Jake was just five, his mother taught him how to cook Kraft dinner.

She used to say, "This is your survival skill when I'm not at home." A dozen Kraft Dinner boxes were stashed in the pantry just in case.

Jake joined Meena. "How's it going?'

Meena placed a Styrofoam box on the table and threw her hands in the air. "Not good." Her face blanched.

"What's the obstacle?"

Meena's role was to get inside information on the guards and prisoners then corroborate it with Jake's findings from the profile scanner, if he could get the damn thing working. "It is hard to get inside information. Even prisoners who've been set free don't want to talk about their ordeals or about the staff in that place."

"Fear."

Meena nodded. "Yes, fear is definitely one answer. Also, before release, each prisoner apparently has to sign a contract stating they'll keep their mouth shut. If they divulge any information about the prison and are found guilty, they will be sent back to Evin *with* their family."

Jake knew that Meena was creative, persistent, and loyal—she wouldn't give up.

"What's your next move?"

Meena pulled a big pot from a bag and deposited it on the table. She opened the lid. "Lots of rice. You're probably getting sick of it by now."

He scratched his head. He did not want to sound unappreciative of their help. "Kind of. But with the problems we have on hand, who's thinking about rice?"

Meena pulled out another bag.

"Ira got a surprise for you."

This whole trip had been filled with surprises.

"What is it?"

She handed him a plastic bag. "Open it. See for yourself."

When he lowered his head, the smell of deep-fried French fries and broiled meat hit his nostrils.

"Hamburgers! Is it legal here?"

He dug his hand in and pulled the burger and crispy golden potato chips out. His eyes danced around the food as his fingers moved to handle this precious commodity. His taste buds anticipated the beef, making his mouth fill with saliva. Jake opened wide.

Meena went to the kitchen counter where one sink was filled with clean dishes and the other with dirty ones. She pulled two plates out and placed on them on the table.

"Back to your question. I've already talked to five people." She lifted one hand with the fingers spread out. "None wanted to talk, let alone give out any information."

"We need to know Laila's cell location."

"I understand. I have to keep digging until I find someone willing to spill." The tone in her voice indicated the pressure she felt.

Ira yelled, "Can you guys come over here?"

Meena loaded rice, roasted tomatoes, and some vegetable onto her plate. "Let's go."

Jake took another bite of his burger. When the beef touched his tongue, a sensation of long-awaited satisfaction zinged his brain. With every chew he savored the sensation. He walked behind Meena in a bit of a daze until they both positioned themselves behind Ira and his computer. He clicked *play* on the screen.

Jake saw a woman behind a glass wall. She wiped tears from her cheeks but continued waving until her palm coincided with that of another woman on the other side of the glass. The taste of the food quickly soured.

"Is that Laila?" He dropped the burger back in the bag and let it fall to the floor as he watched the clip for another two minutes. "Stop. Stop. I can't look at this."

He sank onto the couch by the window. Hands over his eyes, Jake rested his elbows on his knees as his whole body vibrated with despair. Overwhelmed, he cried inside. It took him several minutes to regain his senses, only able to tilt his head towards the ceiling.

"What have they done to my wife?" His sorrow became palpable as he curled in on himself and finally let the tears fall.

Meena and Ira stepped towards him, not quite sure what to do. Motionless and stunned, they didn't know how to react.

With Jake's eyes closed, no matter how hard he tried, he couldn't hold on to the image of the woman he married. Not even the strongest one of her leaving him at the airport. Instead, the pale, battered figure from Ira's video kept flashing behind his eyes, breaking up his carefully preserved memories.

"What has she ever done to anyone? This isn't fair. Not fair. *Not* fair. I have to get her out of that hell hole before they kill her."

"Any progress in finding the prisoner profiler?" Ira asked.

Jake ignored him and focused instead on the situation in Kandahar that he'd witnessed last year—those five men held hostage by the Taliban in a school. The negotiation for their release had failed and intelligence indicated that they'd be executed by their captors. A meeting by the chief of the tactical unit was called to plan their rescue. It ended with the death of two Americans.

"Ira, do you know what the Iranian authorities are planning to do with her? Take her to trial or what?"

"The court recently decided that she's guilty of treason, which is punishable by death. There's no time left."

Meena echoed, "We have to act now."

"I've been trying to get the software to capture pictures of the prisoners so that we can match Laila's image to find where they might be holding her."

Ira took a few steps away to look at the surveillance camera for the safe house. “My hunch is that she’ll be in Ward 209. We know that’s where the women deemed most dangerous are kept.”

“She’s not dangerous. She’s an angel.”

“I’m sorry Jake. I didn’t mean it that way.”

Jake regained his composure somewhat. “We don’t want to shoot in the dark. We need to confirm that she’s in Ward 209. We’ve only got one chance here.”

“I’ll work on it.”

“In the meantime I’ll keep trying to break into the site to find the data files I need. I checked the log and can’t access this folder because they’ve blocked any IP address from Iran accessing that location.”

Ira said, “There’s a software that the Israelis used to scan all the nuclear sites in Iran. It also gave imaging details for everyone working inside the building. That’s how they identified the scientists at the nuclear sites and eventually assassinated some of them. The software was developed in the Ukraine where they may not have the IP restrictions you’re facing.”

“Type in the name of the software for me,” Jake said. Ira nodded and switched over to Jake’s computer before he and Meena left to work on their assignments.

God, I hope I can get Laila out of this alive.

Chapter 31

Meena stepped out of Ira's car into an affluent neighborhood. Startled, after receiving a tender look and best wishes from her friend, she inhaled deeply, fighting back a growing tension in her stomach. After letting the air go, she moved toward one particular house. Ira stayed in the car.

Meena went past a park where children played and parents socialized, a common thing among the well-to-do families. The sidewalk was lined with over-grown beech trees, providing pedestrians shade on a hot day.

She opened the gate in front of a grey house and made sure no one was watching her, before making the final approach. For the success of this mission, she had surveyed this area several times, making note of the houses, traffic, and pedestrians. This was her third trip out here, not an unusual thing when tracking a potential target for a mission.

At the front door, Meena knocked three times. After a long wait, she tried again before finally hearing steps approach. An elderly woman in black slacks with a beige top hanging to her ankles opened the door and adjusted her head scarf by wrapping the ends round her neck and shoulders.

"*Salam, Khanum*. I am here to see Mojgan."

As expected, the woman looked at her with suspicion then shook her head. She did not hide her feelings. "What the hell are you doing asking about Mojgan?"

Meena bowed her head, showing respect for the elderly. Her informant told her Mojgan suffered from severe depression after being released from Evin. A stethoscope hung from Meena's neck, she squeezed the ear pieces.

"I'm from the clinic." When needed, she used deception to get the job done.

The grandma reached for the door, determined not to let anyone inside, but Meena stepped on the threshold preventing it from closing. The woman was shocked and gave Meena a stern look, anger building inside.

"What the hell are you doing? I won't let you into my house. Get out."

It was Meena's last, and perhaps *only* chance, to get the position of Laila's cell. She lowered her hand to the hem of the black robe she wore and pulled it all the way up to her groin.

"See." A Star of David tattooed her inner thigh.

The older woman shot a disgusted looked at Meena, which turned into curiosity.

"Why there?"

"When I turned twelve, I got together with a group of friends for my Bat Mitzvah, and as the party got underway we got silly. One of my friends wanted to give me a present, she wanted it to be this … we did it in secret."

"My husband was Jewish. Come in."

When Meena had researched this family, their Jewish heritage had come up. "*Merci, khanum*. Where is Mojgan?"

She pointed to the second door on her right. "Be warned, she's very angry. She threw a shoe at me."

In Iranian culture, one must be very upset to throw a shoe at someone, an equally disapproving act toward one's grandmother.

"I'm so sorry to hear that."

Meena went through the hallway, past the kitchen, and then knocked twice at the bedroom door. With no reaction from inside, she opened it.

A women curled in the fetal position lay on a bed in one corner of the room. One shoe rested cockeyed near Meena's feet and the other by the bed. A plate half-full of food lay on the floor, the remainder had been flung around the room covering bras, underwear, and pants also strewn about.

Avoiding stepping on anything, Meena made her way to the bed and sat on the edge. "Hello. My name is Meena, and I need your help."

"I'm surprised you're in my room," Mojgan growled. "My grandmother is like a guard dog. Won't let any strangers here since my mother died."

Meena wasn't about to tell her that the star of David tattooed on her thigh opened the door to her. "It was nice of her to let me in."

"Are you from the government? If you are, I am not talking to you and you can leave. Leave now. Who exactly are you?" With every word, the anger in her rose.

"Mojgan, no. Calm down please."

"Oh, you know my name. What else do you know about me?" Her voice was losing energy.

Next to the lamp on the table sat a prescription drug container. It was not surprising to Meena that Mojgan was depressed, as many released prisoners became that way as they unraveled the incidents that led to their arrest. The humiliation and threat to their family made life miserable.

Her face was pale and dry, her hair unwashed, and her eyes sunken with black circles around them; all this told Meena she'd lost her will to live. Antidepressants drained all her emotion.

"How are you feeling?" She did not want to get Laila's cell number and run. At the same time, she thought of Ira waiting for her. Taking too long might spur him to action.

Silence. Mojgan blinked, resisting tears. After a sniff, she said, "Angry." Meena placed her hand on the girl's ankle. "I can't help hating myself to the point of being sick for going to that demonstration looking for my friend."

"Which one?"

"In 2009, following the re-election of President Ahmadinejad. I'm not a political person. I don't give a shit who the president of Iran is." A burning anger made her sit up straight. "I went to the demonstration in search of my friend. We were going to my parents' summer house by the Caspian Sea." She blew air out, then silence.

Meena waited a moment for Mojgan to gather her strength before asking, “What happened when you got there?”

“The Revolutionary Guards arrived in droves and broke up the crowd. Started rounding up people randomly. I was arrested and taken to Evin Prison.” She finally let herself cry.

“For ninety days, *ninety days*, I was barred from making any phone calls and my family got no information about me. Then, they let me go.”

This was good progress. Meena didn’t want to lose the girl’s willingness and so coaxed her toward rising. “Move so that you are sitting on the edge of the bed.”

Meena grabbed her hand and pulled until Mojgan firmly sat on her bottom. The girl swung her legs and pulled herself forward until she rested with her arms on her legs at the end of the bed. It was a good sign.

“You’re doing well.” Meena placed a hand on Mojgan’s shoulder. “Then what happened?”

“I was arrested again in December 2010 and released in March 2011 after securing bail. Not five days later they came to my home and took me to prison again, keeping me for another two weeks, when I was finally allowed out on leave.” She shook her head, mystified by it all.

Meena was familiar with the tactics used by the authorities to break down a person. “You are doing very well. Keep going.”

“A month later the security forces came to arrest me again and they broke a window to get into my home in the middle of the night. But that night I wasn’t here, I was spending time at my grandmother’s home.”

Meena saw a dark shadow on Mojgan’s face.

“My mother suffered a heart attack when the security forces broke in. She died three days later in the hospital.”

Meena felt the pain leach off this young woman and empathized with her plight.

Now the tears rolled freely down this tortured soul’s cheek.

“Take a break. Let’s clean up this room.” Meena started gathering dirty clothes and placed them in a corner. She placed both shoes nicely by the door, took the plate into the kitchen and came back. Mojgan had straightened her covers.

"I hate to make you go through this. But painful as it is, talking about your ordeal will help. I want to help you through this and work toward living a normal life no longer afraid and hopeless."

"They arrested me again and ill-treated me beyond anyone's imagination."

Meena rubbed Mojgan's back. "Take a break any time you want to."

"They beat me up as I dangled from the ceiling by one leg. They degraded me by forcing me to lick a soiled toilet bowl; punched me in the face while I was blindfolded; threatened to have me tried with a charge of *moharebeh* (enemy against God), which could carry the death penalty."

"Were they looking for something?"

"Yes. The interrogators asked me to 'confess' in front of their camera that I had links to the outlawed MEK of Iran. They thought I knew who was targeting the interrogators."

At this point Meena dared to ask, "Which section of the prison were you in?"

"Ward 209, where the most dangerous women are kept—political rebels and other undesirables. Do I look like a dangerous woman? I'm a graduate student. I'm not a murderer or thief."

"Did you mingle with other prisoners?"

She shook her head. "No. It's an isolation area. Days would go by before I saw anyone, except the woman who delivered our meals."

"Did you see or hear of Laila Dareini? Is she still there?"

"As I said, their purpose was to humiliate and break down one's spirit. Trust me, it worked."

"Mojgan, who was the supervisor."

"One mean, fat lady called Fatimeh."

Meena shook her head at the positive intel. "Come. Let's walk to the kitchen."

She helped lift the girl's frail body. Both walked down the hall to the kitchen. Mojgan's grandmother joined them, delighted to see her granddaughter. Eagerly she offered to make tea and brought out some Persian delights.

While Mojgan sipped the tea, Meena excused herself briefly from the home to tell Ira she did not get the exact information they were looking for. He was disappointed but agreed the guard name was a plus.

When Meena returned, Mojgan had progressed to more substantial food. Afterwards, she took a shower and both women went out for a walk, which helped improve the girl's mood. Before leaving, Meena promised to come back daily and walk with Mojgan until her broken spirit strengthened. Meena just couldn't ignore her humanity when the job brought her so close to such pain.

Chapter 32

Jake had difficulty keeping his eyes open in front of the computer after thirteen hours of relentless pursuit. Further to Ira's advice, after scouring hundreds of software companies he found one of interest, a Canadian company called Supportech Inc which earned most of its revenue as a contractor with the United States Military. Also, this company had a major software development center in Dnepropetrovsk, Ukraine, where a program called SkyView was developed and deployed.

This high-tech work was a replica of the American version of SkyDome. Now Jake understood how the US Military circumvented American laws that prohibited companies from sharing or using top secret technologies outside its borders. *Just hire a company to do the dirty work for you.*

With every passing moment as Jake penetrated into the belly of the system and its databases, Laila's tortured face ran through his mind. If saving her from death meant sacrificing every ounce of his energy, he was prepared to do so. He had no desire to eat, drink, or sleep until he found the cell where his beloved was incarcerated—once they had that intel, they could move onto breaking her out.

To his surprise, Jake also discovered that SkyView used the same military StealthSat as SkyDome to take pictures of buildings on Earth. From the screen forms, he enabled the soundwave emitters position at Evin Prison.

These sound waves had a unique property that bent sideways when hitting the surface of the earth. The waves following the horizon in conjunction with Laser beams and sensors, would allow SkyView to produce human profiles inside a building. This sophisticated software, with powerful algorithms, produced photos sharper than one taken by a Canon 4Ti. If SkyView could give him human profiles, Jake planned to then manually match those profiles to the one Ira got of Laila.

SkyView's high definition graphic display was impressive. With the click of the mouse, a form showed the controls of StealthSat. There were Laser, soundwave, and electromagnetic transponders which he enabled with a check mark. When his eyes came to a High Definition algorithm, he pulled up the explanation for the feature. After reading it, he enabled it too. He fought against hacking with great reluctance but it was the sight of Laila's frail body, reduced to a dispirited shell, that won the argument. If he'd had Maya, cracking the software code would've been unnecessary. Jake realized how costly the price was for throwing Maya out of the car window. Totally driven by pain, fear and frustration, he'd lost an ally.

Jake double checked to make sure all the necessary modules were activated. "Let 'er rip!" he cried and clicked the run button.

As the system went into configuration mode, his stomach demanded he use this down-time in a more productive way. He went to the kitchen and opened the fridge—finally able to allow himself nourishment since rejecting the last of his burger yesterday. Pulling out leftovers, he made himself some tea and then hurried back to SkyView.

With an occasional sip of the hot drink and a bite of food, he watched the progress bar move forward. After the software finished scanning and synthesizing the data, an image of Evin spread over most of the screen.

Where are the profiles in the shape of the top of human heads? Where are all the red circles? They weren't there. The food in his stomach turned to stone. His heart ached as if being torn from his chest. He was tired, his mind exhausted. He didn't have much energy left to go forward and was afraid he'd collapse if he did. *It should've worked.* He dropped his head into his hands and groaned.

Then he looked up and examined the image again. This time he saw two lines he'd never seen before. Seemingly both were about two inches thick and ran parallel toward the prison.

Jake activated different parameters in Skyview's control panel, and ran the software again with specific focus on the area where the lines appeared.

After another trip to the kitchen, to put food back in the fridge, and a ten-minute wait, the software came up with a 3D image of a tunnel made of concrete running along the edge of the property parallel to the main building. Through the GPS, he noted the size and co-ordinates of the entrance.

"Yes!" He danced back to the kitchen to celebrate with orange soda and chips.

***

Meena rode the CB1100A Honda motorcycle to the top of a hill and stopped. She watched the tail lights of a vehicle move away in the distance under a moonlit sky. A startling confidence in Jake's tasking of the satellite surveillance over the surroundings of Evin Prison took her by surprise. He discovered several layers of security fencing surrounded the perimeter of the prison; the most outer later contained a barbed wire fence, inside of which lay the prison grounds, and on the outside a dirt road where five SUVs circled the perimeter.

These security vehicles were paced about five minutes from each other and never stopped moving. Along this fence there were guarded towers equipped with machine guns, night vision goggles, and binoculars. Meena shouldn't have been surprised by Jake's capabilities, after all, the man had worked at the best surveillance department in the US military. But the skeptical side of her always made her work harder to achieve success. It had worked for her so far.

In another second she heard the whisper of Ira's motorcycle. With a gentle spur of the engine she turned right into an area surrounded by bushes and trees. Peeling off her helmet, she tossed it to the ground and lowered the motorcycle to its side. She unloaded a bag containing an oxygen mask, tank, night vision goggles, and a miner's hat with headlamp. The goggles were for outside use and the mining gear for the tunnel.

In less than thirty seconds Meena had all three units firmly placed on her body. Ira struggled with the oxygen tank, so she moved closer to help fasten the straps behind his head.

"You should have practiced."

"Yes, *dear*. I hear you. What did you say?"

His sarcastic remark irritated her as always. But Ira had one quality that all women loved: he would listen, without reservation, whenever she spilled her guts—for her, it was better than sex knowing someone *got you* like that.

When the oxygen mask was secure around his nose, she ran the straps around his shoulders and firmly hung the tank across his back. As the commander of this mission, she proceeded to establish communication with command control.

She texted, *"Ready."*

They were on an inspection mission for the tunnel.

Jake's response came as a ding with, *"Let me do a check."* A few seconds later, he gave the all clear and texted, *"You're about 100 meters from the mouth of the tunnel. Proceed."*

Jake was easily able to gather positioning data by tapping into the StealthSat GPS capabilities. For days now he'd been watching the guards circling the perimeter of the prison. He could track the movement of these vehicles and made notes of their routine and shift changes.

Meena and Ira headed towards the mouth of the tunnel, the moon inconsistent in the sky above so they used their infrared goggles to track the terrain. After a minute of walking, Ira lowered his body and worked to pull a five-by-five plywood board from a hidden access tunnel. He'd updated the covering last night during a preliminary external inspection.

Both agents went down a set of concrete steps and slipped inside. Stale, pungent air hit Meena like a punch in the face. She switched the goggles off and activated her minor's helmet. It was dark but she could easily see about ten feet in front with the headlight on.

Meena texted, *"In."*

She was startled by a swift rustling noise. When she pointed the light to the floor, two rats scuttled past, scraping their claws as they went. Lately, rodents ran rampant in Tehran. A program was in place to control the critter population, but truth be told, she was more afraid of the snakes. At the age of twelve, a viper got into her room and then her bed. She was bitten. Only with the quick reaction of her father and neighbors did she survive.

She heard a ding.

Jake responded, *"Can see you."* What he meant was the app he used showed a flashing dot, indicating her and Ira's position. He still couldn't see *into* the prison, but this at least allowed him to keep eyes on her and Ira as they moved forward with Plan B.

Meena looked up; Ira was about twenty feet ahead. The tunnel beneath her vibrated but she didn't know what to make of it.

She slowed a bit to text, *"Floor shaking. Check cause."*

Meena pocketed the phone and shifted to pick up her speed and catch up to Ira when a strange noise fractured the silence. The ground under her feet rumbled more aggressively, a sound familiar but terrifying. She stopped moving but the shaking intensified. A loud cracking sounded several feet ahead as if a tree trunk were being rent in two. The ceiling split open right above Ira. Soil poured down as her partner collapsed beneath its weight.

"NO!"

She fell into the side of the tunnel spreading her arms wide to help keep her balance. Soil and rock crashed down until Ira completely disappeared.

"No," she whispered, then texted, *"Ceiling opened! Ira buried. Can't see him. Covered."*

"Covered with what?"

"Can't see him!" She threw the phone down, dropped to her knees and shoveled dirt with her bare hand as hard as she could.

"Ira, can you hear me? I'll get you out, love."

Several minutes later there was still no sign of a body. The mound over him rose nearly five feet and stretched the width of the tunnel.

"Ira! Ira! Please God, don't let him die. I need him." She drained all her energy scraping and digging the compacted soil. She lost all sense of time. Meena hit a pointed object, igniting a sharp pain running from her right wrist to the shoulder. She ignored the sting and continued shoving both hands deep into rocky soil and gravel until she felt a portion of the concrete that used to be the tunnel roof. Meena moved and swayed to help dislodge the piece. She dragged it to the side as something moistened her arm. Blood flowed from a wound in her palm. It didn't matter. She continued digging.

Some distant part of the agent's brain registered a noise behind her, but she ignored it. She didn't care. Only Ira mattered now. But it got louder, footsteps racing towards her! When she turned, she couldn't see into the dark, her headlamp now caked with moist dirt. *Please don't be the guards. Please!* She dug faster.

The footsteps slowed. She sensed a presence behind her and turned, exhausted. "Jake? You? How?"

"Yes, it's me." He dropped down beside her. "Move over. Let me dig in the middle." With knees firmly planted at the edge of the pile, he sunk his hands into soil and like two shovels he threw dirt to the side. His breathing grew louder. With every inhale his chest puffed up and his hands moved with incredible power for such a lithe man.

Her hands ached; several finger nails had torn off but still she did not relent. Blood seeping out from her palm but dirt caked most of the wound now. She faced Jake, her hands shaking as the pile in the middle became more and more shallow.

Finally, a hand appeared. Jake moved the dirt from around Ira's wrist, following the arm to his waist while Meena focused on the upper body. Jake maneuvered his hand deep into the soil.

"I got his leg." He grabbed it with each hand. "He should be clear enough. I'll pull."

Ira's body shifted beneath the layers of soil, like panned gold, until he lay uncovered on the ground. Meena tore the mask off his face and lowered her ear to his chest.

"He's not breathing. Why? Why? Why did the oxygen mask fail?" Great gulps of tears burst from their frayed restraints, but only for a moment. She reined control over her emotions and placed her hand on her best friend's face. It was warm.

"Ira? Ira, can you hear me?" No response.

On his other side, Jake made sure the agent's body lay flat.

Meena placed a hand under his neck for lift.

"Give him mouth to mouth," Jake said.

She pressed both of his cheeks to force his mouth open and looked inside for a clear passage way before placing her ear close Ira's nose and mouth listening for slight breathing. "Nothing." She tilted his head back a touch more and lifted his chin before pinching his nose. Meena covered Ira's mouth with hers and blew until she saw his chest rise.

"Meena, breathe harder. As hard as you can." Jake straddled Ira's stomach, knees planted firmly on the ground. With both hands, he pumped the man's chest between Meena's breaths. "Ira, buddy, we need you. Come back. Come back. I need your help. Meena wants you to wake up. We have to free Laila. You can't go yet. It's not your time." He timed the chest pumps between Meena's breaths and his words.

Meena stopped and lowered her ear to his mouth. "I can feel something."

Jake stopped. "I saw his hand twitch."

"Ira, come back. You have to come back," she moaned. But his body remained still.

Chapter 33

Ali slid out of his Mercedes E320 in the driveway of his parents' home. With the new-car scent still potent after three months of use, he esteemed this gift from his parents as a jewel in his crown. Walking away from the prized possession, he shot a glance at the shine and shape of the black luxury beauty with admiration.

At the iron-gate, he unlocked the entrance with a push on the latch while his mind still debated whether to confide in his parents his recent life-changing decision or not. As his friends and confidants, he never kept a secret from them, but this time was different.

When he entered the house, his mother got up from the sitting room sofa and approached him.

"Salam, *Madar joon,*" he said

She kissed his cheeks and forehead.

The air, filled with the aroma of Persian spices, tickled his appetite as always; he came for dinner with his parents every Friday. The room sparkled with ornate lighting fixtures on the walls and ceiling. The floor was graced with beautiful, expensive Persian rugs, leather sofas, and antique Egyptian chairs.

She yelled, "Bijan, Ali is here."

His mother knew he was always on a killer schedule. Ali pulled a cell phone from his back pocket. With slowed steps, he made his way towards the dining table while scrolling down the messages on the tiny screen. He stopped to read one text only:

"It's true."

He lifted his eyes towards the ceiling, head shaking he whispered, "What is going on?"

Bijan appeared at the doorway.

Ali approached his father. "*Salam, Babah.*" Then they exchanged kisses on both checks.

His father's eyes opened wide in appreciation of his son. "*Be-farma, be-farma.*" He pointed his hand towards a chair for Ali to sit down at the dining table, then the older man took the head seat.

Ali settled onto the chair to left of his father. Bahiyeh, his mother, came back holding a silver plate of rice which she placed on the table. Right behind her was Niki, the house servant, who placed two other dishes beside it.

Bahiyeh sat across from Ali. Her eyes sparkled with pleasure. She admired her only child. Ali returned a gaze of appreciation. Her face was round with large brown eyes and rosy cheeks, and she wore a beautiful outfit of red and green. When inside, she preferred a traditional set of clothing with colorful, vibrant elegance, but in public she wore a respectable, black hijab.

After Bijan placed a heap of Basmati rice with saffron on his plate, his wife handed him a pot of *ghormeh sabzi*, lamb cooked in kidney beans, spinach, coriander leaves, dried limes, parsley and several other spices—a family favorite. As he often did, while chewing the first mouthful, Ali's father commented on politics.

"Israel's prime minister is making noise about destroying Persia again." The disapproval synchronized with a clicking sound of his tongue. "It won't happen. Like in Israel, prophets of God have walked on our blessed land." The words rolled out with both fervor and disdain.

Ali knew that once his father started on this subject he would not stop. Ali turned and touched his father's shoulder as a way to politely interrupt the lecture.

"*Babah*, I need to speak with you."

"We have divine protection." He placed his spoon on the plate. "I must admit the Israelis—with American help—have been causing a lot of damage to our nuclear facility, but they'll never deprive us from having such a technology. It's our God-given right."

Bahiyeh talked over her husband. "Ali joon, you're not eating." She stared at his plate and lifted the tomato cucumber salad. "Take some of this. You haven't touched the *ghormeh sabzi.*"

Usually Ali would snap back at her for forcing him to eat. In fact, she'd been force feeding him since he was five. As a child, he was chubby and fiercely ridiculed. But today he had an unusually tolerant heart.

"Merci, Madar joon."

Bijan stared gravely at his wife. "Bahiyeh, Bahiyeh. Are you listening to what I'm saying?" Instantly both Ali and Bahiyeh turned towards Bijan. He continued, "Our Ayatollah has predicted that our enemies have a chance to win this battle. That day will *not* come. They will be wrestled to the ground."

As the lecture continued, the text Ali received earlier ran through his mind, weighing heavily on him. As a polite son, he listened to his father, barely, as the urge to express his pressing thoughts grew with every passing moment.

When dinner was over, father and son moved into the living room, a spacious and attractively decorated space. Sweets and fruits in silver and crystal platters already awaited them. Bahiyeh disappeared and within minutes came back with Earl Grey Tea. She left the two men to continue with their conversation while sipping the hot beverage from a delicate, golden-rimmed glass.

When his father was occupied serving fresh dates for himself, Ali seized the opportunity to speak, "Babah, I have decided to quit my job at the prison." His Father dropped a date on the floor, gaze shifting from his plate to his son's face.

"Quitting, you said?"

Ali's stomach turned inside out. "Yes, Babah joon."

Instantly the older man gathered his composure, picked the date up from the floor and placed it on his plate.

Shaking his head, he said, "No, you can't do that." It was a commandment not a suggestion.

"I must. If not, I'll be killed."

His father's eyebrows arched before he grimaced, "Killed? What do you mean?" Bijan placed his right hand on his greying head of hair.

"It has been confirmed. I'm on the MEK hit list." Fear struck Ali's heart hearing the words spoken aloud.

"Next week is my birthday. You can't quit. *After* my party we'll talk about it again."

This was going to be his father's sixtieth birthday. Disappointing his father would not be a good idea. He enjoyed grandiose parties and attention from celebrities and powerful people.

"Who's invited?"

His father got excited, "Who is invited? The list is long." With one hand cupped over his mouth, the other picked food from between his teeth with a tooth pick—a routine custom after dinner. He paused then took a sip of tea.

"The Minister of Justice is coming. Many Imams. And at the top of the list is the Ayatollah himself." He lifted his hand towards the ceiling and said, "God willing."

The Minister of Justice was Ali's boss. At this extravagant event his father would be talking to all the political and clerical powers. How could he deny him such an honor?

"Where's it being held?"

"Esteghlal International Hotel."

Knowing his father, he booked Daryay-e-Nour Hall, also known as the Sea of Light, for its 1000-person capacity. Bijan Mohmed could easily afford this lavish party—all he had to do was sell a thousand barrels or more of oil to finance the event. In his circle of friends, associates, and politicians, he was known for holding lavish gatherings. How could he not have one for his sixtieth birthday?

Ali could imagine mingling with ministers, Mullahs, and friends; they would be praising his father for his service in the Iraq war and for being a devout supporter of the Iranian revolution. But what would really make his chest puff up was the mention of his son as a defender of Islam.

When the dreaming ceased, Ali's stomach turned with anxiety, something he experienced often in the last few weeks. This pain interrupted his sleep, making him wake with regularity around 3:00 am. Then his mind would churn over all the things happening at Evin, then back to the hit list again.

"Why me? I've been a good Muslim and support the Islamic Government. Why would Allah allow someone to kill me?"

The birthday party excitement disappeared from his father's face. "Perhaps it's a hoax."

Does he really know or he is just trying to allay his own fear?

"Many are taking it seriously. Three in my division alone are dead." As Ali chewed on a date, silence filled the room.

After a moment of reflection his father said, "I know government officials have been killed. I think it's the work of the Israelis. But when it comes to Evin, I don't know who is doing the assassinations. I'll make some inquiries. I'll find out about this list, even if I have to talk to the Ayatollah himself."

When Ali heard *Ayatollah* spoken aloud the words, he lived by rang through his mind as if on cue: *If one permits an infidel to continue in his role as a corrupter of the earth, the infidel's moral suffering will be all the worse. If one kills the infidel, and this stops him from perpetrating his misdeeds, this death will be a blessing to him.*

On occasion Ali had reflected on the Ayatollah's belief of death as a "blessing". But from what he had seen, not all of the prisoners were evil people. The system painted *every* detainee with the same brush. What if it was wrong? How could he claim justice was being done? He was tired and didn't want to think on it anymore.

"I should go."

"Stay. Have more tea."

He ignored the request as *Taraf.* His parents knew of his hectic schedule. After kissing them goodbye, he left the house where he was born and grew up, that unsettled pinch in his stomach worsening. At the gate, when he turned around to slide the latch, two beaming faces smiled as his parents waved goodbye.

Nearly twenty feet from his car, he heard a click. Turning toward the noise, two bodies on roaring motorcycles shot like spears at him. He ran to his car for cover. Diving to the ground, gun shots rang through the air. The engine noise thundered past and faded away.

He tried to get up, just managing to lift his body, his stomach wet. *Blood.*

Ali heard footsteps and then screams from his mother, which turned to wailing.

His father shouted, "Call an ambulance!" The man eased Ali's body to the ground and placed his son's head in his lap. Babah pressed his hand into Ali's chest wound. "Oh my God, he won't stop bleeding!"

Ali barely registered his mother hovering over him with one palm choking her wailing. "Oh, my sweet son. Why, why you? Good God, why would someone want to hurt you? Bijan, bleeding … leg."

"Give me your chador."

Bahiyeh unwrapped the head dress and threw it to her husband. Bijan knotted the cloth just above Ali's knee. The interrogator felt his mind clear with a fresh wave of energy but his chest still ached. He opened his eyes wide open. "Two … two men. Black. Dressed in black …"

Bijan turned to his wife, "Stop wailing! Ali's trying to say something important."

Ali continued, "M. E. K."

Bijan responded, "MEK … yes. You would know, wouldn't you?"

Bahiyeh rebuked, "Bijan, do something! Our only son is bleeding. Why isn't the ambulance here?"

Bijan's tears fell across the wound in Ali's chest, "My son, don't leave us. I need you."

"I'm going to die. I can … feel it." Ali closed his eyes as the last burst of energy dissipated and his mind clouded over. He could barely make sense of his father's words.

"Dear merciful God. You see me in tears holding my son's head while his heart is bleeding to death … what more can I do?"

***

In the collapsed tunnel, Meena continued the flow of air into Ira's body, hoping for a miracle.

Jake stopped.

"Wait," he held her shoulder. "His chest is rising on its own, slightly." With a gentle motion, he moved Meena's body to the side so he could get a clear view of Ira's eyes. He lowered his headlamp towards the man's face. "His eyes are shifting left and right under his lids." When soldiers were wounded in the battle, he'd remotely monitored the revival processes. Everything rushed back. "Okay. Give him more air."

Meena lowered her head, cleared the hair from her face, opened his jaw and breathed once more into his lungs. Alternately, Jake pushed with both hands on Ira's chest.

"He's blinking. More air." Jake backed away from Ira, reaching for the man's oxygen tank. After careful examination, he said, "Shit. The strap broke. Here, let him breath from the tank." He inserted the mask on his face and opened up the tap to the oxygen flow.

"Ira, Ira joon. Come back. Come back to me. I need you," Meena moaned.

Nearly ten minutes later, Ira gain consciousness and was able to rise unsteadily to his feet. Jake placed the elastic for the oxygen mask around Ira's head and lifted the man's body over his shoulder. Ira's head hung limp by Jake's back. To share the load, Meena moved in front of Jake, grabbed Ira's legs and placed them on her shoulder. They moved towards the entrance, with Meena in front and Jake following.

At the mouth of the tunnel, they placed Ira on the ground in the fresh night air. Meena turned off her miner's helmet and slipped the night vision goggles up over her eyes. After a 360-degree survey of the surroundings, she concluded there were no other humans in the immediate vicinity. She bent down and lifted Ira's legs while Jake wrapped his arms around Ira's chest and they carried him over to the motorcycles. Meena righted her bike and got on as Jake place Ira on the seat behind her. They could hear the echo of his breath in the oxygen mask but wavered as he sat upright, they needed more security for him. Meena took her chador out and handed it to Jake. He moved Ira's hands around Meena's stomach and tied them together. Jake hid Ira's bike in the underbrush then mounted his own and all three rode off.

Chapter 34

Fatimeh Mohamadi was in her Proton Impian, a locally manufactured vehicle, which she favored over imports. She hated commuting, especially with too many high-testosterone drivers in Tehran. But she had to do it because the travel from her house to work at Evin prison took two hours, one way, by public transportation and only half that time in her car.

She was on her way for the 6:00 pm shift and, as always, a sense of relief ran over her when she turned onto the Chamran Highway and could clearly see the prison buildings in the distance. *Another five minutes.*

An unexpected light flashed off her passenger side-mirror. With a glance out the window, Fatimeh noticed a Toyota Land cruiser maneuver close in the next lane.

A speaker blared, “Pull over, now.”

The flickering white and red beam came from the vehicle’s roof. Fatimeh grabbed the armrest and squeezed it. *Those bastards again.* She’d been stopped many times by the guards of the Revolutionary Guardian, and every time she hated the guts of those arrogant, impolite men.

Through the Land Cruiser’s rolled down window, one young man waved his hand signaling Fatimeh to stop driving. She guided the car to the side of the highway and came to a stop, determined to give these badly-behaved boys a piece of her mind.

The Cruiser pulled in front of her. From the passenger side, a man in a khaki uniform with a gun hanging from his shoulder approached her window. She took the longest time to manually roll it down and then gave him the most disappointing of expressions she could muster.

"*Salam Khanum*, Fatimeh," he gave a nod, showing respect. "Forgive me for stopping you on your way to attend to an honorable duty at Evin."

She was surprised by how well-mannered he was. "How do you know me? Where I'm going?"

"I have bad news, which you may already have been made aware of."

She shook her head as a way to request more information. "What news?"

He placed his hand on his chest. "I am saddened to inform you that brother Ali is in Allah's loving hands." He lifted his hand and head towards the sky.

She placed her hand in her mouth, suppressing a wail. "I heard it from a colleague earlier today. How did it happen? May Allah's blessing be upon brother Ali's soul."

"When he came out of his parent's house last evening, two gunmen shot him. Unfortunately, he did not survive. Forgive me for repeating such atrocities; we stopped you to protect you from the same fate. The prison staff is being targeted more vigorously by the infidels. You understand what I mean?"

She wasn't sure what he had in mind. "What's the plan?"

"We'd like you to come with us. We'll take you to a safe place until it is decided that the danger has passed. When that happens, you will be allowed to go."

A woman going with two strangers in a car was not supposed to happen in Iran. "What do I do? Follow you in my car?"

"No, that would be risky. These killers travel on motorcycles and they can easily plant a bomb on the side of the car and detonate it. We prefer you come with us in our vehicle."

She stepped out of the car. "What happens to my car?"

"Give me your keys and I'll have someone take it to a safe place. When we get the signal that you are not in any direct harm, we'll bring the car to you."

She walked to the Cruiser and sat in the back seat. They drove away.

***

Meena slipped into Fatimeh's Proton Impian and started the engine. She dug up a picture of Fatimeh Mohamadi from her purse. With the visor down, Meena compared the photo with her own face in the mirror. Adjusting the glasses with the brown frames, she then tightened the black chador ever closer to her nose. After making sure the shape of the nose, facial muscles and eye brows were to her satisfaction, she drove to Evin prison.

She went through an overpass leading to the staff entrance where she stopped at a security hut. She flashed a badge at the guard. Compared to other risky assignments, what Meena was about to do at Evin Prison could be the most dangerous task any Mossad agent had ever undergone.

The guard held a machine gun as he approached the vehicle. Meena was as still as a dead body, just as Fatimeh always projected. The woman's classic expression was always dry. When the guard examined her face again, Meena squeezed every bit of anxiety from her mind. He approached the windshield and leaned over to peek at the employee validation permit then waved her forward.

She released a sigh of relief. The iron bar raised and she drove up a narrow winding lane. To her right, she went past the prison security center and administrative offices. As she drove, Meena examined the towers and guards that formed the second perimeter of security. She went past the court house, the first prisoner's structure, and then stopped at Fatimeh's parking spot in front of Korbani building, the location of her ward—209.

Still inside the car, Meena surveyed the area. A bit too crowded for her to risk a chance encounter. Workers left the prison at the end of their shift; two guards each carrying a machine gun. Both replacement guards were now poised at the entrance of the building housing Fatimeh's office.

Meena noticed a corridor of empty space that would take her to the entrance while avoiding eye contact.

She slipped out of the front seat. Moving at a fast clip towards the entrance she pulled the edges of the chador to cover her forehead and checks, leaving only her eyes, mouth and nose in the open air.

One guard said, “Salam, Khanum.”

“Salam,” she replied, and continued walking with her head down but she managed to take a quick snap shot of their faces. The guards took a tired glance at her, perhaps Ali’s death weighed heavily on them. *Or did they notice she was not the real Fatimeh?* She adjusted her gait slightly to compensate.

The hallway unfolded, empty before her except for a woman mopping the floor at the far end. The air was moist. With hurried steps, Meena entered the first door on her right and locked it behind her. The room was barely large enough for the wooden folding chair, small metal table and shelf that decorated it. A picture of the Ayatollah took up one third of the far wall. With a quick glance at the cluttered table she didn’t spot a list of prisoners. *Where can it be?*

Meena examined various piles of paper. There was a copy of the Quran, a stack of brown folders, and sheets with handwritten notes scattered everywhere. After going through many of them, she located a sheet with names and cell numbers. She found another list with the heading: Execution by Firing Squad. Laila Dareini was on it, with a cell number. On the wall behind where the door would open to, rested a board with cell numbers and a key hanging. She pulled molding clay out of her pocket and made an imprint to duplicate the key later. *Things are going well. Hope this keeps up.*

Meena slowly opened the door and scanned the hallway. This time it was empty—it occurred to her it was prayer time. Luck was on her side. She turned right. Inside cell 16 a frail woman lay on a floor bed, on her side, with eyes closed. The noise of the key turning woke her up. She rubbed her eyes. When Meena took a few steps inside, an instinctive reaction in the frail body sent the prisoner into an upright sitting position.

“Is your name Laila?”

She nodded, a positive response. Then her expression laced with fear. “Fatimeh, why are you asking my name? You know who I am.”

Meena bent forward, “Shh. I’m not Fatimeh. Just disguised as her. I’ll be back to rescue you.”

Eyes wide with fear, Laila asked, “Who are you?”

“My name is Meena.” She did not want to tell her about Jake in case the plan was foiled. “Sorry for waking you. Go back to sleep.”

Meena returned to the hallway, relocked the cell and dropped the key off at Fatima’s office before carrying on down the hall, away from the main entrance, to the storage room where the cleaning woman had been mopping the floor earlier. She slipped inside, lifted the hem of her dress and pulled a small flash light from a pouch strapped to her thigh. She pointed the beam from wall to wall until a crease in the far wall caught her attention. She pulled buckets, brooms, and mops out her way until she revealed a hidden door without a handle. The metal was old and rusted, filthy like the wall surrounding it. She gave it a shove; it was wedged in place. *Or locked on the other side.*

Meena searched for something to loosen the door with. The base of the mops were metal. She placed the light on the ground, twisted the wooden handle from a mop head, claimed her somewhat moist prize, and went back to the mysterious door. Wedging a portion of the metal from the mop head into the seam, she pushed and pulled along the length of the door. At a particularly loud groan from the old metal, Meena froze.

A pair of footsteps paced down the hall toward the storage room. Her gaze flitted around the small closet as her mind determined if she had enough time and enough material to hide. She didn’t.

A deep male voice said, “I saw her arrive on time for her shift.

“Her office was locked. She’s probably on rounds.”

“It’s a bit early. She’s supposed to report to Ali first. Maybe she started early knowing he’s no longer with us.”

After a shuffling of feet just outside the storage room door, the man with the deep voice said, “Let’s try the other building. If she’s in room 249 she’ll be a while yet.”

Meena counted to one-hundred, and then again a second time just to make sure the men were gone and no one else had come looking for her—for *Fatimeh*. She turned back to the mysterious door and applied the same pressure to the seams at the top and bottom as well. Her heart refused to calm down. *I told Jake there'd be just as many cons as pros for doing this today.* Ali's death was a great excuse to get Fatimeh out of the way but now others were looking for her for the same reason.

She held her breath and shoved the old door. It creaked but didn't move. *I have to get out of here.* Widening her stance, she lowered her center of gravity and tackled the door, shoulder first. Pain speared up her neck and down her arm but now, moist stale air pulled her mind away from the pain. With both hands she pushed, leaning heavily against the door. It scraped open. Her heart leapt!

Breathing evenly, Meena closed the door again, using the metal mop head to help jam it back into place before reattaching her tool and moving everything on the floor to its original positions. She took a moment to calm her breathing further, then listened with her ear to the door before slipping out and walking from the building.

She drove back through the security gate without hassle. Once off of the Evin property, she took the Chamran Highway but waited another ten minutes before pulling off into an alley and stopping. She took a large, shuddering breath then texted Jake.

"Mission accomplished."

Chapter 35

At 2:55 am Jake stepped out of the van, parked in a spot well off the road surrounded by trees. From the front seat, Meena slid out into the cloud-covered night.

From the driver's side, Ira followed. "Let's do a systems check." His voice was weak. His body wavered as he reached for the roof to regain his balance. The accident in the tunnel—clinically dead for minutes—had caused some health issues, but Ira insisted in not seeing a doctor or resting. He convinced Jake and Meena that it was also integral he take part in this last mission.

"Ira, are you okay?"

"Yes, Jake. I've already told you many times, your wife's life is more important right now. I'm free; she isn't." Ira's irritation when too much attention was given to his personal well-being would not be helpful right now.

"Let's do a systems test then." Jake appreciated Ira's thoroughness, paying close attention to detail—something Jake learned to appreciate during his time training in the military.

Both Jake and Meena already had their oxygen mask, night vision goggles, and miner's headlamp's firmly set in place. Jake took a deep breath through the oxygen mask attached to the tank on his back, then did a quick flick of the on/off switch for the light attached to his forehead. He pulled an iPhone5 out of his vest pocket, and signed onto the device. Tapping on the Dorian icon, an app to track his own position, as well as that of Meena and Ira's, activated. Two bright lights came alive, one connected with a thin line to the word "Meena" in circle, and the other to "Ira." He verified his position in relation to his two friends.

Jake leaned back inside, "I'm good."

Meena had her head lowered towards her mobile device; after Dorian came alive, she said, "Me, too."

Jake and Meena gave each other clear hand signals registered via the infrared night goggles, before moving in through the open area toward the tunnel. The air was humid and hot. In fact, the weather had been the same there as back in Texas.

The cloud cover was good enough that Jake could see ground and the direction he traveled in. At this early hour of the morning, the surrounding silence felt weary—or maybe that was just a side effect of lack of sleep. The dirt road running along the perimeter of the property fence for Evin remained clear of vehicles. They had another two and a half minutes to breach the tunnel before the next patrol came by. Ira drove the van behind a line of shrubs in the near distance, for cover.

Jake turned toward the tunnel, feeling bolstered by their luck. Meena remained a blip on his phone and a quiet breath behind him as they traveled the remaining distance to the entrance. Ira stayed with the van.

Jake got down on his knees to clear the dirt, leaves, and branches off the plywood until it moved freely. He then placed one hand under the wooden cover and lifted it until he saw the steps going down. After lowering himself into the hole, Meena took over holding the plywood then they both moved down into the tunnel.

Dropping their night goggles to hang from their necks, Jake and Meena then turned on their head lamps and paused for further communication.

Meena texted, *"Inside."*

Ira replied, *"Good luck."*

Within five minutes they came to the spot where Ira's body had been buried after soil the size of a truck had fallen from ceiling—a tremor during the inspection run. Jake also recalled just how terrified Meena had been of losing Ira. She knew the importance of this mission—likely understood Jake's conviction more than ever now.

A day after the tunnel collapse, Ira sent a discrete crew to clear the soil and create a path. Wooden supports surrounded the walls and ceiling.

Every minute of this mission had been planned and accounted for, leaving no time to waste, but both Jake and Meena felt compelled to stop at this fateful spot. They stood only inches apart, looking up at the ceiling covered by the wooden frame. Jake felt unbelievably lucky to arrive when he had, to help dig Ira free. Regardless of the collapse, the tunnel was large enough for a medium-size truck to drive through.

Meena whispered, "Had you not come right then, I don't know what would've happened."

"In the military we train for unforeseen calamities, over and over and over again." After another pause, he prompted, "Time is precious, let's move on." Jake took the lead again with Meena only steps behind.

In another seven minutes Jake climbed a set of wooden stairs up to a landing. He pulled at the makeshift rope handle as Meena caught the buckets and brooms behind it. The movement came in small increments to reduce any audible noise to the hall beyond.

Jake slipped through the narrow opening and peeled off his night-vision goggles, oxygen mask, and headlamp, handing them over to Meena who did the same. She placed all the gear on the landing in a backpack.

It was dark but his eyes adjusted to the pencil flash light he pulled out of a side pocket. This time out, his disguise was complete; he was dressed as a prison guard with a khaki uniform, and had dyed his hair brown. Meena took on Fatimeh's appearance once more. Jake motioned Meena into the corridor.

Inside the main building, Meena led Jake down the hall leading to Ward 209. She glanced through the window before entering. Fatimeh had no reason to be here since she'd "called in ill" after leaving soon after her arrival earlier. Meena pushed the door open until she had a full view, studying the hall, cell location, a door at the end, and Fatimeh's office, until she was completely reoriented to the environment.

The space was quiet and dimly lit by a few lamps hanging from the ceiling. Laila's cell was the third on the right.

"I'm going now." She flashed a copy of the key she'd made from her first visit, then walked with purpose to Laila's cell.

Jake stepped to the door and watched her from his peripheral vision while he monitored the other hall through the window. Meena immediately turned back around. Jake opened the door to let her through and followed her back to the storage room.

"Isn't she there?"

Meena waved her hands in disappointment. "No, she's not."

Has she been executed? Where would she be at this hour of the morning? So close, yet so far. His heart pounded as adrenaline spiked through his veins urging him into an action he wasn't sure of. He felt so empty handed. He'd managed to travel from Lackland, Texas to the prison where his beloved was held for months, and except for being shot in the leg once, he made it the whole way alive and well—yet couldn't say the same for his wife.

Meena texted an update to Ira.

"Ira's puzzled. What should we do?"

This was the worst moment of his life. A fierce battle waged between his mind and his heart.

"Jake, Ira thinks we should leave. It is too dangerous to be here."

"I understand Ira doesn't want you to get hurt." Normally, Jake was a very analytical person. There were dangers around him, the risk they'd both be caught and taken to prison, perhaps killed instantly. None of it seemed like a good idea. He recalled how many times missions in Afghanistan were aborted. But in this crucial moment, his intuition demanded something different.

In fact, this wasn't the first time he'd had to trust the prompting of his gut. When he decided to marry Laila, his parents, sister, and friends did not approve, but he'd followed his heart more than his mind and pursued his love. It was the right move. Right or wrong now, he had to trust his instincts.

Meena's nudges to Jake's arm interrupted his spiraling slip into mental paralysis. He was so overtaken by memories he forgot where he was—had lost all sense of time and space.

"Jake, we're aborting this op."

Jake did not like her tone. "No. No way. I can't do that."

"It is too dangerous to stay. We don't know where Laila is." She grabbed his shoulders and made him look at her. "Jake, this is an order. I'm the head of this mission. You should trust my judgement. As a Mossad agent, I'm trained to make an unemotional assessment of any situation and accept failure."

"I won't. I haven't come all this way to go back empty handed. That's not happening."

Meena squeezed his arm. "It *is* happening. Or both of us will be captured and tortured. I don't want that. Shh. I hear footsteps."

Jake shook his head to clear it. He stepped forward and opened the door just enough to view the action in the hallway. A man and woman entered the hall to Laila's cell.

Inside, a voice screamed, "No! Go away! I don't want to die." Moments later the women, held up by one arm, was dragged past the storage closet and out a side entrance. She put up a good fight but her hands were tied behind her back and her mouth now muffled with something. "Let's follow them."

"No. It's too risky. Follow them where? For sure we'll get caught."

He shrugged off her hands and walked towards the far door. As he reached for the handle he was relieved to hear Meena rushing towards him. But she wasn't the only one. The night patrol was making its rounds and neither of them had official clearance to be here at this time.

But Jake couldn't afford to go barging outside without surveilling the area first—he might be following his gut, his heart, but he wasn't an idiot. He cracked the door slightly as Meena slowed her steps so as not to alert the inner patrol that something was amiss. The prisoner was loaded into the back of a van, not completely subdued. She fought her abusers with her feet. The guard positioned just outside the door went to help. With the three of them, they finally got the prisoner inside. The guard returned to his post. Jake signaled for Meena to hold up.

The male and female transport guards headed back towards the building checking a piece of paper. Jake flattened himself against one wall, Meena copied him on the other side distracted by the sound of a door opening down the far hall.

When the guards breached the hallway, Jake grabbed the man in a choke-hold and Meena did the same with the woman. A syringe filled with a tranquilizer jabbed each escort in the gut. It felt longer than it should have for each body to go limp. They let them slowly drop to the floor then pulled them to an obscure area by a staircase just as a set of footsteps entered the hall. There was no door separating the stairwell from the main hall. Meena motioned for Jake to flatten himself against the wall. He did. She was with him again and his trust in her reignited.

Her shoulders tensed and he wondered if she would try to pass herself off to the man as Fatimeh or wait to see how far down the hall he came. Seconds dragged into an eternity. Sweat beaded the brow of Jake's tanned skin—he'd been against using the spray on stuff so Meena had found a cream that darkened the skin a little each day for two weeks. It still didn't look natural to him, but then his usual pale visage would only have given him away.

Meena tensed. The footsteps paused a breath away from the corner of the stairwell when a walkie squawked. Jake watched the guard's hand sweep past the corner as he raised the device to reply. Jake shifted and Meena held up her hand, assuming he meant to engage the guard—of which he held no desire to challenge a riffle to a fist fight.

The guard turned and hurried off. The split second the door shut to hall 209, Meena quietly stepped to the entrance and peeked outside. To one of the guards she said, "Salam, we need your help inside." Then she ducked back in. There was supposed to be two. *Where's the other guard?*

When he came inside, Jake put him in a choke hold as Meena administered another injection. Within seconds, the resistance in his body melted away until he, too lay motionless. Jake pulled the guard into the same area as the others. Each of the three was given another injection, rendering them unconsciousness for several hours.

Jake went outside. Meena gave the all-clear that no one was in the cab. When he rounded the back of the van and pulled the door open, two women in blindfolds raised their heads. Hope flashed through his veins.

"Laila?" he asked, leaning forward to remove her blindfold.

She recoiled.

He stared at her gaunt face and pushed the cloth to her forehead. Laila blinked and squinted in the dark. Her lips parted slightly as she examined his face and the Khaki uniform. Meena pushed up Jake's short sleeve until the monogrammed tattoo of a J and an L became visible. Confusion crossed her face as she opened her eyes to let more light into her retina.

"Hurry up," Meena said, and retreated back to the door to act as sentry lookout.

"Lalouska," he said, the pet name only Jake called her.

"Jake? Jake! Is that really you?" She lifted her bound hands to touch his darkened hair, letting them trail down the length of his tanned jaw.

"Yes, my love." He leaned all the way in over the rear bumper and pulled her into his arms. Just the sight of her made the whole trip worthwhile.

He maneuvered her around so he could place his left hand under her legs. With little effort, he lifted her to the ground.

As Jake moved away, the other prisoner squealed and whined like a toddler throwing a tantrum.

"Jake, Gita. We can't leave her."

Laila was right. He knew the other woman would be executed unless he rescued her too. He pulled her out and all three walked back inside.

Meena gave Jake a grave look at the sight of the two women with him. She was ready to complain, but shrugged her shoulders instead.

"The more the merrier," she said, then lifted her hijab until her legs were visible. From her tool belt she pulled out a knife and cut the women free.

"Meena, you take Gita. I'll take Laila. Let's get out of here."

"Jake. Please, wait," she pulled at his arm. "Can we take Maryam with us?"

"Honey, I'd love to, but we have to leave *now*."

She pointed to the door they'd just come through. "She's right over there. In the other building. I can get her here in one minute."

Meena shook her head. "We just don't have a minute to waste."

"Take Gita to the storage room," Jake said. The wild expression in his love's eyes told Jake something fragile in Laila might break if he denied her this. "We'll be right behind you."

Jake and Laila entered the other building adjacent to the van and over to the first cell on the right. Laila opened the door, glad for Maryam's privilege to sleep without a lock, and went inside. She shook the body lying on the floor.

"Maryam, wake up." Actually she was already awake and rose instantly. Laila grabbed her hand. "Maryam, it's Laila. Let's go."

Jake pulled Laila's other hand and led the women along the corridor. All three hurried back across the quad into Laila's building, careening around the corner. At the staircase, the missing guard caught Jake's attention. The stalky man with a beard blinked, both hands twitching as if unsure whether to call this in or just start shooting. There was a guard accompanying the two prisoners after all. Jake wasn't taking any chances. He let go of the women's hands, pushing them away toward the stairwell where the other guards were still out cold. "Go there and stay back."

Jake whispered, "Shit." As the guard raised his rifle and brought his free hand up to steady the weapon, Jake sprang forward, shoved the firing gun aside and punched him in the chest. His five-six frame bounced off the railing of the staircase as bullets ricocheted off the metal door to the cells. Jake kicked the gun free of the guard's grasp before he scrambled back to his feet. His stance projected defiance not defeat. *We don't have time for this!* Jake bent his knees slightly, one foot forward, one back and two fists raised—as a boxer in a ring.

After a couple of sweeping moves meant to draw the guy out, Jake threw a right punch at his temple. The guard blocked the blow. With fierce anger in his eyes, chest inflated and body straining up, he aimed for Jake's neck. Jake shifted around, avoiding the attack while simultaneously driving his fist into the guard's nose and cracking the man's head against the wall. Jake shifted his weight from left leg to right, planting a hit on the man's stomach with the power of a sledge hammer. The guard staggered. Jake chopped down on his neck—knockout. The guard's body leaned backward and then fell to the ground. Jake pulled a syringe from his pant pocket and administered the tranquilizer. He heard shouts from outside.

"Come on! Let's get out of here!" He practically dragged both women down the hall and into the storage closet just as an alarm screeched to life.

He shut the door behind him and headed to the hidden landing, still pulling the women along. With his pen light, he saw two silhouettes running away down the tunnel. Before closing the access door, he pulled the broom and buckets back into place and yanked the panel closed. Jake grabbed the backpack lying at his feet and distributed one oxygen tank to Laila and the other to Maryam. With his headlamp firmly in place, he stepped down a few stairs and guided the other two into the belly of the tunnel.

"Now, run!"

He made sure he was holding Laila's upper arm. It was bad enough that she stumbled in the dark, but her body clearly couldn't take the stress he asked of it. He followed a dark path, only lit up to five feet ahead. In less than two minutes they'd caught up with Meena, quickly contacting Ira. Jake watched her type something and press send a second time as Laila, Maryam, and Gita's heavy breathing filled the air.

Meena growled, frustrated. "He's not responding."

Jake turned and kissed Laila's head, helping support her frail body. "Try again. If you don't get him, use the app on my phone to see where he is—make sure he's not compromised. Let him know we have two extra passengers. Hurry, the alarm went off at the prison."

"An alarm? What does that mean?" Meena's eyes stared at the screen as she frantically typed.

"I don't know."

She exhaled loudly, "Okay. He'll be waiting for us at the mouth of the tunnel."

All of them rushed, keeping a steady pace for another few minutes to the mouth of the tunnel. The escapees panted and breathed hard but refused to slow down. Part of Jake's heart ached to see Laila tortured like this in her current state but another part of him puffed proud that even in her weakened condition, she was ready to fight for her life, for *their* lives.

Meena took the lead and raised her head until her eyes were above ground. Then she pointed her headlamp back into the tunnel and waved Gita up the short set of steps and out.

"Gita, go into the van."

Jake held Laila close and signaled for Maryam to climb up next before lifting Laila into the open air. He scrambled up after her, holding her tight by his side, not wanting to lose sight of her for a moment. Looking at her from the corner of his eyes, as they hurried over to the open back of the van, her boney arms, spindly fingers, hollow cheeks, and sunken eyes spoke volumes of the torture she'd endured. And yet, somehow those eyes still sparkled when they looked back at him.

Meena helped pull the women into the van, then Jake hopped in and slid the door shut. A strange silhouette moved to the front passenger seat—not part of the plan. *Who is that?* The van gunned forward. The motion forced Jake's body to sway sideways. The women yelled, caught off balance. As Jake fell he reached for the back of the seat.

Laila sat in front of him and Maryam by the window. In the row behind, Gita and Meena took their seats. Jake regained his balance and stood, feet planted. *Something's not right.* The driver's outline was too tall.

"Ira, is that you?"

By now they'd traveled several hundred yards away from the road circling the perimeter of the prison.

The man in the passenger seat screamed, “Jake? Jake Hudley? We finally got you?”

Jake’s heart jumped into his throat.

“Who the hell are you!”

“CIA.”

If you liked Justice Denied, be sure to check out

V. M. Gopaul's first political thriller:

TAINTED JUSTICE

Book 1 of the *Jason McDeere Novels*

V. M. GOPAUL

Fiction writing is V. M. Gopaul's passion. His capacity to dream up ideas show no bounds, with outlines for more than ten books yet to be written.

As a software and database specialist, Gopaul wrote seven books for IT professionals. He then turned his attention to writing books on spirituality, which paved the way for a hidden passion to emerge. When crafting and completing *Tainted Justice*, a lifelong dream of Gopaul's had become reality. *Justice Denied* is the first book in a new thrilling series based around ex-military officer Jake Hudley.

Gopaul is planning to continue both the Jason McDeere Saga as well as Jake Hudley's.

Stay tuned at http://vmgopaul.com.

Made in the USA
Columbia, SC
22 March 2018